WHEN ALL ELSE FAILS, USE A CLUB

As the Humvee hurtled down the road, Shane could see a few of the alien boomerang-shaped probes over them in the air. As he watched, a building collapsed and he couldn't figure out why until he realized the damned things were ripping the rebar right out of the concrete walls.

Nails. Wiring. Cars. It was all going into those damned probes. Every damned scrap of metal. They didn't seem to be killing people except as a byproduct. But they would. Metal *was* civilization. And . . . one . . . three . . . more were headed for them.

"Pull over and unass!" Shane yelled, opening his door. He was rolling on the road before the Humvee was at a full halt.

So was the master sergeant, as it turned out, and the Humvee continued forward, still in drive, as five of the probes came up with a thunder of air. The Humvee began to shake and tear apart and the master sergeant let out a curse as he was jerked into the air. His boots came apart as the eyelets were ripped out and he landed hard on the asphalt. He shook off his ruined boots and looked around for a weapon, finally settling on a timber by the side of the road.

He jumped in the air as the hovering probes drifted over them, apparently searching for more scraps of metal. The four-by-four hit the surface of one, hard. The probe shuddered for a moment, then drifted sideways. It shuddered again and then there was a brief burst of sparks and it dropped out of the air.

"Congratulations," Shane said, getting up from his crouch and examining the fallen probe with interest. "You've proven they can be killed."

Baen Books by John Ringo

The Legacy of Aldenata Series

A Hymn Before Battle

Gust Front

When the Devil Dances

Hell's Faire

The Hero with
Michael Z. Williamson

Cally's War with
Julie Cochrane

Watch on the Rhine with
Tom Kratman

Yellow Eyes with
Tom Kratman

Sister Time with
Julie Cochrane

There Will Be Dragons
Emerald Sea
Against the Tide
East of the Sun, West of the
Moon

Ghost
Kildar
Choosers of the Slain
Unto the Breach
A Deeper Blue

Princess of Wands

Into the Looking Glass
The Vorpal Blade with
Travis S. Taylor

Manxome Foe with
Travis S. Taylor

Von Neumann's War with
Travis S. Taylor

The Road to Damascus with
Linda Evans

with David Weber:
March Upcountry
March to the Sea
March to the Stars
We Few

Baen Books by Travis S. Taylor

Warp Speed
The Quantum Connection

One Day on Mars
The Tau Ceti Agenda (forthcoming)

VON NEUMANN'S WAR

John Ringo
Travis S. Taylor

A Baen Book

Baen Publishing Enterprises
P.O. Box 1403
Riverdale, NY 10471
www.baen.com

ISBN 10: 1-4165-5530-7
ISBN 13: 978-1-4165-5530-8

Cover art by Kurt Miller

First Baen paperback printing, March 2008

Distributed by Simon & Schuster
1230 Avenue of the Americas
New York, NY 10020

Library of Congress Cataloging-in-Publication Data: 2006012260

Printed in the United States of America

10 9 8 7 6 5 4 3 2 1

To the soldiers, contractors, analysts,
scientists, and engineers who press
daily to maintain our nation's security

The Commando's Prayer

Give me, my God, what you still have;
give me what no one asks for.
I do not ask for wealth, nor success,
nor even health.
People ask you so often, God, for all that,
that you cannot have any left.
Give me, my God, what you still have.
Give me what people refuse to accept from you.
I want insecurity and disquietude;
I want turmoil and brawl.
And if you should give them to me,
my God, once and for all,
let me be sure to have them always,
for I will not always
have the courage to ask for them.

Corporal Zirnheld
Special Air Service
1942

CLASSIFICATION:
TOP SECRET SPECIAL ACCESS
NEIGHBORHOOD WATCH

Neighborhood Watch
Final Report
Development and Results of the Mars
Intelligence, Surveillance, and
Reconnaissance Probe "Percival"
Prepared by
Roger P. Reynolds, T. C. Powell, Alan J. Davis

Prepared for the National Reconnaissance Office
Contract # TNW1-01-2007

INTRODUCTION

This document contains all data developed under the Top Secret Special Access Program codenamed Neighborhood Watch. Neighborhood Watch was developed to investigate the albedo-changing phenomenon currently taking place on the planet Mars. Neighborhood Watch initial analysis suggested that a planet-changing phenomena of the magnitude which is occurring on Mars is of non-natural origin. It was also determined to be statistically improbable that all manmade probes that had previously been sent to the planet Mars have gone quiet in a short timespan, including those which had been functioning nominally on the surface.

The Mars Intelligence, Surveillance, and Reconnaissance (ISR) Probe known as "Percival" was developed in a rapid design process and launched. Percival was successful in reaching the planet and returning valuable ISR.

Unfortunately, once reaching the planet all contact was lost with the probe. Analysis of final mission transmissions indicate that the probe sustained progressive failure indicative of attack rather than systems failure.

This report was developed in order to maintain a complete record of the mission history, concept development, mission design components, mission implementation, data retrieved, and data analysis. The authors would like to emphasize here that extreme attention to detail is given where available so that as much data as possible is available if further analysis of the Neighborhood Watch project is made.

The report begins with initial findings that led to the creation of the Neighborhood Watch program. The findings began with analysis of data from ground and space telescopes by astronomers at the Space Telescope Science Institute (STScI). There were also reports from various amateur astronomers claiming that Mars was "changing colors". It was at this point that sequential failures of Mars probes began to alert government officials to the possibility of non-natural actions or activities. A timeline will be given of the sequence of these events.

The next section of the report gives a detailed description of the Percival development effort. Space mission concept architecture, spacecraft design components, and all aspects of the development and implementation of the Mars ISR Probe, Percival, is discussed.

The third section gives the results of the Mars ISR mission. The data is somewhat alarming. The conclusion is undeniable: Mars has been dramatically altered by an unnatural phenomenon. Although Percival is believed to have been destroyed, not "lost," *destroyed*, prior to mission completion, sufficient data was retrieved from the probe to determine that Mars is being altered by an alien entity or entities. No signs of organic life were detected. However, signs of an intelligence at work are evident since major portions of the planet's surface have been converted to mechanical structures, some of them of super-human proportions.

The fourth section is a conclusions and discussions section. The results of the Neighborhood Watch program are summarized and a discussion on the possible outcome and impact of the phenomenon on Mars is discussed along with potential repercussions to Terra and the human race.

Chapter 1

Time: Present minus twenty years

The teachers looked up at the rocket towering over the exhibit and then at each other.

"Duct tape?" the female teacher asked. Usually she taught junior high school science classes, especially "female health" and "earth sciences." It was the first time she'd ever seen a . . . what was it the boy called it . . . a "sounding rocket."

"Only for support of the outer casing," the young man said, smiling broadly and scratching at his nearly white hair. "The primary casing is cardboard. I wanted to make a rocket entirely from discarded and readily available materials. The term is 'off-the-shelf.' NASA hardly ever uses anything that anyone else uses and I think that's a damn shame. There are so many things around that you can make rockets out of. The igniter is a spark plug from my daddy's old Chevy. The energy components, the fuel, are made from common household materials. I made the fins in shop class when we were working with sheet metal; I brought in a hood off a car in my Uncle Bubba's backyard and cut it up. You can see the original paint! And the payload is a sodium tracer round made out of an old Jack Daniels bottle I found under the porch."

"So, when are you planning on putting the fuel in?" she asked.

"Well, it's solid fuel," Roger Reynolds replied, as if she were dense. "You can't just pull it out and put it in."

"So . . . it's fueled?" the woman squeaked. She suddenly realized that all the, many, rocket scientists who were judging the Northern Alabama High School Science Fair had chosen to examine exhibits a *long* way away from this one.

"Well . . . duh."

Roger went on to the International Science and Engineering Fair where he placed in the top five overall and first in his category. He also won a scholarship and a job at the NASA Marshall Space Flight Center. There he was described on his performance evaluation as "precocious." In private he was described as "that young snot-nosed pain in the ass. And keep him away from the fuel. . . ."

Time: Present minus one year—first Russian Mars probe failure

As the improvised explosive device turned his lead Humvee into expensive confetti, Captain Shane Gries, USA, took just one more moment to consider how very much he hated all academic eggheads.

Captain Gries was tall, 6'2", and slim, with a square cut jaw, mild blue eyes and light brown hair cut to stubble at the sides. Behind his back his men called him "The Greyhound" both for his looks and his running speed on morning PT. He had been raised in the Iron Range of Michigan, one of the coldest, snowiest and hardest localities in the entire United States. As a teenager, he'd spent more time hunting the massive bucks to be found in the Iron Range than he had cracking books. Despite that fact, his grades were excellent. Between those, and a friendly congressman, he had gotten an appointment to the United States Military Academy in West Point, New York. His ability at track and field hadn't hurt.

At West Point he'd studied another type of hunting, the hunting of armed enemies of the United States. And he'd studied hard ever since. His first unit assignment as a brand new shavetail lieutenant had been to the First Infantry Division two days before it crossed the Line of Departure and entered Iraq in the first Gulf War. He'd been sent in to replace another lieutenant who had "cracked under pressure" at the thought of actually being in combat.

He'd been carefully instructed by his company commander on his duties the day he arrived. In a flash, as he always did when the shit hit the fan, he recalled the lecture as the first rounds from the ambush cracked across the road.

"You have no clue what your job is supposed to be," Captain Brantley had said. To Shane, at the time, he had seemed immensely old and grizzled, probably, gasp, thirty or so. *"You have no clue what you're supposed to be doing and no clue how to function in combat. It's my miserable*

job to teach you. But I don't have time before we cross the LD. So you're going to have to learn from your NCOs. The way you're going to do that is to ask them what to do, listen carefully, then repeat what they say. Second lieutenants are the lowest of the low. First lieutenants think they have a clue. By the time you're up to captain, if you survive that long, you're going to realize you never will have a clue and all you can do is make it up as you go along. But by then, the ones that are the worst at making it up are gone. And you'll have to make it up as you go along."

The scene flashed as a gestalt while his mind simultaneously processed the nature of the current ambush. Within a second he'd assimilated the nature of the situation, enemy force, friendly force and secondary conditions. Of course, by then his troops were already returning fire.

The American Occupation Force, Iraq, had long experience of ambushes, especially in the Sunni Triangle. The Triangle consisted of the area surrounding Baghdad, situated more or less in the middle of the country, and delineated by the cities of Al-Najaf, Baghdad and Tikrit.

American forces had developed a standard initial response that came down to one phrase: "Overwhelming firepower." As soon as they took direct fire, they returned it with everything the unit had to offer, from pistols to the Mk-19 automatic 20mm grenade launchers on the "gun" Humvees. And they'd been so tightly drilled, and experienced so many ambushes, that the response was automatic at a level that had them returning fire in less than a second. Even if they'd been napping at the moment of the ambush.

It was Shane's job to determine, in brief seconds, what the response beyond "initial" would be. He had to determine from the volume and position of fire whether the best response was to sit it out and return fire or assault the ambush. And he had to do all of this while dealing with the "surprise" of the situation. Moments before he'd been cruising along minding his own business. Now he had to react, intelligently and thoughtfully, but in less time than most people took to decide between a mocha and a caramel latte. While bullets were bouncing off the armor on his Humvee and rocket propelled grenades, which would tear though the armor like paper, were flying past.

But Shane was very good at combat gestalt. Even back in the first Gulf War as a "clueless" shavetail he'd been good at it. He knew he was clueless, but you generally were in war, you never had all the information you'd like, and he was good at working with what he knew.

He knew his primary mission was securing the group of International Atomic Energy Agency scientists that had been "inspecting" a possible covert nuclear site. The group of fifteen international eggheads had been a pain in the ass all day. His job was simply to get them to the site and back, intact. But they assumed that "escort" meant that he was supposed to supply them with food, by which they meant something better than Meals-Ready-To-Eat, water, bottled, not from the five-gallon water cans on the Humvees, snacks, pop, caviar, champagne, candy or whatever they'd thought of that moment. And to carefully lead them around by the hand, bowing and scraping as a good little grunt should.

He figured there'd be a bit of a reprimand in the future for not supplying their every need, want and desire. But not nearly as large of one as he'd get for letting the group get wiped out. And as he considered the situation, he could see the egghead idiots popping out of the Canadian light armored vehicles that were their protection.

He knew that the narrow road they had been forced to use in this section was blocked by the shredded Humvee. Even if the Humvees could creep past—or fly past, the way most of the drivers would handle it—the first vehicle had slewed sideways from the explosion, creating a narrow gap that the LAVs couldn't negotiate. And they probably couldn't push it aside, either. LAVs didn't have the gription. Therefore, they couldn't simply drive out of the ambush.

He knew he had all three platoons of his company that were on the jaunt mounted in Humvees, some armored and some unarmored, with second platoon, that had just lost its lead Humvee, on point, then first, then the LAVs, then his command group, then third as ass-end-charley. Third was short a squad, which was back in Fort Samson pulling guard detail. First and second, except for the usual sick, lame, lazy and wounded, were up to strength. Of course, second had just lost half a squad in a Humvee.

The ambush seemed to be about fifteen to twenty shooters, at least five RPG grenadiers with the rest firing light weapons, AK variants. There did not appear to be any automatic weapons, either light, medium or heavy. The ambush did not appear to have indirect fire support; usually by now there would be mortars crumping down. They were firing from the ground and second level of a three-story building on the right-hand side of the street. The building, based upon usual construction, would have walls made of unbaked brick faced with, in this case, fake marble. Those could be penetrated even by light arms, and the Mk-19s had blown several holes in the walls already. There would be rear entrances and probably windows on the side.

All of this, and the lecture from his first company commander, flashed through his mind in the first moment of the ambush in one continuous gestalt. *Surprise occurs in the mind of the commander.* Shane had learned, long before, to *never* be surprised. He hadn't managed the Zen trick of constant wonder, to be in each moment, treating each new moment as a constant surprise, but he was darned close.

So. And so. He had been carrying his mike in his hand, standard procedure in Ambush Alley, and he picked it up and keyed it exactly two and one-half seconds after the detonation of the IED. One second to assess, one second to plan. Two and a half seconds were a long time in combat, but he'd needed at least that much time to ensure he had all his facts in order. And, hell, the half second was lifting the mike. He'd give himself that as a Mulligan.

"Second platoon, lay down base of fire on ambush. First platoon, deploy and secure the science detail. Ensure the safety of mobile personnel . . ." As he was speaking an RPG penetrated the side armor on one of the LAVs which began to belch diesel smoke and spill scientists out the back like suit-covered maggots, "And recover wounded from damaged vehicles. LAVs, lay down base of fire. Third platoon, set one squad as security. Remainder dismount and assault ambush from right to left, clearing the building."

⚜   ⚜   ⚜

"Top! What are you doing?" Specialist Fort yelled as First Sergeant Thomas Cady bailed out the side of the Humvee into the buzzing fire of the AKs.

"My job," the first sergeant replied.

Thomas Cady was in many ways the antithesis of his commander. He'd been raised in government housing in Decatur, Georgia, where the choice was working in the 7/11 or being a crack dealer. His mother had managed to raise five kids, all from different fathers, on the basis of welfare and occasional child support payments. Thomas was pretty sure "his" father wasn't even his genetic dad; they didn't look a bit alike. But the man, who was white whereas Thomas was as black as the ace of spades, had been the only one of the five to make regular support payments. And he'd even visited his "son" and made sure he had regular presents for Christmas and his birthday.

Maybe it was the example of somebody with some honor and class or maybe Arthur really *was* his dad. But whatever the reason, Thomas had managed to keep his nose clean. His grades in school weren't the greatest, but they were good enough that the Army would accept him. And one of the services seemed to be the only way out of the rat hole that was life in Decatur. He didn't want to chip paint in the Navy, his AGT scores weren't high enough for the Air Force, and the Marines were full up when he tried to join.

So two months after graduating from Columbia High School in Decatur, Georgia, he'd raised his right hand and never looked, or been, back.

Over the succeeding fourteen years, he'd gotten married, twice, divorced, twice, had two kids, both by the first wife after which he got a vasectomy, and made sure he not only kept up with the payments and gifts but that he visited his kids as often as his career made possible. He'd also dialed in on his career and his neglected education, picking up an associate degree when he was still a buck sergeant, then his bachelors a few years later. He was currently working on a masters in history when he wasn't doing his primary job.

His primary job, in his opinion, was to enable his commander's orders. That meant, to First Sergeant Cady, anticipating the captain's orders, then ensuring that all the little details got filled in. Whether the order was "get chow to the men in the field" or "wipe out those rag-head motherfuckers in the building." He'd been with Captain Gries for less than three months but Greyhound was one of those officers with whom First Sergeant Cady "clicked." He knew the primary mission was securing the scientists. But he also knew that Captain Gries wasn't going to sit on his hands. Some officers froze when they got shot at. Some hunkered down and returned fire, hoping that the rag-heads would run. Gries believed in the infantry motto: "In the Absence of Orders, Assault!" Which meant some rag-heads were about to get the shit kicked out of them if they didn't run *now*.

He also anticipated that Captain Gries would use third for the assault. The first sergeant's vehicle was forward with first platoon so if he wanted to get it stuck in the rag-heads, he'd have to make it to the back of the ambush. And along the way, he could do some little things to clean up the captain's orders. If he shagged his ass.

Behind Sergeant Cady's back, the men called him "The Gazelle." Like his commander, the spade-black NCO was tall, 6' 4" and a runner. But unlike the wiry captain, Cady looked like an NFL linebacker with a huge torso and massive shoulders. Despite weighing in at nearly two hundred and fifty pounds, he was, if anything, faster than the captain in a sprint.

He used that speed to good effect less than a second into the ambush, rolling out of the Humvee and darting to the rear, his M-4 in his left hand pointed towards the ambush like a giant pistol. As he ran he spotted targets, firing at them in three-round bursts as he pounded towards the LAVs in the middle of the column. He knew he wasn't hitting anything, but the combined firepower of the unit was suppressing the fire from the rag-head ambushers and that was the point.

As he pounded past the first LAV, one of the scientists stumbled out into the fire and stopped, looking around with an expression of acute stupidity. He was a very smart guy, a Swede who had something like six Ph.D.s. But he was in a situation for which he'd never prepared himself, mentally or physically.

"Get *out* of the line of fire," Cady bellowed. He slung the M-4 and in one continuous motion snatched the scientist off his feet by his suit collar, barely slowing in the run as he lifted the overweight physicist into the air to drag along behind with only his toes touching the ground.

The far side of the road had a low wall surrounding a vacant lot. Cady wasn't sure why anyone would put a wall around a vacant lot, but you saw that sort of thing a lot in Iraq. Some of the guys from Humvees that were drawing heavy fire had already bailed out and unassed to the wall. Cady just adjusted his run to the right a bit, switched hands on the physicist and tossed him over the wall towards one of the defending squads.

"Keep an eye on him, Reese," he yelled as he continued down the wall. He ducked a bit since people were firing right past him, but he figured none of his men would *dare* blue-on-blue him. "And if you see any more of these shit-heads, get them under cover!"

"Top's coming down!" Sergeant Reese yelled to the rest of the fighters crouched behind the wall. "Check fire for Gazelle!"

Two more scientists were out in the road, one down with a bullet in his leg and the other bending over him, waving his hands around as if reciting a magic spell. What was actually going on, Cady knew, was that the second scientist had no idea what to do for a guy with a three finger thick chunk blown out of his thigh. It wasn't gushing arterial blood, though, so the guy'd probably live. If he didn't go into shock and die from that.

Cady just sighed and grabbed them both by their suits, the casualty by the front and the other guy, who Cady recognized as the detail head, by the back, then darted to the wall and tossed them both over. The detail head, a supercilious and scrawny French asshole who'd been a particular pain in the ass, actually spent some time in midair. There was a nasty crack when he hit the ground.

"Medic!" Cady bellowed, heading down-range to third's position. "And bring a splint!"

Captain Gries saw First Sergeant Cady toss two guys over the wall on the left-hand side of the road and nodded.

"Top's up to form," he murmured, as the massive NCO continued his sprint towards the rear of the column.

"Sir, we're taking a lot of fire here," Specialist Reynolds

said nervously. "Maybe we should unass?"

"Negative," Gries replied, glancing over his shoulder. He could see the point of third platoon, which had been almost entirely outside the ambush, heading around the side of the building. And the fire from the ambushers had already started to slack off. They were either running or being effectively suppressed by the counterfire from the infantry company. "We'll be clear soon."

He paused as the first sergeant switched from the left side of the street to the right, actually running *into* the ambush fire, and cracked open his door.

"How's it going, Top?" Shane yelled as the NCO, who was carrying about seventy pounds in armor, weapons, water and ammo, thundered past like an Olympic sprinter.

"Cool as shit, sir!" First Sergeant Cady yelled back, his face splitting in a grin of white teeth that were startling against his skin. "I think I broke Dr. Caseaux's arm!"

"Hoowah!" Shane yelled back. "Don't let 'em get away, First Sergeant!"

He closed his door just as a round bounced off it, then felt the vehicle shake from a series of impacts; someone was trying to track in on the running NCO.

"Gotta lead him more," he muttered to no one in particular as the armor on his window spalled from a direct hit, leaving the deformed 7.62 round stuck in the thick plexiglass about five inches from his head. "Missed me, missed me, now you gotta kiss me . . ."

First Sergeant Cady rounded the corner of the building and got to the side door while third platoon's point, Specialist Charles Walters, was still kicking at the door with his boot.

"Scat," Cady said, slapping the specialist on the shoulder while his foot was in midair preparing for another kick. The slap sent the specialist stumbling to the side four feet and onto his back, but if he noticed, it wasn't apparent; he was up on his feet again before Top had gotten in his first kick.

It only took a single kick from one of Top's size sixteens, though, for the light wooden door to open, splintering away from its hinges and onto the floor.

"Stack up!" Sergeant Gregory shouted. The squad leader of second squad, third herd, Gregory was a relative newbie in Iraq and still worked "by the book." The book said that the point took the door down, then the remainder of the squad "stacked," closed up with each other to enter the room with each member of the squad having a particular area to cover on entry.

He'd never actually *been* in an entry with the Gazelle and wasn't prepared for the actions of the massive first sergeant, who blocked the squad, then tossed a frag through the door.

"Back," Cady said, waving the stack back along the left wall. He'd tossed the grenade well back and to the right, so the fragments were unlikely to penetrate the left wall. But frags were tricky; you never knew how they'd bounce. He crouched by the door with his left shoulder leaned towards it, weapon at tactical, and depended on taking any bouncers on his armor.

The grenade went off with a "crack" and there was a small secondary that blasted dust out of the door and a hole in the right wall.

"They put IEDs in the door," Cady said, glancing over his shoulder at Gregory as he darted into the dust. "You either do a close check or you try to detonate it."

"Got it, Top," Gregory panted as the stack moved into the room. He knew the first sergeant had been at the front of the column when the ambush went off. How in the *hell* he'd suddenly appeared, the sergeant couldn't understand. He kept *doing* that, just appearing out of nowhere. It was uncanny.

The room beyond was empty of anything but junk and cobwebs with an open door on the far side. That led to a narrow corridor but just beyond the door there was a staircase that led up.

"Specialist Thomas," Gregory said, tapping the soldier directly in front of him. "Secure this location with primary direction of security . . ."

"Follow me, Sergeant," Cady interjected. "Bring your squad."

The first sergeant bounded to the first landing in two massive strides, turning to cover the top as fire started to die away upstairs.

"Oh, no you don't," Cady said. "You're not getting away from the Gazelle."

"Romeo Three-One . . . this is Echo Two . . . Five."

Captain Gries sighed and picked up the mike.

"Johnny, this is the CO. We're encrypted. Go plain." The third platoon leader was a butterbar and this was only his second firefight. He tended to get flustered.

"Sir, we've performed entry on the side of the building," Second Lieutenant John Crevasse said nervously. "The first sergeant entered with my second squad. First squad is in support."

"Roger," Gries said, looking down the road. All the

scientists were either still in the vehicles or over the wall and at least out of sight if not out of danger. He could see one trooper down on the road with a couple of troops pulling him out of the line of fire, but so far casualties appeared to be light. "Move yourself and first squad to the rear of the building. Do not enter. Try to find a point that you can interdict movement out of the building. Second platoon, detach one squad to cover the left side of the building. Let Top clear the second floor, then we'll see what's what."

"Specialist Nelms!" Crevasse yelled.

"Hoowah, sir!" Specialist Nelms raised his head up in response and rushed to the lieutenant.

"I'm moving first squad to cover the rear of this building but with all these goddamned buildings in the way I'm not sure we can cover it from ground level. I want you to get the high ground and give us some cover." Lieutenant Crevasse pointed to the south and across the street at the five-story office complex.

"Yes, sir! Got the high ground, sir!" Specialist Nelms hefted his Barrett .50 caliber sniper rifle and trotted across the street, looking for a good snipe point.

He weaved in and out of the shadows like an expert hunter, which he was. He had grown up in central Texas hunting whitetail and mule deer. It was only recently, however, that he had been stalk-hunting terrorist insurgents. Deer didn't shoot back with cheap imitation Russian or Chinese RPG-7s—and cheap or not they still would kill you dead as doornails. Specialist Nelms had just happened to be one of the lucky few who scored 50 out of 50 on the annual corps marksmanship test. Before that he had a pretty cushy job in the motor pool. But a perfect score was a perfect score. The military being short on snipers, he was handed a Barrett and shifted to a line unit.

Nelms moved quickly to an alleyway that led to a blown-out wall in the five-story building. He slipped through the hole in the wall and cautiously made it to the stairwell. It was his job to make it to high ground and cover for first squad, the second platoon detachment, and Top. Specialist Nelms didn't want to let them down—especially not Top. He liked Top and believed in the first sergeant's credo: Do unto others before they do unto you.

First Sergeant Cady stopped again at the second landing. The stairs continued upwards to the third floor, but he hadn't seen any fire from up there. There was a door at the top of the landing and he tried the knob. Unlocked. He opened the door slowly, checking for telltales of an IED and finding none, then peeked around the corner. There was a corridor with several doors. From some of the open doors he could hear Arabic voices and the occasional crack of gunfire.

"We're going to clear room-by-room," the first sergeant said over his shoulder. The guy directly behind him was Specialist Herr, the squad automatic weapon gunner. The first sergeant held out his M-4 and snatched the SAW out of the gunner's hand. "Feed me."

With that he stepped quietly down the hall, moving remarkably silently for his bulk, until he got to the first door. He waved his hand to stop the stack behind him and armed another grenade, tossing it into the room carefully at the level of the floor, then stepping well clear of the door.

The grenade went off with a bang and the first sergeant darted through the door while the fragments were still pinging around the room. There were three tangos in the room, one on the ground screaming from fragments in his legs, most of a body next to him and the third just turning away from the sandbagged position by the window.

Cady targeted the shooter by the window with a burst of fire that spun him to lean out the window, then backed into the hallway.

"Two tango KIA," he said into his squad radio, "one tango WIA. Room clear." Herr darted past him and kicked the wounded tango's weapon aside, dropping to one knee to slip plastic cuffs on the terrorist's wrists.

The stack had passed the first sergeant and he watched as they cleared the next room. As the first two members of the stack entered the room, a tango darted out of one of the rooms down the corridor. He headed for the far end, though, where there were presumably more stairs, rather than trying to fight the American troops in the hall-way.

Cady had too many bodies between him and the tango to target the ambusher, but Privates Jones and Mahoney from the stack engaged him, tossing the terrorist to the floor. He was only wounded, though, and still tried to crawl to the doorway at the end.

Cady moved forward as the stack entered the room, dropping to one knee on the far side of the door to cover the hallway. He'd barely taken a knee when the bulbous round of an RPG peeked around the corner of the third door down.

Now, body armor will stop a lot, but it's not going to stop an RPG. And the grenadier wasn't in sight. That didn't stop Cady, though—he just laid the sights of the SAW on the round itself and fired, throwing himself to the floor immediately afterwards.

The 5.56 rounds from the SAW impacted on the casing of the grenade, throwing it upwards just as the grenadier pulled the trigger. The round fired, frying the grenadier with backblast from the floor and filling the room beyond him with more blast and flame. The round itself impacted with the ceiling and, being within its minimum safe-arming distance, bounced off the ceiling and skittered down the hallway with a whistling sound.

Cady rolled into the doorway, tripping a member of the squad who was on his way out. He grabbed the troop, who turned out to be Sergeant Gregory, and threw him into the room, toppling two more members of the squad in the process.

The RPG slithered down the walls of the corridor until it impacted on the far end. Herr had just stepped out of the first cleared room when it passed and he caught fragments in his legs and right arm while the explosion blew him off his feet.

"I'm hit!" Herr called, rolling back into the room. "Medic!"

"Stay there!" Cady called, rolling back into the corridor. He ignored the intervening doors, pounded down the hallway to the door where the RPG gunner had been and tossed another grenade into the room. As soon as it was out of his hand, he jumped back, throwing himself to the floor with his back to the left-hand wall opposite the previous room.

The grenade went off with a crack followed by a massive secondary explosion; he'd managed to roll it right into the ready ammo for the RPG gunners. The purple-orange explosion blew out the interior walls of the room, filling the corridor with smoke and dust and momentarily deafening the first sergeant. He rolled over backwards, coming to his feet and spinning to the previous room. He peeked around the door but there wasn't anything to worry about there; the explosion had blown in the walls to that room as well and the terrorists were lying on the ground, writhing in pain.

Stepping into the room, he could see into the one that had held the RPG gunner and through holes into the last room in the hallway. He dropped to one knee and scanned the opening, looking for targets. A tango was just getting to his feet and the first sergeant brought him to the floor with a short burst before springing to his feet and darting through the hole in the wall into the RPG room. There was a massive hole in the floor near the corridor wall that he had to negotiate around carefully. There were also two or more bodies, bits really, scattered around the room.

He passed through, staying away from the windows where occasional "friendly" rounds continued to crack, to the far hole. There wasn't any definitive movement, just the one tango he'd targeted on the floor. He tossed a grenade through, anyway, backing away to avoid the fragments, then exploding through the hole as soon as the grenade went off.

There had been one tango by the windows on the near wall, but he was riddled with fragments and coughing blood, his AK on the floor by his hand. Cady kicked it away, then made his way across the creaking floor to the door, peeking into the corridor and ducking back as rounds cracked from the far end.

"You shoot me, Gibson, and I'll put you on vehicle painting duty for the rest of your natural life!" the first sergeant bellowed.

"Sorry, Top!" the private called back.

"Coming out!" the first sergeant yelled. "Somebody come through and tag these tangos! And somebody else get Herr's ammo!"

Specialist Nelms sighted the building that first squad was taking rear cover positions on. He could see and hear a lot of action taking place on the second floor. And a lot of shouting; the first sergeant's accent was clear even through the bellows.

The second room that he came to on the fifth floor had a jagged hole, a remnant from previous street fighting, down near the floor. He set the Barrett down and peeked through, careful to keep his silhouette away from the window. The hole was wide enough that he could cover the entire roof of the building across the way and get an angle into the side street.

Sure about his snipe point, he slid the Barrett forward and snuggled it into his shoulder, peering through the BORS sniper scope and tracking for targets. He scanned the street and the side buildings until an RPG or a grenade going off in the building across the street caught his attention. The walls around the explosion were being pockmarked by fire from somewhere to the side. And it was increasing.

Nelms calmly but hurriedly scanned in the direction of the sound of the AK fire; there they were. Seven insurgents had dug in on the third floor of the building, or what was left of it, and were zeroing in on Top and the stack as they tried to move from the interior hallway to the exterior rooms where the other insurgents were taking cover.

Breathe in . . . out one, two, three, squeeze. The trigger on the Barrett depressed, and Specialist Nelms tracked the round. The rifle used the venerable .50 caliber Browning Machine Gun round or "50 BMG." Developed during the First World War, the round was extremely powerful with massive overkill on "soft" targets like Iraqi insurgents. When the target was hit, the bullet, quite literally, blew the tango apart. The upper torso of the Iraqi insurgent blew upwards and to the left, trailing unidentifiable pieces, while the severed legs and pelvis dropped out of sight.

The Barrett had pushed Nelms back at least three inches, despite the fact that he was stretched out on the ground, but he brought it back into battery automatically and retargeted. *Breathe . . . squeeze!*

This time he'd hit high and the round punched through the terrorist's upper chest, spreading a red stain across the wall behind the muj and covering his buddies with blood. The impact tore away the connective tissue and bone on the right side of the Arab's throat and upper chest and when he fell backwards his head flopped off to the side.

Nelms contemplated the sight for about an eighth of a second with dispassion. It was an interesting example of ballistics and he wanted to make sure he'd seen it correctly. With the exception of casual professional interest, he had no other feelings about the shot. He sometimes wondered if that was because of all the hunting he'd done or because of the nature of the enemy. He, like most of his fellow soldiers, really did *not* like the Iraqi insurgents. They had no particular honor in their fighting methods, most of them weren't even from Iraq and, in general, they were incompetent at anything but setting roadside bombs. To Nelms the man that he had just shot was less than a human, and killing him felt more like stepping on a cockroach than murder.

Nelms pulled the sniper rifle in and up and rolled to the right and then bear crawled to the window at the far end of the room; the signature from a Barrett could sometimes be very noticeable so the experienced snipers had called for no more than two shots from a single position. Quickly he dropped the bipod of the rifle on the windowsill, targeted, and fired twice.

He held still to see what the remaining insurgents were doing. Through the BORS he could see the last two of them scanning for him and covering at the same time. They were preparing an RPG. Nelms didn't pause this time to breathe, he just opened fire on them with the rifle, forcing them to cover. The commotion drew attention to the insurgent terrorists' location and two bursts of SAW fire from first squad took care of them. Nelms ceased fire and continued to scan for targets.

"Top, this is Bravo Six," Gries said, glancing at the building. He had been able to track the first sergeant's movements pretty closely by the carnage apparent from the windows. "I'm sending a squad from second in through the bottom floor. Be advised, there's no more fire coming from the building; the tangos have done a runner."

❈   ❈   ❈

"Roger," First Sergeant Cady said over the tac-net. "We'll just tag and bag, then." He looked down the corridor and thought for a second. "Gregory, we've got this floor, Second's got the bottom. Tag and bag!"

Shane was checking his e-mail when the Third Battalion CO, Lieutenant Colonel Mark M. Markum entered his office.

"Nice job on that ambush," the colonel said, sitting down in a rickety Iraqi chair one of Shane's troops had "liberated" and installed in his office. "The news media is making it look like definitive word we're unable to 'ensure the security of Iraq during the upcoming election' since we couldn't even guard these scientists. But that's par for the course."

"We had three wounded and one dead," Shane said, shaking his head and taking a sip of pop. "I'd like some way to figure out when we're going to *be* ambushed."

"Science fiction isn't reality," Markum replied. "All we can do is keep killing the insurgents and hope they get the picture. When the Iraqis take over for good and all . . . well, we'll see what they can do."

"I'd like another citation for Cady," Gries said, changing the subject.

"He do another Terminator?" the colonel asked, chuckling. "I remember when he was just a sergeant in Second Brigade. Look how little Thomas has grow'd."

"Well, he deserves it," Shane said, sighing.

"You don't look happy," Markum replied. "You didn't take that many casualties this time for how hard you got hammered. So what's up? Oh, your majority?"

"I suppose I shouldn't be pining on it," Shane said. "I

was just hoping I'd have mail. I was on the list. I thought I'd have my leaves by now."

"As soon as you get your leaves you have to transfer out of the company," the colonel pointed out.

"I'm aware, sir," Gries said, smiling faintly. "And, yeah, I don't want to do that, either. Tough call, huh?"

"Giving up your command for the shittiest rank on earth?" Markum said, grinning. "Yeah, it's a tough call. Career or the only fun to be had in the Army, command?"

"Fun," Shane said darkly. "I've got letters to write tonight. But, yeah, command is as good as it gets. I don't know whether I should be hoping I get my major leaves or sorry if I do."

"Well, you're going to have to decide soon," the colonel said, reaching into his pocket and pulling out a small cardboard rectangle with two sets of major's leaves on it. "I got the mail, not you."

"Crap," Gries whispered, shaking his head. "What now?"

"You've got fifteen days to perform change of command," the colonel said, smiling. "Then you're on temporary orders to deploy back to rear det at Fort Stewart. The rest of your orders, I'm given to understand, are somewhere in somebody's inbox awaiting 'determination.' "

Shane frowned at that and glanced over at his commander.

"I'm up for CGSC, right?" Gries asked, referring to Command and General Staff College. The Army's premier course for "middle managers," CGSC was a prerequisite for promotion beyond major, just as War College was a prerequisite for flag rank. It could either be taken as a correspondence course or on-site, the "full" course, at Fort Leavenworth. The latter was much preferred, promotion-wise, to the former and Shane had been given to understand that as soon as he had his majority he was on the list. He'd been a very good boy in the Army, getting all the little merit badges he was supposed to get, the airborne wings, the Ranger tab, and never getting anything short of a "walks on water" review. With the star on his Combat Infantryman's Badge, meaning he'd been to war, as an infantry officer, twice, he was a shoe-in for full bird at the very least, assuming he didn't really screw up. Since he didn't screw the wives of subordinates, the daughters of generals, or males, he figured he was golden. *If* he could get the "full" CGSC course.

"Got no idea," the colonel replied. "All I know is you need to start clearing your company so you can boogie on back to Stewart and the world. Me, I'm stuck here for the next five months."

"How do I get out of this Mickey Mouse organization?" Shane said, trying to smile.

"You can't," Markum admitted. "You're also on stop-loss."

"So, what've you got Mr. Hamilton?" Dr. Simms asked as he flipped through the three hundred pages of data Jack had just dumped on his desk.

"The data from the Hubble Telescope run we made last month on the Martian surface albedo doesn't match the data we took last year," Jack said, furrowing his brow. He had hopes of completing his dissertation with this run of data, but for some reason the albedo he measured this year with the aging space telescope was completely out of synch with last year's data. Furthermore, it didn't match in *very* odd ways. If he had tainted the data some way or if the Hubble was failing again, all his four years of research could be wasted—or at least delayed another year or two. And damnit, Jack was ready to graduate and start making money. As much as an astronomer ever made, anyway.

"Let's not be rash, Jack." Dr. Simms continued scanning the spectral graphs in the stack of printouts. "I know the Earth-based data won't be as defined as this, but have you considered getting Sandi over at Flagstaff to make a measurement for you? At least then we would have something to compare the Hubble data to. You could implement that filtering technique of yours to clean it up some."

"Well, I hadn't thought of Sandi," Jack admitted. "But I did try it with my sixteen-inch setup at home. There just isn't enough aperture for the measurement. I'll call Sandi and see if she can help me out."

"Who knows, Jack, they may already have the data for some other measurement. Don't give up yet." Simms tapped one of the figures and chuckled, "But I don't think this can be right. That is a *lot* of silicon. It looks like a computer factory."

Time: Present minus eight months—first European Mars probe failure

It had taken Jack about four months to collect all of the data he needed. Fortunately, Dr. Sandi Thiaput at the Lowell Observatory in Flagstaff, Arizona, had made several measurements of the Martian albedo for another project the previous year and Sandi e-mailed the raw and post-processed data to him. But a new measurement had to be ordered and put in the experiment cycle. It was more than three months of merely waiting for his turn at the telescope. When the time came and the system had been set up to make new Martian surface albedo measurements, Jack logged on to the telescope control page and took over the system; he could manage the telescope at the Lowell Observatory from his office at Johns Hopkins University via the Internet.

The measurement involved taking several exposures over several hours each and the need for multiple measurements required several nights of telescope time. Jack had lost about a week of sleep by the time the final data was crunched through his filtering algorithms and massaged into a form that made sense to the human eye.

As the algorithm ground to a halt, the computer pinged to alert that it had completed processing the data. The ping startled Jack awake. The graph that was displayed on the screen *really* woke him up.

"Dr. Simms! Dr. Simms!" Jack screamed as he burst into the rotund little professor's office. "It's real! The reflectance albedo of Mars has changed in the past year!"

"Calm down, Mr. Hamilton, and let me see what you have there." Dr. Simms nodded for the graduate student to sit as he took the stack of printouts from him. The graph on the top page showed the reflectance of Mars as of the previous year in black and the most recent measurement in red. The red and black curves were clearly different in both shape and magnitude.

"You see what I mean? The planet is, well, brighter! And it has different compounds on the surface than before." Jack rose from his seat, leaned over his advisor's desk and tapped his finger on the red curve.

"You're certain this data is correct?" Dr. Simms asked, stroking his beard as he pondered the graph. "You sure Sandi isn't just playing a trick on you of some sort? She's been known to do that in the past. This looks . . . This can't be! It's either the most remarkable data in history or . . . but that's the spectrum of . . . This can't be right!" he said as he grabbed a materials reference book from his shelves.

"You can go ahead and look it up if you want, Doctor, but I already did that," Jack said. "It's aluminum and lots of it! There's also steel, carbon-based alloys of all sorts, silicon, and even what looks like gold. And most of all, it must be highly polished for the albedo to be that high. And there has to be *lots* of it!"

"This can't be right—"

"This can't be right," Shane muttered, glaring at the e-mailed copy of his orders.

"What's wrong, sir?" Captain Tyler asked. The two had been in opposite cubicles since Gries had returned from Iraq. From CO of an in-combat company to Assistant S-4 would look lousy on a review, but it was just a holding position while DA figured out what to do with him. Usually, that sort of thing was worked out months in advance of a captain's promotion, but in Shane's case, something had gotten in the works. He'd been on the horn to DA nearly daily, trying to find out where he was going—CGSC, a major's position "commensurate with career progression" or what. In the meantime, he'd been Assistant Rear Detachment S-4 (Logistics) officer, Field Grade

Officer of the Day at Division Headquarters and any other jack-shit detail a field grade officer could get shafted with.

And now this.

"Orders," Shane said, angrily. "I've got my orders."

"And they are, sir?" Captain Tyler asked. He was the "real" assistant S-4, a supply officer who knew his career prospects were limited to *maybe* making full bird colonel in charge of an out-of-the-way depot instead of the strong possibility of stars. Despite that, the slight officer couldn't resent Major Gries; the guy was just too damned *nice*.

"Pentagon," Gries said, steamingly pissed off. "Deputy Assistant Project Officer, Infantry, Defense Design and Acquisitions Bureau."

"What does that mean, sir?" Captain Tyler asked, carefully, aware that the normally laid-back major was right on the edge of going off.

"I have no fucking idea," Shane replied, sharply. "But it's sure as hell not Command and General Staff."

Transcript of the Ret Ball, The Truth Nationwide Show

Nonclass: Open Source

Ret Ball: *You are listening to the Truth Nationwide, the largest syndicated talk-radio program on late night across this great country. We have open callers tonight. Whatever topic you wish to discuss we want to hear it. Kim from Tampa, Florida, you are on the Truth Nationwide.*

Caller: *Oh my gosh, it's so great to be on your show,*

Ret. I listen to you every night and you really do have your thumb on the pulse of the world.

Ret Ball: *Thank you, Kim. What do you want to discuss tonight?*

Caller: *Well, I was wondering about something. With the war over in the Middle East and all we don't see much on the regular news anymore, but have you seen the stories about the European Space Agency and the Russians losing their Mars spacecraft? I mean, I saw a little blurb about it on CNN but there were no details. Why have we lost several probes from different countries all within the past year?*

Ret Ball: *Ah yes, I have seen a few articles about this at SpaceWeekly.com but they explained away any unusual circumstances.*

Caller: *I'll have to check that article out, but isn't that typical. They always explain away everything. Thanks, Ret, keep fighting the good fight.*

Ret Ball: *Thank you, Kim. Let's see, the next caller is, AHA! Our old friend and regular caller, Megiddo from underground. Go ahead old friend, you are telling the Truth Nationwide!*

Caller: *Greetings and salutations, Ret! It's good to hear that there are people out there with their eyes and ears open. Indeed, we've lost several probes at Mars and it's only a matter of time before we start losing all of them there. Have you observed Mars lately, Ret?*

Ret Ball: *Why I guess I haven't, Megiddo. Why? Tell us what is going on, old friend.*

Caller: *Well, I have been watching since the first European probe was lost and something about the little red planet looks . . . different.*

Ret Ball: *Different? How so?*

Caller: *The albedo is shifting, Ret, shifting in a way that is clearly the result of intelligent design. I'm telling you, Ret, the CIA knows about this and they're covering it up, spending all their time trying to track me down instead of facing this critical threat to our very lives! Our solar system is under an invasion from an extraterrestrial intelligence as we speak. The government is never going to warn us in time to take action; it's all up to you, Ret. This is your hour! You must spread the Truth, Ret!*

Ret Ball: *I see. So the government is behind a cover-up of an ET invasion. Typical of them, Megiddo my old friend. Well, I'll have to get my telescope out and go take a look at the red planet for myself! We will speak the Truth! No matter what forces come against us! You're on the air . . .*

Time: Present minus four months—loss of first U.S. Mars probe

"Well, Tom, you work for NASA, you tell us," Roger said with a sly grin. "Alan and I are just lowly space defense contractors and wouldn't know anything 'bout no NASA rocket science."

Dr. Roger P. Reynolds was born, raised, and educated in his home state of Alabama. Although he was well known in the space reconnaissance community as somewhat of a space systems engineering genius, outside of those classified rooms you would never know it. In his late thirties with a runner's build, a more seemingly stereotypical educated Southern redneck you could never find—right down to his slow Southern drawl and his Roll Tide necktie and ball cap.

"That's right. Us here Huntsville Alabama hicks don't know nuthin' 'bout no rocket science," Alan said in his best Southern drawl, laughing. Alan Davis, unlike Dr. Reynolds, whom he thought of as "his sidekick," was only first generation redneck; his parents had moved to Huntsville when he was seven. Now at thirty-seven years old there were still hints of his Yankee dialect in his speech. Alan had stayed a North Alabamian and gone through college at the local university earning master's degrees in mechanical and electrical engineering before "going corporate" and getting a job *doing* mechanical and electrical engineering on space defense projects for the Space and Missile Defense Command and the Defense Advanced Research Projects Agency (DARPA).

"Why would *all* the probes there suddenly quit workin'?" Roger said more seriously as he swirled the pitcher of beer in front of him and started to pour more into his glass. The Hooters' waitress passing by slapped him on the hand and took the pitcher away before he could pour a drop.

"That's my job," the slim brunette said.

"Ha, serious job security issues you got there, honey," Alan said with a laugh as he offered his empty beer glass up as well. "Yeah, Tom," he continued. "You tell us how that could happen."

Tom leaned back on his stool and took a big draw from his beer glass. "Well, personally, I think we should nuke Mars now. There ain't no electromagnetic phenomena or anything that could do it. Haylfahr, iffin' it wore solar flares or somethin', it'd be affecting satellites here at Earth," he said in his horrible attempt at an Alabama accent.

Thomas Conley Powell, Ph.D., was a Californian only recently transplanted to North Alabama. Tom was the elderly "gray beard" of the bunch. In his early fifties and with slightly graying dark hair he represented an archetype of overeducated academician who would rather spend his time solving fourth order sets of coupled differential equations than eating when he was hungry. He was originally from the California Institute of Technology and had been transferred from the Jet Propulsion Laboratory. So, the Alabama "hicks" *had* to give the "expert rocket scientist from JPL" a hard time.

" 'I don't know' is the only answer I can come up with, guys," he said seriously. "And you're not the only ones asking, trust me." With that, Tom shrugged and hit his beer again.

"You know, I've been catchin' up on some of my newsgroups the past few days," Roger mused. "And the weirdest thing is that some of the amateur astronomy groups are saying that the actual color of Mars is changing. Now, I don't know that I believe that since that would require some major changes in either the surface or the atmosphere of the planet." Roger grabbed a buffalo wing by both ends and twisted it counterclockwise, then pulled both bones from it leaving nothing but the meat of the chicken wing in one strip. He dipped it in the hot sauce and then in the ranch dressing in front of him. "I guess we could calculate the surface change requirements, if we knew the extent of change that was being claimed."

"I don't think I believe that shit," Alan replied.

"No, the calcuflation fwool be feasy," Roger said with a mouthful of buffalo wing.

"No, you idiot," Alan said. "I don't believe the color of Mars is changing."

"Well, that part I'm not sure about either. But I know that we ain't talking to any of our probes there anymore." Tom tried the trick with a wing and it squirted out of his hands and onto the floor. "Shit!"

"I got it," their waitress said, swaying over to wipe up Tom's mess.

"All I know is that the newsgroups are saying that there is a visible difference in the appearance of Mars." Roger demonstrated the wing trick once again for Tom. "And, yeah, the guys on the newsgroups are amateurs, but they're not stupid and they can't all be nuts. 'Amateur' astronomers have better hardware than most professionals did in the 1960s and even later."

"Well, then we should try to calculate the significance of that change." Alan demonstrated the trick also, then washed down the wing with beer. "They don't have wings at JPL? Hell, Tom, it ain't rocket science."

"I'll never figure that out," Tom said ruefully. He picked up his next wing and simply bit into it.

"Are y'all talkin' 'bout Mars?" their regular waitress asked with a smile as she approached, picked up the pitcher, and began refilling the glasses.

"Yeah, Rog here thinks its changing colors on us," Alan said.

"Oh, it is!" the waitress replied. The three men stopped what they were doing and gave their undivided attention to the young blonde Hooters' waitress—as if they hadn't been already. She was pleasantly stacked, with shoulder length hair, blue eyes and long legs that ran straight up to a nice pair of assets. Her nametag read: Traci. It was also hard to read since it pointed more or less straight up.

"How you know that?" Tom asked.

"Oh, my advisor and I looked at it last night in PH 489," the blonde said nonchalantly, as she refilled their glasses. "Y'all want another pitcher or anything?"

"Sure, and some more wings . . . PH 489?" Alan said, scratching his head.

"PH 489 . . . hey, ain't that a senior level special topics class?" Roger asked.

"ORDER IN!" Traci yelled as she slid the order for the wings down a wire into the kitchen. "Yeah, it's a senior level physics elective. I'm helping with the Astronomy for Poets class in order to get time on the ten-inch Schmidt-Cassegrain Telescope in the UAH observatory. After the freshman business and art majors are through, I use the telescope to make some *real* observations. I've been watchin' Mars for my project. I've got about two semesters worth of data."

"Traci," Tom said, peering at the girl's breast-perched nametag. "I remember you. You're a physics major or an optics major or something like that?"

"Tom, you *never* pay attention," Roger said with a smile. "That's the whole problem with NASA; attention to detail. She's an *astro*physics grad working on her *master's*. So, you've been watchin' the red planet, hey. What have you found—any canals or little green men, little funny lookin', big-headed aliens that go *aaackk aaacckk aaack*?"

"You're funny," Traci said, smiling thinly. "Over the period of this semester I haven't noted any visible difference. But if you take images of Mars from a semester ago then compare it to the way it looks now, it's different."

"How so?" Roger asked.

"It's less red," Traci said definitely. "The color has blue-shifted significantly. It looks more gray now. It might be my imagination but I *think* the albedo is up, too. Too bad the University At Home can't afford a *real* spectrometer, 'cause I'd really like to see the detailed spectral content from Mars, like down to at least tens of nanometer resolution." She paused in thought, then winked at Tom, springing up and down so her large and obviously unnatural breasts bounced charmingly. "If there *are* big-tentacled aliens coming to town, do you think they'll *like* my hot and spicies?"

"Uh . . ." Tom said, his higher brain functions momentarily circumvented.

"Traci, could I get copies of those im-im-images?" Roger asked. He was just a tad more suave than his fellows, but even he stumbled over "images." The two large images in his mind at present had nothing to do with Mars.

"Sure," Traci said, just as seriously. "What's your e-mail address?"

"Thanks." Roger dug a business card out of his shirt pocket and handed it to her.

"Nuke Mars NOW!" Tom said, coming abruptly back to the moment. "Wait a minute. The University At Home?"

"Never mind him, Traci," Alan said with a grin. "He's a foreigner from the left coast. They're not all that swift iffin' you know what I mean."

"I forget you're from California, *Doctor* Powell," the waitress cooed, causing another meltdown. "I meant the University of Alabama in Huntsville or UAH. We affectionately refer to it around these parts as—"

"The University At Home," Roger and Alan chimed in.

"I get it," Tom said, grinning.

"I'm so *glad* for you," Traci replied, widening her eyes in mock surprise. "After all, it ain't *rocket* science."

Roger and Alan tried not to fall off their stools laughing as the waitress bounced over to get their order. Tom just sighed.

Chapter 2

Time: Present—all contact with Mars probes lost

"Well, sir," the president's science advisor George Fines explained, "scientists at the Space Telescope Science Institute have actually discovered that the bolometric albedo—that is what astronomers call the spectral content or colors of a planetary image—of Mars has changed over the past year dramatically. But what is even more alarming is that within the past month it has changed at an incredible rate. The current spectrum when compared to the previous one shows that there *are* now many different metals, gases, and other compounds on the surface and in the atmosphere. This is an unprecedented change."

"Yes, George. I realize that, but what does it mean?" President Colby replied as he looked out the window of the Oval Office. He was a businessman—top of his class at Harvard. Economic recessions, inflation, hell, even depressions, he could handle. Planets changing colors during his administration was something he wasn't sure he was prepared for. "How's this going to affect *us*? I'm interested and all that, but it's not like there's a great big comet headed this way that only Bruce Willis can save us from. . . ."

"If I may, Mr. President," NASA Director Jess Obannon interjected. "The planet got shiny all of the sudden. We don't know why. Then we started losing probes. That . . . doesn't look like coincidence."

"You're saying . . . what?" the President asked. "Aliens? Little green men?"

"We don't know, Mr. President," the science advisor said, frowning. "That's the problem."

"Mr. President, we're trying to gather more data. But we need more time. And, we need a closer look than we can get with Earth-based telescopes." Obannon rubbed his bald head and looked nervously at the President's back. "But, so far we can think of no *natural* cause for this."

The President rolled up his left sleeve, then began with his right as he turned to face the NASA bureaucrat.

"All right then, I want this gagged. Nobody, and I mean *nobody* leaks this info to the public yet. Anybody that knows about it gets read the National Security Act and the pertinent Executive gag orders. I mean it. The economy is flaky enough as it is right now. No telling what rumors about Mars exploding or little green men will do to the NASDAQ and the Exchange."

"Mr. President, we might need other astronomers and planetary scientists to help figure this out," the NASA administrator said. "If it's classified we might not be able to convince the best ones to help."

Fines had dealt with the planetary science community

long enough to know that NASA "scientists" didn't believe in secrets except when it came to their personal publications. Most of them hated the military and the intelligence community and wouldn't work and play well with them. He remembered the example of a few years before when the National Geospatial-Intelligence Agency (NGA, then NIMA) told them that they had found the failed Mars polar lander in some of the other Mars orbiters' imagery and that it was sitting upright on its landing struts. NASA scientists didn't believe it because nobody is smarter than NASA scientists—and the NASA scientists said it was impossible to make such claims from the data available. NASA administrators at the Office of Space Science didn't care or acknowledge that the NGA had spent a mammoth Cold War budget developing spy satellite image analysis techniques that were decades beyond those developed on NASA's shoestring budget. But since they were not NASA, NGA couldn't know what they were talking about—the "not invented here" syndrome.

Fines knew that NASA scientists were not who he needed. He wanted the *best* scientists, so he knew not to look to the stagnant "white collar welfare" technical community. There were some smart guys at NASA, but most of *them* were involved with the nation's spy organizations in some form or other. Brains go where the money is and for decades NASA's budget was much smaller than the intelligence community's.

"Mr. President, I think we need the space reconnaissance community's help," the science advisor suggested.

The President tapped his phone, "Judy, get me my NSA, the DCI, and the DNRO in my office right now, and the Chairman of the Joint Chiefs, thanks." He smiled at Fines. "You're right, George. Now, let's get this thing quieted down, shall we?" The President smiled and showed the science advisor and the NASA administrator the door.

His phone buzzed as he sat back down in his chair. "Yes, Judy?"

"Mr. President, the national security advisor is here to see you. Should I change your one o'clock meeting with Ambassador Chiaz?"

"Yes, see if you can delay him until sometime next week, will you? And send Vicki in."

"Right away, Mr. President."

"Oh, Judy, as soon as the Chairman, the DCI and DNRO get here, send them in."

"Yes, sir."

"Mr. President, from the data that we have it's my conclusion that this is some sort of preparation for invasion," the Chairman of the Joint Chiefs stated.

"Really, Kevin? How would we know that?" Dr. Vicki Johnson, the national security advisor asked. "What if it turns out to be a natural phenomenon? Or if it's unnatural, then what if they're just moving in or building a home? If it's an alien race, they might *prefer* Mars."

"Vicki," the President interrupted. "I don't know which thought scares me most. Whether we're talking about preparations for attack or just moving in, we might still be talking about strangers—aliens—moving into our neighborhood. And we know absolutely nothing about them."

"We need to know more about what is going on, Mr. President," the national security advisor commented. "But how to get that information is the hard part. Mars is a long way away from Earth."

"John, what do you think?" The President turned to the director of Central Intelligence. "Is there a way to get the recon we need?"

"Not today, not tomorrow, hell, Mr. President, not even this month, maybe not even this year. We would need to complete a Mars satellite design and build and mission implementation in an extremely compressed schedule. I don't know much, if anything, about that. What do you think, Mike?" he asked the director of the National Reconnaissance Office. NRO handled all the satellites used by the intelligence and military branches and developed the new technologies for the next generation systems.

"I don't know, either, Mr. President," the DNRO replied. "I would like a couple of weeks to have my guys run some numbers. We would need some budget for this and I mean serious budget."

"Well, figure it out," the President said. "But if they're preparing for something, do we have two weeks? Hurry. Vicki, John, Kevin, I want y'all to make sure that NRO gets whatever support they need on this. For now this is to be kept quiet. Got it?"

"Major Shane Gries reporting for duty," Shane said, saluting the Navy captain behind the desk. The officer, the equivalent of a full colonel in the Army, which meant a senior division staff officer or brigade commander, occupied just one cubicle in the large room in the bowels of the Pentagon, indicative of just how important the "Bureau" was considered by the real powers in the building. The desk itself had a high-end monitor on it with some sort of blueprint displayed and was just about covered in paper. Shane didn't even recognize most of the forms on the desk but he did see that most had Top Secret cover sheets.

"Welcome, welcome," the officer said, returning the salute lazily. "I'm Captain Sparling, as you can see from that plaque on my overloaded desk. Welcome to Chaos Central. I've been *eagerly* awaiting your arrival, Major. Nay, I can only say how *ecstatic* I am to see you. Do you like traveling commercial?"

"I can hang, sir," Gries said, trying not to shake his head at the greeting. He'd expected the usual "you've joined the best outfit in the division" speech. Or fleet, he supposed, given that his new boss was Navy. Not "I'm ecstatic to see you." That had a note of . . . foreboding.

"I'll give you the quickest run-down in history, Major," the captain said, spinning his computer chair back and forth. Sparling was a short, frankly rotund, officer, which was very unusual to find in the modern military, wearing rather rumpled undress blues. He was balding and entirely unprepossessing, but Shane realized after just a moment that he had about the sharpest eyes the major had ever seen. He gave an impression of casual unconcern, but Shane could tell that there was a mind behind those eyes going a mile a minute.

"The mission of this bureau is simple in concept," Sparling said, smiling broadly. "So simple I'm sure you can keep up, even if I use words of more than two syllables. We're here to look at projects that have reached the preacquisition stage and determine if they have 'real world' flaws. There are two sides to that, Major. The first is that we *definitely* don't want anything going out to the forces that is not enhancing to their mission. The second is equally important. The U.S. is a world master in combat because we have good training and we have the best damned technology in the world. Each new system that is an *enhancement* spreads the gap between us and the rest of the world. You ever gotten something new and gone 'Crap, I wish I had this last week when it would have helped', Major?"

Shane thought about the squad tac-net that they'd gotten just before deploying. It had taken about a week for the troops to really understand it and after that they'd used it to communicate in ways that hadn't been possible days before. He knew guys had been saved by that deceptively simple system; it was far more than just a radio. Then there were some of the new field medical items, like the blood clotter that was made from shrimp shells, that had saved more lives. But he just nodded, continuing to look the officer in the eye calmly.

"You have *no* idea how many great ideas the Beltway Bandits think up," Sparling continued, grinning widely. "There are dozens, hundreds, *thousands* of febrile, bright young minds scattered all over the United States and the world, trying to come up with the 'killer app' for the United States military. Which, next to mass market items, is the largest single market in the world. One item that really catches on and gets wide deployment can make or break a company and certainly those bright young men, and women. If the product gets picked up, they get bonuses and a nice house in the Caymans. If it tanks, they get 'downsized' and have to go into academia where they *don't* get the house in the Caymans. With me still, Major?"

"Yes, sir," Shane said, smiling thinly. "You can feel free

to use words of up to three syllables or even more; I haven't had my mandatory field grade lobotomy yet." He paused as he said that, realizing it might be a slur on his new boss. But it was way too late to take anything back.

Sparling really grinned at that and shook his head.

"You have no idea," was the captain's reply. "The point is that these bright young men, and women—some of the women quite good looking, by the way—will be trying *very* hard to 'sell' you on some wizmo, our in-house word for wiz-bang gizmo. *Your* job will be to see if the item has any *practical* value. You will examine the item carefully, gather all the information you feel appropriate, then fill out a voluminous report, including in it all your experience as an infantry officer with two wars under your belt and a masters in literature with your *thesis* being on near-future potential technologies to be found in science fiction classics."

"That's why I'm here," Shane said bitterly.

"That is why you are here instead of at CGSC," Sparling said, smiling broadly. "Because your *predecessor* was very *very* good at finding things that, in his experienced opinion, would never work. So good he turned in not *one* positive recommendation in three months. And those three months covered over six hundred systems or technologies."

"That's . . ." Shane said, thinking about it.

"And that's the other reason I'm glad you're here," Sparling said, reading his mind. "You're going to the Lockheed Martin facility in Denver on the next plane out. Before you leave see Captain Grantworth, who is our administrative officer. She'll give you your homework. Which, since your predecessor left three weeks ago, is over sixty systems or technologies. Some of them you're going to have to decide upon on the basis of the written or submitted PowerPoint presentations. About fourteen are going to require you to go look for yourself. Ten of those are here in the D.C. area, the other four are at other facilities. That's your workload for *this* week."

"Yes, sir," Gries said, straightening up. What the captain had just told him was that Shane would be working eighteen-hour days for the foreseeable future.

"Of course," Sparling said, grinning happily, "at the end of all that work, in the event of a negative recommendation you'll often find that some congressman disagrees with you and will insert a supplementary appropriation, bypassing our recommendation as if it didn't exist. Because you are, after all, just a dumb grunt and what do you know? Or it may be that you are just one voter and the wizmo will employ thousands of voters in that congressman's district."

"Got it, sir," Shane said, smiling thinly.

"You'll notice I have not used words like 'synergize' or 'transformational,'" Sparling said, suddenly serious. "What you are going to see over the next six to eighteen months, though, depending upon whether we can get a filler while you go to CGSC, is going to be just that. Stuff that can transform the face of the U.S. military and even the world. And it's going to be your job to find that one *nugget* of gold in the crap that might just save your life some day. Have fun in Colorado."

Caller: *. . . and you see Ret, that is why you'll never see the bodies from Roswell.*

Ret Ball: *I see. That is very informative Andrea. Next caller is . . . hey hey . . . it's our old friend Megiddo from underground. Go ahead, Megiddo, you are on the Truth Nationwide.*

Caller: *Hello, Ret, and greetings.*

Ret Ball: *It's good to hear from you old friend. I hesitate, of course, to ask where you are and what you are doing.*

Caller: *Right, and I thank you for that. I am lying low at the moment. My former employers have had enough of me and I them. But they have sent their lackeys from the CIA and the NSA to search for me, saying that the knowledge in my head is a danger to national security. Hah! They shall search in vain!*

Ret Ball: *Ha ha! What can we do for you tonight, Megiddo?*

Caller: *I just wanted to let you know that the situation with Mars has gotten worse.*

Ret Ball: *Ah yes! Mars. For some of our listeners out there that are just tuning in, you need to realize that the color of Mars is changing. I myself have seen this with my own telescope. Our friend Megiddo here, has enlightened us on this subject.*

Caller: *Thanks, Ret. I'll make this short so my burst transmissions are not traced. But the CIA and the right wing conspiracy know about this. They're covering it up and are in fact planning to send a rapid development space mission to the planet to make contact with the enemy and finalize their plans for world domination. They're putting together a set of Boeing Delta Vs with common booster cores that will fling their communications satellite towards Mars on a fast fly-by. This will put them in contact with the masters that are rapidly converting Mars as a base of operations in this solar system.*

Ret Ball: *Really? How do you . . . no, I know better than to ask.*

Caller: *Thanks, Ret. You are a trooper. But I'm telling everybody now. Prepare, be prepared. The world as we know it is about to disintegrate.*

Ret Ball: *Wow! Thanks, Megiddo, we'll keep our listeners posted. Next caller is Ben from Dayton, Ohio. Ben, go ahead you are on the Truth Nationwide.*

Caller: *Ha ha, Jesus H. Christ, Ret! That guy was so whacked he probably wears an aluminum foil hat on his head!*

Ret Ball: *Ah caller, you must be new to the Truth Nationwide. Megiddo has been with us for years. And indeed he does wear an aluminum beanie. He discovered years ago that the remote viewing technology of the CIA can track him otherwise. But to all my listeners, I say this: More times than not Megiddo has predicted something that has actually come to pass.*

Caller: *Well, if you ask me, he is nuts.*

Reference to mission to Mars forwarded to higher security cell for breach evaluation.

Chapter 3

The eight-inch diameter aperture Meade LX90 her father had gotten her for her birthday the previous year more than thrilled Charlotte Fisher. Most fifteen-year-old girls would have wanted something more girly, but not her. The color ccd camera he got her this year might—just might—make up for him missing her birthday again. But ever since the divorce a few years ago when he took that job at Vandenberg Air Force Base in California—to get away from her mom—he began missing things while at the same time trying to make up for it by buying her expensive gifts. In the case of the computer-driven telescope, it did. The perfectly clear evenings in the high altitude at Denver were perfect for stargazing—well, if you could get far enough away from the light pollution of the city. Fortunately, they lived far enough north from the city that a few dark places could be found.

"I think Mars is more, I dunno, gray-colored than red," Tina said as she pointed to the image on the laptop while Charlotte brought the little planet into focus.

"Yeah, I think so too," Charlotte replied.

"Hey, maybe we should go over and ask Mikey about it," Tina giggled.

"I want to do some more observing here," Charlotte fiddled with the altitude-azimuth controls on the telescope.

"Chicken!" Tina said. "You know he likes you. Just go talk to him."

"What would I say? I mean he's a jock and just at this star party for the extra credit he needs in science class and me . . . I'm nobody he wants to talk to."

"Whatever. I'm gonna go see what he's up to."

"You better not!"

"Only way you're gonna stop me is to go yourself." Tina flipped her blonde hair over her shoulder and giggled again as she turned away.

The two had been an unlikely pair since grade school. Tina was a petite and ditsy blonde-hair-blue-eyes cheer-leader type who always wanted attention and Charlotte was the dark-haired-sit-quietly-in-the-front-of-the-class-and-make-straight-A's type. The only time Charlotte ever got loud or aggressive was on the girl's fast-pitch softball team. She was only five feet six inches tall, but she had the super athletic ability of being able to knock the cover off a soft-ball. This made her a deadly homerun hitter. The two girls had been best friends since grade school and neither of them knew why—well, that wasn't exactly true. Charlotte's dad John Fisher and Tina's mother Alice Pike had worked together at the Denver Lockheed Martin facility as long as the two girls could remember. That was of course, up until the divorce and Charlotte's dad had taken a promotion and transfer out to California. John was a booster systems designer, a "rocket scientist," while Alice was a physicist working on advanced microprocessor design, pushing the theoretical limits to find smaller and smaller processors that used very little power for space applications.

"Dingbat." Charlotte shook her head as she went back to work.

She set the computer to capture a long-term exposure of the little red planet, hoping that she would be able to see the redness that she had seen before. Mars had been the first thing she viewed the previous year when she had gotten the telescope from her dad. She had viewed it a few times since but Saturn was her favorite. She had spent most of her time viewing the beautiful rings of the giant gas planet. But their assignment for class was to view Mars.

"What are you looking at, Miss Fisher?" Mr. Anders asked his prize pupil.

"Mars. It'll come up on the screen in a minute. I'm taking a long exposure."

Mr. Anders stood by quietly as the image on the laptop began to appear. Mars' outline and the larger features like the polar ice cap filled in first, then more detail filled in. The image was slightly blurry because of the layers of Earth's atmosphere being turbulent, but the software had an algorithm to remove some of the fuzziness and enhance the edge features of the image. Finally, the computer dinged, announcing the image was complete and post-processed.

"Let's blow it up and look at it," Mr. Anders said.

Charlotte dragged the mouse pointer over to the zoom

controls and expanded the view. The little planet filled the screen.

"Hmmm . . ." Charlotte murmured. "Doesn't look right."

"Have you got a filter on the eyepiece?" Mr. Anders asked her.

"Nope, that's an unfiltered image and my ccd is color."

"Hey, I thought Mars was supposed to be red," Mike said, pointing over Mr. Ander's shoulder. Tina stood behind him pointing and nodding at Charlotte as they approached the telescope. Charlotte tried to ignore her.

"That's right, Mike," Mr. Anders said, looking at Charlotte's telescope and computer camera setup. "It should be."

"Well, unless my brand new ccd camera is broken," Charlotte replied, "Mars is now gray."

"Well, there's a red light on that tower over there. Why don't you look at it with your telescope and see if it's red?" Mike suggested.

"Very good idea, Mike," Mr. Anders noted.

"Yeah, Mike, very good idea." Tina giggled, and moved around to poke Charlotte in the ribs.

Charlotte slapped at Tina's finger, then dragged the mouse pointer down to the scope controls icon. Charlotte bit at her lip while she cycled the scope to point to the tower. After a second or two of refocusing, the red light from the tower filled the laptop's screen.

"Shit, I don't understand." Charlotte realized that she had just cursed in front of her teacher and held her hand over her mouth.

Mr. Anders acted as though he hadn't heard and shook his head. "I don't understand it either."

❋   ❋   ❋

Ret Ball: *Tina from Boulder, Colorado, you are on the Truth Nationwide.*

Caller: *Yeah Ret, oh my God I can't believe I'm on the radio. (giggle)*

Ret Ball: *Well, believe it or not you are on the Truth Nationwide with Ret Ball. What can I do for you tonight, Tina?*

Caller: *Yeah, me and my buddy Charlotte looked at Mars last night through her telescope and it ain't red at all. Like that Megiddo fellow said. It's gray.*

Ret Ball: *Really? How old are you and Charlotte?*

Caller: *Well I'm thir– . . . uh . . . eighteen. Off-phone, female voice, faint: Dingbat!*

Caller: *But we really did see it and it was gray not red!*

Ret Ball: *Out of the mouths of babes. Next caller is Tim from Beantown. Go ahead Tim you are on the Truth Nationwide.*

"I'm glad y'all could make it tonight." Roger held up his beer glass while Tom and Alan made themselves comfortable on the wooden stools. "I went and did some checking of my own. Traci was right. There is a noticeable difference in the surface albedo of Mars. This one paper I found by a J.H. Davis, et al., even had some really good Hubble data from a year and a half ago. Interestingly enough, the paper says there will be another run from Hubble on Mars this past year, but I've looked everywhere and can't find it. I even called up to Johns Hopkins and got stonewalled about it. I wanted to discuss the ramifications of that with y'all."

"You never learn, do you?" Traci laughed. Tom had started to pour himself a beer, but Traci appeared as if from nowhere and slapped him on the hand.

"Yeah, Tom," Alan chuckled, "that's her job."

"Shift change . . . I just got here and I'm running sooo late tonight." Traci smiled at the three men and finished pouring the beer, then adjusted her T-shirt so it was tighter across the front.

"Wings tonight fellows?"

"Nah, just beer, I think," Roger said, sliding his now empty glass towards her.

"Hey, beer *is* food," Alan said. "Cheers!"

"I'll have some curly fries," Tom told her. Traci wrote something down on a piece of paper and attached it to the wire above her head. "ORDER IN!" She smiled, slid the order down the wire, and turned to her other tables.

"So what gives, Rog?" Alan sipped his beer.

"I think it's a muster point," he said.

"*What* is a muster point?" Tom leaned in to listen better.

"It's a point or location where forces gather to prepare for further advancement. But that's not important right now," Alan replied with a grin.

"Be serious for a moment, Alan," Tom said sonorously. "I know it's not in your nature, but you simply have to apply yourself. You can do it. Maybe not *doctoral* level sobriety, but *masters* level should be possible."

"I guess this was the wrong day to stop drinking beer then," Alan said, still grinning as he killed off his beer. He was the only one of the three who had, as he put it, "gotten a real job" after getting his masters. Ergo, he was not a "doctor," simply a lowly schlub engineer with a masters.

"I think that Mars is being used to muster resources," Roger said. He contemplated his beer glass and seemed more serious than usual. "I did a calculation from some of that data I found on the Internet and the rate of change of Mars' surface albedo is so nonlinear that there is no way this is some sort of natural phenomena."

"What, you think it's aliens?" Tom asked with a laugh.

"Yes," Roger said flatly monotone.

Alan put his beer down, picked it back up as if to drink the last backwash from it, and set it down without drinking. "You're serious, aren't you, Rog?"

"Okay, you explain how the entire surface of a planet changes color in a year and how come we've lost all contact with any of the probes we've sent there. And why data from the Hubble Space Telescope that always—*always*—goes on the Space Telescope Science Institute's website is missing. All the other data from the other Hubble runs is there, but not that one. I checked Hubble's schedule. The Mars run was on it. Where's the data? I'll tell you where: It's been classified."

"All right, let's assume that you are right. What do *we* do about it?" Tom asked.

"Well, I think the first and most important thing is intel. We'll need recon of the planet. I mean recon with sub-meter resolution." Roger waited for the implications of his statement to sink in on the other two engineers.

"Yes, yes, that's what Earth should do. But what do *we* do about it?" Tom repeated.

"*We*," Roger emphasized. "We assume that somebody is looking into it, and that it's the right somebody. Then, as I said, I think the first and most important thing is intel. We'll design a recon mission of the planet. And again, I mean recon with sub-meter resolution. Then, I guess, I'll just have to take the mission design and put it in front of the right somebody." Roger nodded to the two men as if they understood what he meant by the "right somebody."

"Sub-meter?" Alan whistled.

"Wow, we can't do that with any telescope from Earth orbit."

"And it takes a half of a year at least just to get to Mars," Tom said, shaking his head.

"Well, I've been thinking about that," Roger admitted. "All we really need is a good old-fashioned spy satellite. Just one that is smaller and lighter and has to go a hell of a lot farther and faster, then stop and deploy itself."

"Oh, well, if that's all. . . ." Tom laughed.

"Here is a strawman design for a recon probe I put together last night." Roger ignored Tom's comment and continued by handing the two men each a copy of some block diagrams for a spacecraft design. "It's similar to the one we worked on for—you know." Roger raised an eyebrow and looked around the restaurant, making clear that they couldn't discuss that here. The two men looked back and nodded in realization of what Roger was hinting at. Then he could tell that they both realized who "the right somebody" must be.

"It's just a block diagram of what we would need, but I

think we could build a probe from off-the-shelf parts in no time. Some of the parts we could rob from that new Discovery program Jupiter probe and some from—uh, you know, other sources." He nodded again, implying that of course the other men did know. In fact, the three men had worked on previous classified spy and communications satellite programs for more than fifteen years together. But few people knew that or ever would know that.

"The problem is the propulsion. Tom, how could we get there faster than six months?" Alan interrupted.

"Hmmm. That ain't easy or we'd be doing it, right? Let's see, if we assume a Delta IV launch, and COTS engines for the probe, and assuming that Mars is in the right part of its orbit, you might do it in six months, but I doubt less." Tom picked up a Hooters napkin and started scribbling notes on it.

"What if we made the probe small enough that we could get two upper stages on it?" Alan suggested.

"That might work, but we would need to know the spacecraft bus size and how much room we would have for the kick stages. And it really isn't a factor of the payload mass as the number of stages, stage efficiency, and thrust needed." Tom drew out a picture of a Delta IV primary payload shroud and drew some boxes of varying shapes and sizes inside it. Then he began scribbling while muttering under his breath.

"*Kick motor1 ~30,000kg, kick motor2 30,000kg, tankage 2000kg, heat transfer100kg, batteries & PCU 1000kg, ACS/RCS 150kg, hi-gain deployable antenna 50kg, low-gain antenna 5kg, main bus 1000kg, GN&C 50kg, IVHM 5kg, science suite 1000kg, structural components 100kg, and pyrotechnics 10kg, braking engine and fuel 1000kg."* Then to the side of the drawing he wrote: *"Total = really heavy."*

"Yep, Delta IV Heavy with strap-ons or an Atlas V with strap-ons. But, I'm not sure that just two upper stages are enough."

"Hey, hold on a minute. If we're gonna see anything once we get into a closed orbit about Mars we still need a pretty good-sized aperture. So don't start eatin' up my room for the telescope with extra kick rockets. And since we're gonna need at least a half meter telescope or better, you probably ought to add another 500kg for the telescope itself," Roger warned.

"Hey, now there is an idea!" Tom got quiet for a second and zoned out in thought. The other two men had worked with him long enough to know that they shouldn't interrupt his process, because he usually came up with something brilliant when he did that. They sat patiently, quietly, and drank their beers. Alan had had to refill his because Traci was busy on the other side of the restaurant, but he made sure she was not looking his direction when he did.

"Let's see . . . ." Tom began to mutter to himself. "The C3 for that orbit's . . . right . . . the I-S-P for that engine is four hundred-eighty seconds as near as makes no difference . . . and the asymptotic velocity would be . . . yep!"

"What?" Roger asked.

"Why orbit Mars? It's a waste of mass to put the braking engine on there. Let's do a super quick fly-by. Hell, we could even crash into it if we want to. Take data right up to the end although you wouldn't have time to send back the data if you impact the planet, hmmm, better fly-by. If the problem is that the entire planet is changing then we should be able to see the phenomenon wherever we look, so orbiting isn't really needed. Yep, fly-by sounds right," he concluded.

"And with the right engines and the right trajectory—I want to check my thinking on my computer later, but—I think we could get a spacecraft large enough to do the job there in four or five months travel time—maybe."

"Can you get me those calculations soon?" Roger asked.

"What's the hurry, Rog?" Alan cocked his head to the left and looked in his beer glass.

"Well, first, if it's aliens we shouldn't just sit around and let them continue on with whatever it is they're doing." Roger sipped his beer and wiped his mouth. "Second, I'm headed back up to Chantilly next week for a meeting with the Director of AS and T at—you know. And I thought I could give him a white paper with the reasoning, strawman, mission architecture, and possible data product description. We should put a short bit in there about CONOPS also. Alan, I'd need you to write up the part on the command and data handling. Figure out how we'd get the data back from Mars." Roger tapped a box on the rough strawman drawing on the napkin in front of him marked C&DH. "And the telecom—both spacecraft and ground stations."

"No problem. We'll probably need a big aperture and a TWeeTA or two. Deep Space Network would be nice, but I'll shoot for some thirty-meter dishes groundside. Who's doing the power generation, conditioning, and distribution systems?"

"I guess I'll handle as much of the nuts and bolts as I

can manage over the weekend. I'm thinking we might be able to grab a spacecraft bus that is already being built for another program. Tom, could you work out the trajectories and such? Figure out what motors and what requirements for the ACS and RCS to hold us on target within say a tenth of a microradian right up until we hit the Martian closest approach point?" Roger asked.

"Yeah, sounds like fun. Assume a Delta IV or Atlas V, right?"

"Yeah, or whatever it takes. Just remember that time is of the essence and we want off-the-shelf stuff. I'll copy and paste standard spacecraft fairing and attachment stuff out of one of our previous mission white papers. We should be able to put together a pretty good mission architecture concept." Roger rubbed his chin wondering if he had forgotten anything.

"What about the cost and schedule?" Tom asked.

"Oh, yeah, we'll need that too, I expect. I'll do a ROM and a schedule. Hey, you know what, I think I still have that Microsoft Project task and work breakdown structure we did on that last mission. I could change it pretty easy to have a pretty good ROM and schedule for this concept. Let's see, is there anything else?"

"Hey, Rog." Alan rubbed his chin.

"Yeah?"

"What about security?"

"Oh, yeah, we best not forget security." Roger nodded. "Let's treat everything we write up in the *white world* as though we're thinking about an idea for a NASA space probe mission. After all, it's always worked in the past. Anything related to the actual mission and components from previous programs, I'll add in at the SCIF at work and take care of the classification then. Let's treat the *real* idea from now on as if it were classified at *special* levels, because if you-know-who buys into this you know that it will become that way. And I don't want to have to do a bunch of back briefings and security stuff later."

"Uh," Tom looked around the room wide-eyed. "Then I guess we shouldn't talk about it here anymore?"

"You're probably right," Alan said.

"Can we meet at my office for lunch tomorrow, Wednesday, Thursday, and Friday to see where we are with this?"

"Fine by me," Alan said.

"Hey, we can pull Project up on the big projection screen in the conference room and y'all can help fix that WBS and schedule up."

"Suits." Tom scribbled a few more notes on his napkins.

"Make sure those napkins are unclassified, Tom."

"Yes, Mother."

Dr. Ronrico "Ronny" Guerrero, the Director of Advanced Science and Technology of the National Reconnaissance Office, listened patiently to the update briefing on one of his many programs. The briefing was business as usual. The scientist in front of the room was smart, precise and had done his homework. What would have been extremely exciting discussions about space-based sparse array antennas now seemed sort of, mundane, because the DAS&T had recently been given another task with a short turn around, which was *way* more exciting— and frightening at the same time. He was preoccupied. However, Ronny was the ultimate in professionalism and would get the job done—*all* of his jobs done—to the utmost of his abilities. It was the only way that he knew to do business. It was the only way he *could* do business. Otherwise he would have never made it to where he currently was. And still be alive.

At fourteen he had been a peasant boy in Cuba and was tired of that life and that place. He had actually lived in a cardboard-and-corrugated-tin house and his living standards were nonexistent. One day after his mother passed away—who knew, she might have lived with better healthcare—Ronny walked out to the ocean and swam north, hoping to cross the ninety miles of water to the United States. He swam and swam. He swam, floated, and swam again for two days and nights until he could go no further. Ronny could still remember, floating on his back and looking at the night sky, how he thought it would be better to die free in the ocean than as an oppressed peasant. He had done the right thing even if he drowned or was eaten by a shark. The next day—sunburned beyond belief, dehydrated and half dead—he thought he was delirious when he saw land in front of him. He was—it wasn't land at all. Ronny had been lucky that a charter fishing boat out of Key West spotted him. The odds of that having occurred were ridiculous but he *was* rescued. God had been with him and Ronny would always thank Him for that.

With a second lease on life, Ronny worked hard to become an American and become accepted by his American peers. A Cuban-American family in Miami took him in and put him into a parochial school where he immediately showed that there was a fine mind in that peasant brain. On his twenty-second birthday—naturalized as an

American citizen and with a bachelor's degree in physics—
he joined the Air Force. Those years developed a mindset
that soon led him into reconnaissance and flight technologies. He enjoyed it and was good at it and used the
opportunity to study graduate level physics at the University of the Air Force. Ronny moved up in the Air Force
and by the time he was thirty earned a tour at the then
totally "black" organization now known as NRO. While at
NRO he completed his doctorate in physics at Virginia
Tech.

Ronny retired as a lieutenant colonel, then took a position as a civil servant with the NRO for a second, arguably
third, career. He quickly moved up and became the
director of AS&T. It hadn't been all easy for him. Being
from a foreign background—Cuban no less—his loyalty
often came into question by adversaries, and his security
clearance investigations always had taken three times
longer than normal. But Ronny kept his nose clean and
maintained a work ethic that made him the go-to guy for
space systems implementation and shut down any of his
opposition. Having taken a, provable, chance on *swimming* to the U.S. also tended to reduce the possibility, in
most people's eyes, that he was an agent. In short, when
it came to building space recon systems Ronny had always
gotten the job done. Now the DNRO had given him the
ultimate challenge—get recon on another planet.

Ronny would get that job done, but he wouldn't let it
interfere with his other tasks either. He felt he had to
continuously prove he was superhuman, or at least better
than the others. So, no matter what the task before him,
Ronny always gave it one hundred percent—even if he
was preoccupied with a more daunting and pressing

problem. Ronny leaned back in his leather conference room chair and placed his hands behind his head while he tried to focus on his multitasking.

"So you see, Dr. Guerrero, the structural integrity of the antenna booms can dampen out the low frequency platform jitter and the higher jitter the piezoelectric system can handle. It's our conclusion and recommendation to you that the Phase 0 design is viable and that the program is ready to move forward to a science readiness review and to Phase 1," the contractor finished in his slow Southern accent.

"That's very good, Roger. I'll take that under advisement. If there is nothing else then . . .?" Ronny looked at his watch and frowned. The contractor actually had about fifteen more minutes scheduled with him so he'd, apparently, sped his brief. Ronny's support staff took that as a cue to end the meeting and they began closing their notes and stretching.

"Uh, since we've got a little more time, just one more thing, Dr. Guerrero, if you please. I'd like to show you an unusual concept that I don't know if you would be interested in or not, but my hopes are that you will."

Roger took four copies of the Mars Recon white paper from his double-locked bags and passed them around the room. He waited for a copy to make it to Dr. Guerrero's hands before he began. Ronny was certain that Roger was trying to gauge the expression on his face. There was no expression. Guerrero had been in the super-secret world long enough to develop a perfect poker face.

"This may sound a little strange at first, but please hear me through on it," Roger began. "It has come to my team's attention that the bolometric albedo of Mars appears to be changing. It's getting shinier and less red. We have data and references here in the white paper to back that claim up—it's real. The intriguing part is that there is a data run from the Hubble this past cycle that is missing from the public domain. Since the Hubble data is usually white, I find it intriguing that a run on Mars has been made 'black.' "

Roger looked around the room at Guerrero and his aids for any sign that they had prior knowledge of this. Ronny and his team, again, displayed perfect poker faces.

"So, given that the surface of Mars is changing on such a massive scale that the bolometric albedo has been altered, then something major is going on there—probably something unnatural. The plot there on page two shows the required increase of certain compounds and metals in kilograms versus time. There are four different good data points and seven from some unverified Internet data. We then curve-fitted that data and you see it matches a simple population growth model." Roger paused again.

"The rate of growth is amazing. We believe that it *may* be a muster point for some alien force. Whether or not that force is friendly or preparing to attack us we have no idea. Based upon that data, we believe it's advisable to perform reconnaissance of Mars. This is recon that could only be gained by sending a recon satellite configured as a probe. And if it's an alien force preparing to attack, then time is of the essence."

Roger paused and Ronny could tell from the expression on Roger's face that he had been half expecting to be laughed out of the room. There were no smiles, frowns, or comments. The room remained dead calm—just like before a storm. Ronny gave nothing away but the very lack of laughter at the preposterous idea said volumes.

"So," Roger continued, swallowing nervously, "we have put together a mission architecture concept that could do the job and be ready for launch in five to six months with a four to five month traverse time."

"Roger," Ronny began in his thick Cuban accent. "Four months to Mars? I'm not sure I believe that."

Ronny realized that he had said too much, because Roger smiled in acknowledgement. Roger was a smart guy and the fact that Guerrero didn't believe the traverse time told Roger that they already had been looking at an interplanetary mission. And Ronny was certain that Roger would surmise that since the NRO had been looking at a Mars mission, something must *really* be going on with Mars.

"That's the clever part of this concept, Dr. Guerrero," Roger said with greater confidence. "If you want to slow down and orbit Mars, it would take longer. But, why orbit? If whatever this phenomenon is has changed the entire planet's surface, then a fly-by mission is all you need. That allows you to remove the need for braking engines and reduces the throw weight tremendously. Instead of a braking engine, we have two kick motors and therefore we go a lot faster."

"That's the answer!" one of the aides in Air Force blues responded excitedly. Guerrero looked at him as if to scold him.

The DAS&T remained quiet for a minute or two longer and flipped through the white paper.

"Roger," he said slowly "what I am about to tell you is Top Secret compartmentalized codename Neighborhood Watch and doesn't go beyond this room. We'll get you some paperwork to sign after this meeting."

Chapter 4

"So, you're telling me that these three men figured this out from information on the Internet?" the President asked Ronny. The new Deputy Director of the NRO—and still the Director of the Advanced Science and Technology Directorate—smiled and nodded.

"That's right, but they're very *smart* guys, Mr. President," Ronny replied. He'd actually been briefed on where one of their "initial verifications" came from, but he decided to gloss over the astrophysicist Hooters' girl. Ronny personally liked that because he knew from his life's experience that you can never judge a book by its cover.

"Fines, I thought you told us that the phenomenon couldn't be detected by small telescopes." The President turned to his science advisor.

"Well, Mr. President, as far as I knew it couldn't," Fines replied and shrugged.

"Mr. President, if I may." Ronny turned the Huntsville white paper to a page midway through it. The page was marked at top and bottom Top Secret/Neighborhood Watch.

"Look at this graph on page two, sir. You see, this curve shows that the growth of the phenomenon is nonlinear. The fellows from Huntsville who figured this out used data that was several months more recent than the Hubble data that NASA showed you. And if you follow this curve it tells us that the change in Mars' albedo is such that it's noticeable now with small amateur telescopes. Don't forget, sir, that some of the amateurs in the world have telescopes as big as some of the professional observatories. I fear we can't continue to hide this much longer. Before long, Mars isn't going to be red."

The President traced his finger over the curve in the graph. It was a growth rate curve, flat for a while then climbing steeply upwards. Economists saw similar things all the time; he understood it well. He also understood that this could be bad. How, he wasn't sure, yet. But he knew it would be bad. Even in stocks, growth rate curves were bad. Eventually, something had to break. Eventually the environment could no longer support the growth and the surplus had to spread. Just where would this Martian growth spread when Mars could no longer support the growth?

"So what do you need, Ronny?"

"Well, Mr. President, the guys down in Huntsville have really spelled it out for us in this brief," Ronny replied, tapping the Top Secret document. "We need to commandeer the ccd cameras from the NASA Jupiter probe, some hardware from three of my programs, a commercial spacecraft platform from Ball, an antenna from a DARPA SPO program, and the nearest Delta IV Heavy or Atlas V launch that we can get. All this is already-paid-for hardware, but around-the-clock effort from about two thousand people for six months is required. The hardware costs are about $100 million plus the commandeered components, launch vehicle with integration is about $150 million, the labor is another $225 million, add about twenty-five percent contingency and we're talking $600 million total for the project. The schedule proposed shows a six-month build time and a four-and-a-half-month mission time. Normally, with spacecraft design and construction you're talking about people working nine to five. Just increasing that to twenty-four hour schedules will cut the time, but the money will go up fast. Dr. Reynolds underestimated our interest, however. I believe if we double the budget and distribute some more of the work we can get the probe ready in three to four months, but after that we'll be looking at diminishing returns. Not much we can do about the travel time to Mars. This is right at the edge of 'doable' boost for current systems."

The President thumbed through his copy of the briefing one last time, sighed and set the paper down on his desk.

"And what will this billion dollar spacecraft buy us?" he asked, leaning back in his chair.

The Chairman of the Joint Chiefs whispered something to the NSA about a "contingency" and Ronny could tell the NSA agreed with whatever he had said.

"Mr. President," Ronny replied, seriously. "I believe this is the only hope we have of getting intel on the situation on Mars. The telescope for the probe will give us a resolution of maybe as good as a few centimeters as it makes its closest approach to the Martian atmosphere. We could see solid detail of the phenomenon at that resolution. It would be like looking at data from a reconnaissance satellite. That's, essentially, what we'd be building here, an interplanetary reconnaissance satellite."

"I see," the President replied. "If there turns out to be something bad there, what then?"

"I don't know, sir."

"Mr. President, Kevin would like to make a suggestion on that point," the NSA offered.

"Well, Kevin, don't leave me hanging."

"Right, Mr. President," General Mitchell said. "We could attach a fairly high yield nuke to the probe and attempt to steer it toward a central activity point. This might slow whatever this is down some," the general said.

"Kevin, I'm not sure I'm ready for that just yet," the President said, rubbing his chin. "Besides, if this phenomenon has changed an entire planet, I'm not certain what a single nuke could do. Wouldn't you agree?"

"Yes, sir," the Chairman replied. "I agree a hundred percent with that assessment. However, it does give us an option. Without it, we can't do anything but look at the threat."

"I agree, sir," the NSA said with a nod.

"Sir, if I may," Ronny interjected. "Adding that much mass to the probe will change the trajectory. How much, I'd have to run some numbers, but it might be enough to slow it down considerably. And as you pointed out, having the option or not might not mean much as we're addressing a planetary scale phenomenon."

"I can see that, Mr. Deputy Director," the Chairman

said, nodding. "On the other hand, if you can throw a probe to Mars, it means we can boost nukes later."

"Look into that," the President said seriously. "I'd like the capability. Let's get this probe on the way to Mars, first, and as fast as we can. Kevin, in the meantime I want you and Vicki to come up with a real contingency plan. Sooner or later, the public is going to find out about this. What do we do then? I don't want to get caught flat-footed by a reporter on this issue a few months from now. And if it turns out that our new neighbors aren't friendly, I want to be prepared for that also."

"One more thing, Mr. President," the DDNRO asked.

"Yes, Ronny?"

"We need this project to be in a location that already has plenty of scientists and engineers available and can support the security requirements as well as the manufacturing and integration. I would originally think LockMart's facilities in Colorado, but I'm not sure there are enough skilled and cleared engineers there to work three or four shifts continuously. If we pulled them from everything they're doing perhaps, but I don't know."

"We need this on a military base in order to keep it protected and buffer it from the public—especially if they find out about it," the NSA replied.

"I agree," the Chairman said. "And it needs an airport on-base or at least nearby. What about Patrick down in Florida? Or Vandenberg—the 30th Space Wing is out there."

"I don't know if there are enough engineers there. Some would have to fly in and wouldn't that cause some suspicion?" the science advisor asked.

"I don't want a lot of suspicion for now." The President

looked at the white paper on his desk. "What are you asking me, Ronny?"

"Well, sir, I think we'll need authority to commandeer a base somewhere, freeze the period of performance on some current space hardware contracts, then fly a lot of folks into that base. That is unless we can find a civilian facility with a lot of technical folks and the infrastructure to support them."

"I see." The President picked up the white paper and handed it to the Chairman of the Joint Chiefs. "Kevin, I think the answer is right here in front of us. Make it happen."

"General Riggs, sir, don't forget your tee-time in forty-five minutes at the officers' club," Sarah said, sticking her head in his office. The two-star was such a workaholic that he would "forget" appearances like charity golf tournaments if not badgered into them. But a certain congressman from the district his base was in would be on his team and his base was on the base realignment and closure list. Brownie points counted, even though the Redstone Arsenal was eleventh on the list. He had warned Sarah not to let him miss the golf tournament.

Riggs looked up from his desk at Sarah, who was still standing in his doorway.

"Thanks, Sarah," he said sarcastically. He looked at the little wooden box on the right side of his desk marked "in" and the stack of paperwork a foot high and leaning dangerously over the edge of the box. Then he looked at the nearly empty "out" box beside it and shook his head. "The things we must do."

Sarah smiled.

"You want me to send Colonel Roberts?"

"Now, Sarah, what kind of message would that send to Congressman Fields? I'll go." General Riggs set his pen back in its holder by his nameplate, then stretched his arms. "I'll just check my e-mail real quick."

Riggs turned to his laptop and looked out his window over the open court of the Sparkman Center at the people having lunch outside below.

"If only it would rain," he muttered, but there was no chance of that; the sun was shining and there wasn't a cloud in the clear Alabama sky.

Sarah turned back to her desk outside the general's door, laughing, and was startled by the phone buzzing. Sarah picked up the phone but knocked her coffee cup off the desk as she sat back down in her chair.

"General Riggs' office, this is Sarah, how can I help you?" She stretched the phone cord down and struggled to hold it to her ear as she attempted to retrieve her cup and mop up the coffee spill with a PostIt note. When that didn't work she reached for a box of Kleenex on the other side of her desk and in the process sent her jar of hospitality peppermints across the floor.

"Hello, this is the office of the Chairman of the Joint Chiefs of Staff. General Mitchell would like to speak with General Riggs. Is he present?" the voice on the phone said. Sarah looked up over her desk quickly to make certain there was nobody hiding there with a candid camera.

"Uh, yes, he is . . . If you'll hold a second I will transfer the call," Sarah replied, unsure if the call was real or not. She timidly pressed the transfer digits. "Sir, I think you should take this call."

"Who is it?" Riggs asked as his phone began to buzz.

"Well, sir, I'm not real certain but they claimed it was the Office of the Chairman of the Joint Chiefs of Staff."

"What? It's probably Fields messing with me." Riggs picked up the phone. "General Riggs here." There was a short pause, then a click.

"Yes, General Riggs, please stand by for General Mitchell." There was another short pause, then another click.

"Danny Riggs! Kevin Mitchell here. How are things down there in Huntsville, Alabama, huh?"

"Great, General," Riggs said, frowning in puzzlement. Redstone Arsenal was a very minor base and he was surprised the general even remembered his nickname. "How may I help you, General?"

"Well, Danny, we're gonna need your help. I've got a couple of fellas that are going to come see you first thing in the morning and explain this in greater detail, but for now suffice it to say that we need to put that base and the whole town around it to work for the next few months."

"Anything we can do, General. What's this about?"

"Well, why don't you call me back in five minutes on your STU at the number I just e-mailed you? I'll talk to you in a minute, bye."

"Sarah! Get me the STU-III key out of the safe and call Colonel Roberts and tell him to put on his golf shoes!"

Chapter 5

More than a hundred scientists and engineers had been gathered by the Neighborhood Watch program leaders in the North Alabama town. Only a week after Roger Reynolds had delivered the white paper presentation to the DDNRO, he had been contacted by the NRO and awarded a prime contract for more than a billion dollars. The company Roger worked for had not expected a contract or even known of the white paper, but they were happy to help the NRO spend its money—if they could figure out how to spend more than a billion dollars in less than a year.

Roger was given the directive from the DDNRO to brief the commanding general of the Redstone Arsenal in Huntsville, Alabama—two-star General Daniel "Danny" Riggs—and the Director of the NASA Marshall Space Flight Center, Dr. Sidney Byron. Roger gathered Tom and Alan and spent the better part of the next day with General Riggs and Dr. Byron developing a plan to choose the right facilities and personnel. Most of the facilities were available either from MSFC or Redstone, but they decided to have two local Huntsville space/defense contractors to "volunteer" a fabrication shop and a clean room, respectively. The civil service and military facilities would be funded via government-to-government funds transfers. The rest would be handled through subcontracts to the prime contractor that Roger Reynolds worked for.

It had taken the better part of the day and most of the night, but a cohesive list of subtask-level team leaders was put together. One of the problems was insuring that each of the members chosen as team leaders had a current Secret security clearance at a minimum. Initially, only people with Top Secret and Special Access or Top Secret and SCI level clearances were considered. The problem that soon became apparent was that although there were plenty of DOD scientists and engineers available with proper clearances who could handle portions of the mission design, most of the NASA employees and contractors that were needed for various aspects were not cleared at any level at all. It was a problem that most Huntsville residents were aware of—the DOD/NASA political dichotomy. Most NASA employees became NASA employees because they wanted to work on public space programs and tended to have the attitude that there shouldn't be secrets. DOD employees on the other hand, held completely opposite philosophies and in many cases the political and philosophical differences created friction between the two groups.

But Roger Reynolds, Tom Powell, and Alan Davis had been straddling the fence between both communities for

a number of years now and personally knew most of the
others in town and within the community who were "strad-
dlers." This experience enabled them to pick and choose
qualified and cleared people with a bit more ease. However, in the end they just couldn't find a complete list and
had to settle for a few handfuls of folks with only Secret
level clearance. They had to get a special allowance from
the NRO. But when he saw the problem, Ronny Guerrero
made it happen.

After a long and exhausting night of planning, the next
morning General Riggs and Dr. Byron, *invited* the list of
Army and NASA civil servants and contractors to attend
the kick-off meeting in the Sparkman Center auditorium,
which would occur in three days. The invitation to the
meeting was hand delivered or secure faxed to each person on the list and read:

> *Your presence at a meeting of the utmost urgency
> and importance is requested. The meeting will be
> held at the Sparkman Center auditorium on the
> Redstone Arsenal, Alabama, this Friday. We apolo-
> gize for the short notice, but again, this is a matter
> of extreme urgency.*
>
> *The meeting will be at the Top Secret level. If you
> are not cleared to this level, arrangements are being
> made to have you cleared in the interim. Please be
> certain to fill out the forms enclosed and appropri-
> ate visit request paperwork and fax it to the number
> given below, immediately.*
>
> *Initial attendance is voluntary; however, all those
> attendees who decide to remain for the briefing will*

be reimbursed for their time and expenses. Direct procurement opportunities are also possible.

Sincerely,
General Daniel Riggs   Dr. Sidney Byron
Commanding General   Director
United States Army
NASA Marshal Space Flight Center
Redstone Arsenal, Alabama   Huntsville, Alabama

No invitations were turned down.

The auditorium, on the other hand, posed a problem since it was only rated for Top Secret level briefings and not for Sensitive Compartmented Information or Special Access Programs. A three-day waiver was authorized by the NRO and the Joint Chiefs, provided that the building was monitored for eavesdropping sensors before and after each meeting session and only individuals to be briefed into Neighborhood Watch were allowed into the building housing the auditorium during the briefings. A security specialist team swept the building for transmitters. General Riggs ordered three days of administrative leave for all of the employees who worked in the Sparkman Center building. No cover was created but if your name was not on the invitation list, then you did not get into the building those three days.

Dr. Tom Powell, Alan Davis, and Dr. Reynolds stood on the stage of the stadium-seating-style auditorium as the final attendees of the meeting filtered into the seats in the upper rows. Armed security guards stepped into the room at each door and pulled the doors closed behind them. Roger nodded to Tom and Alan and the two of them left the stage and sat down in the first row.

"Thank all y'all for coming today. I see a lot of familiar faces here and a few I don't recognize. For those of you I haven't met before, I'm Dr. Roger Reynolds with the local space group office for Space Defense Systems Research, Incorporated. What I would like for everybody to do first is to read the form on the cover of the sealed folders in front of you. Take five minutes and read the nondisclosure agreement carefully and, if you agree to it, sign it." Roger stood at the podium patiently for five minutes.

"Now, if anybody did not sign the form in front of you please leave now."

Nobody stood up.

"Okay, from this point on every person present in this room has indicated that they have signed the documents," Roger said. "It, legally, doesn't matter if you have or not; you're now covered by the security regulations of those documents and the penalties laid out for failure to comply with the security requirements. Very well, open the folders and turn to the first page. Let's have the first slide on the screen please.

"So here is an overview of what we plan to put together in less than five months." Roger cleared his throat as the first PowerPoint slide, a picture of a satellite, appeared on the multiple big screens behind him.

"The reason you are all here is that Mars is being changed by something unnatural. Its surface reflectance albedo has been changed enough so that in the past year these changes can now be detected via small commercial telescopes. We have no idea what is causing this phenomenon, but we suspect that it's not a *natural* occurrence," Roger emphasized.

"Our purpose *here* is to find out what is going on *there* and to find out *fast*. We can speculate all we want, but without recon intel we have no means of truly knowing what's going on there." Roger paused and cleared his throat and scanned the darkened auditorium for reactions. The reactions from most of the room were guarded.

"So, from this slide and from the documents you just signed we see that this information is classified and compartmented. The mission will be referred to from here on as Top Secret codename Neighborhood Watch and our bird will be called Percival, for Percival Lowell who first searched for signs of extraterrestrial life on Mars. I needn't remind y'all of the rules here for compartmented programs. If there are security questions, we'll have the special security officer available after the briefing.

"With the basic stuff now out of the way, let's talk about how we'll do this mission. Each of you here was chosen for your particular talents involved in either spacecraft design or rapid and large-scale systems engineering and integration. You may or may not be the best in the world at your specific talent, but you are good or you wouldn't be here—the time pressure of our situation also indicates that you were available and perhaps others were not. I mention this for a reason. You *are* the folks who will do this job. Whether you are the best person for it or not in somebody's mind, or your own, doesn't matter. You're here; it's your job.

"Each of you will be the team leader for a subsystem or mission task and your particular assignment as we see it now is listed in your specific briefing folder in front of you. You can also see your names listed in front of the headings in the work breakdown structure for each element of the WBS. It will be up to you to put your team together. We'll discuss the aspects of that later this afternoon. For now let's talk about the mission.

"Starting with the project timeline first, I'll go over the rough draft we have put together thus far. Feel free to jump in here and offer input whenever you think of it." Roger glanced around the room.

"We'll talk pre-launch activities first." Roger picked up the laser pointer and slide changer from the podium and began to pace the stage slowly. "Prior to launch, the mission team will be busy planning the aspects of the mission timeline, conducting numerous hardware and software science readiness reviews, preliminary design reviews, and critical design reviews, which will lead to building the spacecraft and its instruments, and finally delivering the spacecraft to the Cape for system integration into the launch vehicle, then launch. During the design and build portion of the pre-launch efforts let's try to make use of as many commercial and government off-the-shelf items as possible. COTS and GOTS might help us reduce our build time.

"The next phase is launch. Our launch phase begins, as you can see from this next slide, once Percival transfers from external power to the internal power on the launch pad. This phase will last until the spacecraft is declared stable, healthy, and ready to accept control commands.

"Percival will launch in August—that's right, your ears aren't deceiving you, that's four and a half months away, folks—from Space Launch Complex 37 at the Cape Canaveral Air Force Station. We're fortunate in that our launch window occurs within Earth's northern summer and that Mars is not that far away at launch date. The spacecraft will use a Boeing Delta IV Heavy with eight solid strap-on boosters. Dr. Tom Powell will discuss the throw weight and trajectories in a splinter working group later." Roger pointed to Tom sitting in the front row. Tom stood and waved in acknowledgement.

"Uh, excuse me?" a man in the audience said, raising his hand. He was clean cut and wearing a jacket and tie, in comparison to some of the engineers present who had turned up in polo shirts bearing the names of their firms. The guy was definitely "big corporate" and Roger made a guess at his identity right away.

"Yes?" Roger paused.

"I'm Dr. John Fisher with Lockheed Martin. Did you say a Delta IV *Heavy*, common booster core, with *eight* solid strap-ons?"

"That's correct," Roger nodded.

"Uh, that's never been done before, to my knowledge," Dr. Fisher said. "Can that be done? I mean, structurally speaking, can you stick eight strap-ons onto the common booster core tubes?"

"If you'll read your spot on the work breakdown structure, Dr. Fisher," Roger said, smiling just a bit, "you will see that it's *your* job to figure that out. It has to be done, therefore it *will* be done."

"I, uh . . ." For some reason, Dr. Fisher's face seemed pale.

"If nuthin' else, thar's always Bondo an' duct tape," Roger said in his deepest, slowest, drawl, eliciting chuckles from some of the people who knew him and a suddenly firmer demeanor from Fisher.

Fisher was one of the men in the room who *had* been

carefully chosen. In his early forties, he was from Denver and had been a rocket systems engineer his entire career with Lockheed Martin. Despite his "corporate button-down" looks, he was a noted outside-the-box thinker and damned fine engineer. One of the things Roger had heard about him that he liked was that Fisher was a "tinkerer" at home as well as at work. Get him in a lab and the suit came off, the well pressed lab-coat came on and he started making things. He was even a skilled machinist, having simply picked it up over the years. If anyone could figure out how to get three CBC tubes linked together with eight strap-ons, then boosting, it would be John Fisher.

"We'll discuss that part of the mission more later in a breakout session, Dr. Fisher. If that is it, we'll continue?"

"Sure." Dr. Fisher sat back down, his forehead furrowed in thought.

"Let's see, where was I?" Roger said as he turned back to the screen and read through the chart to himself. "Oh yeah, our launch window is approximately three weeks in duration over the last three weeks of August with at least a daily twenty-seven minute launch window. So, we're bound to be able to hit one of them." Roger clicked the slide laser pointer button and waved the laser spot over several different trajectory maps showing the different launch dates, times, and trip-times per trajectory. Twenty-one different trajectories curved out from an elliptical Earth orbit and curved directly into Mars' heliocentric orbital path.

"Another thing to remember here, folks, is that launch is a whole heck of a lot more than just lift-off. I've taken the liberty to summarize these steps from the SMAD and various previous mission timelines. You'll find the steps on the next page of the briefing. Launch team, I want you to start breaking them down and populating the steps with more detail."

"Uh, Roger, I hate to interrupt again." John Fisher stood up, again. "But four upper stages on a Delta IV Heavy hasn't ever been done either. I mean, granted I work for LockMart and I know more about the Atlas systems, but they're very similar. I just don't know. And you're showing one of the stages here consisting of three connected and even modified kick motors. How do you think we can pull that off in less than five months? I'm not even thinking design process, bad as that's going to be, I'm thinking *man hours* here."

"John, we'll do it because we have to," Roger replied seriously. "This isn't something that we're doing for fun or because of science that we can let overrun the budget and slip in schedule. There is literally something dramatically changing Mars and what if, just what if, Earth is next? I want to get that point across as sincerely as I possibly can. If this is the beginnings of an alien contact, onslaught, or whatever, we need to know and we need to know it as soon as humanly possible. Sooner."

"We can do it, potentially, but only with dispersed production and every production facility on triple shift," Fisher said, nodding in understanding. "These modifications alone might cost fifty to a hundred million dollars. Do we have that kind of budget?"

"Yes," was all Roger said. Despite his little pep talk it was apparent that many of them hadn't grasped the magnitude of the problem.

"Let me make this clear," Roger said, taking a deep breath. "We have the budget. We have the backing. We have *anything* we want. Any facility, any person, any piece of equipment being produced for the United States government and probably anything being produced for anyone anywhere in the world. That being said, the first company that *screws* with this program since there's so much money being thrown at it will get reamed a new one and probably broken. But we *have* the budget. We have *any* budget it takes to get this done. But we're *not* funding a welfare program for rocket scientists. This is about using off-the-shelf components to get a *mission* completed to find out if there is a threat to the *world*. And we *will* do it and we *will* do it on time, *budget* be *damned*."

He paused for a minute for the auditorium to settle, then he continued with the briefing.

"Okay, cruise phase of the mission begins once Percival is in a safe and stable configuration after the control maneuvers at the end of the launch sequence. The best we've come up with thus far for transit time from Earth to Mars is about four to five months—feel free to discuss with Dr. Powell transit time optimization if you wish. The cruise trajectory will deliver the spacecraft to Mars on a southern approach trajectory where we'll begin taking reconnaissance data. In fact, our plan is to passively collect data for the entire trip. Who knows, it might be useful. We also suggest one active sensor, which we'll discuss in a minute.

"During the cruise phase we'll have time to catch our breath and to conduct some on-board systems diagnostics. We'll have two teams: one for checkouts and calibrations and the other for trajectory optimization and correction maneuvers. Also, at this time the recon operations team will, as I said previously, begin shaking down the passive science instruments and start taking data.

"As a side note here, we've looked for a space qualified 50- to 100-centimeter aperture diameter telescope that was designed for any previous classified or unclassified mission that could be commandeered for this mission. Unfortunately, we have not found one anywhere. So, in the interim we will, today, develop the telescope design parameters. Then we finish the optical design from these requirements within the next two weeks from this kickoff meeting. The structural design *will* be complete a few weeks later. We're already talking to CTI, Lightworks, Composite Optics, and Zeiss optics companies with the hopes that one of these companies can complete the task of constructing our telescope to our design requirements, successfully, within the schedule required. We'll give all four companies a contract with the hopes that redundant teams will give us a better chance for success and less risk. Telescope team, we'll break out after this session and get to work. I have some preliminary design characteristics we can start from. I'm wide open for suggestions though."

One of the optics designers interrupted with a raised hand.

"Uh, Dr. Reynolds, I'm Carla Watts from Zeiss. I have a question."

"Yes, Carla?" Roger breathed an inaudible sigh to himself. He knew that he had to take and answer the questions. But they took *time*.

"Does the primary have to be a build from super lightweight like other space optics?" She paused for a second, removed her glasses, and rubbed her nose. "Or could we hog one out of a heavy piece of glass or Zerodur or something. I mean, the reason I ask this is that, there might be big blanks lying around in this aperture diameter range that could be ground out. That would be a lot quicker than building the lattice, filling, baking and all the rest."

"What would that do to our mass budget?" Roger asked.

"Well," Carla screwed up her faced in thought for a moment. "It might as much as double it. But, and this sounds like a critical but, it would decrease build time by at least a factor of two, maybe more."

"Okay. Let's keep this idea on the table as an option. During the break could you call around and see if you could locate such blanks?"

"Sure. I think I know where there might even be one with a hole already in the center for a Schmidt-Cassegrain design."

"Good, thanks. Back to the cruise phase: the ops guys will train the telescope pointing algorithms on Mars early on so that the pointing and tracking closed loop software will have learned to minimize the pointing jitter by the time it gets to Mars.

"The final phase will be the approach and the detailed recon phase. Since we don't plan to orbit Mars, our goal is to collect data from a few months out and right up until the spacecraft passes by the planet and views it from the other side. We're open to clever ideas about how to extend the mission operation lifetime, but we have yet to come up with anything brilliant in that regard. The spacecraft will pass by Mars at about fifteen kilometers per second, so close approach dwell time will not be very long. During the final phase, Percival will point its active science instruments, such as the lidar, at Mars. During the active part of the recon phase we'll implement an alternate beam path through the primary telescope objective with a lidar system. Hopefully, we can gather some sub-meter three-dimensional imagery from the laser imaging and ranging system. We intend to take the old canceled and mothballed NASA SPARCLE program's lidar instruments, dust them off, and update them."

"Dr. Reynolds," Fisher said, sighing and holding up his hand.

"Go," Roger said, shaking his head.

"SPARCLE's *not* off-the-shelf and has never been successfully tested," Fisher pointed out. "What if it's a dud?"

"Then it's a dud," Roger said. "If we have active recon, that would be good. If we don't, we can live with it. Continuing . . ." he muttered, looking down at his notes.

"Although we'll have had months to keep the batteries charged, just in case, we might as well also try and keep the solar arrays continuously tracking the Sun. I originally considered the use of radioisotope thermal generators, but haven't found any available on such short notice. We could buy some plutonium from the Russians, but that might tip our hand and the nuclear power nuts would probably hear about it, increasing the media presence of the launch. So, solar power it is, again, unless somebody comes up with something brilliant in its place.

"It's our plan that Percival will continue to keep its science instruments pointed at Mars with it in the center of the field of view. We'll use the positions of Phobos and Deimos as part of our GN&C knowledge. The positions of the two moons along with star tracker information should give us extremely detailed attitude determination capability. Once Mars is larger than the field of view of the main telescope system we'll use star trackers for attitude determination and we'll slew the main telescope objective side-to-side via the AD&CS system in order to capture images of various targets outside the field of view. We'll maintain this operation as long as the probe is in range of Mars. Again, if anybody has any clever and light-weight ideas that can be done quickly to increase mission operations time, please let us know."

And the briefing went on.

The meetings lasted from eight-thirty each morning until past midnight each of the three days. By the end of the third day a very detailed spacecraft mission architecture and design were completed. Details of the WBS and the task team leaders were complete and each of the hundred or so attendees of the meeting left with multimillion dollar subcontracts and a list of near impossible action items to be completed by middle of the following week. All said and done, the Neighborhood Watch executive committee—which consisted of the DDNRO, the commanding general of the Redstone Arsenal, the director of NASA Marshall Space Flight Center, and the project scientist, Roger —were tired—very tired—but they were also pleased with their progress. The DDNRO had to brief the President by Monday and so the executive committee worked through the weekend developing the presentation for the President's Daily Brief. Guerrero planned to deliver it in person. Roger planned to take a nap.

Chapter 6

Charlotte could hear her mom's angry voice through the walls of her room. She tried to surf the Internet and ignore the boisterous argument from downstairs, but it wasn't helping. It was obvious to Charlotte that it *was* her dad on the phone—only he could make her mother that angry. Charlotte continued to ignore the heated phone conversation between her parents. To keep her mind off them she visited her usual favorite websites: the Space Telescope Science Institute, the MAPUG site, the SETI League, Kazaa, then the University of Colorado's Athletic Department. Charlotte had hopes of getting a softball scholarship someday, but she was afraid that if she didn't grow a few more inches during her junior and senior years in high school she wouldn't be tall enough to be scholarship competitive. She then clicked through the physics department's site and gave up. The noise was just too much.

"What do you mean it's okay to miss a few days of

school! Don't you realize she's worried about keeping up her grades for a scholarship and that finals are at the end of the month? No, you probably don't because you never come around, do you?" her mother screamed into the phone. Charlotte could image in her mind's eye her mother tapping her left foot and resting her right fist on her hip.

Charlotte's instant messenger dinged at her.

Hello AstroGirl39, what's up! The message was from Tina.

Hey DingBat101! My mom and dad are at it again! she typed.

600 miles wasn't far 'nuf for those 2, huh :).

"Damnit, John! You just can't show up like that and expect her to drop everything just for you. She has a life of her own you know."

Yeah, lots a luv between 'em. Charlotte shook her head as she typed.

Yeah, that's how my parents were just after the divorce. It gets better.

How r u? Charlotte typed.

Got my braces adjusted today, so my mouth hurts. It looks like soup for a few days. Tina replied.

Sorry.

No big. U r lucky you got straight teeth.

Yeah.

Got news on the Michael situation!

Yes? Charlotte typed reluctantly but anxiously.

❖   ❖   ❖

"Well, whatever! Just let her make the decision for herself."

He asked my older brother if U were INTERESTED in anybody right now. So, R U ;-) ???

Oh My God! What did he tell him?

He said he didn't think so. I told bro to tell him that U like him.

U did not!

I did.

"Charlotte! Your father is on the phone for you," her mother yelled upstairs at her.

Call U later. Gotta go. B'bye.

Charlotte clicked X on the Internet browser and stretched out across her bed, knocking over the Louisville Slugger that was leaning on her nightstand, then picked up the phone, "Okay, I got it."

"Charlotte, honey?"

"Hi Daddy, what's up?" she asked.

"How'd the ccd camera work out for your telescope, slugger?"

"It works great, thanks! Odd thing though, I think Mars is turning gray or something," she said.

"Hmmm," John muttered. "Could have been atmospheric interference; perhaps it was lightly cloudy and you just didn't notice."

"Mmmm, nah, don't think it was. What's all the business with Mom about?" Charlotte asked, wondering at the comment. There was no way that clouds could cause the changes she'd seen.

"Yeah, about that, your mom just doesn't understand sometimes about great opportunities and priorities. Listen, I've been down in Huntsville, Alabama, all this week—it's a neat little town. I've got to run up to Denver and see Tina's mom for a day or so, then it's back to Alabama late next week for some meetings and I thought you might could go with me."

"Dad, I'd love to see you, but why on Earth would I want to go to Hicksville, Alabama?" she asked.

"*Hunts*ville, Alabama, and you'd be surprised what all is there. How'd you like to go to Spacecamp at the NASA Space and Rocket Center where they built the rockets that went to the Moon while I'm at work during the days? You'd have to miss about three days of school, but I could call your principal and talk to him about it. God knows it would be educational. Alice is coming down, too. I thought you might get Tina to come down and you two could go to Spacecamp together and hang out at the hotel pool, the space museum—they have some pretty cool rides. And there are a couple of malls a short cab ride from the hotel."

"I'll go if Tina goes; I'd probably get bored out of my head by myself in the daytime." Charlotte thought that getting out of town now that Tina had spilled the beans to Michael that she liked him wasn't such a bad idea. "Can we really go to Spacecamp?"

"Yeah, well, at your age it's the Space Academy actually and it's only three days, but it'll be a blast."

"Sounds like fun."

"Great. I'll come by Tuesday after school to help you pack. Well, let's see." There was a pause as her dad checked something. "It looks like our flight is first thing Wednesday morning and we'll come back on Sunday."

"I'll call Tina and see if she wants to go. B'bye daddy, I love you."

"I love you too, baby."

"Who loves you, baby?" Charlotte laughed and screamed at the same time as the Moonshot launched the two teens ten stories straight up at over three gees. At the top of the ride there was a split second of freefall that made her stomach lurch. Charlotte was fine but she hoped that Tina didn't throw up all over her light blue astronaut flight suit.

"I'm gonna kill youuu!" Tina screamed as the freefall broke and the ride jerked them back downward.

Tina jumped from her seat the second the ride stopped and stumbled around, dizzy for a moment. Charlotte didn't appear to be affected by the thrill ride so she held her friend's arm and told the Space Academy instructor that she needed a break.

"Ten minutes, then back around by the Saturn V out front," their instructor told them.

Charlotte nodded and led Tina by the arm under the rocket engines of the Saturn IB and to the picnic area not far from the ride.

"Wheeeww!" Charlotte wiped her brow. "That was cool. You okay?"

"Yeah, that was all right. I wasn't expecting that thing to shoot off straight up that hard, wow!"

"Well, it's called the Moonshot, you know."

"Whatever," Tina was finally catching her breath. "I could use something to drink."

"Hey, I'll get it, be right back." Charlotte could tell that Tina was still a little pale and was just trying to be bold in front of her. That was Tina's way. Charlotte had learned that years ago and just decided it was easier to play along than to call her on her weakness.

"Here ya go," Charlotte returned with soft drinks and handed one to Tina who was looking at her watch. "We gotta get back."

"You okay?"

"Hey, it's me." Tina punched her on the arm, causing Charlotte to slosh her soda on her hand.

Charlotte just shook her head back and forth muttering "Dingbat" under her breath.

At the front of the George C. Marshall Space and Rocket Center the rest of the teen Space Academy group had collected and was being shushed by their instructors. The instructor was going on about the Saturn V rocket and the Apollo program, then pointed to an elderly man with wild white hair and white fuzzy sideburns.

"Okay, now we're fortunate enough today to have a very special guest here." The head instructor shook hands with the white-haired man. "The man who designed and built the first commercial spacecraft, from Scaled Composites, Mr. Burt Rutan."

"Thank you, Jan. Hi everybody." Mr. Rutan began a short talk about how he had led his team of engineers to build a completely different type of space program than the kind that NASA had done. He talked about how exciting it would be to soon have hotels in space and tourists going to the Moon. He talked about his little composite spacecraft and how there were very few metal components on it. Then he asked if there were any questions. Charlotte raised her hand first and Burt pointed to her.

"Yes, umm, what do you mean by a composite spacecraft with little metal in it? Is it plastic or something?"

"That's a good question. It isn't plastic; actually it's more like fiberglass. In some cases we take a fiber cloth made of something like the Kevlar that bulletproof vests are made of, then we paint it with an epoxy resin kind of like the epoxy glue you can buy. When that hardens, it's lightweight but really strong. In other cases we mix up a resin and paint it onto a mold, let it dry, then repeat the process over and over until we build up enough of the material. The result is that the body and wings of the vehicle can be made cheaper, stronger, and lighter than, say, the body of the space shuttle orbiter. It's called a composite because it's just that, a composite of multiple materials—fibers, resins, and hardening agents."

Rutan answered a few more questions from the group. One in particular from one of the know-it-alls in the group was funny.

"Mr. Rutan, on the first flight of Spaceship One your pilot released a bunch of Skittles inside the cockpit. That seems dangerous to me—what if they'd have gotten into the instruments?"

"Hmm, first of all, it was M&Ms, I believe, and secondly they melt in your mouth not in your spaceship." He chuckled.

Then there was Tina's question.

"Hey, I gotta know something. You guys keep talking about this being the rocket that went to the Moon here." She pointed at the giant Saturn V behind Rutan. "If that's the rocket that went to the Moon there, how'd they bring it back and set it up here?"

"Dingbat!" Charlotte coughed.

"So far, Mr. President, Project Neighborhood Watch is going well," Ronny said, trying not to yawn. Yawning in the President's face was considered a faux pas. "I believe we've put together an excellent team, developed a logical plan, and are implementing it with no glitches at this point. We should hit our launch window of August twenty-first."

"This looks good, Ronny. Are there any problems that the White House can help with?" The President continued to thumb through the Daily Brief.

"None that I can foresee, Mr. President," Ronny replied. "But the engineering on this is going to be complex. If anything comes up, I'll forward it to your attention."

"Good. One more thing, Ronny."

"Yes, sir?" the DDNRO asked.

"Has the situation on Mars, well, has it changed any?"

"Yes, sir, it has, but only for the worse. The change is more or less visible to the naked eye at this point, sir."

"I see."

Ret Ball: *Well, friends. I will have to say that although I respected my good friend Megiddo's insight, I never really and truly could prove he was right. But Hiowa Lend, our investigative journalist, has been investigating the Mars phenomena and she believes she has uncovered something startling. Go ahead, Hiowa, you are on the Truth Nationwide.*

Hiowa Lend: *Thanks, Ret, and that is absolutely*

correct. I recently hired several professional astronomers to make observations of Mars with their telescopes from professional observatories at three different universities across the country. And I can tell you definitively that Mars is indeed changing colors. The astronomers tell me that the surface color albedo has changed. The albedo is the measurement that astronomers use to describe the color and brightness of an astronomical object. And the astronomers I've talked with tell me that Mars has changed. Changed dramatically.

Ret Ball: *That is astounding, Hiowa! Let's get them on the air and let them tell us about it.*

Hiowa Lend: *Well, Ret, that is the catch. It seems that none of them will come forward and speak publicly due to fear of professional ridicule and being ostracized from the community.*

Ret Ball: *Isn't that amazing? I mean, if something is a fact, it's a fact. What harm could come of reporting it?*

Hiowa Lend: *Well Ret, none of my sources will volunteer to come forward, but I can assure you that they're all well-respected astronomers.*

Ret Ball: *Perhaps Megiddo was right. What if this really is a CIA cover-up and a right-wing conspiracy?*

Hiowa Lend: *My sentiments exactly, Ret.*

   � ✖ ✖

"This is funny as hell, John." Roger laughed as John Fisher, who was from Denver, gave him driving directions through his own hometown. "I grew up in this town and never been to the Boeing Delta IV rocket factory just ten miles away in Decatur. I mean, I've fished with my dad by the plant, but I've never actually been there. You know, come to think of it I've fished with him by the nuclear plant, too, and I've never been inside that thing. Hell, I'm glad you know how to drive to it. Otherwise we'd have to walk up the river."

"Yeah, well, turn left there," John said with a smile. "You payload guys never seem to worry about how the rockets are actually put together. That's what I've been telling you all along. This rocket we're building is different from any other Delta IV Heavy; we've had to make extensive modifications to the attachment points."

"So you keep telling me. And the hundred million dollar price tag on the modification didn't elude my notice either." Roger pulled his car into a visitor parking spot. One month into the Neighborhood Watch the first modified common booster core was being rolled off the line. John had led a scaled design "shake and bake" test out at the shake-stand at NASA MSFC and it looked like the hardpoints would hold. The finite-element analysis looked good and the scaled test looked good, but there would be no time for a full-scale test. They were just going to have to hook the three CBC tubes together, then strap on eight solid rocket boosters around them to these modified hardpoints. Roger was not as nervous about that as John was, but both men were at least apprehensive to some extent and wanted to see the manufacturing process in action. And there was still the modified second-stage fairing that had yet to be tested.

It took them about fifteen minutes to make it through security protocols, stop off at the restroom, then find their way around. John had been to the Boeing rocket plant at least once a week since the Neighborhood Watch had started. He had been back and forth between Decatur and CCAFS in Florida routinely. Sometimes he would make the trip several times a week. John was trying to make sure that the rocket pieces got manufactured to design in Decatur, and that they would be integrated appropriately in Florida.

"So, what exactly are we going to see?" Roger asked as he fiddled with the visitor badge on his jacket that read "No Escort Required."

"This way," John said as he led Roger around a corner to the high-bay area. "They're running the third and final CBC outer shell today. We'll get to see that thing manufactured. But what I want you to see is the second-stage fairing-test model. It doesn't work. I mean, I know how to make it in Solid Edge and FEMAP as a finite element model, but we can't figure out how to build the damned thing and fit it in the rocket's aerodynamic shroud with the COTS and GOTS parts available."

"Why not?" Roger raised his left eyebrow in concern.

"Well, we had the three second stage RL10B-2 engines modified to have twice the fuel and oxidizer like Dr. Powell's trajectory design requires, but doing that makes the pressure vessels an odd size and there are no COTS or GOTS space-qualified tanks that will fit in the shroud." John paused in his explanation and started chatting with a fellow running a piece of manufacturing equipment that looked more like a computer than a milling machine.

"Oh, they're about to weld that up now. If you hurry you can catch it," the man told him.

"Great, thanks, Mike." John patted the man on the shoulder. "Roger, this way. That big crane and cylinder down there is where the booster core casing is rolled up. Mike there says they're about to roll off the third CBC. Let's hurry down to that end so we can see this better. Oh, one more thing. Stay inside the yellow painted lines, otherwise somebody will get a briefing about OSHA and safety."

"Yellow lines, got it."

As the two men made it to the end of the high-bay a *large* sheet of aluminum that had a honeycomb structure milled out into it on its up side was slid up under a big roller by an unseen conveyor. The larger roller drum then pressed onto the sheet metal. The aluminum bucked, then rolled itself up into a cylinder about five meters in diameter around the huge drum roller. The former sheet that was now an aluminum tube was lifted upright by its end.

"Watch this part; it's cool as hell." John pointed at the large welding apparatus as it dropped to the seam of the sheet-metal cylinder.

Roger watched as a large welding rod that looked more like a pointed trailer hitch ball was pressed against the aluminum rocket tube while the ball was spinning at God only knew how many thousands of revolutions per minute. The welding rod was touched to the aluminum where it had been rolled together and it spun so fast that when it touched the metal the friction of it was hot enough to force the welding of the aluminum seam. The welding rod zipped down what it was turning into a rocket tube with a screech, sealing the seam with a near perfect joint.

"That is some cool shit." Roger grinned like a kid in a candy store. He allowed himself the break of standing and staring in awe for just a few moments more before it was back to the urgent business of the Neighborhood Watch.

"Now, why don't we get to looking at this second stage model, 'cause I've got to get back to work on the focal plane array packages for the telescope." Roger put his hands in his pants pockets and the little kid's giddy stare turned to a more serious one.

"Right. It's around the corridor here." John led Roger to another room with a shake table in it. Atop the table was a one-tenth scaled model of the second stage system.

There were three scaled engines on the table. The engines were the "stretched" or "extended" RL10B-2 motors from Pratt & Whitney. In order to have twice the specific impulse and burn time, the tankage for both fuel and oxidizer had to be larger. The problem was that the rocket design team had not been able to find available tankage parts that had been flight-proven and were the appropriate size.

Roger surveyed the parts and the various engineering drawings lying on the floor and pinned to the walls around the room. There was one Solid Edge drawing of the engines on a computer monitor. Somebody must have just been in the room and stepped out for a moment or their screen saver was turned off. *How damned hard could this be*, he thought. *We just need bigger tanks! I've got so much shit to be doing!*

"You see, Rog, if we use the tanks from any other engine, the pumps won't fit, the frame will be too large to fit in the aerodynamic shroud without building a new shroud, or the structural design will be questionable, which means we aren't certain about the shake and bake of the larger frame. And if we go to a modified shroud we have to run all new CFD models of the ascent friction and you know that Dr. Powell won't be happy with that."

"Uh huh." Roger frowned.

"There just aren't enough available COTS or GOTS engine parts to solve this problem." John pointed to the model, pointing out the deficiencies in the design. "Open for suggestions here."

"Jesus, John, has this country been wrapped up in paperwork and bureaucracy for so long that just *doing* things is beyond us? Stack a couple of gas tanks out of old pickups together! Whatever it takes!"

"Weeelll." John stretched out the word. "I do have a solution, but it isn't from a space-qualified piece of hardware and both the Air Force and NASA frown on such. But if—"

"John. Let's hear your idea."

"Okay. It really is simple, but you'll have to get a waiver from NRO, or Boeing will never approve or build it. I've been round and round with them about it. In their mind, it's just way too much risk. That's really why I brought you." He pointed to the computer monitor. "Here look at this. I've tried to convince them that this is what we need to do but . . . well, hell, it has been harder than it was getting them to agree to the mods for the strap-on boosters. Risk-averse assholes."

John pulled up a PowerPoint slide file and opened it. He scrolled through the slides to the second stage portion.

"Here is the standard RL10B-2." John grabbed the

tankage portion with the copy tool, then pasted it into a new slide. He then duplicated the tank. "I want to take two tanks and cut one end off each and then just weld the damned things together. Oh, there would have to be some adjustments to the cryo pipes, a little bit of structural integrity support, and stuff like that, but it should work." He finished creating the image on the PowerPoint slide.

"I knew it was simple. Why don't we just do it," Roger said rather than asking.

"I'm telling you, Rog, without you telling them that they would be free of reprisal if the thing fails, Boeing isn't going to even consider it. It took us most of the first week to convince them to add the extra strap-on hardpoints. It wasn't like we really *were* using duct tape and Bondo!" John shook his head in disgust and threw up his hands.

"John, get started. I'm going back to the office to take care of this. You catch a cab back to the hotel." Roger knew John could see that he was angry and that somebody was about to get a good old-fashioned southern *ass chewin'*.

"I don't give a good Goddamn, Charlie. If John says he wants it done, then by God do it. We ain't worried about political fallout here, we're worried about the future of the freakin' human race for crying out loud . . . un huh . . . no . . . no . . . uh . . . no . . . GODDAMNITALLTOHELL Charlie I said NO! If I have to fly to D.C. and get more horsepower behind my decision I'll leave today and you'll be looking for a new fucking job tomorrow. You hear what I'm telling you?" Roger had had enough of the corporate risk-averse culture that was holding back the program.

The bean counters at the top of the culture were a larger impediment to the development of the program than the immense technical requirements and compressed schedule. Roger was irate and working on about a day and a half of sleep in the last month. *It felt good to vent on these bean counting assholes a little*, he thought to himself.

"All right then . . . yes, okay. Well, Charlie I appreciate you getting this done. And I don't want to have this conversation again. I want John Fisher to have a blank check and a rubber stamp approval with y'all from now on. We do *not* have the time to have this conversation over and over every time somebody points out that we're jumping all over the process. Yep, Ronny'll back me up on this." *Back me up on this, Ronny.* ". . . I'll pick up the other line and call him right this minute if it'll help you. . . . No. Okay then." Roger sat down in his chair and exhaled loudly.

"Okay, Charlie, thanks for your help. Hey listen, we're doing great stuff here and don't forget that part of it. Okay then." Roger hung up the phone and screamed at the top of his lungs for about three minutes. Then he opened up his telescope modeling program on his laptop and went back to work.

Dr. Reynolds, Dr. Powell, Davis, Dr. Ronny Guerrero, General Riggs, NASA MSFC Director Dr. Byron and the President's science advisor sat in the VIP bunker at the east coast launch facility at CCAFS with several Boeing and Lockheed Martin higher-ups, USAF 45th Space Wing Program support manager, and other upper echelon contractors and members of the Neighborhood Watch program.

Dr. John Fisher burst into the bunker VIP support room with two hours to spare before launch. He was obviously flustered; multiple beads of sweat had formed on his forehead, and his usually well-combed hair was in disarray. The sweat could have been from stress but maybe not—after all, it was a beautiful August day in sunny Florida, which meant hotter than hell.

John pulled a laptop out of locked double bags, and set it down on the conference table and plugged it into the portable projector he also pulled out of the bags. "This Machine is Approved Top Secret/Neighborhood Watch" was stamped on the front and back of the laptop and the projector.

"Sorry I'm late. There were some last minute hold procedures that I was tending to," he said.

"That's quite all right, John," Roger told him.

"Yes, Dr. Fisher, just as long as we don't miss the big show," the science advisor to the President responded. George Fines pointed out the window at the rocket on the pad. "I can't wait to hear you explain that behemoth to us."

Roger looked out the window across the lake to the launchpad. The fact that they could discuss Special Access Top Secret in a room with a window and people milling around outside in the hallway was a sign of the times. Things were changing in the old ways of doing things. Time and urgency didn't allow for all of the slow security protocols to be followed, so new ones were used in the interim and they were all approved by the Office of the President of the United States of America. Otherwise, some of them would never get past standard security personnel.

John clicked open the slideshow on his laptop and hit the magical keystroke combination that made the projector understand the computer and start displaying the laptop's screen on the big screen at the end of the conference table on the south wall of the VIP bunker support room.

"Okay. I think that's it." He clicked a few more buttons, scrolled to the slideshow and began.

"Well, in order to get Percival to the planet Mars in as short a period of time possible, Dr. Tom Powell developed a strawman design for a launch vehicle. The Modified Delta IV Heavy launch vehicle out there on the SLC-37 CCAFS launch pad is the resultant product of his original design. It's mostly the same as he originally suggested." John paused and cleared his throat and wiped the sweat from his forehead. "It's hot today," he muttered.

"That's right, John," Tom interrupted. "You fellas did a good job and built the rocket I had in mind almost to a T or at least as near as makes no difference."

"Uh, okay." John nodded to Tom and continued. "Dr. Fines, as you may or may not be aware of the typical Delta IV Heavy configuration, this is a modified version of that. This rocket has even heavier capability than the Heavy. The rocket consists of the main common booster core (CBC) tube with a Rocketdyne RS-68 liquid oxygen/liquid hydrogen (LO_2/LH_2) rocket motor base with a thrust vector control nozzle in the middle that can supply up to 650,000 pounds of thrust and 410 seconds of specific impulse. These CBCs were built in Decatur, Alabama, at the Boeing Delta IV rocket plant and they had to be modified slightly, but I'll get to that in a minute." John moved through the slides quickly.

"On either side of the central CBC tube is another CBC tube assembly strapped on. Each of these CBCs has a modified upper stage fairing atop and their engines should produce the same thrust characteristics as the central CBC. This portion of the rocket is the standard Delta IV Heavy that you may have seen before." He paused and noticed that Ronny was nodding in acknowledgement.

"Now, in order to increase the throw weight of the launch vehicle and therefore the mission spacecraft velocity, eight Alliant Techsystems graphite-epoxy GEM-60 solid rocket strap-on boosters are also attached at the base of each of the three larger CBC tubes of the Boeing-built rocket. As you can see from the slide—or better yet from out the window—there are three of these boosters attached to each of the side CBCs: one at zero, ninety degrees and minus ninety degrees. Two solid boosters are placed on either side of the central CBC at ninety and minus ninety degree locations. The GEM-60 strap-ons enable the launch vehicle to accommodate a much larger spacecraft payload than the standard Delta IV Heavy, much larger." Roger cleared his throat and nodded that he was going to interrupt.

"You see, Dr. Fines, this was required because Percival's throw weight to Mars was on the upper limit for a long mission timeline. The half-meter diameter primary mirror for the telescope alone ended up being about eighty kilograms. And with the other instruments and spacecraft structure, there was just no way the Delta IV Heavy and three upper stages would get the satellite to Mars in the hoped for four-to-five-month mission time. Tom here came up with the idea of adding the solid strap-on boosters to the rocket for the added boost. This did it on paper." Roger smirked, then added, "It took some doing and some expensive modifications contracts for Boeing to do it in reality, but they finally got the ball rolling and did it and on schedule." Fines sat quietly and nodded in response without making any facial expressions whatsoever. Roger nodded back to John to take over.

"Above the CBCs we connected three modified and connected Pratt & Whitney RL10B-2 cryogenic rocket motors to make up the second stage. Each of the modified engines will, hopefully, supply as much as 60,000 pounds of thrust over a burn time of 2250 seconds. Then above that is a single modified RL10B-2 making up the third stage. And finally, a standard RL10B-2 with half the burn time makes up the fourth stage."

"Above that," Roger stood and moved to the front of the room, "is the payload." He pointed to the payload shroud section. "The reason we're here is the payload, of course. It's attached atop the fourth stage and housed via the aluminum isogrid payload fairing and shroud. Here is where Percival sits." Roger nodded to John to click the slides.

"This project is a culmination of what mankind can do in a hurry if we really have to," Ronny Guerrero added. He understood that it was a culmination of brilliant design, development, and manufacturing. It was also the culmination of less than five months worth of work that was completed by a small army of a few thousand men and women. Ronny wanted to make sure that the President's advisor understood this.

"Let's hope it's a successful culmination," the science advisor said, smiling faintly.

The Neighborhood Watch team sat quietly for the next

hour and a half. John and Alan were in and out of the room checking with Launch Control to gather any good or bad news. The countdown was going as according to schedule. The men sat listening to the launch countdown protocols, anxiously awaiting the final countdown.

Finally, after four and half months of around-the-clock effort from thousands of the space community's best and brightest, the culmination of that effort was about to go. The Neighborhood Watch was about to happen. Of course, it would not arrive at Mars for nearly another five months.

Tina and Charlotte sat at the Florida hotel's beachfront with the water splashing at their feet as each breaker rolled in. Although school had started that week, they both were excited to miss a day or two of school, to sit on the beach and do nothing. Charlotte's dad and Tina's mother had insisted that the two of them make this trip. The parent's of both of the teens seemed unusually *touchy-feely* to the girls and were acting as though they hadn't seen their girls in years and might not get to see them again for years. Charlotte just chalked it up to the divorce and the amount of overtime her dad had been working. Tina didn't say much about it other than that they were stressing her out.

"You know," Tina dug her toes into the sand as the surf covered her feet. "I like this trip a lot better than the one to Hicksville."

"Aww come on, Tina. The Mars ride was fun. And you nearly wet your panties on that Moonshot thing," Charlotte added with a laugh. "And you gotta admit, flying the Space Shuttle simulator and driving those little Lego Mars rovers was kinda cool."

"Yeah, but this is the beach," Tina said, holding both arms out wide, cocking her hips to the left, and nodding to the ocean.

Charlotte smiled and nodded toward the two young men with about three percent body fat surfing just north of them. Just then one of the surfers wiped out and stood up, shaking the water from his long hair.

"I guess I'd have to agree with you on that one, Dingbat."

"You said it, Astrogirl." Tina acknowledged the two hunky surfers with a whistle.

"Uh huh."

"So when is it going to be?" Tina asked, shielding her eyes and looking to the north as her mother had told them to do, but at the same time not taking her eyes off the two hunky surfers.

"It should be any second unless they had some kind of hold. You know what they're launching?" Charlotte said as she searched the skyline for any sign of a rocket launch.

"Well, Mom just said it was classified. But I don't get why she could bring us to see a launch if it's classified."

"Dingbat!" Charlotte said with a chuckle. "How they gonna hide from all the local people that a big, bright, and noisy rocket just fired off? My dad said it was classified and that I couldn't ask him any questions about what is on it. But the fact that there's going to be a launch isn't classified."

"You think it'll be that bright in the day—look!" Tina stopped midsentence and pointed north-northeast.

"Oh wow! It's really bright! And check out that smoke trail!" Charlotte was giddy and pointing at the modified Boeing rocket as it pulled upward from Earth's gravity well. Both girls had seen smaller launches their parents had attended, but this one was different. The rocket's rumble was a solid body blow, as heavy even as the shuttle launches. Others along the beach turned toward the sky to watch the massive rocket—one of the largest to launch from the Cape since the legendary Saturns. One of the surfers wiped out, but the girls failed to notice. None of them had any idea what was onboard, where it was going, or why. But, they were fascinated by the rocket, its bright glare and rumble going on and on . . .

"Congratulations, John." Roger shook Dr. Fisher's hand and patted him on the back. "Doin' good, right?"

"That's right." John slumped in his chair in the VIP support room. "The launch vehicle functioned flawlessly and the telemetry reports so far tell us that the modified rocket system has pushed Percival into an Earth escape trajectory. Control tells me that the first stage combination of three kick motors fired and completed its burn, then separated. The second kick motor repeated the process from ignition to burnout with no problems. The third kick motor functioned likewise. The telemetry data downloaded from the star trackers to the main bus guidance and navigation computer tells that the software activated the algorithm to optimize the final thrust vectoring for the optimal burn vector to enter into the Mars incident trajectory. So, boss, my job is done. The spacecraft is on its way to Mars." John grinned and loosened his tie and unbuttoned his collar. "I'm gonna go find me an umbrella out there on the beach somewhere and sleep under it for about two days."

"Good job, John. That sounds like a really good idea."

Roger wished he could join him but there were payload checks that had to be run. But, all things considered, there was not really a lot to do over the next four and half months while Percival coasted toward Mars. Maybe the beach was a good idea.

It would be a little less than five months before Percival would fly-by less than a hundred kilometers from the strangely changing planet, but in the meantime the instruments and science suite began to come online for checkouts and operational status. *What should we do now? Waiting sucks.* Roger thought.

Chapter 7

"Waiting sucks," Major Gries muttered under his breath while he flipped through an unclassified white paper about synthetic gecko skin. This small five-employee company in New Mexico had decided that they had a new invention that would allow infantrymen to walk up walls, trees, windows, you name it. But Gries was having a hard time getting in to see the scientist who was supposed to be there to meet him. Apparently, as Carolyn Breese, the secretary of Gecko-Man, Inc. explained to him, Dr. Forrester had forgotten that today was Wednesday and that he was supposed to be there for a meeting.

"Major Gries," the secretary told him. "I just contacted Carl, uh, Dr. Forrester, again and he was in his car on the way here. He apologizes for his confusion and says you should make yourself at home. Would you like some coffee?"

"Yes, ma'am, that would be nice," Shane said.

"Normally, one of the other engineers could show you around, but everybody is at a preliminary design review in Clarendon this week. Sorry." Carolyn Breese finished filling a Styrofoam cup with hot black coffee. "Sugar or cream?"

"Black is fine, ma'am. Thanks." Gries sat back down into the folding chair against the wall across from the secretary a bit annoyed now that he realized there was going to be a considerable amount of time killed in small talk with Mrs. Breese. That was not a real bad thing and Shane was not the type who was too stuck up or important to spend time talking to a little old lady. In fact, she kind of reminded him his mother. But he had a lot of work to get done and he had a three PM flight from Albuquerque to LAX that he had to make. He had hoped he would have time to get lunch from some place other than the airport; that didn't look promising now. Airport food was killing him and making him soft. Shane hoped that he could get in a ten kilometer run sometime tonight but most likely he would end up on a hotel treadmill, which got old fast.

After about forty-five minutes, Forrester finally arrived. Shane guessed he was about five foot nine and weighed in at about two hundred and thirty pounds, not much of it muscle. His hair, although short in length, was extremely unruly and did not appear to have been touched by a comb in years. The most stereotypical part about the scientist's appearance was that he was wearing slacks, a shirt and tie, but at the same time was wearing running shoes. *Running shoes*, Gries laughed to himself. *This guy hasn't run anywhere but to the fridge and back in his life*. Shane smiled and offered his hand.

"Hello, Major. Sorry I'm late. It simply slipped my mind about our meeting today. I'm Carl Forrester." He shook Shane's hand, smiling happily in return.

"Hi, nice to meet you, Dr. Forrester." The humor in the man's appearance was enough for Shane to forget about being angry that he had been kept waiting.

"Come, come with me," Dr. Forrester told him, leading him down the hallway. The little laboratory was located in an old strip mall that had gone belly-up. The walls had holes and raw unsanded white spackle and sheetrock mud splattered at random, as if someone had made a piss poor attempt at fixing them. There were filing cabinets, one Moesler safe with little green magnets on each drawer saying closed, books, and spiral-bound reports stacked all along the floor and on top of the cabinets.

"Here we are." Dr. Forrester pecked in some keys on a cipher-locked door, then swung the door open to a make-shift laboratory that was filled with workbenches, a Snap-on toolbox, a few computers with wires running from them into aluminum boxes, and rolls and rolls of what looked like orange sandwich wrap—Shane had already been to several composite armor companies and recognized it as Kapton, the polyimide material that was used in most of the next generation armor labs.

"This is a sputtering chamber where we grow our synthetic gecko skin." Forrester pointed at a large enclosed chamber with a computer control panel on the front of it. There were several manipulators, spinning tables, and stylus arms inside the large enclosed device.

"Why don't you give me a little background before we get into the show? I'm not certain I understand how this stuff is supposed to work," Gries requested.

"Ah, great, great." Forrester motioned to a workbench stool with a stack of papers on it. "Yes, yes, have a seat."

Shane looked at the bench, then around the cluttered laboratory for a place to set the papers. He carefully picked them up and set them on the floor. Forrester had already turned away from him and was erasing a whiteboard across the room. Shane chuckled to himself again and sat down.

"You see, a few years ago some fellows at Berkeley and at Carnegie Mellon had the idea that being able to emulate a gecko and walk up walls and across ceilings might, and I'm sure you'd agree, be a fun and useful thing." Forrester stopped long enough to grin from ear to ear at Gries. "Think about it. If we could create a material that enabled us to have the nimble little lizard's incredible grip, wow, the applications would be endless.

"The efforts of those fellows made the idea a step closer to reality because they were clever and worked out how to make a material coated with synthetic gecko hairs. Uh, I'm getting ahead of myself. Let me see . . ." Dr. Forrester ran his fingers through his unruly hair.

"Ah yes, the hairs on gecko feet. Biologists call them 'setae.' These little setae are the key to its remarkable grip on just about any surface, rough or smooth, wet or dry, and the things are so sticky that the little lizards can hang from a ceiling with their entire weight held up by a single toe. Isn't that just marvelous?"

"Yes, I've seen little geckos do that trick before. The ones they call leopard geckos are all over Iraq," Shane added.

"Iraq, yes indeed, leopard geckos, hmm, marvelous." Forrester chuckled and his belly jiggled like Santa Claus's. "Well, it wasn't until as recently as last year that we understood how these little guys can do such a nifty thing. In fact, there was some very, shall I dare say, heated, debate about why geckos' setae were so fantastically sticky."

"Really," Shane asked, trying not to let his eyes glaze over or to check his watch.

"Oh, indeed. There was one school of thought that there was some gluey chemical interaction taking place between their feet and the surface they walked on. But that didn't pan out. This really clever fellow, uh, named Ron Fearing, and a few of his colleagues at the University of California at Berkeley finally figured it out. Can you believe that it turns out to be an electromagnetic interaction between a gecko's feet and the surface molecules, wow!" Forrester said excitedly.

"Oh, yes, believe it or not, the adhesion is in fact due to very weak intermolecular attractive forces called van der Waals forces. Amazing, isn't it?" He chuckled again and spent the next few minutes drawing a diagram of the gecko setae and explaining the van der Waals attraction.

While Forrester's back was turned, Shane stifled a yawn and did check his watch. He had no more than an hour he could spend here and it was airport food for sure. If he didn't make it through security, fast, it would be soggy sandwich time.

"The way it works is that the gecko setae measure tens of microns across and at their tiny ends they split into lots of even more tiny, thinner, extremely flexible hairs, each just hundreds of nanometers in diameter; now, isn't Mother Nature just incredible?" the scientist added, looking over his shoulder at his audience and apparently failing to notice that Shane's eyes were creeping closed.

"These little hairs then broaden out into flat spatulas, just like egg turners, at their tips. The wonderful little buggers can bend and conform to the surface of the wall at the molecular level and believe it or not again, this maximizes the surface area contact between the spatula and the surface, which in turn maximizes the van der Waals attractive force. I just can't hardly believe it, can you?" Forrester seemed almost giddy.

"Uh, no?" Shane added uncertain if the question had been rhetorical or not. He restrained the desire to check his watch again. The guy wouldn't be hurried by it, he was sure.

"Finally, these other fellows I've been talking about figured out how to synthesize the gecko skin. Wonderful ingenuity, wonderful," Dr. Forrester said enthusiastically. "Modern vacuum deposition, lithography technology, and some other materials technology allowed them to build synthetic gecko setae made from a material called Kapton that you see there in those orange rolls behind you. They made little gecko hairs that measure about two microns in height and about a tenth that in diameter. That is about the same dimensions as gecko hairs are. They made tape that was covered with this gecko hair with a mold created by a lithographic process. And the most wonderful part is that a piece of tape one centimeter square holds around a hundred million of these little artificial gecko setae and can actually support a weight of one kilogram. Wow! That suggests that a pair of gloves made of this stuff is all it would take to support the weight of a human being!"

"What's the catch? That sounds too good to be true." Shane leaned forward at that statement. Second-floor entry wasn't required *that* often, but various forms of climbing did occur in infantry combat. A pair of lightweight "super climber" gloves would be a great addition to the infantryman's pack. Well, it would add a smidgeon of weight, but . . . no, they could get rid of most ropes, which would *drop* weight. Weight had been a bugaboo in the infantry field all the way back to the days of Sargon.

"Ah, very astute, very astute, Major," Forrester replied and frowned. "The previous researchers have never been able to produce a synthetic gecko skin that worked more than a few times. The little gecko hairs get crushed or dirty or something and the material stops sticking to things. Very astute."

"So, it only works a few times, then you fall off the wall. Hmm, that could be hazardous for Geckoman the superhero, I would think." Gries smiled and was somewhat disappointed. Even if they could draw it out, they probably wouldn't be good for more than one use. Start talking about disposable gloves and it would be a pain.

"Oh, yes, Geckoman, funny." Forrester chuckled like Santa Claus again. "But you see, we've figured it out! I think we can deliver a material that will be completely reusable and work for tens of thousands of uses, maybe even indefinitely if it's cleaned after every few hundred uses. Here, watch this." Dr. Forrester rummaged through some equipment on one of the cluttered work benches and found what looked like a typical toy's remote control box.

Forrester flipped some switches and Shane nearly jumped out of his seat as a bright blue toy monster truck slammed into his stool. Forrester continued to flip the control levers on the box, then seemed to get control of how to steer the little monster truck. Shane noticed that the wheels of the truck were "oversized" to say the least. In fact, the wheels were so large that they stuck out in front of and above the little vehicle's frame. The little toy truck must have been modified with a more powerful motor just to turn those big things over.

"Watch, watch!" Dr. Forrester said as he drove the little monster truck across the room and right up the wall.

"Holy shit!" Gries grinned. "Can I play with that?"

"Sure, go over and pull it off the wall, Major." Dr. Forrester replied.

Shane crossed the cluttered room, being careful not to trip on some piece of equipment and break it or his neck, then grasped the toy truck. Shane pulled at the truck and it failed to unstick itself from the wall. He got a better grip on the truck and pulled harder—the truck stuck steadfast. He wasn't sure he could get it off if he planted his feet.

"I love that bit!" Forrester gave a deep belly laugh. "I'm sorry, Major Gries. I couldn't resist. You see, we figured out that the gecko is clever indeed. He has to twist his foot in a certain motion to release himself—we think. So, you have to do the same with the synthetic material. That's why I drove the truck up the concrete wall instead of the drywall—I take it you noticed all the spackle in the building."

"Yes, I did."

"Well, let's just say we've had a lot of fun with that trick, ha ha." He laughed again. "You know, it took us forever to develop a tire that would spin with just the right motion that would stick when you want it to and not stick when you want it to. Roll the truck forward and pull up and forward at the same time."

Gries did and the little truck went *schaluurrpp* and popped right off the wall.

"Well, I'll be damned." He rolled the truck over in his hands. "How do the wheels get unstuck enough to roll?"

"Like I said Major, that took us a long time to figure out. Geckos do it, so we just studied how they walked on walls and had to mimic that type of action with the wheel rotation. It wasn't easy." Forrester chuckled.

"Can you make me a bunch of this stuff, I mean tires for little recon trucks, boots, gloves, sticky-balls, bags, rolls of the material, you name it?"

"Well, Major, you see we're but a small group. To mass produce this would probably take start-up costs of a few million dollars or more. That little truck alone cost us about four-hundred-thousand dollars, and that's not counting the development cost for the synthetic gecko skin."

"That seems to be the way life goes, doesn't it?" Gries said with a sigh.

"Indeed, Major. Indeed."

Shane looked at the truck, turning it over and over in his hands. They were starting to use trucks like this for recon, especially urban recon. He thought about the ambush he'd been in and running a couple of these, suitably loaded with explosives, up the walls and into the rooms the rifs had been using. If the stuff was *really* durable, it would be useful for way more than just climbing. Hell, it was a replacement for Velcro. Zippers even. Natick was the Army's clothing and gear development center and Natick would go nuts playing with this stuff. Furthermore, they didn't always have to jump through all the acquisition hoops for experimental stuff. This would require a start-up investment, though, and Natick couldn't swing that.

DARPA, maybe. What Gecko-Man really needed was a venture capitalist to jump-start the company. And somebody to actually run it, for that matter. Keep the spackling on the walls, make sure people made appointments.

"I'm just one step in the process," Shane said, slowly, still turning the truck over and over as he thought, "but you *have* my support. I'm going to recommend this for an acquisition investment, but you'll probably get more money, faster, if you could get a private investor." He looked up at the man's suddenly fallen face and grinned. Even frowning Forrester looked funny, like a clown wearing a frowny face.

"Hey, it's never easy," Shane said, still grinning. "But, yeah, this stuff is major interesting and I'm going to *push* for a fast track. But fast-track is usually for acquisition of stuff that's off-the-shelf. I know a guy on the DARPA side, though, the Tactical Technologies Office or TTO. They might be able to fund you, I dunno. I'll talk to my boss and DARPA when I get back; that's all I can promise."

"I appreciate that," Forrester said, almost seriously. "I've been trying and trying to find an investor for this, but nobody can see the possibilities."

"Then they're blind," Shane said, still turning the truck over and over.

The telescope sensors came online and began to slew the telescope's axis. Location information from the star trackers fed into the pointing software and realized that the planet was outside the slewing capability of the telescope mount, so a subroutine triggered the attitude control system of Percival to fire the ACS thrusters and spin the reaction control wheels to align the spacecraft axis with a Mars line of sight. Then the software guided the telescope to bring Mars into the field of view.

The shiny gray planet was centered on the telescope guidance sensor array and the software then activated the ACS and RCS systems to maintain center field of view lock on the little planet. The locations of Phobos and Deimos were mapped to the pixel location on the wide field focal plane camera and the software subroutine began a continuous track on the small moons.

A similar acquisition and tracking routine was completed with the high gain antenna and Earth line of sight. Feedback between Earth and Percival was fed through the omnidirectional low gain antenna until signal lock was obtained with the HGA. Testing of the HGA and the telescope sensors was conducted by ordering the spacecraft to capture images and spectral data of the distant planet and download the data through the HGA-to-Earth link.

After an exhaustive checkout procedure it was determined that all of Percival's systems functioned properly. Neighborhood Watch was operational.

"So, what is it you think we should be doing, Ronny?" Roger looked out Dr. Guerrero's second floor window at the front entrance to NRO that they always showed on the news when referring to the nation's space reconnaissance office. He'd been in the building before but never in so rarefied an environment.

"I don't know, Roger. But we should be doing something." Ronny's Cuban accent was still obvious after a life of living in the United States. Sometimes that caused people to automatically assume he was a bit dim, a mistake they rarely made twice.

"The President and his advisors agree that we shouldn't just sit on our . . . butts for the next four months," Dr. Fines, added, frowning and looking at the wall rather than at the engineer. "We've assembled a team of the nation's most brilliant DOD and NASA engineers, so the President wants them to continue preparing for . . . whatever is to come."

Fines had been in multiple meetings with the President, the national security advisor, the secretary of defense, and the Joint Chiefs since the launch of Neighborhood Watch and everyone had been in agreement with that basic statement. The President had been particularly . . . blunt.

"George," Ronny Guerrero said leaning back in his leather executive chair and placing his hands behind his head. "I think we should take the core group and let them have free rein to brainstorm. Perhaps they might identify more key players that should be involved in the future. But their mission should be to just brainstorm. When we get more data from the probe we can down select to more likely scenarios."

"That almost sounds like a pork barrel, Ronny." Fines shook his head.

"Well, that's what I think needs to be done." Ronny leaned forward, reaching for his coffee cup. It had the NRO symbol on one side and "Boss Mon" imprinted on the other. There were some who wondered about having a former Cuban national in charge of the nation's surveillance satellites. But, on the other hand, he had quite a few people in the building who had been rooting for him for years. The mug had mysteriously appeared on his desk the day after he took over. Given the security on the room, that had taken some doing. He was still considering the security implications.

"Okay then," Fines said with a sigh. "I'll tell the President that we're working on possible scenarios. We'll get the funding, somewhere, to maintain the team with a small material, research and support budget."

"Good. Roger, why don't you get the right group of guys together and start thinking about our situation," Ronny said, nodding at the engineer.

"I'll get right on it," Roger replied. "I'm going to need to get a security waiver, though," he added, trying not to smile.

"What's that?" Dr. Fines asked, seriously.

"We're going to have to get the Huntsville Hooters restaurant designated as a secure facility."

"So Rog, you ever heard of CASTFOREM?" Alan Davis refilled his coffee cup and sat down in the break room of the Neighborhood Watch office suite in one of the commandeered buildings of the Redstone Arsenal in north Alabama. Ronny had missed the humor in Roger's request and had meanly refused to give a waiver for Hooters. It *was* a joke after all. Besides, Hooters wasn't open twenty-four hours and that was, just about, the schedule they'd been running. The team had been brainstorming, researching or cautiously picking the brains of scientists and "futurists" just about 24/7 for the last couple of weeks. And Roger had thought they'd have some downtime!

"CASTFOREM? Cast-forum, Castfor-em . . . Don't reckon I have, Alan." Roger took the empty pot that his friend had just set back down, frowned, then refilled the coffee maker with water, a new coffee filter, and more coffee. He added twice the amount of coffee grounds suggested on the Folgers' bag—he needed the caffeine.

"Well, it turns out that there is this software code that was developed for war gaming and simulating new technologies and how they impact possible battle scenario outcomes," Alan said, yawning and taking a sip of coffee. He frowned at the burnt taste. "Stands for Combined Arms and Support Task Force Evaluation Model. It's *the* approved code for the Army. Here, look at this." Alan handed his friend and boss a printout of some PowerPoint slides.

"Hmm, 'CASTFOREM is a brigade force-on-force, closed-loop stochastic combat model comprised of and captures output data for: Command and Control, Communications, Combat Service Support, Engineering, Surveillance, Engagements, Maneuvers, System/Environment.' " Roger read out loud, then muttered to himself as he scanned the bottom of the page. "Gotta love that bureaucratese. 'CASTFOREM is a highly robust simulation tool that can model individual entities at resolutions required to address the study issues.' In other words, you plug in the parameters and it tells you if you win or lose."

"I've been talking to a small alphabet soup company here in town that's been modeling the Future Combat Systems with this code." Alan pointed out the three letter company logo on the printout. "He thinks that he could modify the code, relatively soon, so that we can simulate damned near any type of magic weapon or concept. And, in turn, the simulation will tell us how it impacts the battle scenario."

"Yeah, but can it model an alien attack from space?"

Roger looked up from the page, raising his left eyebrow.

"Well, I didn't exactly ask him that, but he did say if you wanted to give the enemy rayguns and teleporters you can—with some slight mods to the code that is." Alan mixed sugar and cream into his cup and took a sip. "He did say it would be expensive."

"Oh yeah? How much?" Roger flipped the switch and the coffee maker started gurgling.

"He said about two hundred thousand dollars for a month of modifying and simulation running." Alan smiled as Roger's concerned expression changed to humor.

"Small businesses are great, ain't they? Two hundred thousand, humph; I was expecting you to say something like a million dollars or more." He grinned and opted for a Mountain Dew out of the vending machine instead of waiting for the coffee. "Wish we had Jolt Cola in this thing," he muttered.

"So what do you think?" Alan asked.

"Future Combat Systems, huh? That suggests that they have at least a Secret clearance, right?" Roger popped the soft drink can top.

"Yes. So, do I bring them in?"

"Bring 'em in." Roger nodded. "In the meantime, how many alien invasion movies have we watched thus far?"

"Well, so far, we've seen thirteen of the eighty-seven movies and television shows we compiled." Alan counted in his head for a second. "No, wait, make that fourteen."

"Well, let's keep at it."

"At the six to seven movies a day that we're taking in, it should take us about fourteen or so days to finish. That is, assuming we work weekends. Again."

"Good assumption," Roger said taking a swig of the

soft drink and swishing it around in his mouth.

"Who'd ever have thought that the NRO would pay us to sit around and watch alien invasion movies?" Alan finished off his coffee.

"Nice work if you can get it, right?" Roger said with a smile. "I'll meet you in the conference room and we'll get back at it. I'm gonna stop by the secretary's office and have her order us some pizzas. Why don't you get these CASTFOREM guys briefed and modifying their code? They should be ready to start simulating flying saucers and such in—How long did you say?"

"Fourteen days."

"Right, fourteen days." Roger finished off his Mountain Dew and threw the empty can at the wastebasket in the corner of the break room. He missed. "By then we should be done with the movies. Then we start cracking the books."

Tina had spent the last few months staying with her friend Charlotte since her mom had been temporarily transferred to Florida. Her brother Carl had been staying with one of his buddies—he and his mother hadn't really been that close since the divorce anyway, so the separation from their mother didn't really impact him as much as it had Tina.

Tina, on the other hand was close to her mother and although she liked Charlotte better than a sister, she really missed her mother and wanted to go home for a while. Her mother, Alice, was the quintessential soccer-mom (actually a cheerleader mom in Tina's case) and for her to be away for so long a period of time was hard for both of them. But Tina understood, or she knew that Alice hoped she did, that only something really important could keep her away from her family for so long.

Fortunately, Alice had gotten a two-week vacation and had planned to spend all of it in Denver with her kids. Of course, Tina's sixteen-year-old brother Jason had more important plans than to be hanging around with his thirteen-year-old little sister and his mother on a Saturday night. So Tina and Alice were hanging out by themselves at home for the first Saturday evening in over four months. Oh, sure, Tina had visited her mother in Florida for the launch of the rocket her mother had worked on, but that wasn't the same.

"So, what did you want to do tonight?" Alice propped her feet up on the ottoman in front of the couch. "It feels so great to be home."

"Uh huh." Tina looked up from the television and nodded. Tina tapped the view button on the remote so that the time was displayed on the upper left corner of the screen. "Well, if you don't mind I'd like to watch my show in five minutes. But after that, I don't care. Maybe we could rent a movie or something?"

"Sure, what show is it that you want to watch?" Alice was almost afraid to ask.

"Weeelll," Tina hesitated. "You're not gonna believe this but Charlotte got me hooked on it. It's on the Cartoon Network and it's called *Justice League Unlimited*."

"Oh yeah, what's it about?" Alice had always thought that Charlotte was a good influence on her daughter, so this intrigued her.

"It has all the superheroes in it. You know, Wonderwoman—she's my favorite—Superman, Batman, Supergirl, the Martian Manhunter, Flash, and every superhero you can think of," she replied sheepishly.

"Oh yeah, does it have Spiderman in it?" Alice asked then misinterpreted her daughter's expression. "I just like Spiderman, okay?"

"Uh, no, Mom. Spiderman is Marvel and Wonderwoman is DC. Charlotte had to explain that to me, too, so don't feel bad."

"I see. Well, let's watch it then."

Tina flipped the television over to the Cartoon Network just in time for the animated series to begin. Alice was glad that her daughter's "show" was on the Cartoon Network rather than on HBO, MTV, or some other programming that might have questionable content, because, as it stood Tina was thirteen, but she had all the signs of being a twenty-something girl gone wild sometime within the next week or so.

The program began with a couple of climbers going up the side of a mesa somewhere in a desert in the States. When the couple crested to the top, there was an alien spacecraft there. Alice became more interested in the program.

The spacecraft began producing little probes that would self-replicate and their numbers began to increase nonlinearly.

"Wow! This is a full scale Mega Alert!" Tina said right before Superman made a similar statement in the program.

"What does that mean?" Alice asked her.

"Oh, that means they call *all* known superheroes to the trouble spot!" Tina said, her eyes glued to the television as the costumed superbeings began slugging it out with the alien self-replicating robot threat.

The entire cast of DC superheroes—there must have been hundreds of them—and the military fought these things throughout the program. The extreme might of the comic book legends was no match for the strength of massive numbers and immediate self-replication of these alien bots.

Then one of the superheroes had the presence of mind to send Superman off to find Dr. Ray Palmer, also known as the Atom. The Atom was a scientist who could control his size down to an atomic scale. He recognized very quickly that these alien bots were replicating themselves with nanotechnology and explained that they were most likely Von Neumann probes. He then explained that the scientist John Von Neumann suggested over fifty years ago that self-replicating bots would be the ideal way for interstellar space travel. He went into further details about how the nanotechnology might work. The fact that Tina was watching a show about such high-tech concepts thrilled her mother. It beat E!, MTV, or FUSE hands down. She would never say anything bad about the Cartoon Network again.

In the end the Atom figured out a way to defeat the alien probes from deep within the probes' control computer. Tina was edutained. Alice was excited that her daughter was watching such imaginative and educational programming—she had been right about Charlotte—and she needed to make a phone call to Huntsville, Alabama. Right now.

"The computer just finished running the latest battle scenario, Rog. You want to hear the results?" Alan flipped through a stack of papers, half reading the data.

"Let's hear it." Roger turned away from his laptop for a moment and gave his undivided attention. Besides, checking the status of Percival one more time this hour wasn't going to help get it to Mars any faster.

"Well, in this case we made the aliens ten times harder to kill than human soldiers. We increased the armor coefficient by ten and we gave them rayguns that have an output intensity of a gigawatt per square meter. We gave them terabits per second communications capabilities and unlimited MASINT." Alan continued to read off the list of unbelievable abilities they had given to the alien threat to be simulated as the red forces.

"Yeah, what do we have?" Roger leaned forward in his office chair and tipped the little kinetic desk gadget on the corner of his desk. A little space shuttle attached to a metal rod at one end and a metal ball at the other end zinged around inside a little metal ring in all three dimensions. Roger stared at the motion for a second.

"Well, we started out with just what we can deploy today." Alan scanned the printouts of the simulation results. "Then we added nukes, tac-nukes, RF weapons, directed energy systems, experimental missiles and aircraft, chem-bio, and so on."

"And?" The little space shuttle slowed, then stopped. Roger tapped it with his right index finger and sent it whirling again.

"Blue forces totally consumed by the red forces threat," Alan read from the report.

"No shit."

"No shit. What now?" Alan shrugged his shoulders, looking up from the report and noticing that Roger was only partly paying attention to him.

"That was a two-hundred-and-fifty-thousand dollar obvious answer, huh?" Roger sat quiet for a moment longer, spinning the little desk gadget again. "Let's have some fun with this and model in some other stuff. I mean magic stuff. Try something like in *Independence Day*, or *The Puppet Masters* or *War of the Worlds* or something."

"Well, we tried chem-bio agents like in those last two you mentioned and no luck," Alan said with a frown. "To be realistic, we have no idea about their physiology so there is little way we can put in an agent with a high confidence. Oh sure, we could fudge it in the simulation if you want to win, but it wouldn't be based on reality."

"Like any of this stuff is? We don't have a clue what we're up against here. Hell, there might just be some ten million year alien varmint hatching planet-wide there— who knows?" Roger shrugged.

"Well then, since it's all made up anyway, I'll add some miracles to see what happens." Alan scribbled on the print-outs.

"Do that just to see what happens if we were to find that, I dunno, toothpaste, or bad breath, or something as equally unlikely kills them. Who the hell knows? What about cyber?" Roger sat back in his chair now bored with the desk gadget.

"We tried that and it had little impact. Again, I'll fudge a run for you." Alan scribbled some notes on the print-outs again, then began tapping his head with the pen.

"Hell, give us transporters and antigravity just to see what happens." Roger sort of smiled while at the same time looking disappointed. "Hey, how about adding power armor like in *Starship Troopers* or the veritech fighters, hovertanks, and cyclones in *Robotech*."

"I'll get right to it."

"Oh, by the way, Alice Pike called me Saturday night with an interesting bit of information. Apparently John Fisher's daughter strikes again."

"Refresh my memory . . . John Fisher's daughter?" Alan asked.

"You know, she's the thirteen year old amateur astronomer who captured the images of Mars with her eight-inch telescope—the ones that we're putting in the final report to Ronny."

"I didn't realize that was John's daughter. How about that?" Alan said. "Apple didn't fall too far, huh?"

"Well, like I said, she's made another unwitting contribution to the Neighborhood Watch." Roger said.

"How so?"

"I didn't realize this, but John and Alice have known each other for years and their daughters go to the same school together. It appears that John's daughter has gotten Alice's daughter watching sci-fi and cartoons. Anyway, Alice and her daughter watched an episode of the cartoon called *Justice League Unlimited* this weekend. Alice said that we needed to see that episode."

"Really? JLU? I've seen commercials for that, but I haven't had time to watch it," Alan said. "Did she say what the episode was about?"

"Yeah, she did."

"Well?"

"Von Neumann probes attacking Earth."

"What'd ya mean that nothing helps?" Alan Davis just could *not* believe that the combination of powered armor suits, supercyber weapons, SuperCrest (as they had called the alien chem-bio agent as a joke on Roger), ultrahigh bandwidth communications, and even through-the-Earth transporters were not enough to beat the simulated alien red forces. After a month of modeling, no blue force winning scenario had been modeled.

"Well, watch the big screen and you can see the results for yourself," the programmer from the CASTFOREM simulation group explained. "We used D.C., Atlanta, L.A., New York City, and Seattle as the central points of attack and had the red forces spread radially outward from there as blue forces were depleted. Now, we did have to assume a continuous supply of red forces from space." The software engineer tapped a few keys and nodded to the screen.

The big screen on the wall of the War Room displayed a map of the United States with multiple blue forces gathered at scenario battle theaters scattered across the country. A tiny red dot appeared at each of the cities mentioned and they began growing into red blotches that oozed outward. As more and more red began to spread across the map, engulfing the blue forces, a window on the side displayed a tally of casualties and capabilities losses. The numbers were staggering: in the tens of millions and growing each second.

"This even uses the transporters, right?" Alan asked.

"Right. You see here that just about a year after the initial attacks begin, the war is over. Red forces win and spread to the rest of the world, pretty much no matter what miracles we use."

"There has got to be a way to win this thing." Alan scratched his head while he stared at the big screen.

"Sure there is," the engineer said, shrugging. "It was

obvious. You didn't ask for the scenario, but I ran it anyway."

"Don't keep me hanging," Alan replied.

"You have to cut off their infinite resupply of troops from space."

"Now how the hell are we gonna do that?" Alan asked with a frown. "Where is Superman when you need him?"

"Doing it with Lois Lane?"

"Mr. President, every war game we've run so far says that we cannot win an all-out invasion," Ronny Guerrero explained to the President and his senior staff.

"You mean your boys down in Alabama have come up with no brilliant ways to beat this thing?" the NSA asked.

"Yes, ma'am, and as I understand it, nobody at the Pentagon has come up with anything either. The suggestions of the Neighborhood Watch team is that we need a larger all-out defense development effort to determine if there are possible solutions available." Dr. Guerrero paused to measure the President's reaction.

"You mean something big, like the Manhattan Project, don't you?" he asked.

"Well, sir, I think it would have to be bigger than that and Star Wars and Neighborhood Watch combined," Ronny said trying to make no facial expression, but it was hard for him to hide the grimace.

"Well, keep moving ahead at the level of efforts you have now and add a little to have your team figure out how to set a program like that up. But we'll wait until we get the recon from Mars before we embark on such a mammoth economic drain. Who knows how that would affect the economy right now?" the President replied.

Ronny held his expression blank, but thought that the President should be more concerned about Earth's survival than the economy. *He's not equipped to understand what we are facing. I'm not sure I am.*

The Neighborhood Watch team leaders and data reduction staff gathered around their respective consoles at the Huntsville Operations Support Center at NASA Marshall Space Flight Center. There were others riding consoles at DSN locations around the world and at various relay satellite ground stations. Of course, only people who knew all about Neighborhood Watch were aware that any signal was being received from Mars. In fact, the stations being used were all "shut down for repairs."

Roger Reynolds sat quietly at the HOSC trying to make heads or tails out of the previous image that had just completed downloading. The image was taken minus two hours from Percival's closest approach to the planet's surface. The telemetry data received to that point suggested that Percival should get as close as about fifty-four kilometers from the surface. At that altitude an image from the high resolution point camera would have a resolution of about ten centimeters—small enough to see a license plate but not read it. The probe was approaching Mars fast and would go from 50,000 km away, through the closest approach, and to 50,000 km past Mars in a period of less than two hours.

Data from spectral analysis taken at further distances from the planet had already been downloaded. There were gases and metals but no signs of organic substances such as methane or ammonia. As the spacecraft approached closer to the planet the high resolution camera took priority on the download list.

Mission timeline approached fifteen minutes from minimum distance as the latest image dinged complete. The image had been taken sixty minutes to closest approach and had taken about forty-five minutes to download. As soon as the image download was complete, download of the next image in the sequence began.

Roger pulled the approach-minus-sixty-minutes image up and ran the post-processing software. The image sharpened on the screen in front of him and on several monitors simultaneously throughout the HOSC.

"Holy shit," he muttered under his breath. At minus sixty minutes from Mars the spacecraft was about 50,000 km from the planet and so the image resolution was about 60 m per image pixel. And at 60 m per pixel all Roger could say was . . . "Holy shit!"

"Roger, am I seeing what I think I'm seeing?" Dr. Guerrero asked, pointing at a section of long straight lines interlaced in a gridlike pattern. Years at the NRO had trained him to notice artificial features in space reconnaissance imagery and Ronny recognized what he was seeing. But he couldn't believe it.

"Roads perhaps? Or maybe high-rise buildings? But, these things are a couple hundred meters wide! I don't understand what I'm seeing yet. The scale is just too . . . large," Roger replied.

The next image in the sequence had begun downloading and thus far the mission was going as according to plan. The currently downloading image was acquired at 13,000 km from Mars with a resolution of about 20 m per image pixel. Roger had the raw data displayed as it was downloaded. The first few rows of the image filled in across the screen as the mission timeline ticked by. With no post-processing it was hard to determine what they were seeing, but it appeared to be a cityscape or industrial center, but very, very large.

"How could objects this big be manufactured from Martian soil so quickly and across the entire planet?" Alan asked over Roger's shoulder.

"Dunno?" Roger said, stumped. "Magic."

"Any sufficiently advanced technology . . ." Alan replied.

"Yeah," Roger muttered. "That kind of magic."

"Maybe we'll understand it better when the image is finished and we can clean it up some." Ronny scratched his head and took a sip from the Styrofoam coffee cup in front of him. "But, it looks like a civilization. A *big* civilization. That just . . . sprang up."

"How much longer do we have to wait to get the rest of this 20 meter resolution?" Alan asked.

"Well, it's been downloading about fifteen minutes or so. It'll take about another thirty. I'm gonna grab a Coke, I'll be right back."

Roger stretched and stood from his chair. He pulled the headset off and rolled his head left then right. Tense didn't begin to cover it—his neck felt like a steel wire.

"Mission Command, Watchdog reset on HGA requested. I've got an extreme load on the high-gain dish gimbals." The C&DH console rider shouted over the mike, loud enough for Roger to hear it all the way across the control room.

"Mission Command, we've got an Attitude Determination and Control Systems Alert. The star trackers are giving rapid angular acceleration of the spacecraft." Another console report came in. "Momentum wheels are spinning erratic and the ACS thrusters have fired."

Then multiple alerts at once were being reported. Roger sat back down and donned his headgear.

"Roger that, Watchdog reset. I'm showing no contact with Percival. I repeat . . . no contact with Percival. Has anybody got anything on their monitors?"

"Low bandwidth telemetry shows that multiple Watchdog software and hard resets were triggered. No further telemetry from the LGA is being received," the C&DH console operator said.

Roger waited patiently for reports from all consoles, but he was not at all happy with what he was hearing.

"Nothing from the low-gain antennas?"

"Negative, Roger."

The final assessment was that contact with the probe had been lost.

"Okay, let's start up the reconnect protocols and follow the procedures."

Tom Powell sat back in his chair and made a Jetsons space car noise, blowing air through his pursed lips as he looked at something on his monitor. He muted his mike and turned toward Roger, Alan, and Ronny.

"You know, when I came up with the idea for that 'Nuke Mars Now' bumpersticker when all those probes started disappearing, I meant it then, and I reiterate the sentiment now. Once is happenstance, twice is coincidence, three times is enemy action: NUKE MARS NOW! I knew everybody should have listened to me!"

"Why?" Alan asked.

"Well, I've already compiled the alert signals—there weren't that many of them—and the last one was of massive spacecraft bus structural integrity loss. The first alerts

were from the exterior boxes, then they moved structurally inward to that final alert. All this took place in about
a second or so. It looks to me like the spacecraft was dismantled from the outside inward. Fast. Something took
it apart at a relative velocity of about 15 km/s to the planet.
I mean, something flew up to it, matched velocity with it,
then ripped it apart."

"Tom, don't jump to conclusions," Alan said with a
shrug. "Even if it flew apart, couldn't they—whoever 'they'
are—have just shot it down—not that that's any better
mind you—or couldn't the spacecraft just've failed. I mean
it could have just hit a micrometeorite or something."

Roger looked at the big mission clock on the overhead
screen. The mission time display told him that the telemetry commands sent back to the Mars probe should be
getting there in about eight more minutes. *Be patient*, he
thought to himself.

"Sure," Tom argued. "But I don't think that's what happened. The data doesn't support it. Nuke Mars Now!"

"Tom," Roger said quietly.

"Yeah?" the rocket scientist replied angrily.

"It's on the table. Now shut up."

The eight minutes passed, then another ten, then
another thirty and no response came back from Percival.
More command signals were sent out—still no response.

After hours of searching for signals from the probe,
the team finally decided that the spacecraft was lost. Most
certainly the folks at the DSN would continue listening
for the spacecraft for days, but as it stood at the moment,
reestablishing contact seemed unlikely.

Roger and Dr. Guerrero had continued to check systems, talk to team members and just plain wait. The two

of them had been holed up in the HOSC support room for more than twenty-two hours and it was time one of them said what they both had been afraid to. Roger rubbed his eyes, then yawned. He turned to the DDNRO who was adding another packet of sweetener to his coffee cup.

"Well, Ronny, it looks like somebody didn't want us getting any closer to Mars."

Chapter 8

"Mr. President, Joint Chiefs, advisors." Ronny Guerrero began the debriefing of the top advisors and leaders of the United States of America. The briefing was held in the secure room just down the hall from the Oval Office and was at the highest security protocols. Ronny had completed the mission that he had been asked to do and had done it well. The mission was as successful as it could have been. Success, however, was a bit moot at this point. Ronny had to tell the President of the United States what they had discovered and that the discovery might mean the end of the human civilization. The Mars mission was an easier task.

"Although we lost all contact with the Mars ISR probe, we can report that the mission was a success to some degree. We were able to piece together the timeline of events and the details of the mission and data collected are shown in the classified final report you have in front of you." Ronny held up a copy of the Neighborhood Watch final report.

"Analysis of the alert messages in the telemetry data from the probe suggests that at 1 minute and 4 seconds after reaching its closest approach altitude of about 54 kilometers at a Mars-relative velocity of about 15 kilometers per second the spacecraft was completely destroyed. All systems were functioning properly and no unusual loads were being created by any of the spacecraft systems. Then within a period of less than a second the spacecraft was lost. This at first appears to suggest that the spacecraft was, for want of a better term, 'shot down,' that is, destroyed in an act of immediate and catastrophic destruction. The spacecraft was well above the atmosphere and a micrometeor impact would not have been as catastrophic. An analysis of the sequence of alerts suggests that the spacecraft was pulled apart from the outer periphery equipment inward to the spacecraft structure. In other words, something dismantled it in about a second." Ronny flipped through the report in front of him to the data section.

"If you'll turn to the data section, you'll find there is more startling information. We were able to capture a complete image with 60 meters per pixel resolution and a partial image of 20 meters per pixel resolution before contact was lost with the spacecraft. The imagery was obtained by the spacecraft and downloaded just before its destruction and it shows the change in the surface of Mars."

Ronny flicked his laser pointer at the reconnaissance image on the screen.

"There are vast grids and infrastructure like textures and structures on scales of tens and hundreds of kilometers. There are several single structures many times larger than the Great Pyramids of Giza. Impact craters as large as cities have been excavated and built upon and their specular content has dramatically increased, suggesting refined materials.

"The general reflectance of the region in the imagery shows that the region is much more specular than Mars should be. The large specular regions suggest shiny, most likely metallic, structures, consisting of synthetic, smoothed minerals or concrete, or glass-covered structures.

"Also, a fractal analysis of the imagery has been conducted and the fractal dimension of these images is that of an artificial landscape.

"In summary, it's very little doubt that the changes in Mars are due to *intelligent design*. There are, in fact, now canals, as well as roads and buildings, on Mars.

"Alarmingly, the structures are much larger than human standards and even in Martian gravity must require advanced knowledge of manufacturing principles. Also, these structures must have been constructed in a period of no more than about two years as no changes in Mars were detectable before then. This suggests rapid construction on a planet-wide scale, which is far beyond human capabilities.

"Finally, the Neighborhood Watch team has discussed at great length the data and implications of this occurrence. We have gathered a team of scientists, engineers, mathematicians, exobiologists, cosmologists, and others, and after much debate, it's our opinion that our new 'neighbors' can only be considered as hostile; they first destroyed all of our probes that were already there; second, moved in on a massive scale without contacting us although they knew we were somewhere in the neighborhood due to our probes; and third, they destroyed our ISR probe while they must have been able to realize from its trajectory that it would fly by Mars causing it no harm.

"This conclusion is alarming. The rapid occurrence and large scale of the phenomenon suggest that the implementation was automated and likely mechanized. It's our best guess that self-replicating automatons would be most suited for this task. This suggests either robots or insectlike culture and capabilities. The most likely candidate description that comes to light is that of Von Neumann probes as described by the Hungarian mathematician John Von Neumann in the previous century."

"What are Von Neumann probes?" the NSA interrupted.

Ronny paused and caught his breath for a second.

"Well Madam Security Advisor, the mathematician John Von Neumann described that the best approach to interstellar travel would be to send self-replicating robots to the new star system. One or a few robots would land at the new star system and use in-situ resources to replicate until they reached a critical number. This critical number being that which is required to either construct a civilization infrastructure for the real inhabitants that would arrive much later when the new star system has been equipped and ready for occupation or to create more bots to move on. The implications of that are . . . disturbing." Ronny paused again.

"Disturbing," the Chairman of the Joint Chiefs

muttered. "Nice use of understatement, Dr. Guererro. Can I send a couple of nukes now?"

"All in favor say 'aye,' " the NSA responded. "Aye."

Ronny nodded, acknowledging the comments.

"The worst part, General, is that such automatons would be driven by one of those two goals—replication for further interstellar movement or preparing the new system for colonization. In either case, then we can only assume that Mars is not where they will stop. The Von Neumann probes would use every in-situ resource within a solar system for either goal. The point here being, whether they intend to colonize or simply are 'passing through,' there is no indication that they will not do the same thing to Earth that they have done to Mars. Whether their intentions are hostile or simply . . . uncaring, the damage to the Earth will not be survivable by the human race.

"We suggest tasking the Hubble Space Telescope to look at the spectra and albedos of the outer planets and possibly Kuiper Belt Objects to determine if Mars is the only planet within the Sol system being transformed.

"We also suggest that we begin to prepare for an invasion that could occur at any time. We have no way of knowing or understanding the alien devices' motivation or timeline. What is the critical mass required before they move to the next target planet? Perhaps the Hubble experiment will give us some insight. Or perhaps they will move from Mars to the Moon first, if we're lucky. Who knows? We're not certain of any of these things, but we're certain that these are aliens. We're also pretty certain of the Von Neumann probe theory although it could be some sort of biological equivalent. And finally, several of our team members concur with the Chairman: Nuke Mars Now. However, given the scale of the change and the fact that our probe was intercepted well outside of any reasonable engagement range it's unlikely that we can, in fact, get a nuke onto the ground. Or that any number of nuclear devices would, in fact, help."

"In other words," the President said, sighing. "We're too late."

"Sorry I'm late," Roger said, sitting down at the table in Hooters with a sigh. "Ronny called. He wants us to start using the Hubble to look for more traces in the system."

"We're systems engineers," Alan said, frowning. "Why us?"

"Not we three in particular," Roger corrected, looking over at Tom with a raised eyebrow. "He wants the group that's doing it reporting to us. Then I report to Ronny and he sends it on. And we just got Asymmetric Soldier dumped on us, too."

Project Asymmetric Soldier, from the perspective of the team, might be the critical linchpin of the defense of the world.

Project Asymmetric Soldier was put into play because it was decided that any invasion from space by the phenomenon would be extremely one-sided in the invaders' favor. Asymmetric Soldier was based on the concept of "asymmetric warfare." The general idea was to try to fight battles using your strengths against an enemy's weakness. The concept was much touted by groups that had fought the United States over the years. The known problem with asymmetric warfare was that it rarely worked. The project was already notorious for being referred to by its acronym—AS, pronounced like the name for a male donkey—and various variations.

Asymmetric Soldier was a research, development, and engineering as well as strategic and tactical investigation into how to prepare for the invasion, begin preparations, and search for fast turn-around technologies that could be used against an invasion on a planet-wide scale. While it was probably the only hope of survival of the human race, no one involved, especially given the CASTFOREM data, gave it more than the chance of a snowflake in hell. However, every bit of data they could gather would refine and improve AS's chance of working.

"Why are you giving me the fish-eye?" Tom asked, frowning. He picked up a wing and tried to get the bone to fall out with a twist, ending up with mashed chicken mess. "I *will* succeed in this endeavor. AS GOD IS MY WITNESS, I WILL FIGURE OUT THE CHICKEN TRICK! If I can figure out the chicken trick, maybe I can figure out . . . the rest. . . ." he ended with a sigh.

"We're going to need planetary guys, astrophysicists. . . You're from CalTech, you know all those types," Roger ended with a shrug. He picked up a wing, expertly stripped out the chicken and double-dipped.

"I seriously need a beer," Alan said, sighing and reaching for the pitcher. "I thought we could chill for a while. And now we need asshole physicists—"

"My job," Traci said, slapping his hand away and picking up the pitcher. "And quit bad-mouthin' my future career. Besides, why do you need an astrophysicist? You guys are systems engineers. What the hell do *you* know about stars and planets? Nothing, that's what. You had to get me to convince you the albedo of Mars was changing! Hah. Rocket scientists couldn't even *tell* that Mars was changing color until a *Hooters* girl pointed it out!"

"Funny. But Roger here is really more of a telescope designer than a rocket scientist, although he plays one on TV," Alan said, giving her a forced smile as he picked up the refilled pitcher.

"Hmm." Roger grunted; he was made a little bit nervous by the fact that Traci knew so much about what they had been doing. Security matters were still important. Roger started pondering a debriefing scheme or cover to lead Traci away from the Neighborhood Watch line of thinking.

"Why's everybody so glum? You're at *Hooters!*" Traci said, bouncing up and down so she jiggled pleasantly. "And check out *my* hot and spicies if you need a boost! What happen, somebody cut your funding again?"

"No, funding's not a problem," Roger said, looking at her thoughtfully, then over at Tom who was also looking . . . thoughtful. There was, of course, an alternative to creating a story . . .

"Traci, honey," Tom said, seriously, stroking his beard and not even bothering to look at his nominal boss, "how *far* along are you on your masters . . . ?"

"*Hweet*, Gries!" Captain Sparling half whistled, waggling a finger at the major.

Shane hit the close key on the window showing a new and improved tac-net concept, logged off the secure computer systems, then slid his chair across the corridor to the captain's cubicle. In the last six months he'd tried to keep in shape by running. But his schedule was such that he knew he was getting swivel-chair spread and a beer gut. He *had* to get out of this racket, somehow.

At the same time, he had to admit it was fascinating. Yeah, most of the ideas he'd had pitched, thrown and hurled at him since joining the DARPA Special Technologies Office had been pie-in-the-sky where they weren't downright scary in a "if it's stupid and it gets you killed, it's stupid" way. But a few of the ideas, like the synthetic gecko stuff and the third generation tac-net he was examining, were pretty damned hot. The faster they got in the hands of the troops, the better, although he was still thinking about the uses for that gecko skin. The problem was settling on just *one*. He'd figured out a way to use it for sealing troop doors on personnel carriers.

"I hate these things," Captain Sparling said, waving at his computer. "Sure, they increase productivity. Sure, they make communication easier. But that's a two-edged sword."

"Yes, sir?" Shane said, frowning and carefully *not* looking at the captain's computer. He'd learned that was a bit of a no-no. The team, given the way that data was compartmentalized, really should have had separate *offices*. Instead, they just tried not to read over each other's shoulders. They had been trying to get moved over to the main office in Arlington where there was more room available, but the political nature of this program required them to be stationed at the Pentagon.

"You're on TDY," Captain Sparling said, sighing. "Dump everything you're working on and get packed. You're going to Huntsville, Alabama. Redstone Arsenal. God knows who'll be handling what you're doing now."

"What's there now?" Shane asked. He'd been to

Huntsville a couple of times in the course of his duties looking at projects. Not in the last month, though; the town had virtually shut down from his perspective.

"Something called 'Asymmetric Soldier', " Sparling replied. "The *name* is classified Secret and the purpose is Top Secret, Compartmented. And I don't even have the *compartment* name. But you are detailed to it 'for a minimum of ninety days.' "

"Crap," Shane said, sighing. "Well, I guess ours is not to question why . . . When do I leave?"

Ret Ball: *Aha! Megiddo my friend, where have you been? Did you hear Hiowa Lend's report last Sunday?*

Caller: *Yes Ret, I did. And she was absolutely correct.*

Ret Ball: *How so?*

Caller: *There is no denying it now. Mars has changed. It has been terraformed by aliens. It's no longer the Mars we used to know.*

Ret Ball: *I see.*

Caller: *It's only a matter of time before more happens.*

Ret Ball: *Such as?*

Caller: *Have you noticed that the Space Telescope Science Institute is no longer posting new images from the Hubble of Mars?*

Ret Ball: *They aren't?*

Caller: *No. In fact it has been nearly a year and a half since any new Martian images have been posted. That is somewhat unusual.*

Ret Ball: *Really?*

Caller: *Yes it is. I'm telling you that the CIA has commandeered the Space Telescope Science Institute and corrupted them.*

Ret Ball: *To what ends, Megiddo?*

Caller: *I'm not certain, Ret. I just don't know But I suspect . . . to communicate with their alien masters. The Roswell landing was not a crash, Ret. It was a controller, sent to make contact with our government and begin the conquest. . . .*

"Holy crap," Roger said, quietly, as the image from the Hubble filled the oversized monitor.

The Hubble Space Telescope had been for all intents and purposes commandeered by Neighborhood Watch. Multiple observation cycles were implemented on the outer planets and the data gathered there was not very promising. Albedo shifts had already been measured on Callisto, while the returns from Rhea and Hyperion at Saturn were less conclusive. Titan looked iffy, but the standing hypothesis was that it was a function of that planet-sized moon's dense atmosphere.

The returns from Io and Europa couldn't have been more conclusive. Among other things, Europa and Io both now had noticeable atmospheres; the halos were distinct in the image.

"You're going to owe me a year's salary," Traci said,

chortling quietly at the scientist's disbelief. The current Io image was sharp enough that major features of the distant moon could be distinguished and it was apparent that the entire face had been radically altered. In fact, it looked as if one section had been deep strip-mined. For the change to be visible at this distance, even with the resolution of the Hubble, the structure had to be at a minimum *four hundred* kilometers across. The way things were going, the probes might just *eat* the moon.

"I think we should run a sharpening filter on the—" Roger said, reaching for the mouse on the image analysis computer.

"My job," Traci said, slapping his hand aside. "You rocket scientists and telescope builders can't do planetary measurements worth a flip. I'm not so sure the image can be any sharper. The aliasing seems to me to be due to being at the limit of the sensor's resolution."

"Traci dear, I've been analyzing IMINT imagery for more years than you've been in school," he said.

"You're not that old. And what's mint imagery?"

"IMINT—it stands for 'image intelligence.' Astrophysicists." Roger shook his head.

"Well, all I know is that the astronomical imagery data from the Hubble looked better before you ran that filter again." She pointed at the now blotchy image on the monitor. Traci hit the undo button in the software menu to restore the image.

Traci had proven to be well worth her weight in gold. She had gotten in touch with the *right people* at the Space Telescope Science Institute and was trained on the Hubble-cycling protocols in just a few short days. She had gotten a lot of help from a fellow named Hamilton there. Jack Hamilton had been the first person to really detect the change in the Martian albedo and had been aware of the problem from the beginning. The STScI had been gagged by the President to keep the space telescope data quiet, so Jack and his professors had been briefed into the Neighborhood Watch from early on.

Traci had a command station set up in the HOSC at Huntsville and had it connected and encrypted through the program's protocols. So between the folks at the STScI and the command station in Huntsville, the Hubble Space Telescope was being tasked one hundred percent by the Neighborhood Watch and Traci was doing the driving— with a little input from Jack and, of course, Roger.

She knew, more or less, what was going on at Saturn and its moons. Traci wasn't quite sure what to make of the Titan data.

The moons of Uranus had similar changes. Ariel in particular had a surface albedo much greater than ever before measured. Likewise were the moons of Neptune. Triton specifically had obvious changes.

The albedos of the Kuiper Belt Objects including the Pluto-Charon system were harder to determine changes since there was less highly accurate albedo data available. However, some preliminary investigation suggested that Pluto was slightly brighter.

These experiments took the better part of the month following the Neighborhood Watch final report briefing to the White House. At the same time they'd gotten to work on Asymmetric Soldier.

Billions of dollars were pumped into the project in less than three months. The north Alabama Defense and Space industry infrastructure made a perfect central location for the AS project development and management. The first tactical and strategic suggestion developed from the project was to gather the nation's space/defense talent at multiple locations across the country and in locations as fortified as possible. Asymmetric Soldier wings were set up at Cheyenne Mountain, in Wyoming, at a base in Montana, at Area 51 in Nevada, at Langley, Virginia, at CCAFS, at Vandenberg AFB in California, at Wright Patterson AFB in Ohio, at White Sands, Los Alamos, at Clear Lake City, Texas, at Whiteman AFB in Missouri, at the AFRL in Albuquerque, New Mexico, in two locations in Alaska, at Hickam AFB in Hawaii, at Thule AFB in Greenland, at the old Ramey AFB in Puerto Rico, and three U.S. Navy nuclear submarines and two aircraft carriers were designated as mobile research posts.

. Thus far, with no actual data on the threat, AS was mostly spinning its wheels. With no better than the 20 meter resolution they'd gotten from Percival, they couldn't even determine what the probes looked like. They could be some of the large structures they'd seen on Mars or they could be much smaller. The team had no idea how they moved, how they fought or how they thought. All they could do was look at current and projected military hardware and try to apply it to the little bit they *did* know. It was a frustrating process. And, deep in their bones, everyone on the team knew it was mostly a fruitless one as well.

The aliens were coming and nothing appeared capable of stopping them.

Chapter 9

"Come in, Major Gries, I'm Alan Davis," the scientist said, gripping Shane's hand as he entered his office.

"You guys look busy," Shane replied. The last time he'd been in Redstone was nearly four months before and it had seemed . . . sleepy compared to, say, the LockMart facility in Denver.

But from the careful inspection he'd been given at the main entrance to the repeated security checks he'd endured to get to the engineer's office, the entire tenor of the base had changed. There were more people, all of them looking very distracted, and there was *far* more bustle. It looked more like a battalion getting ready to cross into "Indian Country" than a research base. And he'd seen signs of defensive emplacements under construction—berms being dug on the periphery of the base, construction on the hill that overlooked the Arsenal—that simply didn't fit any scenario he could conceive. It looked as if the base was preparing for a siege. And finally, before Gries got any closer to knowing just what the hell was going on, he was asked to sign a shit-load of National Security Act paperwork.

"Okay, Major, you know all the secrecy stuff, I'm told," Alan said, rolling his chair over to a coffee pot and pouring a cup. "You want?"

"Yes, sir, black, sir," Shane answered.

"Siddown, and stop calling me sir. I've never been in the military, call me Alan—or Mr. Davis if you have to, but Alan is what I prefer," Alan said, waving at a chair and pouring another cup into a none-too-clean mug. "What I'm about to tell you is going to break internationally sooner or later, but details are still going to be TS Special Access. Clear?"

"Yes, sir, uh, Mr. Davis," Shane replied, taking the cup and a sip. The coffee was good at least. Whatever these eggheads had figured out, some congressman probably figured it would win him a whole hell of a lot of votes in the north Alabama district, because from the looks of things there was a lot of money being spent around town.

"About a year ago, people started to notice that the albedo of Mars, the light reflected from it, was changing."

"The gray planet," Shane said, nodding. "There was a news story about it and I saw some stuff online. But I didn't really believe any of it. Sounded too much like UFO stuff to me."

"Well, what is happening is . . ." Alan said, pausing as the door opened to admit a really good looking blonde. Blue eyes, curly hair, fine butt and tremendous knockers. She looked more like a Hooters waitress than an egghead, but Shane had met some fine looking eggheads over the last few months.

"Roger wanted you to see the changes on Mars and the new images of the Moon right away," the girl said.

"Major Gries, Traci Adams," Alan said as the young woman walked behind his desk and hit some keys on his computer. "She's in our astrophysics department." He paused to look at whatever was on the monitor, it was turned away from Shane, then blanched. "Jesus Christ. How big is that thing?"

"Over fifty meters in diameter," Traci replied, tossing her hair over her neck to get at the keys again. "And this."

"It's . . . suspended," Alan said.

"And this," Traci continued.

"Crap," was all Alan said.

"I realize I'm probably not accessed for this . . ." Shane said diffidently.

"You are now," Alan said, spinning the monitor around so the major could see it.

The image was, apparently, from the Moon or at least *a* moon. Airless and gray anyway. But at the edge of a crater was a long . . . cylindrical object.

"That thing is . . . how long?" Shane said carefully.

"Just over a hundred kilometers," Traci repeated. "And it just landed or is landing . . . it's hard to tell."

"Someone landed something a hundred kilometers long on the Moon?" Shane said, closing his eyes. *Surprise is a function of the mind of the commander.* He knew what he knew. He knew nobody had lift capacity on Earth to do that. He knew it was real; you didn't get sent off like this by the Army on total bullshit. "We're being invaded, aren't we?" he said quietly.

⌘   ⌘   ⌘

John Fisher and Alice Pike sat quietly in the hotel room watching the latest reality television programming with their respective daughters. Well, the girls were watching television while the parents were trying to work and also spend time with their kids. They had returned to the Cape for spring break, but unfortunately it had rained for the last two days. John and Alice worked during the days and mostly in the nights, while the girls did whatever teenage girls do at the beach during spring break.

Alice sat at the little hotel table pecking at a laptop and peering over it occasionally at the television, then out the window at the pouring rain. John was reading a technical paper on how to increase the space shuttle's launch capabilities and punching in numbers into a Mathcad simulation on his laptop while at the same time continuously eyeing his wristwatch. The girls lay on their stomachs on the floor in front of the television oblivious to their parents and occasionally poking at each other and giggling.

"I believe it's gonna rain all week." Alice glanced out the window at the downpour; she sighed, closed her laptop, rose, then sat on the couch.

"Come over here and sit with me a minute," she said, motioning for Tina to come sit next to her. She tore off a piece of pizza from the meat lovers thin crust in the pizza box on the coffee table and started to gulp it down. "What time do you have, John?"

"Just enough time for me to refill the ice bucket. Anybody need anything from the soda machine?" John replied, looking at his watch and placing the report and his laptop on the end table.

"Yeah, Daddy, get me a Diet Pepsi will ya?" Charlotte asked.

"Okay slugger. Anybody else?" Nobody responded so John hurried to the vending area. He looked at his watch again, "Five minutes. That's plenty of time."

Once he filled the ice bucket he stuck a dollar bill in the soda machine and pressed the Diet Pepsi button. Nothing happened. Then he realized the darn things were a dollar and a quarter, so he added another dollar bill and this time he got the soda. But the machine informed him that it was out of change.

"You son of a bitch!" John smacked the machine with his fist . . . then he laughed at himself. "What difference does it make?" he muttered and hurried back to the girls' room where they had gathered to watch television.

"Hurry up, John; I thought you were going to miss some of it," Alice told him as he handed his daughter her soft drink and set the ice bucket down. Then, just as they had been briefed would happen . . .

We interrupt this program to bring you a nation-wide presidential address. We were informed just an hour ago that the President of the United States of America will address the nation about one minute from now from the Oval Office. We go now to our correspondent at the White House, Bret Marshall, for insight into tonight's address. Bret?

Yes, Shep, the President released a statement to the press corps about an hour ago that he would make this address and has yet to release the topic. Various White House sources have told us that it most likely has to do with a meeting he had earlier this week with the United Nations' National Security Council. However, the actual topic of this meeting and of tonight's address has been kept from press sources. The White House has been very tight-lipped about it, Shep.

Thanks, Bret. We go now to the Oval Office and the President of the United States. . . .

Good evening, ladies and gentlemen, my fellow Americans and to our friends and allies around the world. Tonight I must speak with you about a matter of utmost importance and the most historic event in the history of humanity. Tonight I am here to tell you that humanity is not alone in this universe.

Approximately two years ago NASA, the European Space Agency, and the Russian Space Agency began to lose contact with probes that had been sent to the planet Mars. Fourteen months ago scientists at the Space Telescope Science Institute and at NASA discovered that the color of the planet Mars was changing. At that time they brought this to my attention and also told me then that they had no idea as to why this would happen. I then asked the National Reconnaissance Office to conduct a rapid mission to our neighboring planet and send a spy satellite there to determine the cause of this phenomenon. This was not a "Mars Probe" in the traditional sense. It was a spy satellite sent to Mars.

The space reconnaissance community under the leadership of the NRO successfully built a spacecraft, then launched it just five months later, a remarkable achievement and proof that our space community is capable of responding as true Americans and problem solvers. Since Mars is so far away, it took the probe about five more months to reach the planet. Once there, the little spacecraft gathered intelligence data for a short period before it was destroyed—and I use that term carefully— by the phenomenon at Mars.

The data the NRO gathered did show us that the surface of Mars has been completely developed into a planet-covering grid of giant, citylike structures. In a period of less than two years, the entire planet has been hyperindustrialized.

Recent studies of other planets in our solar system suggest that the outer planets or their moons, Pluto, Neptune, Uranus, Saturn, and Jupiter, have undergone similar transformations.

It's the belief of the scientists, engineers, mathematicians, philosophers, and military strategists studying the data that this phenomenon is some sort of automated threat. In other words, it's their best assessment that automated robots or robotlike insects have reached our solar system and are transforming the planets within it to meet whatever their goals may be. It has been suggested that the planets are being prepared for other entities to approach and move in once the solar system has been completely prepared for their arrival. We cannot be certain of this, however. What does seem to be the case is that all of the outer planets have been impacted by this phenomenon while no planets from

Earth inward have been . . . yet.

It would appear that Earth is the next planet in the path of this phenomenon, as it appears to be moving from the outer planets inward to the Sun.

I have spoken to the UN Security Council in secret session and shared this information with the leaders of all the planet's major powers. Today at 7:45 PM Eastern Time a worldwide curfew will be placed into effect. For those of you traveling, you will be given one week to make it home to your loved ones. After that, all worldwide travel will be used only for defense preparations against this alien threat.

I have also frozen the securities exchange, and the stock exchange will not open until further notice. Business within the country will be reopened once we understand more about what is happening and what the extent of this possible threat might be. A council based around the Government Accountability Office and the Federal Reserve has been formed to begin preparations for national industrial and financial mobilization.

As of right now, all National Guard units are to be mobilized. Individual members of the units will be contacted through their chain of command. I have authorized the recall of all persons in the Individual Ready Reserve. Individuals in the IRR should anticipate recall orders over the course of the next month. If you do not receive a recall order, a website is being set up for you to update your information and obtain orders through e-mail. I ask that all members

*of the IRR use this resource for obtaining orders if
you do not get them through normal processes.*

*Units deployed overseas are currently under warning orders for redeployment to the United States.
This does not mean that we're abandoning our allies in their time of need, but where and when the
threat might strike is, at this time, indeterminate.
Having our troops in the United States means that
they will be in position to react in any direction,
and as rapidly as possible.*

*Tomorrow, I intend to place a declaration of war
before the United States Congress. A declaration of
war is necessary to begin the process of converting
the U.S. from standard peacetime footing, which
even with the many small wars and cold wars we
have had since the 1940s has never been done since
the war our parents and grandparents fought.*

*Today and in the dark days before us, we must stand
united against this threat. I ask that all Americans
and all people of the world prepare themselves
calmly, thoughtfully and with belief in the ultimate
power of the human soul. And I ask that God be
with us in this, our hour of challenge.*

Briefings expanding the President's speech lasted
thirty-seven minutes longer from that point and John,
Alice, Charlotte, Tina, and the rest of the world remained
fixed to their televisions for the rest of the evening with
hopes of learning more. The government had multiple
news conferences going on but the information was often
repetitious and, with few exceptions, the President's

speech covered the high points. Aliens were coming, probably with bad intentions. Bad times were here.

John and Alice knew more and had a plan. Both of them had pushed to get assigned to the Asymmetric Soldier project group in Huntsville, Alabama. Their intent was to make certain that their daughters were with them when the curfew was put in place. John and Alice would finish their tasks at the CCAFS facility in Florida, then fly to Huntsville from there with the girls.

"Does this mean we don't have to go back to school next week?" Tina asked her mom when the grown-ups finally insisted the television go off.

Charlotte elbowed her. "Dingbat!"

Ret Ball: *My God! Did you hear the President's speech tonight? It would appear that we had the Truth here first before the rest of the world. There really is something going on with Mars and there really is an alien threat. We have exclusively online tonight our friend Megiddo who first turned us on to this. Megiddo, what is your take on the President's speech?*

Megiddo: *I told you so is about all I can say, Ret. The CIA and these right-wing conspirators just couldn't keep the Truth from us any longer. I suspect they tried to cut a deal with their alien masters and when that didn't work, they decided to go to war.*

Ret Ball: *Indeed, Megiddo. What do you propose that our listeners do?*

Megiddo: *I'm not sure just yet. We don't really know*

what these aliens want, except that they seem to have moved in on Mars and took it. What is to say they do not have the same plans for Earth?

Ret Ball: *Indeed!*

Megiddo: *Me, personally, I have moved to a remote and secure location. Perhaps, these things will hit civilization first. That would only make sense, as that is where the resistance will come from.*

Ret Ball: *Ah, you think we can put up resistance?*

Megiddo: *Absolutely not! These aliens have traveled across the deep void of interstellar space and terraformed an entire planet in a very short time. What could we do against a power like that?*

Richard Horton had been driving through and around the suburbs of the old town in northwestern South Carolina for weeks looking for the ideal spot. His real estate agent—himself—had found an old abandoned copper mine on sixty acres bordering North Carolina on Interstate 26, about twenty-five miles west of Spartanburg. After checking the satellite imagery of the region and reading up on the history of the area, he thought it was worth checking out.

Richard drove up the old mining-road-turned-logging-road. There was evidence that some of the timber along the old road had been harvested, but that must have been years ago because the road was overgrown. Without the four-wheel drive Ford F-250 pickup it would have been difficult navigating the old rocky and overgrown road. Richard crested the peak of the mountainside and the road widened slightly, leading up to an old dilapidated and rusted gate with a "no trespassing" sign on it. Richard had a hard time imagining who would be trespassing up this old road, except perhaps mountain bikers and folks on dirtbikes and all-terrain vehicles.

He stopped the truck and walked to the gate to examine its lock more closely. It was a number two MasterLock. He grinned to himself and pulled out the key the real-estate office had given him. It would not have been a problem anyway since number twos were quite easy to circumvent.

Inside the gate and at the top of the hill the road split into two different directions. The map he had gotten from the real-estate office selling the property showed that the right fork went up a few hundred yards more to the old cabin and the left fork went down the hill a few hundred yards to the old copper mine entrance. He took the right fork up the hill to the cabin.

The cabin was run down and had most of the windows busted out. The wood had turned dark gray from weathering. Weeds and briars had grown up on the east side of the cabin around the front porch and would make entering the cabin difficult, but Richard had brought a machete and had every intention of closely examining the building. A few swings of the blade and he had made a clear path to the steps.

The front door was locked and sturdy. The framing of the porch and the post holding up the roof of the porch was in good shape; old, but in good shape. He unlocked the door and stepped into the living room of the little cabin. There was a small kitchen and dining area open to the room and a bedroom and bathroom off to the back of the house.

There was also a closed-in porch on the back, but most of the screen had been torn away by weather and varmints.

Richard turned the sink faucet on; there were some odd sounds but no water. He had expected that. The realtors had warned him that the plumbing was old and the well pump was shot. Richard didn't really care about those details. Things like that could be fixed.

Out the back of the cabin was another grown-up area and it took a few swings of the machete to get through the back door. A few feet away from the back steps the underbrush stopped and rocks took over. The well pump for the house was in a small concrete block housing about ten feet from the cabin. Richard pulled off the cover of the housing and looked inside. The pump was gone and there was only an old handpump attached to the cap of the well.

"What the hell." He gave the pump a few strokes. On the seventh stroke clear, very cold water gushed out of the spigot. Richard cupped his hand under it and tasted the water but was careful not to swallow any of it. The water tasted clean and good, but he would check it out for alkalinity, microbes, and other pollutants later. He spat the water out and rubbed his mouth dry on his sleeve.

There were several trees surrounding the cabin, most of which were hardwoods. But there was a small grove of trees that looked a little out of place. They were evenly spaced and obviously had been planted by a previous owner at least two or three decades before. There were three pecan trees, a persimmon tree, two plum trees, a pair of apple trees, and a pear tree, all of which appeared to be thriving and healthy. The trees were a plus—a naturally replenishing source of food. The realtors had said nothing about the small orchard. Richard didn't plan on telling them when he made his offer either.

"Not bad." He looked around at the cabin and the little orchard from the outside. He pulled a persimmon from one of the trees and bit into it. The tangy tart sweet fruit squirted in his mouth, making him pucker from the taste. He spit the fruit out. "Still a little green. Too early I guess. This will do nicely. Helena will love it."

Chapter 10

Roger Reynolds, Alan Davis, and Tom Powell sat at their usual table for their Tuesday after-work meeting. This time they were joined by John Fisher, Alice Pike, Major Shane Gries, and one of Gries's noncoms, Master Sergeant Thomas Cady. When Shane had been told he could "have anything or anyone he wanted" to help with the program, the first thing he asked for was Cady. Traci was sitting in as well, this time letting herself *be* served instead of serving—for Traci, that took some getting used to.

"I can't believe I'm sitting in a Hooters in Huntsville, Alabama, discussing the end of the world," Alice said, shaking her head and picking at her salad.

"Can you think of a better place?" the master sergeant asked, taking a sip of beer.

"Spazos?" Alice asked. "Marsel's in Paris? The French Riviera?"

Roger did his wing trick and dipped the meat in ranch dressing.

"Been there," Gries grunted. "Nothing there you can't get here and with more friendly service."

"*Poulet au vin et herbs*?" Alice insisted.

"Garcia'll fry you up some chicken breast in wine in a flash," Traci said primly. "I mean, it'll be Sutter Home White Zinfandel, but it adds a touch of extra caramelizing to the onions, anyway."

Alice just sighed in desperation.

"So the data that Traci is telling us about does two things for us," Roger said, stuffing the deboned chicken meat into his mouth.

"Yeah, what's that?" Alice asked.

Roger held his hand to his mouth to say that she should let him finish chewing. He washed the wing down with some beer, then replied.

"We've got this shiny tubule impacting the Moon that she captured with the Hubble. There is *no* dust plume at the surface. This means whatever this tubule is, it's slowing down and landing softly without creating any sort of plume. That means they definitely have reactionless drive systems. No plume, no rockets. The other thing it tells us is that these things have finished with Mars and moved to the Moon."

"That second one isn't certain," Alan said, seriously for a change. "Maybe they have enough in numbers at Mars so as not to matter if they send a few to the Moon."

"No way," Traci said, flipping her hair behind an ear. "Look at the diameter of this tubule. It has to be at least fifty meters in diameter. And the damned thing stretches out about a hundred kilometers from the surface. What the hell is it?"

"Well, I'd say its pretty goddamned obvious that it's a lunar invasion force," Gries grunted into his beer glass.

"No shit, Sherlock!" Traci smiled and hit him on the back, making him slosh beer all over his uniform. "I mean, how or what are the things making up this tube. Is it solid? Is it a chain of sub-vehicles? The Hubble just doesn't have the aperture to resolve what this thing is made of. All we see is a long, shiny, tube. And why does it only stick out a hundred kilometers. I mean, why not all the way to Mars? They've got more than enough mass converted there, based on our calculations. They could just throw a *solid* tube from one location to the other."

"You were right, Rog," Alan said with a grin. "We should've hired her a long time ago."

"Well, Alan, when you're right, you're right," Roger admitted. "And Traci, I have no idea. I could see it as being a relative motion thing, but they still have enough mass to compensate."

"It's a launch window or something," John said, setting down his untouched beer and picking up a wing. "Maybe it's some sort of air traffic control corridor. This has to be a bunch of things in formation. There is no way that is a solid object sticking out of the Moon like that."

Dr. Powell set his beer down and started scribbling on a napkin. It was obvious to Roger and Alan that they needed to ignore him for a while and he would come up with something brilliant. The others had learned to ignore him most of the time anyway.

"I have a question," Sergeant Cady asked. "If this tube sticking out of the Moon is so big, why can't we see it?" Cady, having seen the wing trick, reproduced it perfectly his first try and stuffed the chicken into his mouth. Tom was too busy to notice what he had done.

"That's a good question, Master Sergeant," Alice

replied. "I was thinking the same thing. But I'm not an optics person, I deal with atoms, substrates, junctions, gates, and hole pairs."

"What?" Shane asked.

"Itsy bitsy things down at the atomic level," Roger translated absentmindedly.

"It's simple telescope optics, y'all," Traci stated. "The Hubble has a primary aperture diameter of 2.4 meters. That's a *powerful* telescope, but it can only resolve about 150 meters at the distance from the Earth to the Moon. The tube is maybe fifty meters, max, in diameter. The tube is just too small in diameter for the telescope to see clearly. Now you might see a little bump in the long dimension. I'm not sure why we don't on that one."

Alan rubbed his chin. "Yeah Rog, why is that?"

"Traci." Roger adjusted his Roll Tide cap and turned it around backwards. "Why can't you see the light from a planet around a distant star real easy?" Roger waited a few seconds for the light bulb to go on over Traci's head. He could see in her eyes that she figured it out.

"Of, course! You clever bastard, you," she said. "The Moon is reflecting way more light than the little tube. So it's just washed out."

"Atta girl!" Roger swigged at his beer, proud of himself and his new pupil.

"Is there a way to get a closer look at this thing?" Cady asked. "I mean, it'd be a lot easier to figure out how to blow 'em up if we knew what the hell they are."

Gries nodded approvingly to the sergeant. "Yeah, Doc, how's about it?"

Before Roger could respond Tom slapped the table, "Gravity!"

Alice nearly fell off her stool.

Gries sloshed his beer again.

Thomas choked on a wing.

Roger and Alan were used to it.

"What about gravity, Tom?" Alan asked.

"That's why the tube isn't any bigger and doesn't stretch all the way to Mars."

Roger and Alan had often thought that Tom was autistic because he had a tendency to answer a question that had been asked ten minutes earlier. This was just more data in support of their theory.

"You want to expound on that a little, Dr. Powell?" John asked. Everyone else seemed either indifferent or afraid to ask.

"Most certainly, I shall. You see, a tube this size if it were the length of the distance from Earth to Mars, well, that would have significant mass. That would really affect and effect the things in the solar system that function due to gravity. The orbits of the planets or asteroids or comets might get a little perturbed. Not much, but enough. The tides would get confused and it might even confuse the lunar orbit. These things are smart. You see?" Tom smiled and snapped his fingers.

"Uh, sorry, Doc, I don't see," Gries said.

"Of course," John replied.

"I see," said Traci. "But why not just land all asunder?"

"All right, hold on a minute and let's get everybody up to speed." Roger held up his hands. "Tom is saying that if these things maintained a tubeway from Mars to the Moon this large that it would be so massive that it would fuck the orbits of the planets up."

"Well, I wouldn't have said it quite so crudely," Tom responded with a smile.

"Crude or not, correct right?"

"As near as makes no difference," Tom said. "Also, the relative position of the planets is constantly changing. A solid tube wouldn't work anyway."

"Okay. So these things do not want to f-up the gravitational mechanics of the star system. That makes sense. If they plan to take it over and keep it for themselves, they wouldn't want to muck it up too much."

"Dr. Reynolds?"

"Yes, Alice?"

"Please do me a favor and promise not to speak that way in front of my daughter. She's incorrigible enough as it is," Alice scolded him politely.

"Right, sorry," Roger said with a sheepish laugh. "Anyway, these things appear to fly in a broad sweeping disoriented array then conglomerate when they get close to the planet and all land at the same place. Loosely speaking."

"Sounds right," Tom agreed with a nod. "That's why the Hubble didn't pick up any of the mass prior to landing. For that matter, Spacewatch probably would have spotted it if it was solid."

"Yeah, but what makes no sense to me is why they don't just land all over the place like Traci said. Why would they care?" John asked, fingering his tie-clip and looking at the ceiling. "It would give them broad coverage, they could spread out faster . . . Landing in one spot makes no sense."

"You know, I have no clue. That's alien motivation for you." Roger wiped his hands on his napkin, removed his ball cap, rubbed his fingers through his brown hair thoughtfully, and put his cap back on.

"I never thought of it that way," Traci said with a grin at Roger. "Now we're supposed to read alien minds."

"It ain't hard to figure out," the master sergeant said. "Sir, you want to handle this?" he added, tipping his beer to the major and leaning back.

"Right you are, Master Sergeant," Shane said solemnly. Gries finished off his beer with a burp and waved his glass at the young brunette waitress at the bar, then pointed at the near empty pitcher on the table while holding up one finger.

Roger laughed.

"I'm looking forward to hearing this."

"You see, Doc, this is why you need us," Major Gries said, pointing at the sergeant and himself. "Just like there's a logic to all your rocket science stuff, and calculation to why you can't see that bump on the Moon, there's a logic and precise calculation to combat. The enemy action plan is simple: it's a limited frontage assault. It's the wildest damned LFA I've ever seen, but that is what it's. When you perform an assault, especially on a protected front where you have limited access of movement, you have to push as many fighters into the AC—"

"What's an AC?" Alice asked curiously.

"Hah, you guys have got all your acronyms but the military *invented* them!" Cady said, grinning.

"Access corridor," Shane said, shaking his head. "The idea is to push as many fighters into the AC as you can. Think about the landings at D-Day; we pushed as many soldiers onto the beach as there was room for them. You don't even consider full logistics for the forces, since you *know* they're going to be attrited." Gries stopped for a breath as the waitress showed up with a new pitcher.

"Attrited?" Alice asked again, frowning.

"A bunch of 'em are going to be dead and don't need any more food," Master Sergeant Cady said. "Ever." He started to pour from the pitcher and got a slap on the hand.

"That's her job," Roger, Alan and Traci chorused.

"Oh," Cady said, then grinned. "Now that's what I call service!"

"Okay," Shane continued, sipping his replenished draft. "If there is an entire planet I'm going to attack, the action plan would be to action the enemy's system with either distributed force systemology or direct action—"

"Now you're just making shit up," Roger said, shaking his head.

"He's not, he's not," Cady said, shaking his own. "This is how he always talks when he starts lecturing about killing shit. It's all 'action plan' this and 'directed force structure' and 'attrition phase' and whatever."

"And those are?" Alice asked, leaning back and putting her hand over her mouth as her eyes crinkled.

"What we're gonna do to the motherfuckers," Cady responded, ticking off his fingers. "What guys are gonna do it and the part where we're trying to kill them faster than they're killin' us."

"As I was *saying*," Shane said, clearing his throat. "If *I* was going to attack a planet, I'd either . . . screw around with them for a while using guerilla forces and then take 'em down or I'd drop a bunch of . . . personnel on one spot and spread out from there. Distributed force systemology or directed action. Since you can't sneak down and infiltrate, assault is your best approach. Besides, if you've got the force and don't care about casualties, it's much more guaranteed. If you've got the steam press, crush the walnut."

"Shock and awe, sir!" Thomas added.

"The more you use, the fewer you lose," Gries added with a nod at the noncom. "It also shows that they anticipate defense. They're, I'd say, definitively hostile to whoever holds the real estate. If they didn't anticipate defense then, yeah, it would make sense to drop all over. Since they *don't*, I would say that is definitive indication that they are hostile entities. The thing I don't understand is why they didn't land on the far side of the Moon where we couldn't see them. That's right isn't it, the far side of the Moon is always pointed away from us and we have no idea what's happening there without an orbital probe?"

"That's right," Traci answered.

"Good point, Shane. Why didn't they do that?" John asked.

"Where did they land?" Alice asked.

"Well, it looks like they landed right in the middle of the Mare Vaporum, the Sea of Vapors," Traci said.

"Yeah, for some reason that rings a bell with me, but why I'm not sure," Roger added.

"Well, for whatever reason, and I'm sure you'll figure it out, they wanted something there and put as many troops on the ground as they could manage in a seriously short manner," Shane said. "Standard combat tactics is what it is. I now conclude my lecture on combat assault. Questions? Comments? Concerns? There will be a quiz at the end of the session. You see, Doc, there is a good reason to have us around."

Roger held up his glass in salute to the major.

"Shane, I never once meant to imply that we didn't need you. In fact, the reason I got into this business was to do everything I could—the chicken shit that I am—to protect and help the guys like you and Thomas here."

Thomas and Shane held up their glasses in response. All followed.

"Here, here!"

"Well, we're going to start seeing tomorrow," Shane said, grinning. "Alan's armaments team has some ideas it wants to trot by me."

"We're going to knock your socks off!" Alan promised.

"We'll see," Shane replied, shrugging. "I've rarely seen a first generation idea out of you eggheads that worked."

"I aren't no egghead," Alan protested, waving at the others at the table. "That's them thar. I's just a high-tech redneck!"

"That's even scarier," Alice said, shaking her head. "I can just see your idea of a presentation. 'Hey, y'all, watch this!' " She paused for a moment and frowned.

"I've been thinking about the Asymmetric Soldier concept, too. I've got a few ideas, now that we know they're likely to be cyber systems, that might come in handy." The stereotypical soccer mom paused and picked up a wing. She stripped the meat off expertly and dipped it in hot sauce.

"Hey!"

"I said I don't *care* for Hooters," Alice said, primly. "I didn't say I've never *been* in one."

Chapter 11

"Nice test range here," Shane commented about the missile and munitions firing range on the southwest end of the Arsenal. "So what are we going to see, Alan?"

Alan led Gries and Cady to an M240B set up on a tripod that was hard-mounted to a concrete slab. The range was set up in a valley behind two small hills on the Arsenal and was surrounded by a pasture and a pine grove.

"The range-to-target there is about four kilometers." Alan pointed down range. "I assume y'all are familiar with the M240B machine gun?"

"Top?" Gries said, bowing to the NCO theatrically.

"Yes, sir," the master sergeant said, clearing his throat and taking a position of parade rest. "Listen up, you yard birds! The M240*B* is the primary platoon fire support weapon of the United States Army Infantry Units of Action, *Special* Operations and other units required from time to time to bring direct lethal fire upon the enemies of *Good*! This *ultimate* killing machine is a *belt*-fed, *air*-cooled, *gas*-operated, *fully* automatic chooser of the *slain* that fires from the open bolt position. This weapon of precision *dee*-struction spits out ammo like *hail*, spell that as you *wish*, with an *adjustable* cyclic rate of fire six hundred and fifty to *nine* hundred and fifty rounds per *minute*! It has a sustained rate of fire of one hundred rounds per minute given four to five round bursts and *one* barrel change every ten minutes. This harbinger of the apocalypse . . ." He paused and looked at Alan sharply. "What is the name of this weapon, yard bird?"

"The M240B, si—sergeant!" Alan said, grinning.

"This harbinger of the apocalypse." Cady continued, nodding at Alan as if he was a not-particularly-bright but well-favored pupil, "weighs twenty-seven point two pounds, unloaded. One one-hundred round ammunition box weighs seven point two pounds for a fully loaded weight of thirty-four point eight pounds. The barrel of the M240B *killing* machine, thanks to the fine designers at FN Manufacturing Incorporated and your good Uncle Samuel, is provided with *four* grooves with a uniform *right*-hand twist, one turn in twelve inches giving its seven point *six* two caliber bullets a *buh-listering* velocity of twenty-eight hundred *FEET* per second and a stabilizing spin enabling *you*, the operator, to precisely target the enemy at up to *eight hundred meters* and engage groups of the enemy at up to *eighteen hundred* meters! You may consult FM three dash two two point six eight for further information on this master weapon of all master weapons, this Valkyrie in human form, this brutal engine of total annihilation the . . . M! . . . Two! . . . Four! ZEEEEEEEROOOOOO . . . B!"

"Damn, that was something," Alan said, his eyes wide. "Can you do that with any weapon?"

"Yes, sir!" the master sergeant barked. "Any weapon in the infantry inventory to include specialties in Eleven Mike and Eleven Charlie as well as Eleven Bravo, *sir*!"

"What the hell are those?" Alan asked.

"Bradley, mortars and general gun bunnies," Shane said, grinning. "We've won a lot of money off that memory and knack for weapons statistics, haven't we, Top?"

"Damn straight, sir," the NCO confirmed, his dark face splitting in a broad grin as he dropped out of the tight position of parade rest.

"Well, so you said that the point target effective range was about eight hundred meters, right?" Alan asked, a tad maliciously.

"That's right," Cady affirmed.

"Care to be proven wrong?" Alan added.

"How?" Shane asked, frowning.

"This is a standard M240B," Alan replied, waving at the weapon. "And *that* target down there is at *approximatedly* three *thousand* meters. It's locked in, don't fiddle with the aiming. Just fire off a few bursts. The major and I will watch here on this monitor at how well you do."

"I can tell you what's going to happen," Cady said, kneeling to look through the sight. "They're going to impact about halfway between us and the target, based on this aiming and the lay of the land."

Alan smiled and pointed Shane to the monitor in a weapons van parked behind the firing pad. He thumbed the walkie-talkie that had been snapped to his belt.

"Range clear? Range clear?" Alan asked. When no one

replied he keyed back in, "Range clear, we're firing, firing, firing!"

Cady shrugged, then made himself cozy with the weapon. *BBBBRRRRRRRR BBBBRRRRRRRR!* The weapon ripped out a series of bursts, all but one exactly five rounds. When he stopped he still had plenty of belt.

"Wheew!" Gries whistled. "Top, come look at this," he added, shouting out the back door of the van.

Alan stood back for the two men to get a good view of the monitor displaying the target. The target was a half-meter square metal plate hung from a metal rack in front of a dirt backstop. The square metal plate was full of holes, all within the central third of the half-meter square. More than fifty holes were in the plate and all could be covered with a sheet of notebook paper. There was more hole than metal left in the center of the plate.

"You said that was three clicks?" Sergeant Cady asked in awe.

"That's right," Alan grinned like an opossum.

"How the hell?" Major Gries stepped back over to the weapon and began examining it closer. "It looks the same to me. What gives?"

"Well, sir, look at the belt. The rounds look funny. I didn't want to say anything before; I figured it was part of the show," Cady replied.

"They look like hollow-points or something," Gries said.

"Close," Alan answered. "They're miniature jet engines."

"Like Gyro-jets?" Cady asked. "Those things were inaccurate as hell."

"No, not like Gyro-jets," Alan said exasperatedly. "Hell, everybody always asks that!"

"What are Gyro-jets?" Gries asked. "And whatever they are, how the hell does this work? And why didn't I know about it with what I *was* doing?"

"Here, look at this." Alan reached in the van and pulled out a cut-away version of the round mounted on a board. "The round has an intake vent in the nose that forces the air through the vent down to the throat of the engine here, then the tail is a diverging rocket, er, jet nozzle. The flow of air is accelerated out the back, giving the round a maintained velocity of about Mach three point four. Since the round is spun, it's therefore stabilized and the acceleration thrust vector cancels out lateral motion so it forces the round to stay on a straight-line path. There's a crosswind effect, but even that's muted."

"Wait a minute. A jet engine? Where is the fuel?" Gries asked.

"Oh that. Roger or Tom could really explain it to you in detail, but it turns out that once the intake flow reaches speeds of Mach one or above the flow is continuously accelerated out the back without added energy," Alan explained.

"That sounds like perpetual motion," Cady said.

"Oh no, not at all. It really is just a phenomenon of supersonic flow dynamics. Scientists and engineers have known about this for at least three quarters of a century or longer. The velocity of a supersonic flow increases in a diverging nozzle."

"Well, where do they get the initial energy from then?" Cady asked.

"You said it yourself, Sarge. The muzzle velocity is twenty-eight hundred feet per second. The powder in the round does that for us. Twenty-eight hundred feet per second is about Mach two point nine at sea level. So we see that the shell actually sped up before it got to the target." Alan sounded giddy.

"Ain't that some shit, sir?" Sergeant Cady added.

"How much range do these things have, Alan?" the major asked.

"Well, we don't know. They've only been test fired here. We need to take them out to the desert somewhere and really test them. My guess is that sooner or later they'll reach a speed or spin that the round can't handle and they'll just fly apart. But how far and how fast, I dunno."

"Alan, this doesn't feel like any kind of metal," Cady said as he rubbed the tip of a round on the belt between his thumb and forefinger.

"That's because it's not metal. The nozzle design is too intricately detailed. There are side vents and stuff that I didn't get into. And trust me, we don't need to get into the CFD on this thing. But . . ."

"CFD?" Cady asked.

"Computational fluid dynamics. It's a horrendous amount of math," Alan said.

"Oh."

"Yeah, oh. Anyway, the damned rounds are so complex that we have to build them one at a time in a laser rapid prototyping machine."

"What the hell is a laser rapid prototyping machine?" Gries felt behind the curve. Alan was indeed knocking his socks off. He wished he'd spent more of his time working with stuff like this, rather than some of the silly shit he'd been chasing. Although Geckoman was still really cool.

"Well, you see you design your widget up in this special

CAD software. I use SolidWorks. Then you upload the file into this machine. The machine sprays a layer of this ceramic dust onto a hard steel surface and a laser beam is focused onto the powder. Wherever the part is supposed to be solid, the powder is solidified. The first solid layer is about ten microns thick. Then another layer of dust is sprayed on and the laser solidifies the next layer to the already solid layer. This is done until the complete part is finished. It takes about ten seconds per round."

"I've never heard of anything like that," Gries said.

"Actually, sir, I have," Cady interrupted.

"Yeah?"

"Back about ten years ago I saw this thing on the Speed channel where these fellows were building a race-car engine the exact same way. They started out with a blueprint in a computer and some ceramic dust and ended up with an engine block a few minutes later. They put in pistons and hooked up a distributor and all to it and cranked the thing right up. I remember thinking then that if this technology ever got big it would put a lot of folks out of jobs," the sergeant explained.

"You got that right, Master Sergeant," Alan said, chuckling. "The rapid prototyping technology has been around about fifteen years or so, maybe longer, but is just now getting developed to a useful level of application. I imagine that show you saw was a state-of-the-art system back then."

"Hey y'all, let's go inside the hangar here. I've got more to show you." Alan locked up the van and led them to the hangar just down the footpath from the range.

❊   ❊   ❊

"Now here's one that I think might be useful during the ground occupation phase of an ET attack." Alan Davis showed Major Gries the small missile launcher system attached to the back of a Humvee. "The system implements the miniature nuclear bomb called the W54 warhead, which was designed to fire from the Davy Crockett launcher. It was deployed by the United States during the Cold War and was to be used on advancing Soviet troops if the need were to arise. This missile isn't actually a nuke here, but we should make as many real ones as we can, I think."

"Nukes," Shane said tonelessly. "Nuclear weapons."

"Hydrogen bombs," Cady added. "Teller tea."

"What?" Gries and Alan both asked, confused.

"Sorry," the master sergeant replied, grinning. "Beverly Hillbillies moment."

"Right," Alan said, still obviously confused. "More like hydrogen bomblets. The W-54 weighed about twenty-five kilograms, could be launched from the man-portable or jeep-portable, Davy Crockett launcher. The mini-nuke warhead would cause an explosion about two hundred times smaller than the Hiroshima bomb or about 5×10^{11} joules. Still, it's a hefty bang from such a small weapon. And we think that we can update the launcher, rocket motor, and even the warhead to make it single-man portable to a total mass of about thirty-three kilograms."

"Alan, how much is thirty-three kilograms in pounds?" Shane asked sarcastically.

"Let's see . . . uh . . . about seventy-five pounds."

"And, a single troop is going to carry that, his armor, comm gear, ammo, and so on?" Shane smiled. "Ground pounders are tough, but that might be asking a little much."

"Oh, I see. Uh, perhaps there would be a dedicated

person to carry it and maybe a few others to carry extra warheads?" Alan raised his eyebrows and shrugged.

"Well, the weapon looks good. Your CONOPS needs work. I'll get Top to brief you better on what all the troops have to carry and how they do it."

"Uh, yeah, that would be good," Alan said. "Now, I have some more ideas about this. And, actually Alice's comment about the redneck demonstration of, hey y'all watch this, is what gave me the idea."

Shane laughed.

"All right, now this sounds promising."

"Well, you see, I really think that these smaller nuclear bombs might prove useful as the active warhead on the antistarfighter, antihovertank, and antibattleoid, anti-alien-whatever missiles that we should equip our fighter aircraft and ground vehicles with. It's possible that such compact but high yield explosives may affect the smaller ET crafts' armor. These antistarfighter missiles most closely resemble the AIM-26A Falcon class of air-to-air missiles, some of which were tipped with the W-54 warhead. Now we'll update and modernize the sensor and missile designs so that they will be more effective."

"Are we going somewhere with this?" Shane asked. "Last I heard, we didn't have starfighters."

"Well, here is the fun part. I was thinking about those Saturn missile batteries that I get at the fireworks stands every Independence Day. You know, the little yellow boxes that have ten, twenty-five, fifty, or a hundred little screaming missiles in them?" Alan explained.

"Not sure, but keep going." The major was beginning to see the redneck smile shine through on Alan's professional face.

"Oh, well I'm sure you've seen them. They come screaming out of the little box one right after the other, *yeeeeeaaaak, yeeeeeeaaaak, yeeeaaaak*," Alan made screeching sounds as he moved his hands up and down demonstrating how the missiles launch out of the firework.

"You mean sort of like Katyushas?" Cady asked, smiling.

Alan frowned.

"What are those?"

"Lord he'p me," the master sergeant replied in his thickest accent. "Ah's surrounded by ivory tahr intellectuals!"

"Katyushas are a type of box missile launchers," Shane said.

"Oh, you mean like the Multiple Launch Rocket System?"

"Yeah, MLRS is another example," Shane agreed.

"Got that then. We designed most of that system right here in Huntsville at the Missile Command. And the ATACMS before that. In fact, if you go down the road you came in on and turn back north for a few miles you cross ATACMS Road. But, Katyushas? Why does that ring a bell?"

"They're the Russian equivalent, sort of." Shane was thinking he needed to steer Alan back on topic.

"Oh yeah! Katyushas! Those are the little rockets we shot down with the Tactical High Energy Laser back in the 1990s. I remember seeing the videos."

"Uh, Alan, back to the fireworks and the little nuke, how's that help us?" Shane shook his head, trying not to grin. He thought of Katyushas as "those damned missiles the insurgents keep firing at us." But Alan's referent was "those missiles we're figuring out how to shoot down." It was times like this that he realized just how sheltered Alan and the rest were.

"Oh, sure, sorry. I think we could take something like a Bradley and put a battery of a hundred of these modernized W-54 warheads in the back of it. If you set this thing off all at once, you have a distributed discrete explosion the order of the Hiroshima blast. Hoo-weee! Helluva firework!"

"Uh, yeah," Shane said, sighing. "First of all, the range of the Davy Crockett was within the blast radius—"

"That's an urban legend, sir," Cady interrupted. "I had a sergeant major when I was a wee lad who'd actually dealt with the system. It wasn't *that* bad. But it was pretty damned close. You wanted to duck and cover after you fired."

"And the Davy Crockett launcher was pretty big," Shane pointed out. "I couldn't see putting more than one or two—"

"Not the actual *missile*," Alan said, sighing in turn. "Smaller missiles, maybe based on Stingers. And the W-54 is *old* tech; there are much smaller *and* more powerful warheads now. I was thinking a pack about a meter or two on a side and maybe two meters long."

"That might work," Cady admitted. "Hell of a bang, that's for sure."

"Uh, Alan, if you have this rain of nuclear blasts distributed all around you, how do you expect to *get out*."

"Well, you're in a Bradley aren't you?" Alan said, shrugging. "What's a little radiation between friends?"

Shane and Cady looked at each other, then at Alan and then back at each other. Finally, Cady shrugged.

"What can I say, sir?" the master sergeant said, shrugging again. "This is what happens when you let rednecks play with nuclear weapons."

Chapter 12

"This image here was taken when we first noticed the landing tubeway at the Moon." Traci pushed her glasses back up on her nose and chewed on the end of an ink pen. She had worked so many around-the-clock shifts tracking the lunar invasion over the last ten weeks that her eyes just couldn't handle her contact lenses anymore. She needed a full eight hours of sleep to get her contacts back. She didn't foresee getting that anytime soon. In fact, she had slept on a couch in Roger's office the past two nights and had showered in the fitness facility across the street at least three times a week rather than at her apartment. Her job was monopolizing all of her waking moments.

"Yes, I've seen this image, Traci." Roger looked over her shoulder at her computer screen.

"Okay, now look at this one taken two weeks later. See anything interesting?" She waited for Roger to analyze the image for a moment.

"A dust cloud!" The image now revealed a cloud of lunar dust just large enough for the Hubble imagery to resolve encircling the landing zone. The tubeway was no longer there either.

"Uh huh, now look at the image at six weeks after the landing." Traci clicked a button on the mouse and another image popped up.

"Okay, the cloud is a little bigger." Roger leaned in closer over Traci's shoulder to see the screen better. The scent of the former Hooters' waitress's perfume wasn't lost on him. She might not have been home in three days but she still looked and smelled good.

"And this one taken yesterday at about ten weeks from the landing." Traci didn't seem to mind Roger leaning over her shoulder. He was always all business anyway. Damnit.

"Again, it's larger than the previous one, but the growth in diameter is smaller."

"Yeah, I really need close-up pictures to really track this, but from this data I've calculated a growth rate," Traci said. "The surface area of the moon is about 152,000,000 square kilometers, give or take. So if you turn that into a circle with that area, then the radius of that circle is about 6,956 kilometers. And at the present growth rate of this cloud it will reach that radius at about five hundred and fifty days from the initial landing."

"What is that, let's see five fifty divided by three sixty-five is . . . uh . . . about a year and a half," Roger muttered.

"The size of this thing is still only about six hundred kilometers in diameter right now. The big growth starts sometime around nine months to a year." Traci chewed the pen's cap reflectively.

"Good work, Traci. This tells us we still have a few months more than a year to prepare." Roger patted her on the shoulder. "Hey, why don't you take a couple days off and get some sleep."

"I'm okay. You're the one who needs to take a break. You've been doing this a year or more longer than I have." She took her glasses off and massaged her nose and eyes.

"You might be right. But until I get a closer look at these things I don't see that happening. I wish I could see them with a few centimeters resolution." Roger mulled the thought over in his mind while at the same time considering sleep.

"Well, why don't you just send a telescope up there and orbit the Moon so you can do just that?" Traci put her glasses back on and sighed. "How long would it take to send a probe to the Moon?"

"Well, rocket-wise we could get a small probe there in a few days. It would take maybe three months to build it and integrate it into a launch system . . . hmm . . . and from the Moon we could get basically real-time video— well, maybe a few seconds delayed. That's a really good plan."

"Why haven't you considered it before?" Traci asked.

"Think about it and you'll figure it out," Roger replied darkly.

"Well, you see, Mr. President," Ronny explained, "we really had no way of knowing how long these things were going to stay on the Moon and were not sure we had time to go forward with a lunar mission. Fortunately, Dr. Reynolds has surrounded himself with good people. His lead astronomer was able to measure the growth rate of the lunar dust cloud to project the timeline. If we assume they'll do like at Mars and wait until the planet is mostly covered, that gives us at least fifteen months from today. Also, Dr. Reynolds' launch team has been working around the clock to get as many launch systems ready and waiting as possible since the beginning of Asymmetric Soldier funding."

"Good, Ronny, good. So how long before we can get a better picture of what is going on?" The President looked tired and Ronny could tell he needed to cut this briefing short.

"Within the next three to four months, sir."

"Well, Roger, as far as the propulsion part of the mission is concerned it's relatively simple," John Fisher was explaining. Tom Powell sat beside John in Roger's office nodding his head in agreement.

"Okay, you have the floor."

"We'll launch on a single Delta IV CBC with two solid strap-ons. We use a single standard RL10B-2 to circularize then kick to the Moon and once we get to the Moon we'll use a bi-propellant thruster, just like on the Clementine mission, to put us in an orbit at about ten kilometers from the lunar surface." John paused long enough to gauge Roger's reaction.

"I've already got a team at Ball about two months into a spacecraft bus build that will work. I knew that we would want recon sooner or later so I kept the momentum going after the last mission. All we need are the science instruments and we'll be ready to go."

"Amazing foresight, John. I should have been thinking about this option." Roger hung his head and exhaled. He felt really tired and dull minded.

"Rog, you can't do everything, you know. I mean, that's why you hired us, right?"

"I guess you're right," Roger said, nodding.

"One more thing, Tom here has worked out the trajectories so that we'll come in on the opposite side of the Moon from the landing zone. This might give us a better chance at sneaking up on these things," John added. "Does that cover everything, Tom?"

"As near as makes no difference. I would emphasize that we can really make use of the Clementine science instrument package design. It was small and put together in a hurry, just as we need to." Tom rubbed his beard.

"Yeah, if we find a telescope in the eight-inch range in the next few days, we could launch in less than three months," John added.

"Clementine . . ." Roger mumbled. "Why is it that is bugging me . . . Clementine . . . *That's it*!" Roger pulled his laptop closer to him and started scrolling through files until he came across a pdf file labeled "Clementine Lunar Mineral Survey."

"What's *it*, old boy?" Tom raised an eyebrow.

"I know why they landed at the Sea of Vapors!" Roger opened the pdf file and scrolled down to a figure in the paper showing the near side and the far side of the Moon side by side. The mineral content was color-shaded on each lunar surface image. The far side of the Moon was mostly blue and light green and had absolutely no red on it. The near side, however, had two big red splotches on it and the brightest one was centered on the Sea of Vapors.

Roger turned his laptop around for the other two men to see. He pushed it over to the edge of his desk and let them study it for a while.

"What is the red supposed to be, Roger?" John asked.

"It's titanium oxide. Whatever they are, they like titanium!"

The lunar reconnaissance mission development and launch went off without a hitch. The Neighborhood Watch team had just gone through a much harder drill with the design, build, launch, and mission with Percival and the Mars effort. Compared to Mars, a lunar probe was a piece of cake. Having John Fisher pushing the program and the damn near infinite budget didn't hurt either. The launch went without a hitch and had taken only ninety days to prepare.

"The deceleration burn just started," John heard Telemetry report over his headset. He looked up at the big screen display in mission control showing the graphic for the spacecraft entering into a lunar orbit on the opposite side of the Moon as the centroid of the alien dust cloud. The cloud had grown in the past three months to about six hundred kilometers in radius. Traci's dust cloud growth model was still dead on accurate.

"Roger that," John replied. "Lunar insertion is go. Let me know when the burn is complete."

Roger Reynolds and Ronny Guerrero sat in the VIP lounge watching and listening as the little lunar probe slowed down and circularized its orbit around the Moon. The low resolution near real-time video—there was actually a three-second delay due to the buffer size and the speed of light limit—was continuously displayed on one of the big screens beside the telemetry and tracking map screen. The probe had three small cameras placed around it for star tracking and with hopes that whatever took Percival apart might get captured by one of the small cameras. One image of the Moon filled a screen. An image of a star field filled another. And an image with Earth in the background filled the third one. Ronny and Roger didn't take their eyes off those screens until the imagery from the telescope was brought online.

"Burn is complete! Lunar orbit's circularized and stable at approximately ten kilometers above the lunar surface," came over the speaker in the lounge.

"Okay, the cloud is a little less than half an orbit away so that is about fifty minutes or so. And we're going into the far side of the Moon now and will lose contact with the probe for that portion of the orbit," Roger told Ronny although it was a piece of information both of them had known for months. It was something to say in the silence. The silence seemed to increase the stress.

"It's okay, Roger; we'll get a good picture of them," Ronny assured his junior colleague.

"Right," Roger said, sitting back quietly. After about a minute of that, he leaned forward and began clicking his teeth with his tongue.

"Dr. Reynolds," Ronny said, softly, not looking up from the report he was reading, "if you persist in that annoying noise I will be forced to call in a guard and have you shot dead."

"Yes, sir," Roger said, composing himself and sitting back. After about a minute he began tapping his foot on the floor. Quietly but persistently.

"Dr. Reynolds . . ."

"Sorry, sir," Roger said, concentrating on the blank screen.

"Were you diagnosed as ADHD when you were in school?" Ronny asked, still not looking up.

"No, sir," Roger replied, trying not to grin.

"I believe there's an exercise bike downstairs. Why don't you come back in, oh, twenty minutes."

"Yes, sir."

Roger had just gotten back when the datastream from the probe picked back up. The little lunar spacecraft had made it around the far side of the Moon without a hitch and was sending back plenty of recon data.

"There is the dust cloud in the low res camera's field of view," Traci said over the speaker. "The main high res imagery is coming through now."

Ronny and Roger watched as the image with thirty-centimeter resolution downloaded to the central screen. The low resolution video continued to stream on the other three monitors. The high resolution image was showing that the dust cloud was floating and shimmering with glints of larger objects moving around in them.

"Traci, this is Roger," he said, donning his headset.

"Hey, what do you need?"

"Could you zoom the display magnification on the high res image to maximum so we can see better detail back here?"

"Hold one . . . How's that?" she replied.

The image lurched, then zoomed in to the maximum display resolution with a ratio of one hundred to one, or one centimeter on the screen being the same as one meter on the surface.

Roger popped open his laptop. He had previously hooked it into the video feeds of the imagery display monitors. He toggled a few menu buttons, then the image being displayed on the monitor with the high res data was now being displayed on his laptop. He pecked the left touchpad button and the real-time image froze.

"Now I'll just zoom in a bit here and . . . there." Roger turned his laptop monitor toward Ronny. "Look at that, will ya?"

"Little flying things," Ronny said, a furrow appearing between his eyebrows.

"Yeah, they look almost like a boomerang or something or a flying wing. And at this resolution that must be about four pixels across so that thing is about a hundred and twenty centimeters wide. But, God, they're all over the place."

"Warning Flight! I have a Watchdog reset on telescope gimbals!"

"Flight, I've got three Watchdog resets on structure."

"Here we go, Ronny. Let's hope the antenna holds long enough for us to get a close up." Roger crossed his fingers and stared closer at the three low resolution video streams. He pecked his computer and set it on ready to grab a video frame. Of course if he missed it they could replay the video after the fact.

"There, Roger." Ronny pointed at screen two—the Earthward viewing one.

"Got it." Roger tapped the touchpad.

The image stream stopped.

"Flight, we had multiple Watchdog resets then no telemetry at all."

"Roger that, no telemetry. Continue the reconnect protocols, but I think we can assume the probe was destroyed," John said with a sigh. "Well, at least we know what we're up against."

※   ※   ※

"The best we can tell is that it appears they're made of metal. A composite material most likely wouldn't be this shiny," Ronny explained to the President over the phone.

"So, what does that mean?"

"Well, sir, we haven't really had time to analyze the data completely, but we're certain that they're using in-situ materials from the lunar surface to replicate themselves. That means this thing is most likely made of titanium and aluminum."

"Then that means they won't be impervious to our weapons," the President said.

"Possibly. It might be some sort of super-alloy. But more likely they're simply making themselves from whatever's available. They undoubtedly need some trace metals for their internals, although we have no idea what they are at this point. But, yes, Mr. President, they might be individually vulnerable. However, there are a *bunch* of them. Mr. President, the U.S. needs to go on a full war footing right *now*."

Despite the official declaration of war all that had really happened was an increase in funding and the call-up of the National Guard and Reserves. To the greatest extent possible, it had been business as usual.

"We need a *much* larger Army, more redoubts, we need to throw anything we can at the problem and open it up fully so anyone can get in on the research."

"That's going to need some discussion, Ronny," the President said. "Among other things, you're not the person who should be advising on that."

"Sorry, Mr. President," Ronny said, gritting his teeth but biting back the reply.

"You need to be in the meeting, though," the President

said, sighing. "Get up here and bring Dr. . . . What's his name? The redneck?"

"Dr. Roger Reynolds," Ronny replied. "He's right here, sir."

"Both of you get up here," the President said. "I'll schedule a full Cabinet meeting this evening with the heads of the Senate and the House."

The meeting was in the cabinet room with every cabinet member present as well as the majority and minority leaders of the House and Senate. Everyone except Roger had brought an aide. He supposed he'd be counted as Ronny's aide, or even his second aide, since Ronny had one sitting in a chair behind him, but he was planning on saying his piece.

"We've refined the data a bit since I spoke to the President," Ronny said, concluding his fifteen minute presentation. "We now have a clearer understanding of the threat. They're definitely Von Neumann machines and they're definitely consuming the surface of the rocky bodies in the solar system one by one. There is no indication that they will ignore the Earth. At present, no model that we have shows survival of the human race, or at least civilization, in the face of this threat. We're looking at end game for the ten-thousand year history of post-hunter-gatherer society, ladies and gentlemen."

"It can't be that bad," the secretary for Health and Human Services said, shaking his head. "You can't say that just because they ate the Moon and Mars that they're coming here! And even if they do, we've called up National Guard and the Reserves. What more do you want?"

"We need to rationalize production," the Chairman of

the Joint Chiefs said. "We need a national industrial board."

"We've got one," the chairman of the Office of Management and Budget snapped. "And they're already screwing up the economy—"

"Economy be *damned*," Roger said, trying to bite back the comment as he made it.

"Dr. Reynolds," the President said angrily. "If we don't have an economy, we don't have the money to pay for your pet projects—"

"Mr. President . . ." Ronny started to say placatingly.

"No, let me," Roger said, looking the President in the eye. "Mr. President, there was a book a while back, written by some yuppy economist."

"Yes?" the President said, raising an eyebrow. He very well could be called a "yuppy economist."

"It was a pretty selfish book," the scientist said, shrugging. "Basically, it was about how to plan to manage your money so there wasn't any left over for your kids. 'Die with your last dollar' or something like that. But it's important here, Mr. President."

"Why?" the national security advisor asked.

"Every other time we had a national emergency, we had to keep one eye on what the future might hold," Roger said, looking her in the eye. "If we lose *this* one, there *is* no future. *No* economy beyond glass beads," he said, looking at the chairman of OMB. "*No* agriculture," he said, looking at the secretary of Agriculture. "Not beyond digging small gardens with sticks. *No* housing," he continued, looking at the HHS secretary. "Not beyond caves and stick houses. And not much of that, looking at the Moon and Mars. A few humans scrabbling for survival in the metal monster of a city the machines will create, living hand to mouth, eating *each other* to survive. Mr. President, if the last dollar equivalent in the world is spent to kill the last machine, that will be a *dollar well spent!*"

"Mr. President?" the national security advisor said quietly.

"Yes?"

"We're already looking at the inflation index skyrocketing," she said. "Effectively, in a survival economy, which is what we're approaching, you have to draw money out of the economy or it overheats as there's more and more competition for survival materials. One way to do that is to crank taxes up and put them into non-useful or disposed costs; personnel and equipment that's not going to last. You worry about how to recoup if you win, if the survival situation goes away. You don't print more money, you take it out of circulation."

"There's that," the chairman of OMB mused. "And, frankly, Mr. President, while rather hotly presented, what Dr. Reynolds said makes sense as well. The images from the Moon are more . . . graphic than those from Mars. As are the growth curves. If the same thing happens, unchecked, on Earth, well . . ."

"Agreed," the President said with a sigh. "Senators, Congressmen? We're going to have to pass bills for this. We'll have to increase the taxes, begin a draft—"

"Mr. President?" the Chairman of the Joint Chiefs and the secretary of defense both said simultaneously.

"Yes?" the President said, looking at the secretary with one hand up to the Chairman.

"I think we're both going the same place, Mr. President," the secretary said with a glance at the Chairman.

"There's simply not time, or materials, to make a draft worthwhile. Funneling the money to civil defense and, frankly, organized militias will be more worthwhile. Some increase in Defense, yes, but we're still in the making the tools to make the guns stage. More money and facilities at the scientific redoubts. They'll have to try to survive even if everything else falls."

"And culture," the secretary of the interior said, firmly. "If we lose everything else, let's keep the knowledge of how to rebuild it alive."

"Food," the secretary of agriculture said, frowning. "And storage facilities. Even if these things get a piece of us and we win, food will be at a premium."

"Distribution," the secretary of transportation said, nodding. "That's going to be all screwed up. That was a problem for the Russians, right after independence. They had plenty of food, but the distribution was all screwed up."

"Refugee housing," the director of Homeland Security said, nodding. "And supply . . . On the largest scale ever considered . . . There are never enough tents . . ."

Roger looked over at Ronny and nodded faintly. It was late, but the "government" seemed to finally understand how deep a crack they were in. Maybe, if the probes gave them enough time, there might be a chance.

Ret Ball: *Tonight we have a very special program with both Hiowa Lend and Megiddo on the line. Hiowa, you first.*

Hiowa Lend: *Right, Ret. Jumping right into it. My astronomer friends have been doing an analysis of the Moon for me and they tell me that the surface albedo has changed ever so slightly and that it's now brighter by what appears to be a couple of percentage points.*

Ret Ball: *Really? What does that mean, Hiowa?*

Hiowa Lend: *Well Ret, it means that whatever happened to Mars, is now happening to the Moon.*

Megiddo: *If I may, Hiowa?*

Hiowa Lend: *Feel free, Professor . . . uh . . . Megiddo. Are you sure that your communications are secure, my old friend?*

Megiddo: *I assure you that the government is quite unable to trace my call. I helped design the original Bell system and I know all the tricks.*

Ret Ball: *Very well, my friend, go ahead.*

Megiddo: *I've made similar measurements of the lunar surface color and reflectance albedo as well as its absorption spectra. It's being mechanized, Ret. Something is indeed terraforming the Moon. This is way too close to home and I suggest it's time we all take to remote underground locations. Had the CIA not covered this up for so long we might have been more prepared for it. Ret, you must move immediately to your secure bunker. Time is of the essence.*

Chapter 13

"Mr. President, ten minutes ago we lost all contact with the Transmission and Data Relay Satellite System in geosynchronous orbit. We're getting communications from multiple government and commercial sources worldwide that satellites in GEO are failing," the NSA briefed the President via phone from the Pentagon.

"Vicki, does this means it's starting?" The President sat up in his chair in the Oval Office. "Just a minute, Vicki." He pressed the blinking light on his phone, "Yes, Judy?"

"Mr. President, the Chairman of the Joint Chiefs is here and says it's urgent."

"Send him in."

"Mr. President, the Neighborhood Watch has informed us that most of our high altitude space assets have been lost and our lower orbit platforms are starting to fail," newly promoted five star General Kevin Mitchell warned as he marched into the Oval Office.

"I think it's time to move you to the predetermined safe location." Besides the over forty divisions that had been called up Mitchell was also in charge of the "organized militias." Most of them were more militia than organized, but they gave the vast number of armed citizens in the U.S. something to center around, and while training had been spotty the response had been enthusiastic. Enthusiastic enough that despite increases in production, there was a nationwide shortage of ammunition, which was one of many "survival" items that, as predicated, had been heating up the inflationary indexes.

"Hold on, General, I'm putting Vicki on the speaker. Okay, go ahead, Vicki. General Mitchell is here and has just suggested that I be moved to a safe location."

"Hello, Kevin," the NSA's voice said over the phone. "I agree. Mr. President. We do not know where these things will come down and what they will do, but it looks like it's happening now."

"Mr. President," Kevin interjected. "I think it's time to alert the Emergency Broadcast System while there still is one and we should try to get some recon somehow on where these things are coming down, assuming they plan to hit like they did on the Moon."

"Mr. President, I was just handed a projection from Ronny Guerrero's group at Neighborhood Watch," Vicki said. "At the rate of loss of satellites, they predict that all satellites will be lost within the next hour. And that means all manmade satellites, not just U.S. assets."

"There goes CNN," the President said with a faint, grim smile.

"Mr. President, your orders, sir?" The general stood at ease in front of his desk. He seemed calm. But, then, he'd probably mentally prepared for this moment for a long time.

"What was it the man said? 'I knew this would come, but not so soon'? Whew." The President looked around the Oval Office and sighed. He picked up a small metal picture frame containing a photo of his wife, son, and daughter and placed it in his coat pocket. "Okay. Evacuate the White House and have the civil defense plans put into place. Vicki, we'll meet you at Air Force One."

"Yes, sir, Mr. President. I'm leaving now."

Kevin led the President to the door and informed the Secret Service guards there, "Evacuate the White House. We're moving the President to the safe location." The Secret Service bodyguards went into immediate action.

Tina and Charlotte were watching television from their apartment just outside the Army base in Huntsville. Alice and John were on base, where they had been assigned since the President's speech that warned the world of the alien threat. Tina's brother Carl had decided to move in with their dad.

Since the President's speech Tina and Charlotte had been glued to the television—as had most of the world—trying to learn any and everything they could about the alien threat. The news media had used military analysts, scientists, and, most effectively, science fiction writers for possible speculation about the aliens.

The program Tina and Charlotte were watching was nothing more than the millionth reiteration of things that had already been discussed to death. But then—

❊   ❊   ❊

"We interrupt this program to issue the following warning from the Emergency Broadcast System. The Emergency Broadcast System has been authorized by the President of the United States of America to issue the Emergency Evacuation and Shelter Plan as designated for the pending alien threat. Please respond in accordance with your pre-determined evacuation protocol and report to your designated shelter area. We'll continue this broadcast and issue more information as—"

The screen abruptly went black. A few moments later a local news anchorwoman, looking flustered, sat down at a desk.

"We seem to be having technical difficulties with our satellite system," the woman said, blinking rapidly and then looking off to the side. "We'll be using the ground links to the Emergency Broadcast System to update you. Stay tuned to this station for further word on the alien invasion . . ."

"Let's go, girls," Alice yelled at the two teenagers to hurry into the Humvee.

"Ma'am, we really need to get back to the base ASAP," Master Sergeant Cady urged her.

"Roger that, Thomas. Girls! Now!" she yelled as Tina and Charlotte rushed out the door of the apartment and Tina started back up the stairs as if she had forgotten something but then she thought better of it, adjusted her backpack, and continued into the vehicle.

The base was buzzing with excitement and there were convoys of military vehicles on every roadway. Helicopters were buzzing in and out overhead as Cady drove Alice and the teens to the shelter on the Redstone Arsenal.

The shelters were built back during the Cold War but since then had been used as storage facilities for explosives and chemicals. When the news of the threat of an alien invasion was released, every old Cold War fallout shelter and civil defense location across the country was refurbished and brought back online as part of the shelter system for the populace. The shelter system on the military base was assigned to the personnel involved with the local contingents of Neighborhood Watch and Asymmetric Soldier and their families.

Alice, the girls, and Sergeant Cady met John Fisher in one of the makeshift control rooms for the ISR data analysis team. The room was an obvious afterthought to the shelter. The walls were 2x4 construction with cheap paneling and had been added to the large empty bunker by simply bolting the stud sill-plate to the concrete. The walls went eight feet or so high, then were open to the higher ceiling of the shelter. The makeshift control room had laptops strewn all around it on small tables and there was a bird's nest of cabling and wires running around the room. Four large flat-panel displays were mounted on two of the walls and cables draped from beneath each of the panels to a rack of servers and tele-communications equipment in the corner of the room. This rack seemed to be the nexus of the disarray of cabling.

John Fisher and Alan Davis were staring at the large screens discussing the scrolling numbers and characters as if they could decipher it.

Charlotte hugged her father.

"Daddy, what's going on?"

"I'm glad you made it, darling. I owe Alice and Cady one. It looks like the aliens have decided it's time to move to Earth." John clicked a touchpad a few times and an image of Earth popped up on one of the flat screens. "You see these circular and elliptical lines here all around the planet?"

"Uh huh."

"Well, that is where we used to have satellites. As far as our space debris monitoring radars can tell, none of them are there. On the other hand, this . . ." he clicked a few more times on the touchpad, "is what the radars are picking up." A cloud of blips filled the region around the planet.

"What does it mean?" Tina looked at her mother.

Alice shrugged.

"Dunno."

"It means they're wiping out our eyes and ears and communications capabilities," Alan muttered. "John, I've got to get this to Roger. I'll be back in a few minutes." Alan popped a jumpdrive out of one of the laptops and hurried out.

"Well, Mr. President, the cloud surrounding the planet seems to be gone," Ronny Guerrero explained to the President and the NSA.

"That's good, right?" the NSA asked.

"Not really, ma'am. The latest data that we've been able to get back from radar at various locations around the globe has allowed us to make this composite of the data." Ronny flipped the image up on his laptop.

"Here you can see a large cylindrical swarm of small contacts. Each seems to be less than thirty centimeters across, but there are estimated to be more than three billion of them in this tube that extends out from Earth nearly a thousand kilometers and is about three hundred meters in diameter. Analysis of the multi-static radar data suggests that there is only about one meter separation in any direction between these things within the tube. The cloud that was around the planet seems to have directed itself into the tube. Although there are still some few thousand of the contacts around the globe, most of them have converged into this tubule. And it's coming down. Now."

"Yes, Ronny, I can see that, but where is this thing centered?" the President asked.

"Well, sir, as best we can tell, it looks like somewhere just east of Paris, France."

"Captain Holmes, sir. E-3 is enroute to target zone." Captain Eddie Holmes of the NATO E-3A AWACS contingent from Geilenkirchen, Germany checked the charts velcroed to his left thigh. "E.T.A. of twenty-three minutes."

"Little green men, cap'n?" Lieutenant Tod Alvers said. "Reckon we'll see any?"

"You heard the briefing, Lieutenant. They're machines. That scares me more than little green men. Living things implies that they might be reasoned with or even be sympathetic, but machines on the other hand . . ." The captain marked a checkpoint on his map and keyed the crew frequency. "Davis, are we getting returns from this thing yet?"

"Roger that, Cap'n. I've got the largest passive return I've ever seen. We haven't got the transmitter active and the ambient return looks like God's chaff cloud out there about three hundred miles east," Tech Specialist Davis replied.

"Well, keep us posted up here and clear of those things, you hear me? I want all data live on JTIDS starting now. And as soon as we're in range go active with the radar. The Pentagon wants as much information as we can get."

"Roger, Cap'n. JTIDS link is operational. We're in range now, sir. Going active with JSTARS now." Davis typed in the proper commands on his keyboard to activate the radar systems on board the AWACS aircraft. His screen showed a cloud of metal that looked more like the return from a thunderstorm than from a squadron of flying machines. "Sir, we have zero resolution at this range. Just a large cloud, still trying to get a hard measurement. There must be billions of them, sir."

"What are they doing, Davis?"

"They're—" Davis stopped abruptly. "The cloud is changing shape . . ."

"Captain," Lieutenant Alvers said, quietly but urgently, pointing toward the cockpit window.

"Holy shit! Bank! Bank! Bank!"

A swarm of meter-long boomerang shaped metallic objects consumed the aircraft and began ripping it apart. The aircraft metal on the empennage of the aircraft was rapidly stripped away. The cockpit and cabin pressurization gave way.

Banking and diving the aircraft seemed to have no effect on the swarm's ability to match velocity and attack. Captain Holmes and Lieutenant Alvers banked and juked until the plane was pulled apart. Eddie looked out at the right wing and shook his head as it buckled; it was covered with meter-long boomerangs.

✻   ✻   ✻

"This is Bob Campbell in Paris," the CNN reporter said. "The reports of the alien landing are spotty at this time but it appears that they're approaching Paris. The French military has issued a statement saying that they're in position to defend the city and citizens should remain calm and in their homes. Thus far we have no reports of how the fighting is going and all communications from the area are cut off."

"Probably because they lost," Roger said, sipping a beer as he watched the streaming video. With all the satellites down, the report from Paris was being fed through Internet pipe over trans-Atlantic cable links and it was flickery and scratchy, with the reporter's words occasionally coming in either before or after the video. "Our intel feed says that the French military's already lost contact with them. Lost it right after they said they were engaged. Nothing since then."

"They're going to fight hard," Shane said. He was sipping a Diet Coke since he considered himself "on duty." Even if duty was watching the world end, live. "Everybody disses the French military. And, okay, their generals and politicians are fucked. But the troops are good and the junior officers are first rate. The good ones just can't get promoted past colonel."

The producer had set up a shot with the Eiffel Tower in the background. The reporter was yammering about defense plans and evacuation plans, just to fill the dead air. But he paused and turned as dots came into view over his shoulder.

"There appears to be something happening . . ."

Campbell said as a Mirage jet thundered overhead, distorting his voice again. The cameraman swiveled to catch the jet just as it fired an air-to-air missile. The jet followed the missile in and as it passed over the tower it seemed to be swarmed by dots. More were descending on the tower, and in the background there was a wash of dust as a large building appeared to collapse.

"I'm not sure what's happening," the reporter said nervously, then looked up and blanched. The screen suddenly went dark.

"We're experiencing technical difficulties with our feed from France," the anchorwoman in Atlanta said, looking up into the teleprompter. "We'll try to get Bob Campbell back with his live report in a moment. We'll go temporarily to our expert military analyst retired Colonel . . ."

"That was quick," Roger said, frowning as he picked up the remote and lowered the sound. "And somehow I don't think we'll be hearing from Bob any time soon."

"Were those things all over the Tower like it looked?" Cady asked. "And I never saw the missile impact."

"No, I didn't either," Roger said. "We were recording so we'll run it through some filters and tighten up the images as much as we can. But I'm not sure what we'll get. They were all over that Mirage like stink on a hog, though."

"There's a Stryker brigade deploying out of Le Havre in a day or two," Shane said musingly.

"You want to go have a close up look?" Roger asked, askance. "I mean, we don't know if anybody in France is alive or dead at the moment. I don't even know if we're in contact with the Stryker brigade. And I definitely don't know how long they'll last."

"Yeah, I want to go look," Shane said. "If I can get a good look at what they're doing, that's going to help, right?"

"If you can get the word *back*," Roger pointed out. "We don't know if these things are eating people or what. I mean, that one report is as good as it's gotten. Nobody has gotten more word out than that."

"I wouldn't mind going, sir," Cady said, setting down his beer. "But I'd like to get back, too. I don't want to die in France if you know what I mean."

"How high a priority can you get us?" Shane asked.

"For a Neighborhood Watch observer?" Roger replied. "Pretty damned high. Why?"

"I think we should go," Shane said. "But I agree with the master sergeant. We definitely want to get back if there's a chance."

"I'll make some calls," Roger said.

United States Air Force Lieutenant Colonel Matthew "Bull" Ridley had only been assigned to the multinational NATO-Euro F-16 "Fighting Falcons" squadron as an instructor/observer. His main objective in soliciting the assignment had been to reach "full bull" colonel; the multinational position was a good resume builder. As an instructor, it also meant that he'd get plenty of cockpit time, which was a nice bennie. But promotion was the last thing on his mind at the moment; his present mission made survival a much higher priority.

When the alien threat entered European airspace the NATO "unified defense" protocols were automatically activated. NATO had been toying with a combined force ever since the failure of the "EU Deployment Group."

The EUDG had never really gotten beyond a very expensive headquarters and some garrison troops but the concept still remained. Accepting the inevitable, the European Union, virtually all of whose members were also members of NATO, revamped the concept as a NATO force. The division-sized "deployment force" was designed around the "pull-and-pick" scheme; when a mission was assigned it would pull available ground and support forces from the supporting countries.

However, the force intended to have some dedicated units, notably support and air forces. After an exhaustive testing program, the "EU" unit chose, of all things, the American F-16 as their primary strike and air-to-air fighter.

There were mutterings that the air forces should, by right, have come from a European country. However, since the "EU" force was composed primarily of American and British ground forces, had an American commander and was primarily funded by the United States, having an aircraft that could electronically interact with the American and British forces was paramount. The British Tornado was the only "European" system that met the requirements, European avionics being at least two generations behind the U.S. The F-16 was a far superior air-to-air fighter and a tad more capable at ground attack.

Thus the assignment of an American colonel to instruct and, in this case, command, a "European" squadron made perfect sense, at least to NATO.

As soon as the report came that the attack stream was headed for Europe, all the remaining seventy-two F-16s in the multinational fighter wing were called to action.

The squadron of multilingual and multinational fighter pilots were to bring support from the northwest toward the alien tubule that looked as if it would encompass Paris.

Lieutenant Colonel Ridley decided that he couldn't leave the one F-16 that he had been training and instructing from on the ground. That just would not do. And besides that, this might be the best chance to gather intel on the threat that the U.S. would have. Matt hoped he could live long enough to get the intel home.

Rumors were coming in that multiple French Mirage squadrons had been lost on the southeastern front and the Falcons were beyond nervous. Very few of the European air forces had been as blooded as the Americans and Brits. Americans and Brits had maintained the Iraqi No-Fly Zone in the face of Saddam's ground-to-air missiles, had carried the brunt of the battle in Bosnia and had operated against the Iraqi air-defense in Operation Iraqi Freedom. Ridley, alone, had more total "combat stick" time than the entire French air force. And the Belgians and Germans on the mission totaled exactly zero combat stick. Matt had decided early on that his primary mission was to try to keep them calm. Sangfroid. Just another training exercise. Right.

"Okay boys, just like we been practicing. We're a gonna go in low at high Mach, pull up through those alien bastards to slow us down to firing speeds and let loose hell on them." Lieutenant Colonel Ridley nodded at his wingman and keyed in his weapons code.

Weapons cache online, the computer told him with a ding.

Ridley adjusted the radar controls and set the system on wide target search.

"That's odd, there's no AWACS data," he muttered to himself.

"Bull, I've got multiple bogies in-bound on us from the south, Mach Three Dot Five, Angels fourteen!" Belgian Flight-Lieutenant Rene "Low-Boy" Lejeune said over the radio in very good English. Rene had done well in training on the plane and had the instincts of a good fighter pilot. He kept good wing, for that matter. But he got a tad excited over the radio. Belgians hadn't figured out the "phlegmatic" approach. Ridley looked over and could see his wingman waving at him and pointing downward and to the south.

"Roger that, Rene," Ridley replied laconically. "Let's take it to 'em boys. Follow me through."

Ridley eased his stick all the way forward and throttled up the F16. As the g-forces pushed him back into his seat his stomach tightened and the airbags around his thighs slightly inflated.

"Radar contact shows multiple bogie, vector one-one-seven, Angels fourteen. Careful, the system is showing them as vampires. Visual range . . ." the lieutenant colonel tried to keep both eyes on the radar and both eyes on the sky. That was a trick that most humans failed and at which fighter pilots excelled.

"Contact, contact," a calm, French accented voice said. "Visual, two o'clock, low."

"Zehn Uhr!" a slightly more excited German voice said hastily.

"TWELVE!"

The two formations were closing at a combined rate of nearly four thousand miles per hour. One second there was only a shiny, slightly gray cloud. The cloud, like coming closer to a pointillist painting, suddenly became billions of dots and then the dots became a cloudy sky filled with meter long boomerangs that . . . were . . . freaking . . . *everywhere*!

Ridley began yanking and jerking the joystick control at his side in a desperate attempt to weave in and out of the cloud of alien probes. The F-16 was in a supersonic dive at the edge of its operational capabilities, but the alien metal boomerangs zipped up effortlessly into the squadron and began tearing the manmade vehicles to shreds. Ridley watched as one of the boomerangs passed right through the empennage of the F-16 flown by Luftwaffe Captain Heinz Zwack, sacrificing itself to destroy the fighter. Two more exploding Falcons was all it took to tell him this was not a survivable tactic.

"Full throttle and push through, push through!" he yelled.

"Bull, we must slow to firing speeds!" Rene exclaimed.

"Push through the first wave, Rene! Then bank just like we trained!" Ridley ordered. His orders were doing no good. The less seasoned pilots were anxious to go to missiles and guns and to do that they had to slow down. At Mach speeds the alien boomerangs seemed to have a hard time maneuvering with precision, but as soon as the F-16s banked and slowed the little alien probes matched velocity vectors and ripped them apart.

Ridley pushed the F-16 nose down so fast he thought the wings would fly right off and Rene stayed right with him. Maybe twenty or so of the other pilots matched the tactic as well. Ridley's eyes rolled up as a shiny metal boomerang zipped by his cockpit in a blur.

"Jesus, that was close!"

At the bottom of the dive the F-16s did a slow curving bank with little juking maneuvers thrown in to avoid the boomerangs. The dive took them mostly below the initial cloud of the alien probes, giving them a few seconds to slow and maneuver to firing speeds.

"AAAARRGGGHHH . . .   AAAARRGGG . . . UUUMMMPHHH!" Ridley grunted and squeezed his abdominal muscles, calves, and thighs as the air bladders inflated as tight as they would go. Ridley bit down on the bite block hard and grunted again.

Warning, warning, excessive g-forces, blackout danger! The cockpit chimed.

"Nooo shhhiiittt! AAAARRUMMMMPPHH!" Ridley grunted through the bank and immediately went to the Joint Helmet Mounted Cueing System to fire the Aim-9X Sidewinder air-to-air missiles. "Fire one, fire two, fire three . . ." Ridley rolled the fighter upward and painted as many targets as he could. His wingman and the other remaining twenty or so fighters were following suit.

The Sidewinder missiles left sinewy and twisted contrails at Mach 2.5 upwards through the belly of the cloud of alien boomerangs. At the supersonic velocity of the deadly missiles the alien probes seemed to have some—not a lot mind you, but some—difficulty matching their velocity and attacking the missiles until it was too late.

Ridley watched for the split second it took for his first missile to explode and fragment just in front of a subswarm of boomerangs. Several of the alien probes were blown into fragments and scattered into several other probes nearby, killing them with fratricide. Ridley also noted that as soon as the handful of probes were destroyed several handfuls filled the void and swooped up the flying debris like a magnet picking up iron filings.

"There are too many of them, Bull! I'm out of missiles and guns seem to have no effect!" Rene said frantically.

That was apparent. Rene had taken an angle shot at a stray boomerang. The probe flew right into his fire cone, actually seeming to bank towards the tracers, but the bullets just seemed to disappear as they closed the target.

"Roger that, Rene! Let's make a dive for the hard-deck and try to get away from these goddamned things! Falcons evade and escape as best you can! Retreat!"

"*Oui*, Bull!"

Twelve of the F-16 Falcons remained and dove as hard to the surface as they could manage. Bull looked up and back, fighting the Gs to get a look at the enemy. Incredibly, the damned boomerangs were banking inside their curve. The F-16 was the most maneuverable fighter on the face of the earth at these sorts of speeds and the damned things were *inside* their maneuverability envelope! A good bit of the swarm had already banked around and were closing from the rear at well over the max speed of the Falcons. They looked like boomerang-form air-to-air missiles, without the smoke trail.

Evasive maneuvers at subsonic speeds were proving fruitless. The boomerangs had the ability to match speeds and simply attach to the fighters' surfaces. One of the fighters behind him, Bull thought it was Lieutenant Granz's, was surrounded by six of the 'rangs and seemed to simply come apart. The mostly aluminum and sheet metal fuselage and wings of the fighters stripped off like friable plastic and vanished in midair.

"Stay fast Falcons, they're closing!" Ridley warned. "Afterburner!" He kicked in his afterburner and yanked and banked to treetop height, then pulled up hard again, nearly blacking out. He couldn't look back at these speeds; all he could do was hang in there. He was flying practically nap-of-the-earth at high Mach and the ground effect buffet was shaking his fighter apart.

High inertia structural damage, the warning system cooed. *Warning. Warning.*

"AAARRRGGGHHH . . . AAARRRUUUMMMPPHHH . . . UMMMP . . . UMMPPHH!" he grunted and squeezed his muscles as hard as he could trying to curl his toes right through the bottom of his boots. Ridley bit down hard on his bite block as a black spot appeared in the center of his vision and the tunnel started closing in. Then *Thud*!

"WOOOHH . . . WOOOOHH . . . SHEEWWWWW!" he breathed and squeezed as another *Thud* and then *Spang* sounded through the aircraft. The fighter was already bucking from the air compression around it but these were solid hits. It sounded and felt like he was taking flak. Hell, he could be hitting treetops, he didn't know. He pulled up a bit to try to get out of the ground buffet and there was another, hard, *Spang!*

"Bull, I'm hit, I'm hit. Ejecting!" Rene screamed over the net.

Ridley rolled his head slightly to the right and saw his wingman's fighter fly into thousands of pieces just as his ejection seat fired. Almost at the same time he saw his own right wing fly apart and the ship immediately begin to go into "out of control" condition.

Still not completely out of his tunnel vision and his mind hazy, Lieutenant Colonel Matthew "Bull" Ridley instinctively reached between his knees and pulled the eject handle. The process had been drilled into him and it had served him well once during the first Gulf War. The training would save him this time. *Thwack, bang!*

Ridley was flung out of the fighter jet into the evening air at several hundred miles per hour just as the jet came apart below him. Fortunately, the fuel load didn't detonate. The g load and the spin were worse than any roller coaster. To Ridley's bemused astonishment and distaste, it seemed a lot worse than it did a decade and a half ago. Of course, that time he hadn't been at damned near Mach One and below Angels Seven.

Then his chute popped and things slowed down for a second. Ridley could see the chute from several of the twelve remaining NATO squadron pilots already deployed. He had made it much closer to the tree line than the others and most of them were a thousand or more feet above him. And then one by one their chutes began to fail. Ridley tracked the closest chute to him; he thought it was Rene. Then he realized why the chutes were failing.

The boomerangs swarmed the chute and the dangling payload and almost as soon as the swarm surrounded the downed pilot, his chute collapsed and he began a plummet toward the ground. The plummet appeared to Ridley to be more of a controlled dragging and tossing, like a dog shaking a chew toy in its mouth.

Ridley strained hard to pull his right leg upward so he could reach his pistol. Just as he grabbed for it something invisible jerked it right out of his hands. The carabiner on his right shoulder ripped away from the harness. Then his clothes seemed to explode and be pulled away from him. The invisible force that grabbed him flung him sideways, slamming him into two shiny boomerangs that ripped the buttons and hasps from his flightsuit, again tossing him upward.

Ridley's helmet *thwacked* hard into something. And then he felt a sharp stabbing pain in his left shoulder as he was spun face first into the top of a tree and into another alien probe. The faceshield of his helmet cracked and flew off as the buttons and other metal fasteners were ripped from it. The probe tossed him up and outward into another one and this one yanked the shoes right off his feet, breaking three bones in his left foot and dislocating all his toes on his right. With all the metal gone from his body, the probes left him plummeting downward.

Fortunately, he was at damned near tree height. A final plummet through several thick tree limbs spinning and smacking him around ended with a skipping, scraping, bouncing, and rolling stop on the ground at the base of a tree. Ridley lay there on the edge of consciousness in pain from head to toe staring up at the sky.

"So much for making colonel," he muttered, then passed out.

Chapter 14

Roger had been as good as his word. In less than fourteen hours Gries and Cady had been flown over to France on one of the C-17s that was supporting the Stryker brigade out of Stewart. Only one battalion had been off-loaded and mated up with their vehicles but there was another already queued up to land.

Shane had stopped by the local French "unified defense" headquarters, which was located in a small industrial building on the outskirts of Le Havre. Even in the worst conditions in Iraq, headquarters units had always been pretty button down and operational. When he went to the headquarters to try to get some intel on the situation, he'd found utter chaos. Nobody recognized his priority, or cared. Nobody seemed to have any idea what was happening or what to do about it if they did. He'd seen one three star French general wandering around the operations room asking everyone if they had a pencil sharpener; he seemed to have forgotten why he needed a pencil sharpened and was simply concentrating on a task he could perform.

While there were plenty of people willing to talk, nobody seemed to have picked up *any* information about the probes. Repeatedly, units had reported contact and then gone off the air. Areas where probes had hit—they sort of had those mapped out through negatives: military and police units that didn't respond—had lost all communications. Refugees that had made it to units still in contact reported that the probes were "eating" vehicles and even buildings. That was about all the intel they had.

After a fruitless hour in the command center, Shane and Thomas, who had managed to use their priority to secure a Humvee, joined the convoy of Strykers and support vehicles headed to the Calais area. Nobody knew why they were heading to Calais and after seeing the chaos in the headquarters Shane was pretty sure even the French weren't sure why the Strykers were heading to Calais. But those were the orders.

The drive was unpleasant. Despite cops trying to stop people using the limited access highway, civilians were out in force. Everyone seemed to have some place to be they thought better than their homes in the emergency. The convoy was caught in a traffic jam for an hour outside Calais before the battalion commander ordered the combat companies to head off-road. The support vehicles and logistics could catch up later. They thumped down off the limited-access highway, cut through some fields ripe with winter wheat, hit a few side roads that weren't quite as crowded and finally reached their assembly area, which was another light industrial park near the town of Coulogne.

Cady drove the Humvee over to where the battalion staff was setting up a forward tactical operations center. Shane had paid his compliments to the battalion commander, Lieutenant Colonel Walter Schon, when he'd first linked up with them in Le Havre and scrounged a vehicle. Schon was a bright officer with the tall, lean, clean-cut look that was de rigeur for modern infantry commanders. Shane had recalled a paper the commander had written in Command and General Staff on operational maneuver in the defense and had mentioned it, which the commander took as the intended compliment. They got along. They knew some of the same people and they both came out of the same school of modern military hard-knocks. Schon had had a company in Iraq as well and saw in Shane a fellow, only slightly junior, up-and-coming officer. He'd spent a few minutes picking Shane's brain about the anticipated threat and had come away if anything more depressed.

Now they were in position and Shane got out to watch the battalion maneuver into defensive positions. Nobody knew exactly what they were defending, as such. But they spread out with a defense geared on a generally easterly axis, the Strykers and a platoon of Abrams tanks that had been sent in support finding hide positions along the slight slope of a hill.

"How do these things attack?" Major Forrester, the battalion operations officer, asked as Shane and Cady walked up to the huddle by the command Humvee. "Ray guns or what?"

"Major Gries?" the colonel asked, looking over at the attached "expert."

"That's what I'm here to try to find out, sir," Shane

admitted. "We've never seen any evidence of directed energy weapons, but the views we've gotten have all been on dead planets and the Moon. And not many of those, sir."

"We have gotten no word on their method of attack as well, sir," Lieutenant Leroie said. The French liaison shrugged. "Every unit has gone off the air shortly after contact. Including the Euro-NATO F-16 squadron."

"What's the update on the invader's position?" the colonel asked Captain Carson, the intel officer.

"The last update I got was when we left, sir," the captain replied. "They'd apparently wiped out everything around Paris and Tours as well as entering Belgium and Germany. It's all negative intel, though, just where units weren't responding. They have picked up some swarms on radar, but they're mostly staying low and the radar has all gone down, quick. So have radio, land-lines and even cell phones. We had an AWACS up with F-15 escort, but they took that out nearly four hours ago."

"Where was it?" Shane asked. "Where was it orbiting, that is?"

"I dunno," the intel officer replied, shrugging. "Why?"

"Well, if they were in and around Paris and it wasn't, why'd they go for it?" Shane asked.

"Good question," the colonel replied. "I guess we'll have to find out, won't we? How hard are these things to kill, do you think?"

"They're flying, sir," Cady interjected. "Hard to hit even if what we have can kill them."

"We don't have a clue what they're made of," Shane admitted. "It could be super unobtainium for all we know. No data at all, Colonel."

"I guess we'll have to gather some," the colonel said. "Major, I'd like to speak to you for a moment."

He put his hand on Shane's shoulder and led him a bit away from the staff.

"Did I put my foot wrong, sir?" Shane asked.

"No," Colonel Schon said. "Not at all. I wish we knew more, but that's like wishing this wasn't happening. No, it's about your mission. Could you define it for me, again?"

"To observe first contact, evaluate the threat and report," Shane replied. "Basically, we're an eyeball recon for the Neighborhood Watch team."

"Exactly," the colonel said, his face working as he considered his words. "So, when we first make contact with these things, what are you going to do?"

"Observe the effect of our weapons, sir," Shane said, confused.

"Major, every single unit that has made contact with these things has dropped out of the net shortly after first report," the colonel pointed out. "What does that tell you?"

"That they're pretty damned bad news, sir," Shane replied.

"What it tells me is that we're going to get butt-fucked," Colonel Schon said. "Fast and hard. I don't know how, but we will. And your job is to . . . ?"

"Get the word back. Why, sir?" Shane said, his stomach sinking.

"That's right," the colonel said. "Concentrate like fire on that mission, Major. Concentrate hard. Nobody, but *nobody*, has succeeded in it. And the United States *has* to know what these things are. How they fight. How *we* can fight them. I'm going to lose this battle, Major, sure as God made little green apples. Sending us here is pissing in the wind. My one and only hope is that while *I* may fail in my mission, *you* succeed. If you do, it *might* make losing my battalion, losing my troops, worthwhile. *Do not fail me.* Do you *fully* comprehend what I am saying."

"Yes, sir," Shane replied, swallowing.

"I didn't have many Humvees to spare," the colonel said. "I gave you that one for a reason. Use it."

"Yes, sir," Shane repeated.

"That's all."

"What was that all about, sir?" Cady asked when Shane waved him towards the Humvee.

"The colonel was clarifying our role in this battle," Shane said, sitting down in the passenger seat as Cady climbed in the driver's.

"And that is?" Cady asked.

"Master Sergeant, I don't often say this," Shane replied. "But when we make contact, you just obey my orders like lightning. Understand?"

"Yes, sir," the master sergeant said, uneasily. "I usually have a fair understanding of them, anyway, sir."

"Well, here's a portion of your commander's intentions," Shane said. "Keep a careful eye on how to drive the fuck away from here and get to someplace where we can make it back to the States. Or at least England. You work on that for the time being."

"And what will you be working on if I may ask, sir?" Cady said, trying not to smile.

"I'll just be sitting here and worrying like hell."

"Lieutenant Colonel, can you hear me?"

Ridley felt a searing pain in his left shoulder and decided

to lie still and pray it would go away. His head still hurt, badly, and he had quit trying to cope with the pain in his feet and toes more than ten or more hours ago.

"Bull! Can you hear me, sir?"

"If I open my eyes there had better be somebody there and this not be a hallucination!" Ridley said. He cracked his eyelids slowly, and instinctively tried to hold his left hand in front of them to shade his eyes. That didn't work. His left shoulder complained by sending a sharp twinge of pain through his upper body. "Fuck!"

"Sir, don't move until we know how bad you are," Rene said.

"Rene! I thought you were dead?"

"Uh, yes, sir, same goes for you. Although, you *are* the first survivor I've been able to find." Rene leaned slowly over Ridley and surveyed him. His helmet was cracked completely through all the way from the front of his forehead to the back of his neck. Rene separated the helmet and threw it aside. There was a tree limb about a half-inch in diameter sticking out of Ridley's left shoulder and his upper left side was covered in blood, but he didn't seem to be bleeding any longer. Rene slowly removed Ridley's socks. His left foot was swollen and likely broken and three of his toes on his right foot were turning brown and blue.

"You look rough, sir." Rene straightened and adjusted the makeshift sling around his left arm.

"Shit, Rene, you don't look so hot either." Ridley opened his eyes completely and waited for his vision to adjust. He wiggled his fingers on both hands and realized he had complete control over his right arm and hand. He moved both legs and wiggled his toes—that hurt like hell.

"I'm not sure you should move, Bull."

"Aw shit, just superficial stuff, I think." Ridley adjusted the way he was lying on the ground and then forced himself to a sitting position with his back to the tree. He rolled his neck left and looked at the stick protruding his left shoulder. "Reckon I ought to pull that out?"

"No, sir, I wouldn't do that. It might start bleeding again. From the looks of it you lost a good bit of blood from it going in." Rene sat down and leaned against the tree beside the lieutenant colonel.

"How bad are you, Rene?"

"Left collarbone is broken and I have some cracked ribs I think. My right knee is twisted pretty badly, but I can walk. My left eye is hard to keep open but I'm managing it."

"Yeah, you look rosy. I don't know if I can walk or not, but I can try if we need to." Ridley felt the stick in his shoulder and decided to leave it the hell alone.

"That's just it, Bull. I'm not sure where we would go." Rene sighed and closed his eyes for a moment.

"Any idea where we are?"

"Yeah, I think we're about eighty kilometers north of Bethune and maybe ten or twenty south of Calais."

"What about the aliens? You seen any since you been on the ground?" Ridley felt through his torn garments hoping to find water or an MRE or something—no luck.

"None. They all seem to have headed off to the east right after we went down."

"Hmmm. Hey, tell me something. Just how the hell did you survive that fall?" Ridley tried to grin.

"I was tossed into one of those things chest first. I bear-hugged it and hung on for dear life, until it crashed into the treetops. I fell from there. And you?"

"Hell if I know!" Ridley laughed and then grimaced in pain.

The two men rested in silence against the tree for a few minutes more. Ridley finally decided to test his strength and forced himself up to his feet. He could put all his weight on his right foot with pain that he could endure from his toes, which were mostly numb now. But his left foot would not support his weight for more than a few seconds without sending unbearable pain up his body. Ridley sat back down.

"Rene, you think you could tie a splint around my foot with that bum collarbone of yours?"

"We'll do what we can, sir."

Ten minutes later the two men were hobbling along through the woods of France, trying to make their way north toward Calais. They had been told that would be the rearward evacuation point for the attack. Ridley leaned heavily on the rough walking stick that Rene had found for him, but was able to walk slowly. At their present pace they figured to reach Calais in a couple hours, but with any luck they would find help long before that.

"No, sir, it doesn't sound good," the medic replied to Ridley and Rene's questions. "Everything I've heard so far is that all communications have been lost with the troops as soon as they make contact with the aliens. You two are the first survivors I've come across yet." Fortunately, the two of them had stumbled across a highway and decided to follow it. Before long, an evac convoy heading north to Calais came along and rescued them.

"That sounds about right, Specialist. We lost contact

with the AWACS long before we ever made contact with the boomerangs," Rene said.

"Boomerangs, sir?"

"That's what they look like," Ridley grunted. "Shiny, metal, and the shape of a fat boomerang about a meter or so across. The damn things ate our entire flight squadron of F-16s. The two of us are, as far as we can tell, all that's left of the NATO-Euro Falcons."

"Just sit tight, sir," the medic said, tying a last bandage in place. "They'll take care of you in London. I wouldn't want to mess with that stick if I didn't have to."

"There," Specialist Werry said, waving at the treeline. "What was that dot?"

Werry was twenty-two, with light brown hair cropped to stubble on the side, fair skin that refused to brown no matter how much time he spent under searing desert skies, and a scar on his cheek courtesy of an Iraqi improvised explosive device. His unit had been one of the last to leave Iraq and he found it odd that they'd been chosen to "show the flag" in France. Couldn't somebody *else* have been chosen to help out the French? Preferably somebody that didn't still, literally, have desert sand in his boots?

"What dot?" Sergeant Cordette asked. The light-brown infantry sergeant wasn't much older than the specialist but he had two extra tours of being shot at and blown up. In about a month he would have been trying to decide whether to end his second hitch and try the college and civvie route or reup and become a "lifer." But with the state of emergency the choice had been made for him. One less stress in life was fine by Eshraka Cordette. He was looking north and looked to the east as the specialist waved in that direction.

The two soldiers were forward of their company, holding down a look-out point a hundred meters towards the treeline. It could have been worse, but Cordette wasn't sure how.

"There was a dot," Werry said. "At about eleven o'clock. It just popped up then back down."

"I don't see," the sergeant said, shielding his eyes. Then he did. Everyone did.

His mind immediately identified it as a flock of starlings; that was sort of what it looked like climbing up over the trees. But it wasn't; starlings didn't fly like that. Starlings swooped and whorled as they flew. These things moved around within the . . . flock but their movements were erratic or responding to some pattern he couldn't identify. And the . . . swarm wasn't swirling as such at all. It was flying in a straight line for their position.

"Contact!" Cordette bellowed, dropping into the belly of the Stryker and swiveling the M240B towards the swarm of probes. "Open fire!"

Shane saw them even before the lead units, because of his slight elevation over them. He listened to the familiar rattle of M-4s and machine guns start up and watched for a moment to gauge their effect. Not damned much.

"You watching the tracers, sir?" Cady asked, not taking his eyes off the approaching swarm.

"Yeah," Shane replied quietly. You couldn't see bullets, of course, but you could follow the red lines of the tracers. They were approaching the swarm, and the probes were tight packed enough that some of them were going to be hit, but they would just . . . disappear.

And there wasn't much time to fire. The probes had seemed to be moving slow but they weren't. They were on the lead unit in less than a second after it had opened fire and they swarmed around the Strykers like bees attacking a wasp. Shane could see portions of the armor flying off and as it approached the probes it would . . . deform and then just *vanish*. Six or seven of the probes had stopped in the air over each of the Abrams and as he watched, the refractory metal, mostly depleted uranium, of the powerful tanks was peeling away like skin from a grape. A soldier, probably a medic, was running across the battle, if this massacre could be called a battle. As he did so a probe swooped down and he was suddenly decapitated then levitated into the air. His rucksack seemed to explode outward, his weapon flying up towards the probe along with bits from the ruck and LBE. Then the sodden corpse fell thirty feet through the air to slump to the ground.

Shane had only gotten a brief glimpse of all of this, fragmentary images, when one of the probes dropped right on the command Humvee. It had broken away from the swarm and seemed to ignore most of the vehicles around the Humvee, making a beeline for it. It was followed by a handful more. He saw Colonel Schon and Major Forrester along with the Humvee driver all similarly decapitated and levitated as the Humvee shuddered and began to dissolve.

Surprise is a function of the mind of the commander . . .

"Get us out of here," Shane said. "NOW!"

"What?" Cady asked, looking over at him.

"GO! Go west! Now!"

Cady put the Humvee in reverse, made a flying three-point turn, and headed down the road through the light industrial park.

"You know where we're going?" Shane asked, pulling off his dogtags and tossing them out the window.

"I don't know why they sent us here," Cady said, looking over at him as the captain similarly began tossing ammunition magazines out of the window. "But there's a . . . What are you doing?"

"I'll take the wheel," Shane said. "Start getting rid of every scrap of metal you have on your body, starting with your dog tags. Right NOW!"

Cady blinked, then relinquished the wheel with a blurted: "Holy shit!"

"Those things eat formed metal," Shane said, trying to steer the Humvee down the twisty road. "They ripped the dog tags off the colonel so fast his head went with them. We need to get rid of everything. As soon as one gets to us, we're going to unass this vehicle, too."

"We should call in," Cady said.

"They zeroed in on the command track," Shane replied tightly, as Cady took the wheel back and started tossing magazines out the window one handed. "Why?"

"I dunno," Cady said. "You're the brains of this outfit, sir."

"Radios," Shane snapped. "They eat metal but they zero in on radios. Unless you're radio silent you're just a big metal popsicle to those things." He popped open the hatch for the gun mount and climbed through.

"Keep pulling metal off your body!" he yelled, pulling off his watch and tossing it away. "Rings, necklaces, bracelets, watches. Like you're going through a scanner at security!"

"Coins!" Cady yelled back. "What are you doing?"

"Keeping an eye out for them," Shane yelled, emptying his pockets by the roadside. He thought about what other metal he had and then looked at his West Point ring. Graduates were disparagingly referred to as "ring knockers" because you weren't anybody unless you had "the ring." He contemplated losing it. Then contemplated losing a finger. The finger won. But instead of tossing it aside, he put it in the shoulder pocket of his digi-cam uniform. Even if they ripped it out, all he'd lose was a pocket.

The battalion had been obscured by the buildings but Shane could see a few of the probes up over them in the air now. As he watched, a building collapsed and he couldn't figure out why until he realized the damned things were ripping the rebar right out of the concrete walls.

Nails. Wiring. Cars. It was all going into those damned probes. Every damned scrap of metal. They didn't seem to be killing people except as a byproduct. But they would. Metal *was* civilization. And . . . one . . . three . . . more were headed for them.

"Pull over and unass!" Shane yelled, dropping into the Humvee and opening his door. He was rolling on the road before it was at a full halt.

So was the master sergeant, as it turned out, and the Humvee continued forward, still in drive, as five of the probes came up with a thunder of air. The Humvee began to shake and tear apart and the master sergeant let out a curse as he was jerked into the air. The seam on the seat of his pants ripped and his boots came apart as the eyelets were ripped out. Then he dropped through the air to land hard on the asphalt.

"Son of a BITCH!" Cady snarled, looking up at the probe, which was hovering not much above head height. His wallet was firmly attached to the underside.

As Shane watched, the wallet ripped apart and a bit of metal was briefly visible, then the wallet dropped through the air, just another scrap of useless garbage to the probe.

"My COIN!" the master sergeant raged. He looked around for a weapon and finally settled on a timber by the side of the road. "That was my battalion coin you BASTARDS!"

The master sergeant hefted the heavy construction timber and jumped in the air as the hovering probes drifted over them, apparently searching for more scraps of metal. The four by four hit the surface, hard, and rebounded leaving a large dent. The master sergeant cried out in pain as the timber vibrated in his hand and he dropped it.

The probe, however, shuddered for a moment, then drifted sideways. It shuddered again and then there was a brief burst of sparks and it dropped out of the air.

"Congratulations," Shane said, getting up from his crouch and examining the fallen probe with interest. "You've proven they can be killed."

As the master sergeant hefted the timber again, the remaining four descended on their fallen brethren. Before he could get in another whack they lifted it, whole, into the air and began to strip it apart. Shane could see bits flying off towards the other four probes but as they approached them the bits seemed to dwindle and then disappear. One thing he noticed was that the probes seemed to be getting . . . fatter. They were sleek boomerang wing shapes but as the fallen probe was disassembled they seemed to be getting more material on their surface.

As soon as the wounded wing was fully disassembled three of them flew away. The last one, however, continued to hover at about ten meters off the ground and Shane watched as it seemed to change shape. The center got thicker, the metal appearing to move inward from the wings towards its middle. Then a dimple appeared and the thing began to twin, joined wings stretching out from the middle, which got flatter and flatter. Finally, all that was left was a small joining between two of the probes and then that separated.

As soon as it did, the two flew away, ducking down to rip apart Shane's boots and shoulder pocket in passing. The stone from the ring dropped to the ground about fifty meters away, carried in a ballistic arc as the things accelerated to cruising speed in an instant.

"Bastards," Shane said, walking over to the stone. It was a synthetic ruby, all he could afford on graduation. He buffed it and pocketed it in thought. Rubies were nothing more than pretty aluminum dioxide. Either they didn't like aluminum or unformed metal . . . There was a thought there, but he wasn't sure what it meant.

"You were saying you had a plan for getting out of here?" Shane asked Cady distractedly.

"Well, I was *planning* on driving back to the airbase at Le Havre," Cady replied, tossing the four by four back to the roadside. He'd been holding onto it in case the damned things got lower. "But as a last ditch, it's all lost, go to hell plan, we're about five miles from where the Channel Tunnel comes out on this side. I figure that might be why they put us here; to defend the tunnel. If they're not to England, yet, we can run the thirty or so miles from one side to the other. Better than swimming."

Shane thought about the long tunnel, then about the things eating the very metal out of the walls. Flooding. Refugees. On the other hand . . .

"I don't have a better idea," Shane said. "Where's this tunnel entrance?"

Chapter 15

The Army standard for the five-mile run is forty minutes. Shane figured it had probably taken them somewhat less than thirty to reach the massive entrance. And that was with a stop at a devastated town to pick through a store for running shoes. Ones with no metal in them.

The channel tunnel was a miracle of modern English and French cooperation and engineering. The "Chunnel" in actuality consists of three tunnel-railroad connections that run under the English Channel, connecting Folkestone, England, and Calais, France. When the Chunnel was being constructed both French and English citizens had a fear of being so far beneath the water and there was a popular myth that the North Sea would collapse it and fill it in with disaster-movie effect. That myth was explained away once the public realized that the Chunnel was actually constructed beneath a *mostly* water-impermeable layer of chalk at 150 feet below the bottom of the English Channel seabed. The odds of water from English Channel leaking into the Chunnel were proven to be basically nill—that is unless structural integrity were lost in the super high density shotcrete reinforced regions of the tunnel.

The tunnels are 31 miles long with two rail tunnels, each 25 feet in diameter, and a central tunnel, 16 feet in diameter. The central tunnel is used for maintenance and ventilation. Two of the tubes are full sized and accommodate the various rail traffic. The smaller service tunnel has several "crossover" passages that allow trains to switch from one track to another. These connecting tunnels serve as emergency escape routes when necessary. In fact, they were used as refuge by thirty-one people as a safe haven during a Chunnel fire back in the late 1990s. The escape route system worked well and all of the trapped people survived. But the Chunnel escape system was designed for fires in sections of it, not for metal-eating alien probes swarming through the entire construct. Most likely, the cross-over escape tubes would only appear as that much more tasty metal for the bots to gather. Shane was considering what would happen to the tunnel's structural integrity when those bots started yanking metal support from the concrete walls.

The entrance, and indeed the entire track, was walled off by a high metal fence. It was proof positive to Shane that the probes hadn't gotten there yet that the fence was still standing. It was also a hell of a thing to try to cross.

Others, however, had had the same idea and already holes had been dug under the fence. There was only a trickle of people going through the holes and Shane and the master sergeant, apologetically, pushed their way to the front and through one of the holes.

As soon as they were in the tunnel, they began to run again, weaving in and out amongst the light crowd. There was a two-meter wide walkway on the north wall with a meter-and-a-half drop down to the railbed. About a hundred meters inside the entrance there was a door on the wall with an "exit" sign.

"Take that?" Cady asked.

"Clear enough in here," Shane said. "I've been on this thing, I know where it goes. But there's a spot up here about five or ten miles on where we'll have to do some climbing. Some sort of big cavern."

They saved their breath for running the rest of the way. They were among the few who were steadily running. Most of the rest looked as if they'd run as far as they could and now were just grimly determined to walk the rest of the way. But about a mile into the run, Shane heard the rapid pad of feet behind him and a man in running clothes passed them at a good clip. He was shorter than either of them, but he had long easy strides and easily outstripped them, disappearing back into the crowd ahead.

"Marathoner," was all Cady said.

"I never thought the Army running program would come in this handy," Shane replied.

Cady just grunted.

Shane had gotten well into the rhythm of the run. He was feeling good about that if nothing else; there was a mind numbing pleasure to just running. But dodging the people around them, young, old, male, female, mothers carrying their children, was a pain in more ways than one. Shane had seen civilization end in less than an hour. And even if these people made it to England, the Channel wasn't going to stop *this* invasion. Nothing would. Most of the people he saw around him were going to die. Of starvation. Of exposure. Of disease. At each other's hands. The fabric of society was going to crumble and with it everything that had kept these shocked people alive in a technological womb. The law of the jungle was here again and probably here to stay. Unless somebody, and he knew *which* somebodys he was thinking of, could figure out a way to *win*. At the moment, he didn't see one. But that was what the eggheads were *for*. All he wanted to do was get back to the States and dump it on them. Strykers and Abrams clearly weren't going to win this one.

As they got deeper into the tunnel they began to see vast condensation-covered pipes lining the walls, which radiated cold. Shane glanced at them and then at Cady and shrugged. He wasn't sure, but he thought they probably went through to the ocean high above. The pipes were steel and the concrete in the walls most undoubtedly had steel rebar in them. That was all he needed to know.

They passed through the French crossover tunnel, which was a bit of a pain, though uneventful. They had to hop over the train rails of the scissors crossing at the crossover point, which slowed their pace. The slowing of their pace and the widening of the crossover cavern allowed the few runners who were still pushing through to spread out a bit. It also gave Gries and Cady the opportunity to isolate themselves a bit from some of the other runners. Not that they did not want to help, but their mission was more important on the scale of helping humanity survive as opposed to helping a few humans survive.

Shortly after they'd gotten back into the rhythm of running, they began to see the first signs of organization since the battalion had been wiped out. A group of English soldiers in camouflage dress were clustered around one of the pipes, rigging it with explosives. The group of sappers were surrounded by guards who directed the hurrying refugees into the exit doors rather than let them continue down the walkway.

Shane and Cady slowed to a walk as they approached the soldiers and held up their hands as they walked forward.

"Please enter the car, sir," a British private said politely, gesturing at the open door. "Buses are being shuttled down to—"

"Bad idea," Shane said. "Private, I'm Major Gries with the Neighborhood Watch organization. I need to talk to your officer right GOD damned now."

"Sir, we're supposed to—"

"I said right *now*, Private," Shane snapped.

"Yes, sir," the soldier replied unhappily. "Sergeant!"

"Leftenant Porter," the lieutenant in charge of the demolition squad said, saluting the disheveled American major in ripped uniform and pink and blue running shoes. "Royal Sappers. Pleased to make your acquaintance, sir, but—"

"We don't have time, Leftenant," Shane said, saluting in return. "Do you have commo to higher?"

"Yes, sir, there's a phone—"

"Get me to it," Shane said. "And get ready to pull out. You do not want to be here even as we speak."

"Lieutenant Colonel Forsythe, Royal Engineers. To whom am I speaking?"

"Colonel, this is Major Shane Gries, Neighborhood

Watch," Shane said, sighing to finally be in contact. "Sir, you need to pull out your demo squads, right now, sir. We were present for the assault on the Stryker battalion as observers. If we don't make it, please *immediately* inform the Neighborhood Watch group that the probes simply *eat* formed metal and then reproduce. That is their only attack. But, sir, your men are going to die down here. The probes rip rebar right out of concrete walls and will *eat* those big pipes as soon as they find them, flooding this tunnel. And they're going to find this tunnel, soon, sir. They also pluck bullets fired directly at them right out of the air. They appear to ignore carbon—the master sergeant killed one with a stick. But, sir, this tunnel is about to start flooding as soon as one of those things finds a pipe. Sir, is this clear, sir?"

There was a pause and then a sigh.

"Thank you, Major, yes that is clear," the colonel replied. "My orders, however, are also clear. The pipes have to be rigged. However, I will give orders that you are to be brought to the surface as rapidly as humanly possible. And I will send on your observations. That is the first clear intelligence that we have gathered on their attack method. Did *anything* work?"

"Shooting them didn't, sir," Shane said. "There's a type of bullet I saw that might work, but . . ., sir, I don't have time for this, sir."

"Agreed, Major," the colonel replied. "Give me the leftenant."

"Was it bad over there, sir?" the private driving the truck asked.

The vehicle was a railway support truck that ran on

the rails of the bed. As they drove down the tunnel, Shane could see soldiers rigging pipes every mile or so. It seemed like overkill. And unnecessary.

"It defies description, son," Cady responded for him. "And I'd put your foot down if I were you."

"Why, Master Sergeant?" the private asked nervously.

"Because these things eat metal, Private Thorgate," Shane replied distantly. "And as soon as they get in the tunnel and find one of those pipes on the French side, it's going to flood. How well can you hold your breath?"

"Not well, sir," the private said, pushing his foot down. "Sir, all those sappers—"

"Are dead as yesterday's news," Shane replied.

"Oh fuck," Cady said, quietly.

Shane looked over his shoulder and could see lights going off behind them in a shower of sparks. But in the sparks he could see, as well, a wall of water.

"Floor it!" Cady yelled, pushing his foot down over the private's and shoving the accelerator of the truck all the way down.

"The sappers!"

"They're dead!" Shane yelled. "And so are we if we don't make it out of this damned thing!"

"Probes," Cady said, looking over his shoulder. There was no "driving" the truck; it was on rails. All you had to do was push the accelerator or the brake. The private had taken a look over his shoulder and made the decision not to try to use the brake.

Shane looked back and he could see one of them. But it seemed to be caught in the water rather than flying or . . . assimilating. As he watched it was slammed against the wall of the railbed and began to come apart like a child's toy. He got a brief glimpse of the interior, which was just so much metal bits. He also could see bodies being washed on the wave, which was still down in the railbed. Of course, so were they. And the bodies were being torn apart just like the probe. Some of them were civilians from the clothing, but others were in uniform. The sappers hadn't made it out.

The water got closer and closer despite the fact that the truck was hurtling along at well over a hundred miles per hour. But just as it seemed the water would catch up—it was less than thirty meters behind—they entered the broad crossover cavern and it spread out through the cavern, receding in the background as they started to climb up the slope to light and air.

They rocketed out of the mouth of the tunnel doing nearly a hundred and twenty and as soon as they were out Cady took his foot off the pedal.

"I'm getting damned tired of running away from these things," the master sergeant said, angrily.

"Then figure out a way to fight back," Shane said.

The C-130 lifted from London just as the probes began to spread across the English Channel. The giant cargo plane was filled with shell-shocked and wounded soldiers and civilians packed in as tight as they could fit. Gries and Cady made their way to the back of the plane, taking stock of the people on board and gathering intel from their stories. As they made it to the back of the plane Shane noticed in the dim lighting of the cabin a lieutenant colonel in flight gear with a bloody stick poking out of his left shoulder. The man looked like he had seen better days. Shane saluted him.

"Major Shane Gries, sir. This is Master Sergeant Cady."

"Lieutenant Colonel Matthew Ridley." Ridley half saluted the major and the master sergeant. "This Belgian fellow here is Flight-Lieutenant Rene Lejeune."

"Sir, if you don't mind my saying, you look as though you could use some medical attention." Gries nodded to the stick.

"Well, they promised to take that damned thing out in London, but I guess it's been in there for more than a day now so it can wait till we get to the States," the lieutenant colonel said dryly.

"What happened to you, sir?" Gries asked.

Ret Ball: *We have yet to hear any word from Europe. We can only pray that the NATO troops there are holding their own. Next caller, Frank from Albuquerque, you're on the Truth Nationwide.*

Caller: *Hi, Ret! The media is only coming across on local stations and over Internet broadcasts! My satellite dish gets no signal and my cable company only has the local channels active. I don't think the infrastructure is there any longer to get the news from around the world. Are we being pushed back to the pretechnology era?*

Ret Ball: *That is a really good question, Frank. Are we? What is the intent of this alien threat? Aha, Megiddo is on line two. Go ahead Megiddo, old friend, you are on the Truth Nationwide.*

Caller: *Hello, Ret. I've been listening to all of the military channels with my spectrum analysis equipment and I can tell you that the units that were deployed have stopped transmitting.*

Ret Ball: *How could you know that, Megiddo? The forces were deployed in Europe.*

Caller: *Oh that, I've been DXing by listening to signals bouncing off the ionosphere. I'm sure others out there have noticed this. Not long after the deployment there was plenty of encrypted communication taking place. But now . . . there is nothing.*

Ret Ball: *And why do you think that is, Megiddo?*

Caller: *I think it's obvious, Ret. Those units no longer exist; they have been destroyed.*

Chapter 16

"They wanted to keep you in Washington," Roger said as Shane settled into the chair in the hastily made conference room. The "core" of the Neighborhood Watch group was seated around the table, which was really a dining table, to debrief the two soldiers. "But we convinced them you'd be better utilized giving us the skinny directly."

"Thanks," Shane said, sighing. "I really don't want to be in D.C. when those things get here."

"I don't know where I want to be," Cady interjected. He'd gotten a new uniform and a new set of sergeant major's insignia to go with it. "Maybe on a mountain somewhere in a log cabin with some wooden farming implements."

"What's the word on England?" Shane asked, nodding at the sergeant major's comment.

"You made it out of England just in time," Tom answered somberly. "They crossed the Channel when your flight was still in the air. All contact has been lost with the south of England and it's spreading north. All of northern France, half of Germany, all of Belgium and the Netherlands are gone."

"Belgium, huh. I guess Rene will be staying with us for while," Shane said. Cady nodded in agreement.

"Who's Rene?" Alan asked.

"Long story, you'll meet him sooner or later, but he was one of the two surviving pilots of the northern aerial assault. He and USAF Lieutenant Colonel Ridley were both part of the NATO-Euro Falcons. They were on the plane with us from London. They were really banged up. I told him they should come visit us when they were better."

"They had a rough go of it," Cady added.

"Go ahead and tell us what you saw," Roger said, nodding at Shane and turning on a digital recorder. "Start from when you first saw the probes. When you're done, we'll get to the questions. We'll send the recording out on the net so everybody can get a look at it. There's not going to be any securing data from this point on; that decision has already been made. But you're the only people we can find who got an accurate look at the probes and made it back to tell about it."

Shane related the story of the fallen Stryker battalion and the flight through the tunnel, shaking his head as he did.

"I didn't want to just run away," he admitted. "But Colonel Schon made it pretty clear that that was my job."

"That's what he was telling you," Cady said, "when he drew you aside."

"Yeah," Shane replied. "That's what he was telling me."

"And he was right," Roger said firmly. "There's important stuff in what you just described."

"How long do you think it took those two to twin?" Tom asked. "It sounds like mitosis, just like a bacteria."

"I was thinking the same thing," Shane admitted. "It was just like watching a cell divide. I wasn't timing it but maybe thirty seconds, a minute. No more."

"How close did they get?" Tom asked, his eyes narrowed.

"What do you mean?" the sergeant major asked.

"How far away were they from the metal when they . . . sucked it up?" Tom expanded.

"Oh," Shane said, frowning. "Not far. They got down to within a meter or so when they were ripping apart the Humvee. I . . . you know, I never saw them . . . pull from farther away than a meter or two."

"They were right above head height when they attacked me," Cady said. "They seemed to stay down at that level most of the time when they were . . . searching, I guess."

"Two meters or so?" Tom said, nodding. "Interesting."

"You think the . . . what is going on with that?" Roger asked. "Tractor field?"

"Something like that," Tom said, nodding again. "Call it that for now. *How* is the sixty million dollar question. But it *appears* to be range limited."

"Yeah, point," Roger said, making a note.

"And they were only going for formed metal?" Alan asked.

"Yeah," Cady said. "But they went for everything. I mean, they were ripping the dog tags off so fast people were getting their heads cut off."

"No dog tags," Roger said, making a note.

"Way beyond that," Shane replied. "They ripped out everything. Wiring, torn-apart cars. And you should hear Lieutenant Colonel Ridley describe how they tore apart their F-16s."

"They really liked the armor on the tanks," Cady pointed out.

"Heavy metals," Tom said, nodding. "Makes sense. Heavy metals are going to be universally in short supply due to the way they're made."

"Well, all you need is a lot of heat, right?" Cady asked. "You sort of melt it and roll it out—"

"He means how the atoms are made," Roger said, smiling slightly. "Not how you form the metal. You know how atoms are made?"

"No," Shane admitted. "Does it matter?"

"If they need heavy metals it might," Roger admitted. "All atoms except hydrogen are formed by fusion. Two hydrogen nuclei fuse in a star to form a proton, a neutron, a positron, and a neutrino. This picks up another hydrogen nucleus running around and there you have it— helium. Our sun is currently in the proton-proton cycle. The lower weight stuff, up to iron, is formed just like that in other still fairly common regular stars that are in the CNO cycle. Uh, that is for carbon, nitrogen, and oxygen. These CNO stars are more massive than our sun. Above iron, though, it takes a supernova. So, the heavier the metal, the less likely it is to be produced. Some of them are more likely, on a quantum level, than others as well. But it makes sense that if they have to use certain materials in their production, reproduction whatever, that they'd concentrate on heavy metals."

"They like it," Shane said. "But they seem to go for

everything. I mean, they stole the sergeant major's battalion coin and my ring. They left the stone, though. It was a synthetic ruby."

"And that doesn't make a lot of sense," Alan pointed out. "Ruby's aluminum oxide. They were working with titanium oxide on the moon. Why use ores there and not here? I mean, there's *iron* in blood, lots of it. Why not rip that right out of our bodies?"

"They've got all this formed metal," Tom said, shrugging. "Why bother? And there's as much concentration of iron in soil as in blood. They might get around to strip mining iron out of the very soil in time, it sounds like they have the ability, but why bother? There's more iron in a knife than in the human body. They fed on the damaged probe?"

"Yeah," Shane said, nodding.

"And another one," the sergeant major interjected. "I don't know what happened with that. It was right after we were leaving the town. I don't think you saw it, Major. There were two of them attacking another one. Happened so quick I didn't bother to point it out and we were sort of hurrying at the time."

"Why?" Roger asked, a crease appearing between his eyes.

"Well, we'd just gotten new shoes . . ." Cady said, his face sober as a judge.

"No," Roger said with a sigh. "Why were they attacking it? Was it damaged?"

"It didn't look that way," Cady replied, smiling at having gotten a yank in on the eggheads. "They were all three flying along, but they took it apart like a lobster."

"That's odd," Tom said, frowning.

"That's what I thought," the sergeant major said, shrugging. "But they ate it."

"And they appear to be ignoring carbon," Roger said, making a note on the sergeant major's observation. "They need that for steel at least."

"It's everywhere," Tom said, shrugging. "And they don't need much since they don't appear to be using composites or plastics. They also appear to be ignoring silica. You mentioned broken windows scattered on the street."

"In the town where we got the shoes," Shane said, nodding. "They didn't really touch most of our gear. It was all screwed up, mind you. They'd even ripped open the MRE pouches, which kind of confused me until I remembered they had metal in them. But the plastic and cloth was all there."

"So how do we attack them?" Roger asked.

"Sticks," Cady said. "I'm getting me one of those staff things."

"Not a winning option, I fear," Shane pointed out.

"Bullets don't work," Cady said. "I think what was happening was they were just eating them out of the air. I don't know how, bullets go damned fast."

"They intercepted the Mars probe at somewhere around fifteen kps," Tom replied dryly. "That's much faster than any bullet, Sergeant Major."

"You know, that is interesting because Ridley said that the Sidewinders were somewhat effective and that the probes didn't pluck them out of the air as easy. He also said their guns were ineffective. Why would that be?" Gries asked.

"Don't know, we need to talk to him. But you know bullets don't maneuver and missiles do . . . hmmm?" Tom pondered and rubbed his beard.

"But they don't go for plastics," Alan said. "And they don't appear to . . . see a threat to them. The sergeant major hit them with a stick. Rubber bullets?"

"That's an idea," Roger said, making another note. "More."

"I was thinking about the sergeant major's wallet . . ." Shane said, then paused uncertainly.

"Go on," Roger said, his eyes narrowing.

"They picked it up," Shane went on, his eyes unfocussed. "Because there was metal in it. And I remembered thinking I wished it was a bomb . . ."

"They'd just rip out the detonator," the sergeant major said. "They're made of metal."

"But . . ." Shane said, still looking at the far wall. "What if you had say a slab of C-4 with a friction detonator in it. All plastic or whatever. Hell, a match with some gunpowder. Attach a sort of pin to it, something solid metal like the sergeant major's wallet . . ."

"They pick it up," Alan said excitedly, "pull the pin for you and . . . BOOM!"

"Okay, now we have a weapon," Roger said, making another note. "An anti-probe . . . mine?"

"Yeah, a mine," Shane said, nodding.

"You could throw them," the sergeant major said. "Slingshots . . ."

"Potato guns," Alan said, grinning. "I'm not sure you'd want a lot of velocity on them."

"Proximity detonators," Tom said. "If your tanks or whatever fired explosive rounds with proximity detonators, the probes would catch them in the air and blow up. You'd have to tinker with the timing, but . . ."

"Good," Roger said, making more notes. "This is good."

"Those super bullets," Cady said. "You said they were made from ceramic, right?"

"They can be made from metal," Roger said. "But they're usually ceramic."

"They won't intercept those," Cady pointed out.

"Put a bit of metal in them and they might fly right into them," Alan said.

"They'd probably try to match velocity," Tom pointed out. "Like they did with the probes. Our probes, that is."

"Be interesting to see them try," Alan replied. "In atmosphere."

"Ah," Tom said, nodding. "Good point. That's probably why they couldn't stop the Sidewinders."

"Directed energy weapons," Shane said. "Lasers. They're vulnerable. I don't see why you couldn't shoot them down with lasers."

"Technology hurdle there," Roger said but made the note. "And we're going to need *a lot* of whatever we use. We need to figure out how these things work. To do that, we have to capture one. Alive or dead. I'm not sure it matters."

"I wouldn't like to try to keep a live one," Cady said. "Dead . . . hit it with a stick. I'm telling you, we need a staff corps."

"We already have a staff corps," Shane pointed out, grinning. "The Chairborne Rangers."

"But the other ones just eat it," Alan pointed out.

"Get around that when the time comes," Roger said. "We need one for study."

"Capture one . . ." Shane said, his eyes narrowing. "You know what I was doing before you feather merchants roped me in, right?"

"Looking at wild-eyed projects?" Cady asked.

"And some of them were pretty wild," Shane said, nodding. "There's two I'm thinking of right now. One of them was Gecko-Man and the other was Coyote glue."

"Gecko-Man?" Tom asked, smiling. "Coyote glue?"

"They were both pretty screwy," Shane admitted. "Gecko-Man was synthetic gecko-feet skin. It sticks to just about anything. If you had gloves made of it you could climb right up a wall. You can stick it and then unstick it with a sort of rotational motion. Think super, stick-to-anything Velcro."

"I can see where you're going with that," Roger said, nodding. "Figure out a way to get them to stick it to them and attach it to something."

"Have to be a pretty strong something," Tom pointed out. "I'm not sure what the energy budget of these things is but they can fly into and out of a gravity well. That means one hell of a lot of pull."

"I wonder how resistant to electricity they are?" Alan asked. "Get them to stick to a live wire?"

"They'd just eat the wire," Cady pointed out.

"Coyote glue was really, *really* weird," Shane said. "DuPont had come up with it. One of those things like super putty. They were working on something else and got this. It's an adhesive, very sticky, but it's elastic as well."

"Like the Coyote gets his foot stuck and it pulls back?" Alan asked, grinning. "Tries to pull it off with his hand and gets the hand stuck?"

"Just like that," Shane said, smiling back with a nod. "It only starts to set when it hits air and it never really gets hard or dry. Just . . . stays sticky for a long time. They wanted to use it for a crowd control system. The current glue they use for that, if it gets over a person's face they suffocate. They were pretty sure they could tinker Coyote glue so a person could pull it away from their face but not get entirely away. But I was thinking . . ."

"Put out a trap with some of it," Roger said, nodding. "They get stuck to it. Like flies on a spider web."

"Energy budget again," Alan pointed out sourly, looking over at Tom. But Tom was clearly gone somewhere, with an abstracted expression on his face.

"Yeah," Roger argued. "But you can tinker that. Admix some high strength materials in it like Spectra 1000 fishing line. Give it a good foundation, just a big ass concrete slab."

"It's really elastic," Shane pointed out. "Really, *really* elastic. I could see one of these things, well, *pulling* really hard. And then getting pulled back just as hard."

"Okay, we've got some good stuff here," Roger said, nodding. "The probe mines—"

"And potato guns," Alan pointed out.

"And . . . low velocity kinetic bombardment devices," Roger said, writing carefully. "What's the status on Gecko-Man materials?"

"They're going to need funding," Shane said. "Fast and a lot. Hell, with all the money flying around they might have gotten it already."

"We're up on that," Roger said, nodding and making a note.

"Spring traps," Cady interjected.

"Say again?" Roger asked.

"The super Velcro," the sergeant major said. "Think about, oh, I dunno, a ball of this gecko stuff. With some metal in the middle and some sort of plastic spring thing or a bungee cord. The metal releases the plastic spring.

They pull it up, the spring goes off, they're wrapped in super Velcro. I'm not sure what happens then . . ."

"Bombs," Shane said. "They're tied to something. You name it."

"Spring traps," Roger said, making a note. "Proximity fuses. Coyote glue."

"They've got some high falutin' name for it," Shane said. "But that's what all the engineers called it."

"Ceramic scramjet rounds," Roger said. "Directed energy weapons."

"Staffs," Cady insisted. "Everybody gets a big stick."

"I've got a friend who's into that SCA stuff," Alan said. "I'll get you a good one."

"Thanks."

"Spikes!" Tom said, excitedly.

Roger and Alan just looked at him, used to the sudden apparent nonsequiturs, but Cady and Shane were clearly confused.

"Volleyball?" Shane asked. "Like hit volleyballs at them really fast?"

"No," Tom said. "Although it's a thought. Take some of your Coyote glue. Make a holder with a carbon fiber spike in it. Bait it with metal. Attach it to something strong, but not incredibly strong. Maybe put a capacitor on the spike. The probe grabs the bait, pulls away, can't, pulls harder, the attachment breaks, the spike goes through the probe and it's history. *Then* we study it."

"I can see that," Alan said. "We could get one to study that way, assuming we can keep the others off."

"Surround one of those traps with mines?" Cady asked. "Winner of the mine avoidance contest gets to be dissected?"

"If it's a small swarm that might work," Shane said. "As tactics if not strategy."

"Okay, I'm gonna write up the notes and send it to the working group," Roger said. "We'll have to see what happens on communications when they get here. This is even going to screw Internet communications."

"Oh, that's another thing," Shane said. "They zero in on RF. Anything broadcasting gets eaten. Fast."

"Very important note," Roger said. "Let's take a break while I get this out and then we'll come back and look at some of these ideas in more depth."

"You think any of this is gonna work?" Cady asked Shane as they filed out of the room.

"It'd take a miracle."

"It's gonna take a miracle," Alan handed Roger the latest CASTFOREM models that had been tailored to Gries's and Cady's debriefing information.

"Red consumes blue," Roger read the printout and sighed as he tossed it onto his desk.

"Yeah, it just took a little longer this time." Alan made a Jetson's car sound with his lips as he plopped onto Roger's couch and lay back with his hands behind his head and his feet propped up.

"What would you do, coach?" He glanced at his autographed picture of Coach Paul "Bear" Bryant on his office wall and muttered to himself.

Alan smiled in response. "He'd probably call for a run right up the gut."

Roger grinned and nodded in agreement.

"The problem with all these *great* ideas Alan, is scale." Roger toggled the Mathcad simulation on his laptop to calculate and then kicked back in his chair. He considered spinning his little desk gadget but thought better of it.

"What do you mean, Rog?"

"Well, Gries and Cady were thinking tactically about how to kill one or a few of these things. We need to kill *billions* of them. We need to be thinking strategically. And a potato gun just will not do it. Even the supersonic F-16s and missiles only made a microscopic dent in their population before being destroyed. That reminds me; get somebody making completely composite fast airplanes. Don't know how to power them, but get somebody on it." Roger shook his head at the graph that was drawing on his computer screen. Alan rose up and took his little notepad from his belt, grabbed the stylus, and jotted some notes down.

"Well, the ideas may only be a drop in the bucket or spit in the ocean, but it's a start." Alan shrugged as he continued jotting notes. "We can't just sit around and do nothing."

"Sure, but according to my calculations here, which consider death and growth rates of the probes, we would need a million potato guns with thousands of rounds each to keep up. Looks like CASTFOREM agrees with me." The temptation overwhelmed Roger and he decided to spin the little space shuttle gadget. He flicked it with his index finger and it went spinning.

"So, we make that many. And I've already figured that out. We don't use potato guns—well, maybe a few as larger grenade launchers. Instead we use paintball guns. Sarge and I've found three different manufacturers of them that can make canned air powered full auto systems that fire up to fifteen balls per second. The balls just have a liquid paint in them anyway so . . ." Alan paused and looked up from his PDA to see if Roger was paying attention. "So, we fill them with a high explosive. And here is the good part. I only had to come up with two very simple modifications to make them completely out of a carbon polymer material. No metal. And Sarge found one company—couple of enthusiasts really—that has a minigun that can fire nearly three hundred rounds per second!"

"That's good work, Alan. How long before we can get delivery on them?" Roger asked.

"Two weeks for the first thousand rifles and first hundred thousand rounds. But we're building up manufacturing capability at all the redoubts now that we know what we're dealing with. We'll have millions of rounds and hundreds of thousands of guns within a month and a half. The minigun needs more mods since it had more metal in it and the first twenty will be delivered in a month."

"Great, let's hope we have that long. Triple the efforts on that if you can. But we still need a Hail Mary play or a hook-and-ladder kick-off return to use if we're behind by a touchdown and only five seconds left on the clock." Roger was subconsciously upset with the fact that there would be no more SEC Football and his game analogies and euphemisms were starting to surface as a symptom. Others had symptoms of the under-siege society in other ways. God only knew how Alice's and John's little girls were handling it.

"Well, I'd say we're a couple of touchdowns back and its time to pray for the onside kick," Alan added to the analogy.

"I've been thinking about what Shane said about them

attacking the radios and the report of the AWACS going down and the probes hitting the Falcons when they went active. You know, they hit the probes around Mars and the Moon, which all had transmitters going. Sure we shielded the lunar probe good, but it was still radiating like a bastard out the back lobe of the antenna. Hmmm . . . what if they weren't taking out our eyes but were just hungry for radio?"

"Maybe, but that might just be a good way to accomplish knocking out our eyes." Alan pondered the radio emissions point for a second. "So, where are you going with this?"

"What if we took a nuke or some other BMF explosive and attached it to a huge radar transmitter? Or several distributed radars with a bomb each? We wouldn't kill them all but we might could contain their movements and reduce their numbers. Gries was telling me something about a so-called *killing field* tactic that comes to mind."

"Killing field, yeah, I see. Well, if they rebuild themselves with nanotechnology, blowing them up might be a bad idea," Alan replied.

"Would it really? Wouldn't the fireball vaporize most of the material or carbonize it? I'm asking here, I don't know."

"Well, you know what the Martian Manhunter said in that episode of *Justice League Unlimited*. The nanomachines would just get spread out all over the place and the threat would be spread that much further. Of course, that was just a cartoon. Who knows?"

"But what if they don't use nanotech to replicate?"

"Okay, I'll bite. But if they don't use nanomachines

what do they use?" Alan shrugged. "Tom was right a long time ago. We should've nuked Mars when we lost the first probe."

"We need some of these things to study."

"Mr. Sergeant Cady," Tina tugged sheepishly at the back of the large intimidating black man's shirt. "You walk fast."

"Hello, Tina. And it's Sergeant Major Cady. Just call me Top, like everybody else. That's really what a first sergeant is supposed to be called, not a sergeant major, but my troops are used to it. What can I do for you?"

"See I told ya, Dingbat." Charlotte punched her on the arm.

"Charlotte," Cady nodded at the other teenager, amused.

"Well, uh, Charlotte and I have been hearing all of you guys talk about these metal-eating alien robots. Is it true?" Tina asked.

"Well, I'm not supposed to talk about it, but don't you worry your pretty little head about it. You should talk to your mom and see what she will tell you."

"Well, I would but her and Dr. Fisher, you know Charlotte's dad," she nodded at Charlotte. "Well, they flew off to somewhere to build a new rocket or something. They won't be back for a few days and, well, we're worried about something."

"Oh, who is watching y'all girls?" Cady was surprised.

"Oh my God, Top. We're both fourteen years old, and surrounded by the Army, what could happen to us?" Tina held her hands in the air palms up and cocked her head sideways.

"Right, uh okay," Cady said, trying not to think about various songs he'd sung over the years. The answer was: a lot. "There are alien robots in Europe, on the Moon, and Mars and the other planets in the solar system as far as we know and they eat metal. Good enough for you? Nothing to worry about; we're all working hard to find a way to stop them. I need to get back at it."

"Uh, we were afraid of that." Tina smiled big at Cady and Charlotte pointed at her braces.

"Metal like this, perhaps?" Charlotte said as she pointed.

"Jesus Christ!" Cady realized her concern. Some of the horrible images from his and the major's trip to Paris of soldiers being decapitated flashed in his mind. What if a bot got close enough to pull the metal out of this poor kid's mouth? If the damn thing pulled the metal straight out of her mouth she would likely lose some teeth and have her lips, and tongue ripped to shreds. And what if she was facing the wrong way when the bots pulled the braces free? Cady had seen the damned alien things pull rebar right out of concrete; braces through a little girl's head would be nothing for them. And as far as he could tell, the goddamned machines would care less. Then it dawned on him, *Why didn't they take the fillings in MY teeth when they had the chance?* Cady remembered that the bots had not taken Gries' ruby at the same time. He also seemed to recall something about fillings being made of silver, tin, copper, and mercury. *Dog tags are stainless steel*, he thought. With all the dog tags and iron rebar around, the bots were eating buffet style and not getting to everything on the table—just eating the treats, perhaps. Sooner or later, Cady was certain, they would. The damned bots would eat every piece of metal on the planet, including the metal fillings in his teeth and the braces in the cute little fourteen year old girl's mouth in front of him. Goddamn heartless bastard machines!

"Come with me, girls." Cady about faced and headed back down the hall toward the major's office. "Jesus Christ!" he muttered again careful not to add further expletives in front of the teenagers.

"Roger, the sergeant major and I need a minute with you." Major Gries pecked on Dr. Reynolds' door and peeked in around the door frame.

"Can it wait, Shane? Ronny is breathing down my neck for a progress report to go to the President this afternoon." He looked over his laptop at the major. It had been some time since Roger had gotten plenty of sleep and he suspected it would remain that way for, well, years. He felt haggard and hated putting off his more real duties of interacting with the people working for him, but he was conflicted by the fact that he also wasn't going to turn in a half-assed report that was going all the way to the President.

"Uh, actually, I think this ought to be in your report." The major stepped fully into the doorframe and leaned his shoulder against it.

"Okay, what is it?"

"Sergeant Major," Gries turned away from Roger.

"Yes sir!"

"Bring in exhibit A, please." Gries half grinned but only at the theatrics. The thought of kids around the world having had their faces destroyed by these alien things really pissed him off. Though he and Cady had only seen

the aliens attacking military and only caught their interaction with a few civilians, he knew that countless kids
with braces and other medical metal implants must have
been tortured and killed by the damned mindless alien
robots.

"Exhibit A present yourself in front of Dr. Reynolds'
desk, please." Cady winked at Tina, who marched and
stood at attention in front of Roger's desk.

"What's up? Hi Tina." He leaned back in his chair,
amused at the parading teenager.

"Hi," she whispered while still at attention.

"Miss Pike, please smile real big for Dr. Reynolds,"
Cady instructed her.

"Roger that, Top!" She grinned as big as she could at
Reynolds.

Roger looked her up and down for a moment still side-
tracked by the report he was working on for Ronny, but
then it hit him like a ton of bricks. The report that Gries
and Cady had given him upon their return from the initial attack in Paris came foremost to his mind.

"Awww shit! I hadn't even thought of that."

"Mr. President as far as we can tell, most of the major
cities have been evacuated to redoubts and refugee centers in the Midwest plains and in the large expansive areas
that have no major infrastructure and are near lakes and
rivers and other water sources. All refugee centers were
built with wood, plastic, and other synthetic material construction and all personal vehicles were moved to locations
at least five miles from those encampments." The
President's national security advisor Vicki Johnson
continued through the President's Daily Brief or the PDB.

"Are they living with no power or other things that metals enable?" President Colby asked.

"No, sir. There are areas set up outside each encampment that are several hundred feet below the ground. Hopefully, the bots will not find the underground locations before we can figure out a way to beat them back. The Neighborhood Watch group also believes that the cities will be enough bait for them to keep them busy for a little while. All of these underground locations have modern facilities, wireless and wired Internet, ice machines, laundries, hospitals, and so on. The problem is that the number of refugees at each camp far exceeds the amenities and capabilities within each of the underground facilities. So a rationing and sharing protocol has been put in place."

"That's right, Mr. President," General Mitchell agreed with the NSA. "We have implemented the largest evacuation and survival center in distributed locations across the country and the U.S. territories in the history of mankind. It has taxed every service, civilian, and military, beyond their limits, but we believe we can survive a full occupation for an extended period of time."

"Are all of the people out of the cities and in either the redoubts and refugee camps . . . refugee camps, God Almighty I hate that term." The President sipped at the coffee mug before him. He paused and looked at it. It had been his favorite mug: he'd kept it on his desk in the Oval Office. The mug had a picture of the White House on it and the official seal of the President of the United States of America etched in it. Across the presidential seal was etched the autograph of all four of the currently living former presidents. He couldn't stand the fact that the White House—the entire country—would be occupied by an outside threat during his watch. *What would they have done?* he wondered as he considered the names on the mug.

"Well sir, many are. Those that didn't go to the official centers decided to chance it on their own and fend for themselves. Some stayed behind in the cities. Some have become nomadic, and some have moved to the various desolate and unpopulated regions of the country. Dr. Reynolds calls them Farnham's Freeholders for some reason. He has also created some models that have tried to estimate their numbers. He guesses between five and fifty million citizens are Freeholders." Vicki closed her notebook, which usually signaled the President that the PDB was coming to an end.

"Is that all?" President Colby looked around the War Room at his advisors.

"No sir, there is one more thing. Dr. Guerrero and Dr. Reynolds have brought to our attention—" Vicki crossed her hands over her notebook in front of her and sighed. "There are estimated some seventy-five million people in the United States under eighteen. At any given time about a third to a half of those have orthodontic braces of some sort. Add in Americans older than that with orthodontic braces and then those with some sort of surgical metal implant, we end up with between fifty and a hundred million Americans that have metal physically attached to them somehow . . ." She paused to see if the president was catching on. He was.

"God Almighty! We've got to get those damned things off every single one of those kids before those damned alien machines get here! Oh Christ, how many kids must've been killed or maimed in Europe?" The President put his face in his hands and began to weep. Then he wiped his eyes, stood, and pounded his right fist into his left hand, "Vicki, you do whatever it takes to take care of this. This takes first priority over everything we're doing. If we can't protect our children, then Goddamnit what use are we!"

"Roger, the President wants to know what is happening worldwide. Our over-the-horizon radar doesn't seem like a good idea. All aerial missions we've sent have been completely lost. The only real recon we've received is from Major Gries, Sergeant Major Cady, and the two pilots who survived the disaster in France. Oh, we've put together reports from the many survivors but a lot of those accounts are jumbled and don't really include much useful intel beyond what we got from Major Gries."

Ronny sat in his makeshift headquarters office at the Huntsville redoubt. The accommodations were about the same as the office he had had in Virginia before the major cities were evacuated. Instead of moving him to the CIA redoubt in Langley, the President had ordered him to stay with his Neighborhood Watch team that had served so well to this point.

"I understand that, Ronny. I've got the guys working on just how in the hell to get aerial or space recon without metal and radio. That's not an easy task, mind you." Roger squirmed in the leather guest chair making it squeak as he did.

"Could we build a nonmetal refractive telescope and nonmetal film camera?" Ronny asked.

"Sure, we could even build the camera with a clever

plastic spring-wound timing system. The optics on the telescope would be heavy, though. Most of the glasses would only work worth a damn in the visible spectrum. Infrared would be possible with some glasses and the right film. The wavefront error would be horrible without being able to put a deformable mirror or tip-tilt corrector in there to take out atmospheric distortion." Roger thought out loud while removing his ball cap and rubbing his fingers through his hair.

"Yes, yes, Roger. But could you do it? Fuzzy images would be better than none." Ronny rested his elbows on his big metal desk as he steepled his fingers together and leaned his chin on them.

He laughed to himself at the thought of all the metal inside the redoubt. In the wiring, the computers, the monitors, the structure, and even the furniture. He considered that ironic or crazy; old construction habits must be hard for the corps of engineers to break. But at the same time he knew that if the redoubt fell a metal or a plastic desk would make no difference.

"Sure we could. How do we get it up and back is the question."

"Perhaps we should learn from history, heh?" Ronny smiled.

"What do you mean?"

"KH-1 through KH-7 ring a bell?"

"KH-1 through 7," Roger mouthed. "Hmm, KH is Keyhole, oh, sure the Corona project, but . . . heh." Roger knew exactly where Ronny was going with the comment. Corona was the first spy satellite program. It was a little satellite that was launched into a decaying low Earth orbit. The little satellite had a camera in it that snapped a bunch of pictures on a timer and then it fell back to Earth. The camera box was caught by a big net that was pulled behind an aircraft. Roger knew that aircraft were out of the question, but parachutes or something similar might work.

"I thought you would get it." Ronny laughed. "How do we get it up and back?"

"A rocket with completely composite components and mechanically driven guidance systems with no metal, no radios. The satellite takes a couple orbits worth of photos and plummets back to Earth. We use an air pressure gauge to release a chute with all-composite parts and then we just go pick up the film canister." Roger started running the idea through the design process in his head. The last two missions had made him very sharp with the process and he was already thinking about the mission components.

"Can we do it?" Ronny asked.

"We can do it. I better get to work." Roger ran out of Ronny's office, looking for Tom Powell and John Fisher.

"Good lad." Ronny leaned back in his chair and sighed.

Dr. Richard Horton rummaged through the antechamber of the old copper mine looking for his RJ-45 connector crimping tool. He had sworn that he had set it on top of the spool of Category-5 Ethernet wire that he had brought with them.

"Is dis vat you are looking for?" Helena asked holding up a coaxial cable crimping tool.

Richard paused for a second to take in her sexy thick Russian accent before responding to his very young and very beautiful wife. He had found her a year before on RussianWives.com. It had only cost him sixty-three hundred dollars and a plane ticket to pick Helena Terechenkova from the catalogue and fly her to the States. Getting a lawyer to straighten out the paperwork had taken another two thousand. After staying with Richard Horton for three weeks, Helena decided that he would do and married him. That translated into: living with Dr. Horton was less of a hell than living under the oppressive thumb of the drug lords in the bad part of St. Petersburg. Richard could care less why she stayed; just that she stayed and married him was enough to satisfy him. The occasional treat of sex with Helena made it more than satisfying, at least for him. From Helena's standpoint, the sex was worth getting out of Russia—but just barely. She knew that Richard Horton meant nobody any harm and that he was a nice person, but besides that he was a crazy conspiracy nut, which meant that they moved around, used assumed names often, and lived in the oddest places. Helena tried to tell herself that his paranoia was just *entertainment*.

Entertaining or not, he eventually got on her damn nerves. Had aliens not come to take over the world, she would have probably left him. But for now he seemed like her best bet for survival. Who knew, he might even eventually grow on her. That part was unlikely, but Helena was a survivor and she was going to make the best out of the situation—no matter what.

"Sorry, dear. That's for crimping connectors onto television cable. We're looking for the crimping tool for putting one of these onto this." He held up an RJ-45 Ethernet connector and the frayed end of a piece of Ethernet cable.

"Oh, dat one, yes I seen it over dere," Helena pointed

to the tool box sitting on the tailgate of the pickup truck parked in the entrance to the mine.

Richard walked over to the truck, stumbling over several other packs and boxes on the way, and stopped to kiss Helena on the cheek. Helena smiled and squirmed a bit from the roughness of Richard's long, unruly, graying beard.

"You should shave dat ting."

Richard ignored her and made his way through the tools in the truck until he found what he had been searching for. The little blue crimping tool was there and finally he could get back to running the network on his equipment. Just in case he needed another tool once he got down to the bottom of the mine shaft he slung the little backpack shaped toolbox over his shoulder and snapped the restraining strap around his waist.

"I'm going back down, you coming?" Richard grabbed the hundred-foot spool of Ethernet wire.

"*Nyet*, it's too dark down dere right now. I tink I'll drive back up to the cabin and make some dinner. You vant?"

"Maybe in a few hours. I've got a lot to do today."

"I still don't see vhy you don't go vireless." She brushed her long black bangs off her soiled forehead. "I vill go down . . . go into the cave . . . when you get finished."

"Suit yourself, but wireless would probably not be a good idea," he said.

"Why is dat?"

"The alien probes use it." Richard shrugged and started the long winding half-mile trek to the bottom of the mine.

Although he had already been working on the mine for months, it was just now becoming a true shelter with real necessities of life. He had lined all the shafts with touch-on battery operated lights—the kind you could buy at the hardware store for a few dollars each. He had placed them about every fifty feet or so and had strung low-voltage rope lights between them to mark the walking path.

He followed the path deeper into the mine for another quarter mile or so before he had to stop and shift the weight of the spool of cable to the other arm. He started rolling off his list of things to do out loud to himself.

"Okay, let's see, first I need to connect the waterwheel to the torque control circuit and the optical encoders to the laptop. Then I can control the gearing mechanism electronically." He adjusted his headlamp with his right hand and nearly dropped the cable spool on his foot. "Shit!" He caught the spool just in time.

Several times in the past he had considered buying an electric four-wheeled vehicle to carry equipment up and down the shaft to the shelter, but it was either the four-wheeler or a spectrum analyzer. Then it was either a four-wheeler or a computer-controlled waterwheel—batteries or gas-powered generators just weren't going to do. It was unlikely that the waterwheel would put out enough power continuously for him to operate the equipment and life-supporting things he needed, but it was his best shot.

Then it was either the four-wheeler or digital microscope setup. Then it was the four-wheeler or a very fast digital oscilloscope card. Then it was the four-wheeler or the Bell jar and vacuum pump. Then he started entertaining the idea of putting together an electron microscope down there, but that would be heavy and he'd probably need the four-wheeler just to haul it down there. The electron microscope would be too expensive just then and would require a more *creative* funding source—maybe later. So he decided on a mass spectrometer. Then it was a well-equipped chemistry lab, including stills, condensers, centrifuge, and such. And so on. Richard just could not force himself to sacrifice a piece of scientific equipment because he didn't like the long walk down the shaft. After all, he could only generate so many credit card numbers a month without getting caught. And he didn't want to get his proverbial red wagon fixed.

But at the same time he wished he had his little red wagon with him. What he had been doing was pulling a beefed up heavy duty RadioFlyer filled with the stuff up and down the mine shaft. But he had forgotten and left it at the bottom of the shaft on the last trip down. He continued to wrestle with the idea of buying that four-wheeler.

"The uninterruptible power sources are already connected to the generator, but the UPS diagnostic is Ethernet and goes from there to the hub." He continued talking his plan out loud to himself. "Right. Then it goes from each of the computers and the printer to the hub. Let's see, there're three computers, a printer, and the scanner, oh and the eight different Internet wires from the river . . ." He ticked off the list.

Richard had searched for a month to find the most secluded and deep underground Internet service providers in the area that ran close to the river that wound through the mountains. He found one switching hub from the phone network at the edge of the town just below the mountain. He found a server that was operated from a small service provider a few miles up river on the other

side of the mountain. He found two different cable/
Internet companies that had brought high speed wireless
up the mountain along with digital cable. One connection he hacked into ran beneath a power line that ran
across the mountain ridge on the other side of the valley.
Two ran from Park Ranger stations at either end of the
river on each side of the mountain. His final and perhaps
most robust connection was to an abandoned SCADA
network running the old railroad system that wound
through the mountains. Richard expected it to be the most
likely system to survive.

SCADA, or Supervisory Control and Data Acquisition
systems, weren't actually full control systems or Internet
connections. Instead SCADA systems were typically designed for use on the supervisory level. Fortunately, most
supervisors would rather use Internet connectivity and
simple browsers to supervise such systems. It was just
easier for them.

Richard knew that the good thing about SCADA control systems was that they were basically all software that
had been overlaid on top of a networked hardware system. SCADA was a fairly common and commercial
approach that used COTS devices that could be inter-
faced and programmed easily. Their robustness and
versatility had made them quite popular as the program-
mable logic control system of choice since early 2000.
Not only were they used for railroads and factories,
SCADA systems were ideally suited for any large manufacturing facility that had thousands of input/output
interface requirements, such as car manufacturing plants,
nuclear plants, power generation and transfer plants, and
even some airport systems.

Unfortunately, the only one that came near the Appalachian Mountain chain that Richard could find was the railroad system. It was easy enough to hack into since there was little need for network security from bears and raccoons. Most of the older SCADA systems ran on DOS, VMS and UNIX; this one used UNIX. Richard spoke UNIX just fine. So he hacked in and got connected and then only had to drag a line back to the river, then through an access shaft to the mine. The portion running up to the access shaft was pure optical cable, so the bots should leave it alone.

Thus Richard had eight different routes to gain Internet connectivity. Once he had identified his closest Internet service provider locations, he either set up accounts or hacked into the cables. Mostly he hacked into the systems by splitting the cables at junction boxes. Where he could get line of sight he set up lasercom relay systems to the river and then he dropped cable downriver to the mine. This all sounded simple, but it actually involved several months of very tedious and sometimes clandestine work. He also found that he had to run power cables up to the edge of the river to power the lasercom systems. Fortunately, he only ended up using three different lasercom routes and was able to drop cable all the way from the other six connections.

Bandwidth was his big problem. He knew the long drops would only supply low bandwidth connections. He hoped to mitigate that with a couple of different approaches. The first was to multiplex the eight different connections, thus effectively increasing his bandwidth by sending IP packets out sequentially on dynamic IP addresses. This would help some.

The other way he planned to increase his bandwidth was by placing a big amplifier at each end of the connections. Under normal circumstances the companies would have eventually found the hacks, but nothing about nowadays was normal. Richard was planning on the companies basically dropping out of customer service and such matters altogether. So looking for hacks would be low on their lists of things to do. And if they did find them all, which he doubted, he would fall back on bursting transmissions through the amateur radio repeater networks. But there was still something nagging him about that.

Thinking about the repeater networks made him subconsciously look at the rope light to make sure the coaxial cable from the radio transceiver antenna was still running along beside it. It was. As a last ditch effort he could use the amateur radio network to com-municate and connect to the world. But he was not even going to turn that system on if he didn't have to. Radio . . . he still wasn't sure, but there was something about radio that made him nervous. Radio and telecom seemed to be the first thing to go at Mars, the Moon, around the planet. Was there something about radio? Most all telecommunications that were left on the globe now were over the Internet. There were occasional burst transmissions of radio sent from Australia, South America, parts of Africa, and still here in the United States, but they were limited. As soon as he got set up, he was going to do a full analysis on the RF spectrum and see if he could figure that out.

He continued to talk himself through his things to do and after about eight minutes of walking he finally made it to the entranceway to the shelter. He shined his light up and down the walls of the mine shaft at the doorway he had built. He was quite pleased with his handiwork. He was somewhat displeased with the empty red wagon parked beside the doorway. Richard punched in the code on the cipher lock and pushed the door open. He tapped the battery-operated light by the door and illuminated the front room of his shelter

The front room was nothing more than a section of the mine shaft about fifty feet long. There were three other shafts on the right side of the main section and one on the left. Between the shaft entrances on the right were plastic garage storage shelves with every inch of space filled judiciously with plastic storage bins, cardboard boxes with various item titles handwritten on the side in marker, and various other hardware and supplies.

On the left side of the main tunnel were more shelves and some folding tables. On the folding tables were a coffee maker, a microwave, a hotplate, a blender, and a toaster oven. There were folding chairs placed in front of the tables. Near the entrance to the left-side shaft was also a large plastic shop sink. There was a plastic gallon container with a pump dispenser top marked "antibacterial soap" sitting on a shelf beside the sink. Two one-inch pieces of PVC pipe ran up the mine wall behind the sink and turned down the left-side wall of the entranceway to the shaft on that side of the main room. Alongside where those pipes entered the shaft were several other one-inch PVC pipes that came out of the entranceway and ran across the top of the shaft and over to the other side entrances. A green garden hose ran out of the bottom of the sink, then along the bottom side of the shaft and out the left side. There were several other garden hoses meeting at that left-side entranceway.

On the other side of the shaft entrance—the one on the left side of the main chamber—were several bundles of Cat-5 cable and several very thick high amperage electrical power cables running along the corner of the wall. Richard tapped another couple of battery powered lights and followed the left shaft.

About twenty feet down the shaft the sound of running water became overwhelming. Richard continued to tap lights on the wall of the shaft. He had placed them much more densely in this tunnel. Under most of the lights were more folding tables with various pieces of equipment stowed in boxes. There were also a few large plastic bins stacked on top of each other. On the left side of the shaft, about half the way down it, a PVC pipe ran into a sixty-gallon water heater. The inflow pipe to the water heater continued down the hall with the rest of the pipes.

There was also a five-shelf plastic garage storage rack on the right side of the shaft with router and switching hardware. They were not powered presently. Eight coaxial cables came in to the hardware from further down the shaft. Several Cat-5 cables were connected to a bank of hubs. The Ethernet cables then ran back out toward the way he had come in.

Finally, he reached the end of the shaft at an old rusty metal pier and ladder. The PVC pipes all connected into a string of tees that were converted to two-inch PVC that was then converted again three different times until it was finally an eight inch pipe that ran upward alongside the ladder. The large pipe was zip-tied to the ladder. The bundle of coaxial cables wound around the pipe and upward.

He stepped out on the pier and shined his light across

the large underground chamber. The chamber had to be at least thirty feet across in any direction and at the bottom, which was another twenty feet below him, was a small freshwater pond that was several feet deep in the middle. He knew because he had surveyed it several times with snorkeling gear. In the light there was a flash of silver as the small trout he'd stocked reacted to his presence. People meant food to the little trout. When they were larger, the reverse would be true.

The rushing water was very loud in the pond chamber because a small underground stream flowed from thirty or more feet above over a falls into the pond on the left side. The stream flowed from left to right and went out somewhere under the rocks on the far end of the pond. There was very cold spray that misted the area near the ladder and pier. The cool mist and the rushing water sound were quite tranquil and sometimes Richard would just sit in the folding chair on the pier for hours and relax. But today, he had a lot of work to do.

He climbed the ladder to the metal pier above him where his waterwheel and generator assembly sat. The main eight-inch PVC water line and the coaxial cable bundle ran up to the edge of the falls to the bottom of a large galvanized metal hundred-gallon animal trough. The Internet cables split off and disappeared into the water. The trough was positioned in such a way that part of the falls fell into it and it was full and overflowing. This is how he ran water through the mine.

The waterwheel was positioned in the middle of the falls and the axle, slip-ring connectors, and control circuitry wires ran out along the periphery of the axle to the power conversion unit sitting on the pier. Richard tapped the lights on that pier level and set about running the Ethernet wires. In the dim lighting it was tedious work.

After a few hours Richard had the waterwheel spinning free and the clutch being controlled by a laptop in the main chamber. He activated the system and a rechargeable battery powered gearbox slipped the main drive of the waterwheel into gear. Richard watched the UPS units against the wall of the main chamber eagerly. After a few seconds the little green lights on the front of the boxes kicked on and then the chamber lit up.

The fluorescent lights hanging from the ceiling of the chamber hummed to life and Richard could hear the refrigerator compressor kick on. The microwave beeped and a video tape ejected itself from the VCR that was set up in the end of the main room where Helena had established a "living room." There was an inflatable couch and chairs set, a small folding coffee table, and a small entertainment stand. The entertainment stand housed a stereo, a VCR, a DVD player, a Playstation2 and a nineteen-inch color television. All of which came on and were blinking *12:00 AM* on their respective displays.

A few more hours of connecting systems and checking Internet and file-sharing protocols and he was too tired to think straight. Then he looked at his watch and realized it was pushing eleven PM.

"Oh God," he said looking at his watch. "I better hurry or I'll miss it."

"Hurry up, Charlotte or you're going to miss it!" Tina said loudly in Charlotte's ear as she looked over her shoulder at the computer monitor.

"Dingbat, the show lasts four hours. We're not gonna

miss it." Charlotte giggled and shook her head. "There we go." The speakers chimed on and the RealPlayer software finished setting itself up.

"I know that, geek-brain. But I like how it comes on. I hate missing that part." Tina punched her friend on the shoulder.

"Okay then, shhhh. Here it is."

Ret Ball: *Welcome friends across the country and those across the world who can still hear us through the wonders of the World Wide Web. I know that we have lost contact with most of Europe and our prayers go out for those folks and for the rest of humanity. Although there are phone lines still working in this country, they're mostly overwhelmed with emergency services. If you can manage to call in, we will take your calls. Also, now we're set up for the real-time online audio chatting as well as using instant messaging. So we're still on live with you and can still hear from you. God bless us all and let's get to the Truth Nationwide! Caller one is talking to us online from New York City. Go ahead, Mike, you are on the Truth Nationwide. . . .*

Chapter 17

"Mr. President, this is Dr. Carolyn Mayer from the National Security Agency's ELINT branch. She has compiled some information that we thought you would want to see," Vicki Johnson said as she introduced the forty-three year old blonde analyst to the President and the secretary of defense.

The two men had been in the War Room looking over possible defensive and offensive strategies in the event the probes made it to the U.S. That would happen soon enough as far as anybody could tell, but with no recon on the situation in Europe nobody had a clue how bad the situation was. There were no orbital platforms and it appeared that the aliens were enforcing a no-fly zone over most of the Atlantic and eastern Eurasia. The Americas still had air travel below thirty thousand feet—nobody had tried to go higher. Naval boundaries seemed to be about the same. Anything traveling eastward past about the forty-five degree latitude line was never heard from again.

The President looked up at the NSA and the pleasingly plump lady she had brought with her. He always found the diversity of individuals who came together in times of crisis to be intriguing. This young lady could have been a model for an oversized-women's clothing store, not a black-program analyst.

"Nice to meet you Dr. Mayer. This is Secretary Stensby." He motioned to the secretary of defense. "What is this all about, Vicki?"

"Dr. Mayer," the NSA motioned for the analyst to begin.

"Uh, right. Here, Mr. President," Carolyn said. She pulled out her laptop and toggled to a map of Europe. "Here is where the probes have gotten to."

The map of Europe was a standard map package with an overlay of red growing on it. The red blotch covered all of Western Europe and even had spread to Iceland. On the eastern side of the region the red covered parts of Russia all the way from Rostov in the south to St. Petersburg in the north. Stockholm and Helsinki were red also. Due south, all of Morocco, Algeria, Tunisia, Libya, Egypt, Jordan, Syria, and parts of Saudi Arabia were red.

"How do you know this, Dr. Mayer? We've been trying to get recon for weeks with no luck. About all we can discern is the no-fly zone." The SecDef shrugged his shoulders in disbelief.

"Right. Well, you see, before all of this it was my job to track Al Qaeda operatives using electronic intercepts. Most of that has been using Ferret satellites, but I specialized in Internet communications. I spent the better part of the last four years finding and geolocating every Internet hub and router and every webcam in existence around the world. Oh, I only made a drop in the bucket, but I made a pretty good map of the world and had several known routers and webcams per region." Dr. Mayer paused for a second and toggled some keys on her laptop.

"I see, so how does this help us now?" The President looked over at the painting on the wall behind his desk in the War Room. He missed the Oval Office. He missed being above ground and he hated all this hiding and waiting.

"Ah yes, it's actually kind of simple, Mr. President. This map of red is a map of lost Internet routers, hubs, power grid stations, phone hubs, webcams, etc., all compiled into one graphic. I've even got several images from many of the webcams before they failed. Here." Carolyn turned the laptop back around for them to see.

"What is that?" the SecDef asked.

The President nodded.

"It looks like a battleship aground."

"Well, actually it's one of the aircraft carriers that we've been missing from the Mediterranean. And if you look here in the background you'll notice the Coliseum." She paused to let that sink in.

"Rome! These things have picked up an aircraft carrier and set it in Rome!" SecDef Stensby was stunned. "What on Earth for?"

"I don't know, sir. I'm a data collector and analyst not an exoroboticist. But this is just one image. Look at this one." Carolyn tapped the touchpad button.

"Hundred of ships, airliners, trucks, and cars and God

knows what. It looks like a junkyard," the NSA said. "And from this image the landscape can't be identified. I've tried."

"Then where is it, Dr. Mayer?"

"It's Cairo, sir. This is a webcam that used to have the Pyramids in view. They're still there probably, just under a mountain of junk," Dr. Mayer said.

"Jesus Christ!" the SecDef and the President chorused.

"Vicki, has the Neighborhood Watch seen this?"

"Not yet, Mr. President."

"Get her down there. And I want a real-time feed of this map right here in this room. Hell, I want it in a similar room in every redoubt across the world."

"Right."

"They've spread too far to nuke now, Mr. President." Jim Stensby sat back in his chair looking at a printout of the map. Technicians were hard at work putting together a real-time version of the analysis for a display console.

"You and I know that, Jim. And besides, we don't know if the people are still alive there or not. Nuking was never, *is* never an option until we know where all the people are." President Colby shook his head at the map. "What the hell do we do now? What about the plan developed by the Joint Chiefs to have a firewall of nukes set up on each side of the country?"

"The contingency is set in place, sir. If the probes cross the sixty-degree lat line moving west we'll fill the sky with nuclear airburst. If they cross the one-hundred-fifty degree line moving east we'll do the same."

"Do you think that will work?"

"Perhaps the first time, Mr. President. It might be a good tactic to buy us time. Without destroying the majority of them around the globe though, I'm not sure what good it would do. And like you said, what about all the people there? Like in France, are they still there? Are they still alive? Have all of the survivors resorted to cannibalism like the recon team discovered?"

"Right. Those poor people . . ." the President muttered.

"Well, let's pray the eggheads come up with something before the Chinese or the Russians or the Indians or whoever decide they're threatened enough to start setting off nukes willy-nilly," SecDef Stensby said.

"I've relayed my concerns to the UN Security Council on several occasions but I'm not certain they listened. I'll resend a message across what is left of the world hot lines again with my concerns here." The President felt somber and was not sure of the chances that even if the message went through to the remaining world leaders that it would *get* through to them. "I just wish we knew more about what is going on around the world."

"Okay, Ronny, this should give us a better idea of what is going on around the world." Roger Reynolds, wearing a clean suit and latex gloves, sat what appeared to be a miniature model of a satellite about the size of a coffee can with small solar panels wrapped around it on the clean room table—the culmination of about seven weeks of work.

"How so, Roger? This looks like it would be any other satellite when it's built. Why won't the probes eat it, too?" Ronny adjusted the paper bonnet on his forehead so it would be more comfortable.

"This is so cool," Alan said as he rolled the device over and examined it closer.

"Uh, Ronny, you don't understand. This *is* the actual satellite. It's a picosat. We've minimized the metal content and made it mostly of composite and semiconductor materials. What metal it has is in the computer portions and only microns thick. Dr. Pike figured out a way to build a motherboard and bus with minimal amounts of metal. We used fiber optics to relay signals where possible. We've also shielded all radio emanations from the CPU so that it's damned near undetectable from a meter or two away. There are no radio transmitters on it. It's all optical. And our hope is that there isn't enough metal in it to interest the probes." Roger smiled at the little spacecraft.

"How did you shield it without metal for a Faraday cage?"

"Oh, that's the neatest part," Alan interrupted. "We used RAM."

"Yeah, Ronny. We thought on that one a while and came up with making a cage out of radar absorbing material since we couldn't use metals. It works pretty well, actually; we're starting to use it in some places where we want shielding but don't want to put in Faradays." Roger pointed out some of the RAM materials inside a panel on the little spacecraft. Ronny's eyebrows went up as he nodded. "We even used inefficient highly resistive carbon wiring on the major wiring harness from the panels to the power supply to reduce the need for metal there."

"How do we get intel down from it?" Ronny asked while taking a more detailed look at the little spy satellite's articulate components. "And what type?"

"Okay, it has a ten-centimeter glass optic aperture. We plan to orbit at LEO around four hundred kilometers so that will be about three meters per pixel on the ground.

We're gonna try a real ccd camera instead of film—well shielded from emissions. We also added a little commercial-off-the-shelf tip-tilt atmospheric distortion corrector in the optical path to clean up atmospheric scintillation and such. We should get good three-meter resolution images." Roger paused for a second and pointed out the primary optic and the optical train of the telescope.

"I see," Ronny nodded again. "Very interesting, fellas."

"And this little gadget here," Roger said, pointing to a black-composite material box with three small windows on the side, "is how we'll get the data out. It's a little diode laser communicator. We'll download each time it comes over our ground stations in the U.S. and that means any place in the country with a meter aperture telescope or bigger will work. We've also built several portable ones."

"Uh, Roger, how does the picosat know where the ground stations are if they're mobile?" Alan asked.

"That is the beauty of it," Roger said. "Tom has worked out the orbit model and each time we get a download it will get better. All we do is drive out in the path of the thing and send up a quick coded laser pulse train. The input to the optical system of the satellite detects it and turns on the downlink."

"Won't that tip off the aliens?" Ronny asked.

"Possibly, but we'll send a weak signal and only for a few hundred microseconds. Besides, Ronny, this is laser. It's monodirectional as hell. In fact, if we use a one-meter aperture beam-directing telescope on the ground, the laser spot size at the picosat including atmospheric spread of the beam will be less than four meters in diameter. We can spot the satellite passively with a telescope and fire the laser on boresight. And in case we can't get the mobile units in the right place at the right time, the onboard system tracks landmarks of four ground-station locations. When the computer recognizes those landmarks it'll link up automatically."

"What type of bandwidth can we get?" Ronny asked.

"Well, we based the point-to-point laser communications system on an old Ballistic Missile Defense Organization program called the Space Technology Research Vehicle-2. That system could achieve 1.2 gigabits per second at eighteen hundred kilometers. We'll only be at four hundred kilometers. So, rough calculations suggest about 2 to 3 gigabits per second. That's about one 4 megapixel image per second. We'll be in line of sight with the sat for about two minutes with each downlink, so, that's over a hundred images per orbit and that's about all the solid-state memory capacity the little picosat has anyway. We can also use them to send up a communication and downlink them back to a ground station. It'll give us some minimal satcom capabilities back." Roger watched for Ronny's reaction, but wasn't sure what he was thinking.

"I like it," Ronny said, nodding somberly. "I mean, what's the point of being the DDNRO if you don't have any satellites? How are we going to put it up?"

"How are we going to put *them* up, is the right question, Ronny," Roger said, raising one eyebrow and smiling. "*Them?*"

"That's right, *them*. We already have ten of them finished and ready to go." Roger grinned from ear to ear.

"Very nice indeed!"

"They're so small that we can put them all into two fairly small sounding rockets. John and Tom have already worked it out and one rocket is being put together out at Vandenberg and the other at the Cape right now." Roger said.

"Why the two different launch sites?" Ronny wiggled uncomfortably in his paper jumpsuit.

"We'll put half of them in staggered polar orbits and half of them in staggered standard orbits. We'll maximize our coverage that way. For that matter, we're moving the tech to make the sounders not on site into the redoubts. As long as the redoubts hold out, we'll continue to have limited sat-com and ISR."

"Good, Roger, good," Ronny said, sighing tiredly. "We need the eyes. Although I'm almost afraid of what we'll see. When do we launch?"

"Two weeks from today."

"Good. Let's hope it works. You got a backup plan if it doesn't?"

"Yep. We're almost through with a composite Corona setup. But I hope we don't need it because the information from that will be much less useful than from these little bad boys right here." Roger patted the little satellite lovingly as if it were his child.

"Cady, you awake?"

"Yes, sir?" the sergeant major answered as he raised his cap to look over to the major. Gries' feet were propped in the window of the open Humvee door and Cady could tell he was focusing on something in the sky.

"They're here. Time to dance."

"Yes, sir." Cady rubbed his face and straightened up in the driver's seat. "Where, sir?"

"There!" Gries pointed at a spot in the sky just beyond

the Tennessee River south of the airport. Then two F-16s zipped over the trees and touched down side by side. Those two were followed by two more and then two more and so on. The fighters taxied in to the parking area and parked in formation about a hundred meters from where the Humvee was parked.

"Let's go, Sergeant Major."

"Sir." Cady started up the vehicle and drove them up to the base of one of the fighters that had "Colonel Matthew 'Bull' Ridley" painted just beneath the cockpit. There were also eight shiny boomerangs painted on the nose of the plane. The sergeant major noted that they were unusually small. The pilot obviously intended to add lots more.

"Colonel Ridley, sir! I didn't expect to see you so soon, and congratulations," Major Gries saluted the colonel as he climbed down from the F-16. "If the Major may make so bold, Colonel, sir, you're looking one fuck of a lot better than the last time I saw you."

"Greetings, greetings Major," the colonel said, smiling as he returned the salute. "Good to see you too, Sergeant Major. At ease, gentlemen. No need to stand at attention for the newly promoted full colonel; kissing my ring is sufficient."

"Yes, sir," Gries replied, grinning. "I'll keep that in mind. How're the shoulder and the feet, Colonel?"

"Hurt like hell before it rains, but other than that I'm good to go according to the flight surgeon."

"Hard to keep an old dog down, right, sir?" Cady smiled.

"Damn skippy, Sergeant Major. Now, let me find Rene and get my boys situated and one of you two can buy me a drink."

"We'll have to skip the drink, sir," Gries replied, shrugging. "Dr. Guerrero told us to get you and Rene over to the AS HQ asap. There's a liaison here waiting to get your squadron situated."

"A woman she work from sun to sun but a cunnel's work is never done?" Ridley tucked his flight gloves into his new all composite helmet and started loosening the g-suit.

"Sir, let's make sure your fellows are taken care of. That seems soon enough for me." Shane grinned thinly and turned to Cady. "Sergeant Major Cady?"

"Sir?" Cady barked, snapping to attention theatrically.

"Sergeant Major, it looks like that damned motor pool gave us another Humvee with shit tires. Looks like that right rear is running on the run-flat. How long do you think it will take you to get it fixed?" Shane asked.

"Yes, sir, Major, sir! That is so totally my fault. I should've given that damned specialist at the pool an earful when we picked up that shit-ass vehicle this morning! I guess it should take, oh . . ." Cady paused and consulted his watch. "Carry the two . . ."

"About an hour and a half," Ridley said, smiling.

"I'd say about an hour and forty-five minutes, Major, sir!" Cady finished.

"Good, see to it, Top."

"Colonel," Cady winked and saluted, then boarded the Humvee.

"Now Colonel, let's see about your squadron."

Support for the Huntsville Redoubt Air Support Squadron had been trickling in for the better part of the week before Colonel Ridley and the "Rednecks," as they were calling themselves, landed. Ridley had decided if they were going to be assigned to protect the rednecks down in Huntsville, Alabama, that they might as well fit in.

An equipment hangar had been designated on the commercial side of the airport where the FedEx aircraft had been maintained before the alien invasion. The USAF was in full swing, commandeering and operating the fighter wing out of the commercial side of the airport.

On the other hand, somebody had dropped the damned ball figuring out where thirty new pilots were going to bunk once they got there. Shane and Colonel Ridley spent the better part of an hour kicking people out of the Airport Hotel and having them relocated to hotels farther away, Ridley's reasoning being that in case of an air attack, the pilots had to be right there on call and only minutes from take-off; civilian contractors could stay anywhere. The entire town had pretty much been turned into a redoubt, so moving folks farther from the center of the base or the airport was not a major issue from a protection standpoint. Hell, Gries or Ridley didn't think it would matter much anyway having seen first hand how the probes attacked. But, of course, they never said anything like that.

At times Shane had wished he hadn't sent Top off on a boondoggle, as there was nobody better at rattling cages than Sergeant Major Thomas Cady. Oh well, the colonel and the major did all right for themselves in that regard and the pilots were well taken care of.

"Nice to meet you, Colonel Ridley. Major Gries has told us a lot about you." Ronny shook the fighter pilot's hand and offered him a seat.

"Thank you, sir. The major here told me I should come visit but I had no idea that I would be assigned the fighter protection here." Ridley took a seat in one of the leather guest chairs in Ronny's office.

"Well, we have the task of spearheading development of the technologies that might give us the edge we need to defeat these alien probes. And you, your Belgian friend, Major Gries, and Sergeant Cady are the only folks with any real experience with them. So I got you pulled down here."

"I see," is all Ridley said, realizing that this Dr. Guerrero must have pretty big pull. The squadron had originally been designated to the defense of Washington.

"We hope you saw something that when you relay it to our team here, it will mean something to us. And at the same time we plan to use your squadron as a test bed for any new weapons or capabilities we can come up with," Ronny said. "Normally we'd run that sort of thing out to Dreamland for testing. But since most of the work is being done right here, we can shorten the feedback cycle by putting your squadron directly in touch with the designers."

"Great, sir, we're gonna need something," Ridley admitted darkly. "My pilots are ready and willing to take on the enemy, sir. But I'll admit that right now we don't have the chance of a sparrow against an eagle. They took our ships apart like ants eating a grasshopper, but faster. Anything we can do to improve the situation has my full and complete support, sir. What do you want me to do?"

"There are some very bright minds running around on this base and they'll be picking yours for anything that might help. Let the major show you around and get another debrief. He understands the lay of the land around here. And in general, pitch in however you can. Don't hesitate to ask questions; don't hesitate to make suggestions. Be foolish if that's what it takes."

"Clear, sir. Can do. I'll have my guys do the same." Ridley began thinking about any way to fight the probes. Off the top, nothing came to mind.

"Hey, Colonel," Shane said as he walked in the squadron office. He gave the Air Force officer a gesture that was more wave than salute. It wasn't disrespectful, just a friendly greeting between warriors. "How're you settling in?"

"We're good," Bull replied, returning the waved salute. "We've gotten our full delivery of squadron equipment and we're finally at over ninety percent on personnel. We're missing some critical areas, but since they include weapons techs and avionics . . ."

"And you're in one of the nerve centers for both . . ." Shane said, chuckling.

"We've got civilian contractors out the ass in the area," the colonel replied, nodding. "So we're farming out most of it. I mean, the contractors around here come up with the *next* generation gizmos."

They seem to enjoy working on "off the shelf" equipment for a change." The "off the shelf" equipment was the most advanced installed in any aircraft in the world. But the reality of electronics advances made it already obsolete by the time it was installed.

"There are some big brains around here."

"Tell me about it," Shane said, shaking his head. "As an infantry officer I, of course, can never feel the slightest hint of doubt about my overall intelligence, good looks and sex appeal. But I'll admit that from time to time I feel challenged in the intelligence area when dealing with some of these guys. But, speaking of which, is Rene around?"

"Down in the briefing room," the colonel said, nodding. "He's conducting a class on threat assessment."

"Well, it's nearly quitting time," the major replied, glancing at his watch. "What say we have our first debrief with the Asymetric Soldier team?"

"A woman she work from sun to sun . . ." Bull said, shrugging. "Over at the comm facility? We've got secure rooms set up now."

"Nah," Shane said, grinning. "We've got a better place . . ."

"ORDER IN!"

"Your primary debriefing area is *Hooters*?" Rene asked, grinning.

The Huntsville Hooters location had been changed. While a large portion of the Huntsville area had been designated "protected," the actual location of the Huntsville Hooters was outside that zone. After a certain amount of wangling, Roger had pulled the strings to get it moved into the secure zone and it now was placed directly outside the gates of the Redstone Arsenal, which was the inner ring of the redoubt.

If Hooters fell, for all practical purposes the world was lost.

"Take a look around," Roger said, sipping at his beer. "You'll see most of these same faces over the course of the next month or so. At this point, practically everyone in this *city* is working on one defense project or another.

Most of the waitresses work over at the base or for one of the defense contractors and moonlight here. For that matter, most of the stuff we're doing isn't even classified anymore. The probes don't seem to care and the news media is too worked up about the city defense plans to pay much attention to what we do. So most of our security restrictions have been tossed. They always got in the way of communication anyway. And would you prefer to be sitting in a secure room sipping cold coffee?"

"No," Bull said, laughing. He reached for the pitcher and a passing waitress slapped his hand.

"My job, Colonel," the girl said, winking. "You're the CO of the Redneck squadron, right? How's the arm?" She moved on without actually waiting for a response.

"See," Roger said. "There ain't no such thing as secret no more. So, Alan, Tom and I have read your reports. Why don't you and Rene give it to us again," he suggested.

"I . . ." The colonel paused and frowned. "I know what you were saying about clearances, but . . ."

"You want me to call Ronny?" Roger said, frowning. "I suppose I should have gotten you briefed in. I'm not sure what my current title is . . ."

"Deputy Secretary of Defense for Advanced Defense Concepts and Testing," Traci said, picking up a wing. "You never read memos, do you?"

"Who's got time?" Roger asked frowning. "Did you say *Deputy* Secretary? Not assistant deputy's assistant secretary?"

"That's right," Tom said. "You didn't get the memo?"

"I dunno," Roger replied. "You're sure there wasn't an 'Assistant' in there, somewhere, or an 'Undersecretary'?" he asked, almost plaintively.

"Nope," Tom replied. "You're on the manning chart as reporting to the secretary of defense."

"I haven't talked to him but *twice*," Roger argued. "Who the hell said I was a deputy secretary?"

"Uh, the President?" Alan replied. "I read the memo. You were appointed by the President, confirmed by the Senate and it was in the newspapers. Hell, it made the evening news, briefly. It was a nice little write up."

"Crap, I have *got* to start reading my e-mail." Roger sighed. "Anyway . . ." He paused at the expression on the colonel's face. "What?"

"You're . . ." Bull paused and swallowed. "Somebody had better not be pulling my leg."

"Somebody better not be pulling mine," Roger said, frowning at the far wall. "How the hell can I be a deputy secretary?"

"They're not, Colonel," Shane said, grinning. "I read the e-mail, too. Hell, I saved the link to the *Washington Post* article."

"You don't remember anything about this?" Tom asked, laughing. "I thought *I* was checked out!"

"Ronny said *something* about coming to work directly for the Defense Department," Roger admitted, frowning in thought. "I just asked if I'd take a cut in salary and he said, no, the salary would be the same or better."

"There was paperwork," Traci pointed out. "Sally put it on your desk. You signed it."

"Sally's *always* putting stuff on my desk," Roger said, shaking his head. "I don't have time to *read* it!"

"Colonel," Shane said, laughing and shaking his head. "You can assume that Roger has need-to-know. Director Guerrero said that I was supposed to show you around.

These are the guys I was supposed to show you around to."

Bull looked at the three, Tom with some chicken from his latest failed attempt to strip it off the wing speckled on his shirt, Alan with his Roll Tide ball cap and Roger, the "Deputy Secretary of Defense for Advanced Defense Concepts and Testing," in his jeans and polo shirt with a hole on the sleeve, and shook his head.

"Any other deputy secretaries of defense sitting at the table?" he asked and laughed.

"Nope," Tom said, shaking his head. "I'm an assistant under deputy secretary and Alan's just a flunkie."

"Hey!"

"I told you you should have got that Ph.D."

"So *anyway* . . ." Roger said, stripping off a wing and stuffing it in his mouth. "Whu doh ou sta't ah uh be'inin." He swallowed and washed it down with some beer. "I mean, why don't you start at the beginning and just tell us the story. What's a better place for that than Hooters? And have a beer, for God's sake! Who knows how long beer will be available. I mean, hell, we've already lost football! Hell, I'm so strung out I'd even watch a Canadian game, or arena, or Division II colleges, or high school, or shit, even NFL Europe at this point."

"Yes, sir." Bull laughed, taking a sip and looking at the far wall. A Hooters' girl was just getting up on her tiptoes to shoot an order in and the thought that went through his mind was that she had very little metal on her body. If she got rid of the necklace she'd survive. At least the probes.

"It was a couple of months ago," he temporized, picking up a wing. "My memory's not as clear as it was. I was debriefed then—"

"It was a crappy debrief," Tom interjected. "They didn't know the questions to ask. And we're not going to be saying: 'Colonel, are you sure that your memory wasn't affected by the high Gs that you sustained?'"

"You *have* read the report," Rene said bitterly.

"Oh, yeah," Alan said, taking a sip of beer and shaking his head. "I'm pretty sure they wouldn't ask the same questions now, but it was a crappy debrief. Tell us. Have some beer, tell the story, then we'll toss it around."

Bull nodded and took another sip.

The replay of the events took about an hour, he and Rene contributing about equally, their hands occasionally rising in the air to show the maneuvers. Through it all, Tom carried the majority of the questions. He'd clearly studied the original debrief. Roger, Alan and Traci just listened, nodding from time to time.

"Okay, let's go back over that," Tom said as Bull reached the point that he hit the ground. "You were closing at about—"

"Seven hundred knots," Bull said, nodding. "We picked up a bit of speed in the dive, then bled off as we pulled up. Then we went to afterburners when I saw the attack plan was useless."

"After," Rene pointed out. "We'd cleared the cloud when we went to burners."

"After," Bull said, nodding.

"And they *banked* to follow," Roger said.

"Yeah," Bull replied, nodding again. "Definite bank. *Tight*, mind you. Motherfucking tight. I was in a good sixteen-G bank and they were turning *tight* inside of me, and I think they were at higher velocity. They had to be pulling twenty-five, thirty Gs."

"Thirty Gs would be nothing to those things," Tom said,

frowning. "They should have been able to stop on what would look like a dime and then come after you so fast you could barely see them."

"Why?" Rene asked. "You knew they could do this?"

"It's based on their interplanetary movements," Tom said. "We can, to a limited degree, trace their projected movement time from Mars to the Moon. And we can *definitely* trace their acceleration in and around the Moon and on their approach to Terra. They have an accel capability of at least one *hundred* Gs. There's no reason to think they would be limited . . ." He trailed off in thought.

"Gravity interference?" Traci asked. "Does the reactionless drive react to gravity?"

"It's what I'm thinking," Tom admitted, coming partially out of his trance.

"Nah, I think it's simpler than that," Roger said, taking a sip of beer. "Atmospheric effects. At those speeds, the atmosphere is *dense*. There's significant nonlinear compressible flow. At those speeds and short darting maneuvers the flow might even become unstable and nonlaminar. They just can't *move* as fast in dense atmosphere. Or maneuver as fast. They've got loads of potential delta V, but that's counteracted by the atmosphere so their attitude correction and control is limited."

"Makes more sense than gravitational interference," Tom admitted.

"Then the higher they get, the faster they're going to be," Rene pointed out. "Get above about forty kilometers and they're going to be nearly as fast as in space."

"Maybe," Roger said doubtfully.

"Nah," Alan said. "They're not made out of superunobtainium."

"Plasma," Tom said, nodding.

"Say again?" Bull asked.

"They're not going to be able to move at interplanetary velocities because of heating," Roger translated. "Like the SR-71? It had to be designed to stretch in flight because of atmospheric heating. Until they're completely out of the atmosphere, they're going to be somewhat limited. And that explains why they had trouble with the missiles, too."

"It does?" Bull said. "I'd been wondering about that. I guessed it was maneuvering, but I wasn't sure why."

"They've apparently got a limited range on this tractor field or whatever," Roger said. He looked at his nearly empty glass, looked around covertly and then reached for the pitcher.

"I'll tell Casey on you!" Traci said. "CASEY!"

"I've got it," the waitress said, walking over to their table. She topped up everyone's glass, looked at the depleted tray of wings, filled out a form and hooked it to the overhead wire. "ORDER IN!"

"So you guys going to save the world today?" Casey asked. She was a tall brunette with hazel eyes, pleasantly mammalian, with narrow hips.

"We're sure working on it, sweetie," Roger said.

"Hey, congratulations on your promotion," Casey said, grinning. "This is the first time I've ever served a deputy secretary of defense!"

"He's not letting it go to his head," Bull said solemnly.

"Good thing," Casey replied, winking. Then she looked at him seriously. "Any word on when they're going to cross?"

"We're looking at it," Roger said. "But right now, we're

trying to figure out how to stop them when they do." He turned his attention back to his colleagues. "Okay, they're going to be maneuver-limited in atmosphere. That's good news. Not great, but it's something. And you said that when they were hit, the secondaries took out others."

"When the Sparrow hit, it usually took out about three or four," Rene said. "But all the Sparrows didn't survive."

"So far, they've apparently been ignoring carbon," Tom said. "We can probably tweak the Sparrows so they're less tasty. But it will be a major redesign."

"Why not combine the mine concept with the Sparrows instead?" Traci said, frowning. "When they detect probes in the vicinity, they blow out mines."

"Works," Roger said, picking up a Hooters napkin.

"You've had a few, Mr. Deputy," Casey, who was still listening to their conversation said, grinning, and pulling the napkin over. "Let me. Sparrow, mine. That work?"

"Works," Roger said, nodding. "But you've got other tables."

"Not tonight," Casey replied.

"You're packed," Alan said, gesturing around.

"Not . . . tonight," Casey repeated. "What's next?"

"The guns definitely didn't work," Rene said.

"They're depleted uranium," Roger sighed. "Those things *really* like heavy metals."

"Ceramic?" Cady asked. He'd been quietly sitting sipping his beer, waiting for the big brains to stumble.

"Way to go, Sergeant Major," Roger said, nodding. "Casey."

"Ceramic bullets, Falcons."

"Another major redesign at the plant," Alan pointed out.

"Can't be helped," Roger said. "But I think we're staying way inside the box. What about directed energy weapons?"

"They've experimented with mounting chemical lasers on Falcons," Bull said dubiously. "But you only get about twenty shots if I recall correctly."

"Hell with that," Alan said loudly, then belched. "Use a shit load of dah-odes!"

"Pardon me," Rene said. "A *what*?"

"A diode array laser," Tom replied, taking a sip of beer as Roger pulled out another napkin and started sketching. "Instead of using chemicals to produce the laser, you use electrical energy and a diode. You can fire for as long as you have power and keep the diode system cooled."

"Won't work," Roger said, shaking his head and looking up from the napkin. "You need at least a hundred kilowatts. The F-16 hasn't got the juice with all its other systems. And I can't see a way to shoe-horn in another generation system."

"It would work for ground defense, though," Traci pointed out excitedly. "Really *really* well."

"Put the diode in a high place," Alan said, his accent thickening. "Get a bitty nuke generator, one of them pebble-bed thingies from General Atomics. That'd give you all the power you need fer sure. Hell, we could even hook 'em right into the hydroelectric turbines on all the dams up and down the Tennessee!"

"We could cobble together a multi-diode hundred kilowatt system pretty easy," Roger said, nodding. "Hell, multi *mega*watt for that matter. Targeting would be a bitch."

"You're talking about if they attack, like, here, right?" Casey said.

"Yeah," Roger admitted. "But, hell, if we could just fix the targeting it would be another good city defense system."

"This is a laser, like in a laser light show?" Casey asked.

"Well, lots more powerful," Roger pointed out. He knew that Casey wasn't up to the smarts level of Traci, but he didn't want to hurt her feelings.

"And there's lots of them?" Casey asked, waving her hands as if to get people to see where she was going. "The probes I mean."

"Yeah," Bull said, sighing. "They damned well fill the . . . Oh."

"So you get one of those things that, like, moves the laser around . . ." Casey said, as if speaking to a moron.

"And just paint the whole fucking sky," Roger said, slapping his forehead. "Jesus, you could just use any optical targeting system with cooled optics! Alan, see about getting the design specs for the SEALITE Beam Director off the MIRACL laser. We're gonna want something like that."

"They're going to close *fast*," Bull pointed out. He gestured out the window to the general east. "If they're closing here, from the east, they're going to be coming over that big ridge. You won't have more than a minute from when they come in view and when you're under attack."

"Well, we could mount it on top of Monte Sano Mountain; that's the highest point around here. And we could put one on Madkin Mountain and shit what's the name of the mountain out in Harvest with those towers on it?" Roger said.

"Rainbow Mountain?" Traci asked.

"We'd have to cut a bunch of trees." Tom tried another wing—no luck.

"Balloon," Cady said.

"Airborne, Sergeant Major," Shane added, grinning.

"Sure," Alan said, looking up from his chicken wing. "Mount it on one of them barrage balloon sort of things. You'd have to stabil . . . stab-l . . . you know . . ."

"Stabilization's easy," Roger said, frowning. "But that won't be all-weather. Why not just mount it in a plane? One big enough to carry the diode and the generator?"

"C-130 would do," Bull said, nodding. Then he blanched. "Shit, I'm going to end up fighting from a trash-hauler!"

"You missed something," Shane said.

"What?" Roger asked. "I think it will work."

"Back a ways," Shane replied. "The sparrow-thingy."

"Sparrow-mines?" Casey asked.

"What you got?" Roger said.

"I was thinking about that nuclear Katyusha Alan was pitching," Shane said. "What about mounting the mines in some sort of rocket? One that released cluster bomb mines into the swarm?"

"And it would be easy," Roger said, nodding. "Hell, why use cluster bombs? Mount them on K engine rockets. You can make those like . . ."

"We could probably get up to about ten an hour, if we were just making K engines," Casey said, nodding.

"What?" Alan asked blearily.

"That's where I work, Rocket Ram-Jets, down off James Record Road by the quarry where the divers dive and the boys play paintball and the sheep are nervous," Casey replied, smiling. "I mean, my day job. And we've been really falling off. Not many people are making home-built rockets right now. The K line is about shut down and we're mostly making Es. They've got some sort of military application. But if we hired some people, we could probably make about ten K engines an hour, twenty-four hours a day. Maybe more if we set up another line and could get the raw materials in place."

"Casey," Roger said carefully. "Make a note for the . . . what am I?"

"Deputy Secretary of Defense for Advanced Defense Concepts and Testing," Traci said, grinning.

". . . the Deputy Secretary of Defense for Advanced Defense Concepts and Testing to call your employer and give him a spec contract on full K production and probably upgrade of the line tomorrow. Please. Thank you?"

"Call Rocket Ram-Jets," Casey said, slowly filling out the napkin. "K engine production. Good news, I even know the number."

"She's feeding you beer," the colonel said, smiling. "Does this fall into the category of lobbying?"

"I'm paying for it," Roger said, reaching for the pitcher and then pulling back as Casey, without looking up, reached out with her left hand and poured him another beer. "I think I'm covered."

"Right you are, sir," Bull said, grinning.

"An ABL," Roger said, nodding. "I'd say that's going to give us a throw to about sixty klicks. Inside that we've got the Falcons using modified Sparrows and ceramic bullets. Inside *that* we'll have the K rockets. They'll go to six klicks, straight up, so that gives us a linear ballistic of—"

"About a factor of two as near as makes no difference," Tom replied without thinking. "Fired at a forty-five degree angle."

"Twelve kilometers then," Roger said, nodding. "Then inside that we've got the probe mines, Gecko mines, Coyote glue, the M240B with ceramic rounds, what have you."

"And if they get inside of that?" Traci asked.

"Staffs," Cady, Shane and Alan all choroused. Then Alan hiccupped and slid off his stool onto the floor.

"I think the meeting is adjourned," Roger said, picking up his glass. "Time to toast my promotion!"

"Mr. President, from these satellite images taken by the Neighborhood Watch's new birds we can actually determine where the alien machines have spread." General Mitchell pointed at the flat world map on the flat screen.

"That group down there in Alabama has come through again, sir," the NSA added. "Those are some very bright rednecks."

"That's why I appointed Roger to his position, Vicki," the President said mildly.

"Well, sir," Mitchell continued. "We see that the expansion wave has begun to touch into northeastern Greenland and that is getting close, sir. The AS Program has developed a first generation set of weapons that are entirely nonmetallic that they believe will be effective against the probes. Dr. Guerrero and Dr. Reynolds continue to request a recon team to capture and bring back some of the probes to study. I think northeastern Greenland would be the most likely place to make such an attempt."

"Why do they want to catch one of these damned things?" the President asked.

"It's Dr. Reynolds' theory that bullets and bombs might, and he emphasizes might, hold them off for a while," the

NSA answered. "But simulations say that they'll have a limited long-term effect. The theory within the AS team is that we'll need something new, some tool that attacks the probes specifically and on a very large scale. To have any chance of doing that, we need one or more to study."

"As the NSA said, sir." General Mitchell flipped the slide to a map of Greenland. "We can fly in low and fast to God's Thumb. The team will go from there to the edge of occupied territory and try to find regions with low concentrations of the probes. The plan is to find a small subswarm of the probes and kill or capture all of them. They intend to bring back any and all debris that can be managed and hopefully one or more full probes. The Huntsville AS team is leading the way on capture methods while the Denver and Boston teams are point units for analysis and countermeasures."

"Jesus Christ, what if that just pisses them off and makes them follow the team back to the U.S.?" SecDef Stensby asked.

"Well, sir, they've been building a pretty extensive underground bunker at both the Huntsville and Denver Redoubt and the plan is to do all of the research as deep underground as possible," General Mitchell said.

"Okay." The President held up his left hand. "Peace, gentleman. We can argue this if we want, but the AS and Neighborhood Watch have done their job thus far. Let's not get in the way of that. Approve the mission, General, with whatever resources it needs."

"Yes, sir." Mitchell moved on to the next slide. "One more bit of info from the spysats, sir, shows us that the aliens are doing something other than just creating replicas of themselves."

"And that is?" The President put his hands on the table and thought to himself, *Oh God, what now?*

"The Neighborhood Watch scientists took the hot spot data given to them from the NSA analysis and made those points the first targets for the space recon." Mitchell pointed the mouse at a spot in the center of a picture of Italy and it zoomed in on Rome, specifically the Coliseum. "Here, sir, there is obviously a major construction taking place. Where there used to be ruins there now stands a large metal infrastructure nearly a hundred kilometers across. It's similar to the images of Mars and now the Moon."

"That is not good!" NSA said, biting her lower lip nervously. Where Rome used to be looked like one gigantic metal building.

"This is only a small part of the story. The AS analysts have put together a mosaic of the red area from the spysat data and from that you can see that there are major central infrastructure regions tied together with vast pathways."

The image of Europe showed bright spots where most of the major cities had been and they were all linked together like a giant shiny spider web. The probes were un-terraforming the planet—fast.

"There are four extremely large concentrations of alien activity, Mr. President. The largest is just east of Paris where they first came down. The other three are in Casablanca, Morocco; Cairo, Egypt; and Moscow, Russia. The terraforming of Rome is small compared to what has been done at these other cities." Mitchell showed slides of each of the metal cities that were now hundreds of kilometers across.

"Holy shit!" resounded through the briefing room.

"Yes, sir, holy shit, sir. Zooming in on Paris we can see even more. In this image we see this big rectangular object here. This object is about a kilometer long and about half that wide. You see this shadow here, sir?" Mitchell paused to see if the President responded.

"Yes?"

"Well, from the angle of the sun at the time the image was taken, the analysts were able to determine that this thing, whatever it is, is about a thousand meters above the ground. It's flying, sir."

"Flying?" the SecDef said.

"Yes, sir. And from the data we have so far, there are many such mammoth objects that appear to be just floating in midair above these larger centers. They're not swarms; they're flying cities, Mr. President."

Chapter 18

"Hey, Danny," Roger said as he made his way into the general's office.

Most of the personnel of Redstone and the Huntsville Redoubt had moved out of the rather cramped "secure" quarters and back into the buildings and offices of the base. Newly promoted Major General Danny Riggs was once again installed in his office in the Sparkman Center. And now was clearly too busy to play golf with any congressmen.

"Hello, Mr. Deputy Secretary," the general said, grinning.

"Am I the *only* one who didn't read the memo?" Roger asked plaintively.

"Apparently," General Riggs said, still grinning. "I'm not supposed to know there was a pool going on how long it would take you to notice that people were calling you 'Deputy Secretary.'"

"You grow 'em up, you let 'em wear shoes . . ." Roger said, shaking his head. "Besides, aren't deputy secretaries supposed to be pushing paper, not electrons?"

"You've got some good administrative people around you," Riggs said seriously. "I made sure of that. And you're running most of Neighborhood Watch *and* Asymmetric Soldier. It's not a small program anymore, in case you hadn't noticed."

"I had," Roger said, sighing. "And I'm going to see what I have to do to make it larger. We need a probe to study."

"That's going to be interesting," General Riggs said, raising an eyebrow. "But I suppose we can get with SOCOM and see about infiltrating a CAG team into Europe . . ."

"You sort of lost me past SOCOM," Roger said, frowning. "CAG?"

"Combat Applications Group," Danny replied. "Delta."

"Oh," Roger said, his brow furrowing. "Do we need to use Delta? I was wondering if we could just get some guys for Shane. He has some guys from his old command he says would be pretty good for it. And he knows the systems we're working on for it and the mission."

Riggs leaned back in his chair and looked at the scientist soberly for a moment.

"There's some operational issues there, Roger," the general said carefully. "I'm tempted to say 'Mr. Deputy Secretary' because, technically, you're my boss. This base is part of Northern Command, now, but you're, effectively, calling the shots for us and the rest of the redoubts."

"I need to read that memo carefully," Roger said. "So if I am, what's the problem?"

"Major Gries isn't part of my command," the general

said, ticking off a list on his fingers. "He's temporary duty, as is Sergeant Major Cady. I'm not his commander. For that matter, I don't even know who does his evaluations. Maybe we should get that changed, but that's the way it is for now. And the base is not part of FORCECOM. I'm not somebody that they put in charge of shooters. Then there's the authority to perform a combat action in a foreign country—"

"We're planning on Greenland," Roger said, sitting down and listening carefully.

"Greenland more or less obviates that," Riggs said, nodding. "Planning on staging out of God's Thumb?"

"Yes, sir," Roger said, nodding.

"I call *you* 'sir,' sir," General Riggs pointed out. "Okay, but what you're talking about is forming a direct action group under the control of this base, more or less under your direct control. That's . . . not how civilian control of the military is supposed to work and there are actually regulations to prevent it. And then there's the question of movement priorities, funding and all the rest."

"We sent Gries to France," Roger argued.

"He wasn't going in command of a group of shooters," Danny said with a sigh. "He was an observer. That's different. Lethal force and all that."

"Danny, all we want to do is send ten guys or so to Greenland!" Roger said plaintively. "We're developing the weapons and trap systems right now! What do we do, rent a plane?"

"It's not that simple and you know it," General Riggs said definitely.

"So what do I do?" Roger asked. "Call Ronny?"

"You don't work for Ronny anymore," the general

pointed out. "And it's not impossible to do, don't get me wrong. But when you said 'make your team larger' you weren't just talking about size, you were talking about profile, whether you know it or not. And you'll be stepping all over a lot of feet."

"I've been doing that since Alan, Tom and I came up with the mission, General," Roger said, shrugging. "I'm not afraid to step on a few more. Who do I call, or whatever?"

"I know the way this is supposed to go," the general said, breathing out. "But I'm not sure how to do it fast. Except make some calls. How can I reach you, Mr. Secretary?"

"On my cell?" Roger asked. "If it's secure, I'll move to one of the secure areas."

"Right," Riggs said, looking distracted. "Let me make a few calls. Who does Gries want?"

"I'll send your secretary a list," Roger said, standing up. "Thanks for your time, Danny."

"Any time," the general said, giving him a half salute. "Oh, what are you planning on using to catch these things?"

"The most incredible mish-mash," Roger said, shrugging.

"Have you figured out how to track them yet?"

"I think, I dunno. I'm workin' on it." Roger raised an eyebrow Spock fashion. "The solution will be . . . fascinating."

Roger had been analyzing the data from all previous engagements including the loss of the probes at the Moon and Mars and the telecommunications sats around Earth. And he agreed with Shane that radio was the culprit. If it was an emitter in the RF through to microwaves, it went first. That meant something, perhaps something even more sinister than he could put his fingers on and his mind around, but . . . but it was lingering in the back of his mind that there was more to the radio emission attraction than he had completely grokked.

What he had figured out was quite unfascinating technologically, but extremely fascinating from a "go figure" point of view. Roger had put together a team of electrical engineers and RF specialists including a group from the CIA's Directorate of Science and Technology's Measurement and Signatures (MASINT) division. He had also gathered some expertise from the NSA's ELINT group and AFRL's MASINT branch that used to be the so-called Central MASINT Office or CMO—the CMO had been renamed years ago, but it was still the CMO to Roger. And to round off his team he had found a group of wireless networking engineers and several amateur broadcasting enthusiasts. His team had been working for months behind the scenes trying to detect and even hack into the alien machines' communications. Finally, one of the ELINT engineers found their communications method: Radio.

That sort of surprised people. Most of the group figured that it was some sort of unobtainium quantum whatchamacallit but it turned out to be, more or less, plain old radio.

More or less. Actually, it was a spread spectrum signal that worked a lot like 802.11b wireless data transmission protocol, only it was centered somewhere around 1.42 gigahertz. Roger could not place it but that particular radio frequency meant something to him.

After weeks of analysis they had a real good handle on the signal the bots used to communicate with each other. Centered at 1.42 gigahertz in the frequency spectrum there was a string of very fine bands—almost impulse functions with zero width—all of which were spread from the kilohertz all the way up to the terahertz. The frequency spike transmissions did not remain locked at the same frequency either. They randomly jumped from one frequency to the next along the many spikes that the bots used spread across the radio and microwave spectrum.

The unfascinating part was that spread spectrum technology was well understood and was a basis for ultra-wideband communications technology. The 802.11a, 802.11b, 802.11h, and 802.11g protocols used the technology, although their allocated spectrum was not as spread out as the ones the bots used.

The fascinating part was that the damned aliens used such a mundane technology that seemed so . . . so Earthly. Perhaps radio was a universal constant. After all, there were so many sources of RF in the universe that any advanced civilization should understand the technology quite readily. But, and the but here was significant, why would an interstellar traveling species limit themselves to speed of light communications? Perhaps the bots and their makers were limited to the speed of light limit. Once upon a time scientists would have said "Duh" to that pronouncement. For many decades the light limit was considered a hard and fast rule in physics. Recent theories, though, indicated that it might be possible to go faster than light, or at least to have FTL communications. But the alien probes still used radio. Perhaps it was a clue, and a good one if it was true, that the probes were not that much further advanced than humanity. Who knew?

Now if he could just figure out that unobtainium grab-ber field that Shane had noted.

What Roger did know was that they now had a way to track the bots' movements. Hopefully, before long they might even be able to decrypt the hopping spectral broad-casts and therefore learn more about them. But the spectrum hopping sequence seemed basically random or at least more encrypted than anybody at the NSA and the CIA had ever seen. They kept trying, though; maybe, just maybe, somebody would figure it out.

"Hey, Major, Sergeant Major," Alan said, waving them towards the covered range. "We're still working on some of these weapons, but this is what we've got for you so far."

Shane looked at the collection arrayed down the line and shook his head.

"They look like toys," he said. "Or a redneck's back yard."

There was a weapon that looked vaguely like a bazooka with a magazine that was apparently constructed mostly of PVC and duct tape. There were two plastic rifles that clearly had ancestry in something bought at a local Toys R Us, and a covered object on the far end. Waiting by the weapons was a large person Shane hadn't met yet. Very large. He both overtopped Cady and outweighed him. The guy was a fucking mountain with black, shaggy but short hair, massive hands and shoulders, and a long, lugu-brious face. He looked like Abraham Lincoln on a bad day.

"Well, that's what they is, Major," the man said in a

slow Cajun drawl. "We'uns done did the best job we could with the time we got. When you guys go we'un gonna give you better stuff. But this is what you might call the prototyping period."

"Major Shane Gries, Sergeant Major Thomas Cady," Alan said, waving at the two soldiers. "Doctor Phillip Krain, Ph.D. Lurch, Shane and Cady."

"Pleased to meet you, Major," the man said, slowly reaching out and shaking his hand. The Ph.D.'s paw absorbed Shane's.

"Pleased to meet you, Doctor," Shane said, realizing that if the guy wanted to rip his arm off he was going to be going around the rest of his life with a stump. "You're a . . ."

"My specialty's chemistry," Krain said, shaking Cady's hand as well. "Exothermic reactions."

"He's really good at getting things to blow up," Alan translated.

"Call me Lurch," the doctor said. "Everybody does."

"So what do you have for us, Alan?" Shane asked, looking at the weapons curiously.

"Well, we've got the potato gun," Alan said, hefting the PVC and duct tape construction. "No metallic parts, fires either contact explosive or Coyote rounds."

He lifted the device to his shoulder and fired downrange at a man-sized target. The round landed behind the target with a puff and a *CRACK*! at which he grimaced.

"It's not terribly easy to aim . . ." he admitted. He looked back downrange and on the third round managed to hit the man-sized target at fifty yards. When he did, however, the center of the target disappeared in the resultant explosion.

"Very nice," Shane said, frowning.

"Change out the magazine," Alan said, pulling out the magazine and slipping in one marked orange, "and you've got . . ." He fired and this time managed to hit a target to the side, covering it in orange goop. "Coyote glue. It's reinforced with Spectra 1000. Small snips of it are mixed in and they interlock to increase the strength of the glue. The glue bonding itself is massive; it's the actual tensile strength of the glue, especially as it extends, that will cause failure. That and the site it's bonded to."

"DuPont was pretty close about that stuff, as I recall," Shane said, his brow furrowed. "You get it from them?"

"Uhmmm . . ." Alan said, looking over at Lurch.

"Somebody sent me a sample," Lurch said, shrugging. "It was easy enough to reverse."

"Oh," Shane said.

"Under current government operating rules, that's okay," Alan hastened to add. "Critical defense needs and all that. DuPont, pardon the pun, was getting sticky. So Lurch—"

"Fixed it," Shane said, nodding and then grinning. "Great. I guess you really know your chemistry, Lurch."

"I like exothermic reactions," Lurch said, shrugging. "But I can do the rest."

"He also did the contact explosive design," Alan said. "You've got no idea how hard it is to make a stable contact explosive for something like this. It helps that it's low velocity. You realize these things are going to be *very* short ranged, right?"

"Yeah," Shane said. "What's next?"

"These are paint-ball carbines," Alan said, hefting one of the small guns. "They've got internal air-packs, all polymer, and we've got back packs for more air. Air's the real killer with these, not the rounds. The rounds are very light, all things considered."

He aimed the carbine at a new target and fired a series of rounds. These mostly impacted on the target, causing small bits of it to be blown out.

"From the description the sergeant major provided we think these will take out a probe," Alan said. "They're a binary explosive. Making the paint-balls with dual chambers was the tough part."

"It warn't that tough," Lurch said. "Makin' a lot of 'em's going to be tough."

"We're working on an assembly line technique," Alan admitted. "But it's going to be . . . tricky."

"Exothermic reactions," Lurch said, suddenly grinning. "Big exothermic reactions."

"So what's the cover on?" Cady asked.

"Well, that's Lurch's idea," Alan said nervously.

"I like it," the chemist said, smiling again, his eyes lighting.

Alan looked at the two and went over and removed the tarp.

The weapon, if that was what it was, was the most bastardized thing Shane had ever seen. It had a long plastic barrel, a large breech and three lines running into it. The breech had a circular rear portion that looked something like the cylinder of a revolver. There was a trigger assembly and a shoulder stock, so it was clearly designed to be fired. But the lines ran to three large canisters so it was at the very least only semiportable.

"We're working on reducing the size of the canisters," Alan said hastily, interpreting Shane's first question. "But right now, they're marginally portable with straps."

"That I'd like to see," Shane said. Two of the canisters looked somewhat like SCUBA tanks while the third was simply a large plastic box.

"I done it," Lurch said. "Black boy could."

Shane blanched at that and looked over at Cady who apparently hadn't noticed the slur.

"I bet I could, if it's worth it," Cady said, nodding.

So much for not noticing.

"Worth it," Lurch said, lifting some straps down from the walls and hooking them up. When he was done he had stuff dangling all over.

He lifted the rifle, for want of a better term, and pointed it at a target. The weapon discharged with a rapid series of "phuts" that sounded like one continuous hiss. But that was quickly overridden by the sound of the rounds hitting the target, which began to disintegrate as the exploding rounds tore it apart in a continuous explosion.

Lurch continued to play the weapon around the area, blowing away targets, target stands and a few wholly innocent bushes. The whole time his face was creased in a giant smile.

"I *like* it!" Cady said, grinning just as widely.

"It's basically a Gatling gun," Alan said, pointing to the cylinder on the breech. "The box is the ammo feed and the tanks supply air. It takes two air points to drive it, thus the two tanks. We should be able to double mount them with the feed box underneath."

"I think you've made the sergeant major's day," Shane said, shaking his head.

"He can probably heft it," Lurch said, setting the rifle down and then unslinging the canisters. "You wanna try, boy?"

"I'll even let you get away with that 'boy' crack," Cady said, smiling. "But not forever, you Cajun hick."

"We gonna get along," Lurch said, smiling and holding out the weapon.

"Okay, Mr. Deputy Secretary," Danny said over the video link. "You're set up. Advanced Research Testing and Scouting Team Alpha has been authorized with a manning of one field grade officer, two company grade officers and fourteen enlisted personnel as direct action specialists and a group of support and administrative personnel."

"Translate?" Roger said, smiling as his brow crinkled.

"Shane's got a new command," Danny said, smiling in turn. "He requested certain personnel from his former command and they're on their way here as we speak. I've drawn a few clerks and support personnel from my boys and girls. He's only going to have about half his TOE personnel when those people are in, so he can pull for more personnel. Their primary mission is reconnaissance and analysis of alien methods and materials. Secondary mission is testing of new equipment and materials to analyze their utility for anti-probe defense. Tertiary mission is primary security for advanced design concepts personnel."

"I thought we had lots of soldiers around to do that," Roger said with a grin.

"We do," Riggs said, still smiling but this time a bit darkly. "But if the redoubt falls, their mission is to get you to a remaining redoubt, with your material and knowledge, alive."

Chapter 19

"You know what they say about Greenland, Top?" Major Gries adjusted the collar on his parka and pulled his toboggan down over his ears better as he tore open one of the new plastic-wrapped MREs and tried to eat the PowerBar without breaking his teeth. Even though he'd held the damned thing under his arm for the last fifteen minutes it was still hard as a rock from the extreme cold.

"Other than it being goddamned cold, no, sir, what's that?" Cady asked as he bit down into some armpit-warmed granola.

"Well, Top, legend has it that there is a beautiful woman hiding behind every tree in the land."

Cady scanned the horizon in front of him and didn't see anything taller than a yellow poppy. He knew from the fifteen kilometers that they had already hiked that there hadn't been any f'n trees nowhere.

"Right, Major." Cady nibbled on the granola and worked his frozen fingers. Shane surprised him by handing him his new issue plastic field binoculars.

"Would you look at that?" Gries nodded to the west and choked down the bit of frozen PowerBar.

"Son of bitch. You think that tundra bird even knows what he's sitting on?" Cady laughed at the sight. Specialist Nelms had crawled to the peak of the next ridgeline to take up the forward recon point and had remained so still that Cady and Gries were taking bets on if he was frozen to death. The specialist had been still for so long a small flock of tundra birds had wandered near him and one of them was presently perched on his head.

"Why doesn't he move?" Gries asked.

"Look to the north of him about two hundred meters, sir." Cady handed Gries back his binoculars.

"Hmmm." Gries scanned to the north of Specialist Nelms and found the rest of his squad.

Staff Sergeant Gregory was moving fast through the tundra valley toward Gries and Cady, his fully automatic HE ball gun at the ready. Gregory stopped about halfway between Nelms and Gries and started making hand gestures and signals. The ground around him started to come to life as the rest of the squad rose from their camouflaged positions. Staff Sergeant Gregory continued giving orders to the seven soldiers and then suddenly he stopped, knelt, and became motionless.

"What the hell? Want me to check it out, sir?"

"Let's hold it up, Top. Something's going on here." *Surprise occurs in the mind of the commander*, Shane thought. He scanned the edge of the ridge from north to south. Top had his binoculars out now and was doing the same.

"I don't see anything, but something has them spooked, sir." Cady didn't like this damned tundra. There was nothing to hide behind. No place to take cover. There was an occasional yellow poppy, grass, lichen, or sedge bush, but nothing substantial enough to stop a bullet or just to simply lie low behind.

A flock of birds rose up squawking from the other side of the ridge, startling Gries at first since they seemed so much closer through the binoculars. Once his sense of distance adjusted he noticed the birds around Specialist Nelms take flight as well. Then a herd of reindeer crested the ridge. The reindeer ran at a ground-eating canter past the troops in the valley southwestward and did not appear as though they would be slowing down anytime soon.

Then Shane noticed more movement on the crest of the ridge on both sides of the specialist. And the ground continued to look as though it was moving. Gries focused the binoculars again, thinking they were out of focus, and then he realized what he was seeing as the sunlight started to glint and glare back at him from the ridge.

Forty or fifty little shiny boomerangs crested the ridge one after the next, right past and over Nelms. The boomerangs looked as though they were walking on the surface but from what Gries could see the things had no legs. The alien probes were moving slowly and although in random paths they all seemed to be moving in the same general direction—right for the troops and directly at Gries and Top.

"Shit!" Top muttered and reflexively grasped the big ornate oak warrior club that Alan Davis had given him.

"Well, we wanted to get close." Shane watched as the alien boomerang-shaped probes skittered and swarmed like ants over the hill and poured down over his squad in the valley. "Don't move, boys. Don't move."

The subswarm of boomerangs made no noise as they moved except occasionally when they would do something that would cause the dirt to roll, churn, and be blown aside like from a leaf blower. But they didn't do this often.

"I think the little dust clouds must be when they find something they like," Gries whispered.

"Well, I hope there ain't nothing on a ground pounder that they find appetizing, sir."

"Roger that, Top." Shane nodded. "Looks like they're gonna head right for us. I guess we're gonna find out if the shakedown worked."

"Should we move, sir? Or are you wantin' to dance with 'em again?" Cady asked.

"Too many to dance with, Top. But they don't seem to be bothering the rest of the squad and we came here to get intel and a bot!"

"Somehow, sir, I knew you were going to say that." Cady felt his HE ball minigun to make sure it was ready to go. The geeks had done a good job with the first production model. It wasn't even a fourth as heavy as a real minigun and Cady could carry it and all the air packs and HE ammo for the thing he wanted without being weighted down. Then he felt up his warrior club one more time, fondling it for confidence. "We wait, sir?"

"We wait . . . quietly and very goddamned still." Gries made himself comfortable on the ridge as if he were getting ready for a nap. A light bead of sweat rolled on his forehead even though it was only five degrees above zero.

"Yes, sir! Still as a goddamned rock, sir." Cady didn't like this at all.

Shane was quiet as a mouse, but he was nervous as a freaking cat as the subswarm of shiny meter-long stubby boomerangs blotted out the sky as they crawled over him. Although he could see very closely—very closely—that the bots had no legs, it felt like they were walking over him as they went by. He could literally feel something stepping on him. And he could hear the faintest rustling of the tundra from the alien bot herd. Whatever they used to stir up the ground made a slight perceptible noise from that close a range.

He and Cady had seen the things rip metal right out of concrete with some sort of invisible grasp, so he figured that they used the same force for crawling and flying. Dr. Reynolds would be better at answering that question and Shane knew he had to catch one of these things so that Roger could do just that.

The fifteen minutes it took for the boomerangs to crawl over them seemed like at least seven years. Shane could no longer hear the faint rustling noise but that could mean they were only a few tens of meters away. He raised his neck slowly so he could see the subswarm over his feet. The bots had gotten more than thirty meters away and appeared to be paying them no attention. Shane motioned to Cady to hold fast for five more minutes.

By the time Shane thought they had given them enough time Staff Sergeant Gregory was easing quietly up beside them. He tapped Cady on the shoulder and made some subdued hand gestures and then pointed to the southwest.

Cady relayed the same message to the major. The probes were now two hundred meters southwest of them.

"Good work, Gregory." Shane rolled over to see the small swarm of the alien boomerang-shaped probes still traipsing across the tundra as though it were an evening stroll for them. Who knew? It might have been just that. "Gregory, are there more behind them gonna come over that ridge behind us anytime soon?"

"No, sir," the staff sergeant whispered. "As far as we can tell the main swarm is still four or five clicks northeast."

"Good," Shane whispered. "Then that's our target."

"Understood, sir," Top whispered and nodded. *Down to business*, he thought. "Orders, sir?"

"Let's stay on their tail. Get me two or three runners out ahead of them and set the trap. Then we'll ambush them, trying to kill all of them but one completely and we'll just knock that remaining one out. We better do it all at once, since those damned things can fly. Let's do it, Top."

"Yes, sir."

Cady grabbed Staff Sergeant Gregory by the shoulder and motioned for him to crawl back over the ridge. He dragged the minigun beside him with one hand and eased over the edge. As the two men crested the ridge and out of sight of the probes Cady rose to his feet and slung the composite HE ball minigun on his back. That was one piece of equipment he was never letting go of.

"All right Gregory, you heard the boss. Go fetch Specialist Nelms and have him meet me down the valley five clicks south—and tell him he better beat me there. You and three others get back here and stay with the major. Put your two fastest long-distance runners on the west side of the probes and tell them to get a half click ahead of them and stay that way until they can see us through the binoculars closing in on them. When they get the signal they're to put out the friction mines as fast as they can and then hunker down, ready to fight. Put the other two on the west side pacing with the probes. Make sure all of them are ready with the riot grenades. Got it?"

"Got it, Top."

"All right then, move!"

The President and the Joint Chiefs studied the spysat photos of the European and Asian continent in dismay. There were already major central "hive-like" structures that were a hundred to three hundred kilometers in diameter at several major cities in Eurasia. The largest still seemed to be Paris and now that city was growing upward. More and more the recon photos showed the mammoth floating structures around the large central hive cities. Nobody had any clue what the giant floating structures were or what they were for. The alien probes had completely transformed Europe and were stretching into Russia, the Middle East, Africa, and were starting to stretch across the Atlantic into Greenland.

"Mr. President." George Fines, the presidential science advisor entered the War Room with the SecDef.

"George, Jim, what's happening?" The President could detect the look of urgency on their faces.

"Sir, about seven minutes ago our nuclear watch seismographs detected seismic wave activity that could only be caused by multiple detonations around the globe. The detonations were of very large nuclear devices and it appears that there must have been more than fifty of them.

Following that by about four minutes there were several more, perhaps ten, detonations detected," Fines reported.

"Where were the detonations?" General Mitchell asked.

"There's no way to know until the next downlink from the Neighborhood Watch sats come in. That'll be in about twenty or so more minutes before we get any pictures that were taken after the detonations." SecDef Stensby looked at his wristwatch to mark the time.

Specialists Jones and Mahoney had been the two unfortunate enough to be the fastest long distance runners in the group. They had to get back up the valley and over the ridge where Major Gries was waiting, pace faster than the men taking the west flank, and cover about ten kilometers in the same time the other men covered five. They had to do all this while not giving their positions away to the alien probes—if the things were even paying attention to them.

Major Gries understood what was being asked of his men and he set the pace at an easy march with light bursts of run here and there. Fortunately, the terrain of the early springtime Greenland tundra was easy to make time over and only the occasional ridgeline would put his other troops or the bots out of sight. Without radio communication they had to make certain that each member of the squad was in sight of somebody else within the squad so they could daisy-chain the communications back and forth to the major. Normally they could have used watches and timed it, but they left all metal at the evac point about fifteen kilometers east before this mission, watches included.

Major Gries still wanted to give the alien probes a wide

berth and be cautious about letting their rear position overtake the alien subswarm of the boomerang-shaped bots. Gries slowed the rear group to almost a stop and surveyed the tundra through the binoculars. *At least this time I'm running after the damned things instead of from them*, he thought.

"Sir, it looks like Top is in position, but he hasn't signaled that he's seen Jones and Mahoney yet," Staff Sergeant Gregory whispered while looking through the binoculars at the large man brandishing a minigun like it was a paperweight. Of course, this one was, compared to a minigun that shot real bullets instead of paintballs filled with impact-mix-detonated HE.

"Right. I can see our men on the west flank. Top is set up on the east. As soon as we get the signal from Top, we'll start closing in on the metal bastards." Shane rested for a second and tightened the lid on his plastic canteen. The subswarm of Von Neumann probes still looked like a herd or swarm or flock of creatures milling about the tundra and in no particular hurry. They seemed uninterested in the troops at the moment. Shane hoped it stayed that way. It would make their job a whole hell of a lot easier.

"Sir," Gregory whispered.

"What?"

"Top's giving us the go-ahead signal, sir. Orders?"

"Staff Sergeant Gregory, check that all team members are in position and signal the slow advance." Shane tucked the canteen back in his standard insulated carrier pack and hoped it kept it from freezing since the sun would be going down soon.

"Team's ready, sir!" Gregory said quietly.

"Move out."

⚜   ⚜   ⚜

Jones and Mahoney had just enough time to catch their breath when Top started signaling for them to get set up. The probes were headed in their general direction and would cover the kilometer or so up the small valley to the ambush point in probably fifteen minutes at the pace they were traveling. That would be just long enough to plant the special riot mines that Major Gries had brought along for the trip.

The mines, as with everything else, had to have exactly zero metallic content. The weapons could be activated in several ways, all of which came down to direct motion and friction.

Mahoney dropped to his knees, looking around and figuring out the best configuration for the mines. Among other things, they didn't want to "paint themselves into a corner." The only way to do it was to start at one side and work back to their position. They'd practiced extensively before deploying, but he still needed to get the lay of the land.

"Mine one here," he said, pointing. He pulled out the carbon fiber digging tool, which looked like a cross between a knife and a spatula, and stabbed it into the ground.

"Crap," he said as Jones dropped to his knees nearby.

"What?" Jones asked, stabbing in himself. "Hey! It's fucking rock!"

"Permafrost, you hick," Mahoney replied digging some of the soil aside. There was only about four inches of soft soil at the point he was digging and then it turned to solid permafrost.

"This sucks," Jones said, hacking at the ice-bound soil. "What the hell do we do now?"

"Mound them," Mahoney said, thinking quickly. He dug down as far as he could get, opened up the hole so that the mine could slide in, slid it into the hole and then dug soil from around it until there was a large mound. Packing it in on the sides held the mine in place.

"Now for the tricky part," he said. He took a long piece of carbon fiber that looked something like a thin whip and screwed it into the top of the mine. With the whip trigger in place he carefully pulled out the safety pin and pocketed it.

"This really sucks," Jones said, as he got his second mine in place. "Nobody said nothin' about no permafrost shit."

"I guess they thought it'd be melted off," Mahoney said. "Now shut up and dig."

With the last of the sixteen mines planted, Mahoney tapped Jones on the shoulder and motioned to back off to their cover point. The two specialists slipped back up the valley about thirty meters and took cover in a low spot in the tundra. Jones lay flat on a bed of yellow tundra poppies.

"Did you signal Top?" Jones nudged the other specialist and pulled out his binoculars.

"Shit, I thought you did. Hold," Mahoney raised to a knee and made a couple of quick hand motions. "Did he see it?"

"Top gave thumbs up. Do the same and get the fuck ready." Jones set the binoculars on the poppy bed in front of him and took aim with the HE ball gun. Mahoney signaled and readied his HE ball gun and loaded a riot grenade canister in his potato gun.

⌘   ⌘   ⌘

"Nelms, when you get the word I want you firing that potato gun as fast as you can, got it?"

"Right, Top! Ready." Nelms had all ten of the riot canister magazines he and Top had brought strapped across his shoulders on their bandoliers and his potato gun at the ready.

"Okay, hold one." Top looked to the north and gave the major the signal that they were ready to go and waited for the return signal to go ahead.

"Sir, west side is ready," Sergeant Gregory informed the major.

"Good." Shane readied his potato gun and the Kevlar and Spectra 1000 net that the Huntsville scientists had put together for him.

"All right, troops, remember your orders. We shoot the motherfuckers dead! Every goddamned one of them but the one the major shoots with his special bag. I want suppression fire to keep those damned things from flying away and stay ready with the potato guns." Staff Sergeant Gregory gave a nod to the major. "Ready, sir."

"Move out!" Shane gave the go signal to Top on the east flank while Gregory motioned the west flank on.

The first two or three minutes were uneventful and nerve-racking as the rear and side flanking positions closed in around the little alien probes. The forty or fifty some-odd shiny metal boomerangs skittered over the ground as if they were cattle grazing. Perhaps that's what they were doing.

But the ambush plan was perfect. The little bots sauntered unaware right into the minefield.

The long whip was attached to a detonator. As soon as the first bot touched the whip it was bent slightly sideways. This released a shear pin, which in turn released a spring-loaded firing pin. The firing pin detonated the primer, which triggered a pre-charge. The pre-charge traveled downwards to a launching booster and a moment later the primary charge detonated.

The first riot mine erupted upwards, then the primary detonated, spreading the Coyote glue into a small spheroid cloud that settled over several of the probes.

"Fire!" Gries gave the word and the rear flank opened up on the unsuspecting bots.

FWOOOMP! FWOOMP! FWOOMP! FWOOMP! Sounded the potato guns from all directions. Several riot grenades detonated just above the small swarm of boomerangs and spread the Coyote glue, covering a majority of the swarm sparsely, but enough to stick them to the ground and temporarily prevent them from flying away. And then came the rapid *spikt spikt spikt* of the HE ball guns, followed by the *kerpow* of the HE balls detonating against the bots and the tundra.

FWOOOMP! FWOOMP! FWOOMP! FWOOMP! Several more riot grenades detonated and the confused bots triggered several more of the mines that Jones and Mahoney had emplaced. Top rushed to the edge of the gooey cloud, spattering away at the loose bots with the minigun. HE balls exploding at more than two hundred a second made an interesting visual and sound effect. The HE balls were proving effective against the bots. It appeared that the alien boomerang-shaped probes were no more or less fragile than earthbound vehicles and materials and the HE balls disposed of them in a nice little fireball of scattering bot shrapnel.

Jones and Mahoney held their positions, firing both HE balls and riot canisters as fast as they could. Gries and the rest of the rear flank pressed inward until the major didn't think moving closer was a wise idea.

"Check advance! Round 'em up!"

Privates First Class Gibson and Letorres pushed the west flank inward. The Coyote glue would hold an individual bot for a few seconds while it tried to spin and wriggle out of the glue's grip. When that would fail, the alien boomerangs would propel upward very fast, stretching the glue to its elastic limit. Where a bot was held by a thick glob of the riot glue it would be yanked back downward into the tundra hard. The impact would render the probe useless in a shower of sparks. Gries noted how it looked like a special effect from a cheesy science fiction movie when the things malfunctioned or were knocked down.

Several of the bots nearly reached the elastic limit of the sticky mess to freedom—nearly. But the flower that rises above others is cut down. Out of the mix they were natural targets for the HE ball guns, and the entire herd of the alien probes was nothing but cattle to the slaughter. The HE ball guns were performing well above Gries's expectations in dispensing destruction on the probes. He owed Alan Davis a beer.

"That one on the edge, there!" Gries pointed. "I got that one." Shane took aim on the bot and depressed the trigger of the compressed air cannon. *FWOOMP* went the potato gun. Just as the bot stretched to the edge of the Coyote glue trap the canister Gries fired exploded open into a thick spider web of Kevlar and Spectra 1000 filaments with synthetic gecko-skin patches mixed in. The hi-tech net spread open and wrapped and tangled around the alien thing. The bot started spinning wildly, trying to free itself. Pieces of the composite fiber net began to fly off in multiple directions. And it looked like the bot had some capability of cutting through it since large portions were disappearing. If the thing had not been doused in Coyote glue before Gries fired the net, it would have gotten free.

"Riot grenade!" Gries yelled and pointed at the nearly escaping bot.

"Got it!" Staff Sergeant Gregory hit it with another net grenade, giving Major Gries time to reload his potato gun.

As the last bot was blown the hell up, Gries flung his last net grenade around the captive one. It wasn't going to hold and Sergeant Cady realized this at about the same time Gries did. Like an Olympic sprinter Cady rushed the little alien probe, wielding his custom battle club. With one muted blow from the club the bot stopped resisting captivity, sputtered silent with a shower of sparks and fell back into a pool of the thickening riot glue with a subdued *thud*!

"Cease fire, goddamnit!" Gries ordered as one of the specialists on the west flank fired an HE round way too close to Top. Cady dropped and covered as the explosion sent an aftershock through the cold and hardening Coyote glue. A finger of the glue plopped a few inches from Top's face.

"Goddamnit Gibson, what have I told you about blue on bluing me?" Cady yelled.

"Don't do it, Sergeant?"

"You bet your ass, don't do it!" he yelled at the private.

"Uh, Top," Gries grinned, offering him a hand up from the ground. "Thought we were gonna take home a live one."

"Sorry, Major, but I just couldn't see anyway we were gonna catch a live one. It was eatin' right out of that net the eggheads made us. I figured if I just banged it lightly, they might could put it back together. And I sure as hell didn't want that thing gettin' away and bringing back a few hundred thousand of his buddies. Besides I just tapped it."

"Concur, Top." Gries knelt by the dented alien probe and poked at it with the barrel of his potato gun. There was a buzzing like an angry wasp inside and then another brief crackle of static electricity on its surface. It shuddered for a moment and then was still.

"I think maybe we do have a live one," Gries said musingly.

"Mr. Secretary, after making a quick analysis of the most recent spysat photos and comparing that data with the NSA Internet data as well as the seismograph detections, we believe we can say what is going on now." Ronny Guerrero's image came through the T1 datalink in realtime to the President's underground headquarters in Wyoming.

"Well Ronny don't keep me hanging," SecDef Stensby replied. The entire presidential staff had assembled in the War Room of the underground headquarters for this debrief. They all were hoping for good news, but none were expecting it.

"Right, sir. It looks like it was a firewall along the sixty-degree eastward latitude line. We've got signs of detonations in Mashhad, Iran; in Turkmenistan; Uzebekistan; Temir, Kazakhstan; Ural, Samara, Ufa, Izhevsk, Perm, Magnitogorsk, Tagil, Ukhta, Ifdel, and many other Russian cities with the first wave of detonations. There were also a few in Yemen, Oman, Pakistan, and Saudi Arabia. It appears that there were a total on the near order of one hundred and sixty strikes, most of them from multiple reentry vehicles," Ronny explained.

"My God!" President Colby shook his head. "General, check me if I'm wrong but that's a significant portion of Russia and China's nuclear arsenal."

"About that, sir," General Mitchell said.

"Are we going to have nuclear winter on top of everything else?" the President asked angrily.

"Uh, sir," the national security advisor said, then looked at the secretary of defense.

"Mr. President," the secretary said, carefully but definitely. "Let me state for the record that most secondary analysis of the original nuclear winter scenario indicate that it's overstated."

The President frowned for a moment, then shook his head.

"How overstated?" he asked.

"The terms that comes to mind are deliberate 'political tinkering' and 'junk science,' " the Chairman of the Joint Chiefs said bluntly. "Then a descent into urban legend. The total energy output of all of the nuclear weapons in the world at the height of the Cold War is lower than the output of the Mount Saint Helens blast. Even with fudging hard on secondary effects, nobody except the original scientists could come anywhere near a 'mini-iceage' scenario from a full-scale nuclear war. Upon review, even most of the physicists involved in the original study repudiated it. What we'll get from this blast is a slight reduction in temperatures, hardly noticeable except by fine study. As a matter of fact, given the destruction of the worldwide sensory networks, I'm not sure it will be testable at all. Oh, and some spectacular sunrises. And a slight increase in background radiation, but nothing that's going to cause two-headed babies; possibly a slight increase in cancer rates. Given that if we don't win, the human race is going to be wiped out, a slight increase in cancer rates is the least of our worries."

"Point," the President said, nodding. "Did it work?"

"Not the way they intended, sir." Ronny paused to flip through his data. "Uh, if you will flip to slide four of the package we just sent you, you'll see that the second group of detonations that took place a few minutes after the first were located in India, China, North Korea, and the far eastern parts of Russia."

"Why does that mean that these nukes didn't work?" the SecDef asked.

"We did not fire on those locations. Ergo, they must have fired upon themselves. We suspect the initial detonations tipped off the Von Neumann probes that the launch sites for these nukes were a threat and then they must have attacked those locations. That is the only explanation for nuking yourself that we can figure, sir," Ronny finished and waited for a response.

"We were planning a similar tactic," General Mitchell said quietly. "I hate to say it, but I'm happy as hell that the Chinese and Russians beat us to it."

"Do we know how effective the bombs were at destroying the probes?" the NSA asked.

"All we know is what is in slide five." Ronny waited for them to flip to the last slide the Neighborhood Watch had sent over the T1 hotline. It was a slide containing several images from the last ten or so spyphotos they had received. The compilation slide showed multiple tubules of alien probes descending on Nagpur, Calcutta, Chengdu, Si'an, Beijing, Novosibirsk, Bratsk, Omsk, and Chita. The probes were consuming the Eurasian continent.

"One of the most interesting things here is that the probes let the missiles fly and detonate as if they had no clue as to what they were or that they didn't care if they lost millions of bots. We guess that the missiles were launched from beyond the occupied regions and flew to the edge of the bots' territory."

The President nodded. "I see."

"Until now the bots had only imposed the no-fly zone over the occupied regions with a bit of cushion around it." Ronny let that sink in for a second and then continued.

"It looks like now from data we've been able to gather that they're imposing a global no–fly zone. This is going to limit operations severely. And, of course, as reported in the media and on the Internet, contact has been lost with most of these areas," Ronny continued. "The last significant contact was from a blogger in Singapore stating that the probes had been reported approaching across the straits from Malaysia. Internet pings from the National Security Agency indicate that there are no remaining Internet nodes on the Eurasian landmass. With the exception of South America and areas of Africa, we appear to be alone in this fight, Mr. President."

⚙ ⚙ ⚙

"Home," Jones said, sighing as he lowered his end of the mesh "stretcher" to the ground. The bot had turned out to weigh a good two hundred pounds, despite its small size, and they'd taken turns carrying it back to the cached Humvees.

Besides the bot they'd managed to pick up about another two hundred pounds of assorted bits, including one bot that was blown in half, revealing the interior. It was, as far as anyone could tell, just a mish-mash of metal and what looked like glass, damned near solid, which explained the weight. The small team had had a time humping all the bits, and their gear, back to the Humvees.

The bots had been carefully observed by satellite and it was noted that they'd stopped, presumably temporarily, on a strict line. For safety the Humvees had been left twenty kilometers west of the line and the attack point had been set up about two kilometers inside. It had been a long twenty-two klicks humping all those bits over the tundra.

But the Humvees were still there, which meant they didn't have to hump it the whole hundred and fifty to the Thumb of God.

"Keep moving," Cady said, grasping the whole bot and lifting it into the bed of the Humvee. "I'm not going to be happy until these things are back in the States. And not very then."

"They're not radiating," Mahoney said. He was the team's designated electronics and intel geek and already had the devices the scientists had loaded them with out and operating. "No radio signals. No gravitational signals. No apparent subatomic particle stream."

"Doesn't mean they're not talking to somebody," Cady growled. "Load it up and let's move."

He dumped his ruck and the minigun in the back of the Humvee and got in the driver's seat, picking up the squad radio and donning the headset. The new system they'd been issued had no carrier wave for the bots to home in on and only radiated when used. The system worked over short ranges using the so-called ultrawideband *Pulson* chip technology and was theoretically too low-level and spread-spectrum a signal to pinpoint. Alan and Roger had really geeked out on them. Hopefully, they wouldn't have to use it.

Shane climbed in next to him as Mahoney and Gibson climbed in the back.

"Mahoney, you getting *anything* at all?" Shane asked as Top put the vehicle in gear.

"I'm getting intermittent radio from east of the line, sir," the specialist replied, looking at the readout on the Gateway laptop. "Multiple frequencies, very short bursts. It'd be interesting to set up a full radio intercept site somewhere near here. I think Doc Reynolds is right; these things use plain old radio." As the Humvee bumped over the springtime tundra he kept hitting keys and nodding.

"Interesting," the specialist said. "There was a big burst of signals about six hours ago, sir."

"That when we hit them?" Shane said, then shook his head. "No, that was about four hours ago. Any idea why?"

"Negative, sir," Mahoney replied. "Big burst of signals that went on for about three minutes. There was heavier signal traffic before, then it peaked in number of transmissions and power, went down to still increased levels. Then it fell way off. It's still down."

"Let's hope that's a good sign," Cady said.

"Concur, Top," Shane replied, pulling out one of the new combat field ration packs. The replacement for the MRE had a heater pack built in using a friction tab starter. He pulled the tab on a packet of fettuccine Alfredo with chicken and set it on his thigh to warm. "I've got beef stew and chicken romaine, Top. Take your pick."

"I'll take the stew," Top said, his eyes scanning the horizon. "That romaine shit gives me the shits."

The sergeant major was just finishing his beef stew, controlling the Humvee's wheel with his knee while spooning up the stew, when Mahoney made an interrogative noise from the back.

"Sir . . ." the specialist said, hesitantly.

"Go," Shane said, pitching his finished alfredo out the window.

"I've got increasing probe signal strength," the specialist said. "Could we stop for a second?"

"Hold it up, Top," Shane said, sticking his arm out the window and signaling with a closed fist for the two following Humvees to pull up.

"What are you doing?" Gibson asked, pitching his own finished entrée out the window.

"Trying to pick out the stronger signal," Mahoney said. "And get a direction and maybe a location. I don't want them to have moved on us and have us run right into them."

"That would be bad," Cady admitted, opening up the door and stepping out to look around the tundra. Overcast had moved in, turning the land into shades of gray.

"Yeah. Sir?"

"Go," Shane said, turning around in his seat to watch the specialist.

"We've got a large amount of noise to the southwest of us, sir," Mahoney said, nervously.

"Shit," Gibson said, opening up his own door and getting out.

"And I think it's moving . . ."

"Top!" Staff Sergeant Gregory yelled.

"I see 'em," Cady called. "Sir, we've got probes inbound from the direction of God's Thumb!"

"No word from the bot recovery mission yet sir, and uh, there is more, Mr. President," Vicki hesitated.

"Let's hear it."

"Well sir, SEAL Team Six has returned from the French Riviera and have some very . . . disturbing photos."

"Disturbing?" the President said, shaking his head. "Vicki, alien metal-eating probes are taking over the world. We're evacuating every major city in the U.S. My daughter just started sniffing around boys. Try to up the ante, Vicki. Feel free."

"Yes sir. If you recall we sent in a team along the periphery and into the occupied zones with hopes of conducting recon on the areas with an emphasis on determining what happened to the people in the occupied territories. Well, Alpha Platoon SEAL Team Six was the only platoon that returned. And they suffered two casualties."

"Yes, Vicki, quit beating around the bush about it." The President was getting tired and was ready for this nightmare to end. He didn't expect that to happen anytime soon—if ever.

"Right, here." Vicki set a folder in front of him and then sat quietly.

President Colby looked at the folder and at first was almost afraid to touch it—as if it were tainted with something bad. He glanced around the room at his top advisors and realized that they had all seen the pictures in the folder and they were nervous about letting him see it. He sighed, opened the folder, and spread the pictures out before him.

"Jesus Christ!"

Roger sat in his office looking at the photos that had been e-mailed to him from the SecDef's aide. He topped his glass off with a little more Old Number Seven and then thought about adding some Coke to it—but it was a passing thought. The Tennessee whiskey was nowhere near strong enough to make him forget the images in the photos. At first he had thrown up in his garbage can, then he cried, then he started drinking.

He couldn't believe that the human race had been reduced to what he was seeing. But, seeing is believing. The thousand words these photos told were alarming, disturbing, very sad, and . . . grotesque.

"Roger, do you have a minute?" Alice Pike tapped on his office door.

"Uh," Roger looked up and tried to compose himself but Alice had already noticed the open whiskey bottle on his desk.

"Is this a bad time?" Alice asked.

"I guess the answer to that is yes. But they're all bad times now, aren't they. . . ." Roger shook his head and then capped the whiskey bottle and put it back in his desk drawer. "I'd offer you a drink but I know you don't really like the hard stuff."

"What's happening, Roger?" She could tell he had been crying or sick or maybe both. "Is it Major Gries and Sergeant Cady? Are you okay?"

"There is no word from the bot recovery team yet. But that ain't it. Shane and Thomas can . . . will . . . take care of themselves. If worse comes to worse, they'll kill a walrus, tan the hide and make a kayak to get back." Roger rubbed his chin, then pulled up his Crimson Tide ball cap and ran his fingers through his unruly hair.

"Sit down for a minute. I need to tell somebody this . . . I guess I need to tell everybody but I just don't know where to start."

"Tell everybody what?" Alice sat.

"This." He slid his laptop around for her to see the scanned photos.

"Jesus!" Alice gasped at the sight of a naked, lifelessly pale, and bloodied little girl or what was left of her hanging from a metal spike on a metallic wall. The spike protruded from her chest between her breasts where blood had dried around the impaling shiny metallic stake. Her left leg had been cut off above the knee and her right arm was missing. Her abdomen was open and her entrails were hanging out.

Alan toggled the image viewer and a second image with a wider field of view showed several such bodies. The bodies ranged in age and sex and some were dismembered and naked. Some looked as if they had been butchered, their bodies carved open and their organs removed. And there were two healthy bodies still clothed in military attire reminiscent of SEALs or other recon forces uniforms—American uniforms. One of the SEALs had a spike protruding from his throat and the other was leaned against the wall beneath him with his forehead bashed in and bloodied. His head leaned limply to the left.

"God, what is that!" Alice turned away.

"This is France." Roger toggled the images again.

"She can't be much younger than Tina . . ." Alice turned pale.

The third photo showed an even wider field of view. The background appeared as a vast metal landscape. There were obvious engineered structures and there were piles of junk—metal junk. There was a large metallic box the size of a coliseum hanging effortlessly above the metalscape. The fourth and fifth images zoomed in below the floating object to a group of humans in rags and all of whom looked as if they had been starved to near death. Their bodies looked like something from a World War II film of the Nazi concentration camps.

The starved humans were gathered around the wall where they were hanging bodies. Others were milling around with metal shards, scraping the bodies clean of skin, flesh, and muscle. The wall was a butchery block and the meat was human.

"Cannibals?" Alice whispered.

"Cannibals." Roger nodded.

"We've got a problem," Riggs said over the video link. He was clearly unhappy about whatever information he was about to impart.

"Are they on their way already?" Roger asked, frowning.

"No, but God's Thumb's been taken down," Riggs said. "About an hour after the nuke attacks, a probe group hit

the base. The base sent out a distress call over the land-
lines and then went silent. They're working on getting
somebody in there right now."

"Does it appear to be related to Shane's mission?"
Roger asked.

"Might be, might not," Riggs said. "But we have to
assume that Major Gries's team has been lost. We'll try to
get some recon assets in there to see if they can be recovered but . . . it doesn't look good."

"It ain't over 'til it's over," Roger said, unsmiling. "Like
I told Alice, I'm sure that Shane and Cady will make it
through. They're . . . resourceful."

"This is so not good," Gibson moaned.

Surprise happens in the mind of the commander, Shane
thought. *And you never know what the hell you're doing.
So do something.*

"Unass the vehicles," Shane yelled, watching the
approaching probe swarm. There were at least a hundred
probes in the swarm, but they didn't appear to have
detected the team, yet. They were just tooling along at
about a thousand feet above ground level and headed
vaguely northwest. They might even head right by. Then
again, they might not. But if they acted per normal probe
SOP, they were going to home in on the Humvees. He
looked around and nodded. There was a *very* small
promontory off to the left, about fifty meters away. Perfect. "Grab the samples and all the spare ammo and mines,
including the scatterables! Head for the hill!" He gave
Gibson a shove towards the rear of the Humvee. As soon
as the p.f.c. was moving, it seemed to break everyone else
out of their frozen immobility.

The major hefted his potato gun and started hastily pulling gear out of the back of the Humvee. They had brought far more ordnance than they could pack into the ambush for reasons Shane hadn't considered at the time. Included in it was the scatterable "probe killer" mines *designed* to be picked up.

"Leave the emplaced mines," Cady yelled, expanding on the commander's intentions. "Take the catcher grenades for the potato guns! Leave the food! Mahoney, grab as much of your gear as you can carry! Concentrate on the data you've gotten and anything that can let us track!" He grabbed his minigun and two spare ammo canisters, then picked up the intact probe. "Jones! Forget the glue mines! Grab the case of scatterables and you and Letorres get ready to lay them in along the line to the hilltop. Nelms, grab your BDL and the case of ceramic rounds."

All of the gear that wasn't to be carried was dumped out of the backs of the Humvees in an unmilitary mish-mash. But they had time to unload all the critical items and get most of the way to the hilltop before the probes seemed to notice the cluster of Humvees and turned towards their position, suddenly accelerating.

"Nelms, get in position right on top of the damned samples," Cady said, pointing to the three bags of probe parts. "Jones . . ." he said, looking around.

"On it, Top," the specialist said. He and Letorres hadn't even made it all the way up the hill. They'd stopped about halfway between the Humvees and the hilltop and now had the top off the case of mines. The scatterable mines were fist-sized bright-orange tetrahedrons, packed into the case in a solid mass. He dumped the mass out on the ground and then he and Letorres started spreading them out in a rough crescent around the defensive position. There were sixty of the mines in the case and spreading them took less than two minutes. The last few were tossed away to widen the crescent. They didn't roll far.

In the meantime, Top had spread the rest of the troops into a rough cigar-shaped perimeter with the heaviest group in the direction of the Humvees. The troops carrying potato guns were on the outside of the perimeter with the four troops carrying carbines on the inside. He and Shane were in the center with the samples and spare ammo and then Nelms actually sitting on top of the pile of probe parts.

The probes were stooping onto the Humvees by the time Letorres and Jones were back in the perimeter. The two were hastily pushed into position as the first Humvee started to shake and was lifted off the ground by the probes.

"Okay," Shane said softly. "Wait until they're all down feeding and then open up. Nelms, I'll designate your targets."

Cady had forgotten the case of glue mines in the third Humvee, which had been commanded by Staff Sergeant Gregory. Gregory had heard the sergeant major's order not to bring glue mines so he'd left them behind. But these weren't the whip-detonated mines. These were "probe trap" mines that they'd brought along in case there was a chance to test them. The chance occurred by . . . chance.

A probe, detecting metal in the plastic case, swooped down and exerted enough pull to rip the case open. The pull on the metal within also released several of the friction pull triggers embedded in the mines. This, in turn, detonated the mines.

Each of the mines was a quarter kilo charge of Composition B surrounded by about another half kilo of Coyote glue. While not quite as explosive as the more common C-4, Comp B was the standard filler in military rounds and about ten percent more powerful than TNT.

The case erupted in a titanic explosion that made the Coyote glue within quite redundant and, indeed, virtually all of it was vaporized by the detonation of the twenty rounds in the case.

The explosion, besides causing the troops to cringe and get a ringing in all their ears, not only vaporized the Coyote glue, it also vaporized the probe that had attacked the case and six others in the immediate area. In addition, fourteen more were rendered hors de combat, tossed away from the explosion to fall to the ground, shuddering and spitting sparks.

The Coyote mines were not the only ordnance in the back of the Humvee, and the rest detonated in a long series of secondary explosions that threw material all around the area, concussing and impacting on more probes. A Coyote potato round was thrown from that Humvee to Shane's and detonated a small pile of other potato rounds that cast Coyote glue all over the probes assimilating the Humvee. Another case of "regular" grenades was caught in the explosion and a half dozen detonated sympathetically, killing most of the entrapped probes.

Two probes, blown away from the series of secondaries, were pushed towards the hill while the soldiers on it were still cowering on the ground and trying to dig into the soil with their fingers. They instantly detected the nearest metal, which happened to be the same scatterable mine, and lifted it in the air.

The probe on the right of the line of view happened to win the brief tug-of-war and lifted the half pound orange device to its base, ripping the metal from within.

The metal was glued in place along one of the faces of the tetrahedron. As soon as the mine impacted on the surface of the probe a small packet of super-glue was ruptured, gluing the mine to its surface. The metal, when removed, opened a channel between two otherwise nonreactive chemicals. However, when they came into contact they immediately detonated, causing the surrounding C-4 to detonate in sympathy.

The explosion tore the winning probe to bits, sending more metal scything in every direction, and the detonation and flying shrapnel ripped apart the wing of the accompanying probe, hurling it to the ground.

The swarm and the soldiers recovered at about the same time. For just a moment both groups seemed to pause, as if to take stock and a breath. Then Shane opened his mouth.

"Open fire!"

Each of the potato gun "catcher" rounds was designed much like the scatterable mines. As they flew through the swarm, the probes, sensing metal, swooped down and caught them, pulling them into their metal embrace and then . . . died. After a bit of aiming, each of the potato gun firers stopped bothering and just threw the rounds towards the reduced swarm. Those that missed the swarm entirely were often picked up by probes while they lay on the ground, acting much like the scatterable mines.

The probes were going absolutely frantic. Here was this huge target of metal and . . . at every turn there was MORE! Of course, the "more" was their fellows being blown to bits, but they didn't seem to care or even notice. They were flying all over the place, picking up bits of metal, reassimilating probes and . . . dying.

Each of the potato-gun firers only had five magazines and they expended them in less than three minutes, reducing the swarm to a bare thirty or so individuals. Of course, the probes were assimilating the metal flying around them very quickly, but it took a bit of time to "twin." When one started to twin it tended to float upwards away from the fray. Each of these Shane picked out and had Nelms target with his 7.62 BDL sniper rifle. The rifle fired standard ceramic rounds, although he had a packet of "super rounds" if he needed more range. But at this range he was ignoring his scope and firing under it over open sights. The probes entirely ignored the ceramic round but the rounds did not ignore the probes. One round of 7.62 was more than enough to take down a probe. He got most of the "twinners" and those that he missed Cady directed the carbine teams to engage.

Twenty, then ten, then only six probes were left, all of them trying to breed. The carbine gunners, Nelms, and Cady with his minigun took care of them with only two managing to twin and those two staying in the area to assimilate until blasted apart by the sergeant major.

With that probe down, there were no more functioning probes in sight. Just a twisted field of shattered metal.

"Damn," Jones said, standing up and looking out over the "battlefield." "We won." He paused and that didn't seem to be enough. "WE WON!"

"Yeah, we did," Cady said, looking out at the masses of twisted metal scattered around the tundra. "But they got our wheels."

"Alien bastards," Nelms shouted. "You killed our Humvee!"

"Boss," Mahoney said, quietly. He'd set up his laptop, then taken a place in the line, but as soon as the fighting died he'd hurried back to his beloved electronics.

"What?" Shane asked, somewhat loudly. His ears were still ringing from the detonation of the case of mines.

"I think we've got a live one out there."

The probe was upside down, lying sideways on another much more damaged boomerang. The only probe was missing the tip of one wing, but the wing looked . . . odd. The wing narrowed towards the tip, then flared outwards to a jagged break.

"It was breeding or whatever," Jones said, bending down and prodding the thing with his carbine. It was shuddering and sparks were shooting off the exposed interior but it couldn't seem to fly.

"There's something seriously wrong with it," the sergeant major said, frowning.

"Yeah, Top, it can't fly," Jones pointed out.

"More than that, shit for brains," Cady replied. "It's sitting on a big hunk of metal and it's not tearing it apart."

"I guess we're going to find out if they can repair themselves," Shane said, his hands on his hips as he surveyed the trophy. "Top, tag and bag this thing. If we've got to dump some of the pieces out, we'll do it. Mahoney!" he yelled.

"Sir?" the specialist called from the small hill where the rest of the team was still waiting.

"Any sign of more of 'em?"

"Negative, sir," the specialist called back. "There's some

radiating off to the northwest and a lot to the northeast. But it's all more than twenty klicks off. That one's radiating, but *very* weak."

"Keep an eye on it," Shane yelled. "Tag it and bag it—and make sure it's wrapped so it's not radiating—and then we're going to go find out if there's anything left of the base."

There wasn't.

They'd kept up a steady pace, walking through the strange arctic twilight and into the "dawn" as the sun began, once again, to ascend into the sky. As they approached the base at God's Thumb, though, it was apparent that the probes had been there before them.

The region around the base was flat as a pancake so the control tower was normally visible from at least ten miles away. However, nothing of the base was apparent until they got into the last kilometer.

"Holy shit," Jones said. The approach brought them in close to the massive runways that had been the original reason for the base's existence.

Used as far back as WWII for antisubmarine patrols, the facility had been heavily upgraded during the Cold War to support long-range bombers. The runways were designed to launch loaded B-52s on their way to gut the Soviet Union, thus they were very long and made of very thick concrete.

They were now . . . long, plowed-looking sections of dirt and crumbled concrete.

"They pull the rebar out of the concrete," Shane said, balancing his end of the pole. There had been long carry-poles in the Humvees. On the way to the ambush it hadn't been worth carrying them, in Shane's opinion. But once the Humvees were trashed they'd picked them out of the debris. The long poles could be run through the handles on the catch-bags so the soldiers detailed to carry them didn't have to use their hands the whole time.

And Rank Hath No Privileges when there was over three hundred pounds of probes and parts to carry sixty kilometers.

"What are we going to do, sir?" Jones asked as they continued to follow the edge of Runway Road. The road itself had been torn to bits.

"Get down to the main base," Shane said, gesturing tiredly at the cluster of buildings. "Find something to spell out 'Come Get Us!' Then leave it up to Roger and the rest of the guys to figure out how."

The specialist nodded and continued to trudge forward. They hadn't been able to carry all that much ammo with them—it had been a trade-off between time, ammo and probe bits. Shane had edged towards time and probe bits over ammo, so if they had to fight the probes off again they wouldn't have all that much of a chance. Of course, the old man knew that, too. So mentioning it would be pointless.

As they approached the main base, which was connected to a small port by road, it was apparent that it was, essentially, rubble. Not a single building was standing and all of the concrete roads had been torn up. Some of the roads, those with asphalt surfaces, were intact.

"Jesus," Mahoney said as Shane stopped, raised a closed fist and lowered the burden to the ground.

"Well, they don't rape or burn," Letorres said, drifting over to pick up a piece of paper that was blowing by in the incessant wind. "There's that."

"But they sure as hell do loot and pillage," Sergeant Gregory said, nodding. "Anything useful?"

"Training schedule," Letorres said, flicking the paper to blow towards the ocean. "About as useless as it comes."

"Top, see if you can find anything to improve sheltering," Shane said, rubbing his shoulder. "Get out some perimeter. Mahoney, set up your boxes. I want at least thirty percent personnel up at all times; these things don't care about day and night."

"Gregory," Cady said. "Take Jones and Letorres and do a survey for any shelter that's still standing. Just a couple of walls will do. Angle down towards the port. The rest of you, get the gear in a huddle and put in a perimeter. Nelms, center up again, potato guns out and carbines in. Let's get it moving, people."

"Nothing, nada, zilch," Jones said an hour later. The three soldiers had moved southward through the base, looking for anything that could be used for shelter. But the vast majority of the buildings had been concrete from which the rebar had been pulled. They weren't even sure *where* on the base they were; the road signs were gone and most of the roads had been dug up for metal.

"We need to get heading back," Gregory said, looking at the sun. Despite trying, the Huntsville team hadn't been able to come up with any really good nonmetallic watches.

"I could use some rest," Letorres said, shaking his head. "I could swear that bit of rubble just moved," he added, pointing to a section of what had probably been wall.

"Me, too," Jones said, drifting sideways and then taking a knee to target the pile of broken concrete.

Gregory spun slowly in place, taking in the sky and ground, then turned back to the pile.

"Slow advance," the staff sergeant said. "Jones, keep it covered. Letorres right and rear, I'll take left and rear."

The three spread out in a rough triangle and approached the rubbled wall, which was about seventy meters away.

When they were about fifty meters from the pile or rubble, Jones raised a closed fist, then stopped and took a knee.

"What?" Gregory asked, keeping security left and to the rear.

"Shit," Jones said after a moment. He stood up and let his weapon drop on its sling, cupping his hands around his mouth. "HEY!"

The rubble seemed to shift slightly and then Gregory realized that it was a gray suit of ghillie cloth.

"What the fuck are you guys doing over *there*?" the soldier under the ghillie cloth asked, raising up to take a knee. Except for wearing a mottled gray digi-cam uniform he was outfitted in essentially the same manner as the capture team. "You were supposed to be approaching from the east!"

Gregory realized that in their perambulations they'd gotten over to the west side of the base and, apparently, snuck up on someone that was looking for *them*.

"We're setting up camp over on the east side by the runways," Gregory said, waving in that direction.

"Why?" the soldier asked, waving over his shoulder, then stepping down off the rubble. "Don't you *want* to go home?"

❈   ❈   ❈

"Lieutenant Cragar, Alpha Platoon, SEAL Team One, sir," the SEAL officer said, saluting Shane.

"Good to see you, Lieutenant," Shane said, wearily returning the salute. "And, especially, additional bodies to carry all this crap. Don't get any metal around the red-marked bag; it's got a live one in it."

The SEAL platoon had been set up near the port, with OPs out to watch for Shane's team. As it turned out, the teams had been less than two hundred meters apart and in the cratered landscape of the former base they had missed each other entirely.

Cragar, though, had picked up the whole platoon and moved it to the recon team's site when the SEAL sentry had brought in Gregory and his team.

"Holy shit," the SEAL said, shaking his head. "Good work, sir!"

"It was an accident," Shane admitted. "We got bounced on the way back. They got the Humvees, we got a live one. I call that a win."

"No shit," Cragar said, his eyes wide. "You *won*?"

"Beat the crap out of them, sir," Cady said, his face split in a broad grin.

"We can do it," Shane said, quietly. "We've proved that. The question is, can we do it *enough*."

"Well, we've got transport out to the sub, sir," Cragar said, waving his platoon forward to help carry the probe samples. "It's going to be a bit rough. And you'll want to put these on," he added, holding out a plastic packet.

"What's this?" Shane asked, looking at the pack. "Scopolamine?"

"As I said, sir, it's going to be a bit rough," Cragar said, grinning.

"Just climb in," the SEAL said to Cady, gesturing at the ocean kayak. It was colored in gray-blue digi-cam that made it almost disappear into the lapping water. The kayak had been drawn up on a pebbled shore but beyond the small cove the waves were crashing in foaming white water. "Keep your weight down or you're going in the drink and you *really* don't want to go swimming, even in the suit."

The team had been hastily stuffed into immersion suits as soon as they got to the beach and now were boarding the kayaks as the SEALs loaded their samples and equipment.

"I don't care for water, much," Cady said, clambering cautiously over the bow. "I'm too solid to swim good. My massive, godlike penis drags me down."

"Got it," the SEAL said, grinning. He hung onto the side of the kayak and made his way into the waist-deep water by the side of the small boat. "Slide your legs, and your godlike dick if it will fit, into that opening," the SEAL said, gesturing to the front seat.

Cady managed to get into the opening although it was a tight fit. The SEAL pulled up something that looked vaguely like a cross between a poncho and a harness and hooked it over the sergeant major's shoulders.

"Cinch that buckle in if you would, Sergeant Major," the SEAL said, gesturing at an unbuckled clasp. "Not too tight, but it's what's going to keep you from getting soaked."

"Works for me," Cady said, sliding the straps out so

they'd fit around his chest and then hooking up.

"These things are stable as hell," the SEAL said as he pushed the kayak into the water. He slid along the side, using lines that were laced there for the purpose, until he got to the rear. Then he slid over the side and into his own compartment, hooking up and picking up his paddle. As soon as they were out from the beach he spun the kayak in a circle and made his way into the cove where several of the other kayaks were assembling.

"Why kayaks?" Cady asked. "I thought you guys used Zodiacs. And do you want me to help paddle?" He'd noticed that there was one lashed by his seat.

"I can handle it," the SEAL said. "You're pretty solid but this takes a certain set of muscle groups and it'd probably kick your ass after a while. And the reason we're using these instead of Zods is that the sub is about ten miles out. Paddling a Zod for ten miles is a bitch and a half. This isn't *easy*, but it's a fuck of a lot better than paddling a Zod. Especially in this shit."

The kayaks had assembled about fifty meters offshore and about the same from the opening to the cove. As soon as the last kayak was with the group, Lieutenant Cragar waved to the south and they headed for the opening.

"This is pretty rough, huh?" Cady asked as the kayak swooped up and down on the waves in the cove.

"Light chop," the SEAL said. "Now, out there, we've got seven to ten foot waves. There's a storm coming in from the southeast, which is why they're running so high. It's gonna be interesting getting out to the sub. We surfed most of the way in."

"There wasn't anybody at the base," Cady said as they cleared the cove and the first real wave hit them. The nose of the boat pitched up until it was pointed at the sky and the kayak rolled slightly to the side. Then it headed for the trough like a rocket, the bow digging into the oncoming wave and covering the front of the kayak in green and white water. Then they headed back up the next wall of water. "Jesus!"

"Think of it as a free roller coaster ride!" the SEAL yelled against the stronger wind that was blowing in the open ocean. "Once we get out a bit it will get less choppy! We might even be able to use the sail!"

"Sail?"

"Hey, you want me to have to paddle the whole way?"

Through the maelstrom of water Cady saw a spout and at first thought it might be a whale. But when two more came up he realized it was something else.

"Is somebody throwing grenades?" he yelled.

"Right," the SEAL called back. "Signaling the boat mission accomplished. We'll head out to sea a ways and then signal them in. It'll take a few hours. You just sit back and relax."

The kayak was still pitching around like a live thing, but the SEALs seemed to have things in hand. And he wasn't getting seasick, which was a blessing. He never seemed to get air-sick, but the one time he'd been in a boat deep-sea fishing with a retired buddy, he'd gotten sick as a dog despite the pills he took. Whatever that patch was they'd put on him, it seemed to work.

Not for Jones, though. He saw the specialist was bent over puking up his guts.

The seat in the kayak was pretty comfortable and there was enough room for his feet. It was also warming up from his body-heat. Since the water was going to be around freezing, it must have been insulated somehow. It was nice and comfy except for the constant up and down, side-to-side motion.

It had been a long damned mission. The sergeant major crossed his arms in front of him, bent his head and went to sleep.

"We're here!"

Cady lifted his head and rubbed his eyes to get some of the encrusted salt off. Sure enough, there was a submarine on the surface with people up on the conning tower.

"We sure there are no probes around?" Cady asked.

"No," the SEAL admitted. "But we better hope they ain't."

The sub was big. Vast even. And the sides were rounded and looked very slippery. Then there was the fact that the waves were washing over the side.

"How the hell are we going to . . ." Cady said, then shook his head again as the rear portion of the sub seemed to bulge upwards. In a moment two vast clam-shell doors had opened up and big cranes were lifting into the air.

"They'd been working on this before the probes got here," the SEAL said. "It's an Ohio Class converted for covert ops. They changed the design a little for the new missions, but not much."

One of the kayaks had paddled up to the side and the cranes let down lines that were hooked up to hard points on the front and rear of the kayak. Then the whole thing, kayak, people and gear, was lifted into the air and over the side of the sub to disappear behind the doors.

There were two cranes in operation and before long it

was Cady's turn. He grabbed the swinging line and got the hook attached to the eyelet on the front of the kayak then held on as it was lifted into the air. The kayak was swung over the doors and then hung suspended for a moment over a huge cavernlike hold that must have been three stories deep.

"This is the old missile compartment," the SEAL said as they were lowered into the hold. "Go ahead and unstrap; we're going to unass as soon as we hit the bottom."

Cady got the straps and poncholike arrangement off and as soon as the kayak settled into a cradle he climbed out. Some SEALs and sailors grasped the lines on either side of the kayak and lifted it off the cradle. The lines from the crane started retracting upwards to pick up another boat.

Cady grabbed one of the handholds and helped the group carry the kayak to a rack, setting it on the third tier. Then he and the SEAL opened up the cargo compartment and he retrieved his pack and minigun.

"Nice rig," the SEAL said, nodding at the weapon. "You'll want to clear it in here. The armory is on the forward bulkhead. We're bunked forward, I suppose I'll see you around."

Cady wasn't too sure which way was forward at this point, but he saw the CO in conversation with a Navy guy with captain's bars. That made him a lieutenant in the Navy and since he was in khakis he must be from the ship.

"The next one is the live one," the CO was saying as he approached. "How are you going to handle it?"

"I'm not sure," the lieutenant said, shaking his head. "We'll leave it suspended away from metal and in view.

But if it goes live once we're underway, we're going to have to take it out. And fast. If that thing eats a hole in the pressure hull or, hell, some of the pipes, we'll sink for sure."

"We can destroy it easy enough," Shane said. "We'll just leave someone on watch at all times with orders to destroy it if it so much as moves."

"Hook a mine up by it, sir," Cady suggested. "That way if it goes back to pulling metal, it'll pull that. Hopefully. And that will take it out."

"And someone on watch," the lieutenant said.

"Agreed," the major replied. "But not my people; we've been on continuous ops for the last few days. The SEALs aren't much better."

"We just happen to have a spare platoon," the lieutenant said, grinning. "I think they've got a new mission."

"Great." Shane nodding tiredly. "In that case, let's get my people cleaned up and bunked down. How soon are we going to reach the States?"

"About forty hours," the lieutenant said. "We're going into Portsmouth."

"Wake me up when we get there."

"Hail the conquering hero," General Riggs said, putting a hand on Major Gries's shoulder as he stepped up behind him.

"You know, sir, if this was a science fiction movie, there'd be all sorts of cool readouts and blinking lights and stuff," Shane said, shaking his head and waving at the window.

"Sorry, Major, this is as cool as we could make it," the general replied, smiling.

The room beyond the window looked like a cross between a very messy toy-maker's cottage and a metal octopus convention. Wires ran everywhere, tools were scattered at apparent random and there wasn't a cool read-out in sight. Well, one. There was a plasma fusion screen with some sort of complicated control screen up. But the rest were mostly monochrome monitors that looked like somebody had raided a museum.

All of this stuff was concentrated on the bits of probe scattered around the room. The "live" one was being kept under careful observation in an underground bunker wired with command and automatically detonating mines. It was still radiating in the RF spectrum but as deep as it was there was no way that radio was getting out. Since being brought off the sub it had been surrounded by Faraday cages to prevent communication. Assuming it didn't have a secondary "magic" communications system, the probes shouldn't know where it was located. Whether they would care was another question.

Work on the "live" one could wait. For that matter they weren't even messing with the "whole" one that Cady had knocked out. The engineers and scientists gathered in the clean room were having a hard enough time with the bits that Shane had brought back.

"You can tell they're baffled," Riggs said quietly. The glass was two-way and not particularly thick; he didn't want them being thrown off by the comment. "They don't scratch their heads, but they have other tells."

"Roger tries to stick his hands in his pockets, and he fidgets," Shane said, nodding. "And Tom rubs his beard. Alan just throws his hands up in the air like . . ." He waited a moment and then chuckled as the environment-suit clad engineer straightened up and threw his hands up in the air, gesticulating wildly and clearly on the edge of shouting.

"But I'll say this for them, they just won't give up. Roger has been in there almost twenty-four hours a day. I'm not even sure he has slept this week. He probably wouldn't have eaten if his girlfriend, uh, what's her name . . . Tami . . . you know the one with the huge knockers . . ."

"Traci?" Gries asked.

"Yeah, that's it, Traci. Anyway, she has brought them food and occasionally makes Roger quit to take a shower or a nap or something," Riggs grinned.

"Damn, Traci, huh? I had no idea."

"Anyway, since Roger briefed us on France he's been . . . different. Hell, we all have, but Roger . . . well, I think he thinks it's his fault somehow."

"France?" Gries asked.

"Nobody has briefed you?"

"Sir, we've been pretty much spinning our wheels since we returned. And like you said, Roger has been busy."

"Shit. I'll get somebody to brief you as soon as I can. Europe is . . . bad."

Roger looked over his shoulder at the two observers and shrugged. Then he tapped Tom on the shoulder and waved to Alan.

The two soldiers met the engineers at the exit to the clean room and Danny raised an eyebrow.

"Not going well?" he asked neutrally.

"Not at all," Roger admitted. They'd been studying the probes for a week and hadn't been able to give one progress report. "We think we've found their motivator, the inertialess drive. But supplying power doesn't get it to work. And we've found something that looks like the brain, but it's a solid mass of silica and metal, mostly metal. And we've found what *has* to be their power source. But it's . . ." Roger paused and rubbed his bloodshot eyes.

"Impossible," Alan said, flatly. "F'n impossible! It's a ball of hollow metal about the size of a baby's fist. No fuel, no external supply. Just . . . a ball of metal."

"And it's got to, somehow, supply power equivalent to a multistage rocket," Tom pointed out. "The runs from it shouldn't even be able to handle the power. We *know* these things can accelerate at something like a hundred gravities. Even with their relatively low mass, we're talking about terawatts of power and there's *no* way that the power runs that we're seeing could handle that load. And we're still not sure what the tractor beam is generated by. Nothing in this thing makes sense."

"The brain is the worst," Roger said. "It's unbelievably complicated. I mean you'd expect it to be, but this thing is light years beyond our current tech. I think it's basically a controller chip, but it's constructed in three dimensions. We've been trying to do that for decades but, besides the sheer difficulty and expense, the programming algorithms are a bitch. And the actual processing seems to be at the atomic level. We don't have the instruments to study it, here, much less make head or tail of it."

"What do you want to do?" Riggs asked.

"Give it to other people," Roger replied definitely. "We've got three of the brain cases, if that's what they are. We'll send one to the redoubt at the LockMart facility in Denver, another to MIT, and the last one to Georgia Tech. Tech's setting up a redoubt using some of our plans, so they could hold out even after Atlanta gets hit. Hopefully they can make some sense of it. I'm also going to request that all the data be turned into open source. We need anyone and everyone looking at this data. We don't know who might have the right way to look at it."

"That will need authorization," Riggs pointed out.

"I'll bring it up with the secretary, but I think I have that authority though I'm not sure," Roger said. "But we need to make this information open to the public."

"They're going public with the fact that we sent a team into Greenland and it won a small battle with the probes," the general said, nodding. "If we start putting out data about the probes it will be obvious where it came from. I'll suggest making it a two parter. Do a dog and pony show with Shane and his team along with the bits of probes that we recovered. Civilian morale needs a shot in the arm; it's getting really low."

"I couldn't believe the media when I got back," Shane said, nodding. "It's all doom and gloom."

"There are plenty of people who have just given up," Riggs admitted. "All of the media included."

"Not that I particularly want to do a dog and pony," Shane added. "But I think it will help."

"I'll call the Chairman," Riggs said musingly, then chuckled. "You know, a few months ago I was surprised he knew my nickname. Now I'm calling him just about every day. Or, more often, he calls me. Strange."

"Hell," Roger said, trying to be humorous with his deepest accent, but his tiredness, fear, and somberness was hard to overcome. "Ah's a deputy secretary with the weight of the world on my shoulders. How strange is that?" He said through a very thin, pursed lipped, halfhearted smile.

"As strange as getting invaded by metal probes from beyond the solar system?" Shane asked, shrugging.

Chapter 20

Ret Ball: *So my friends, if you are still on the Internet then you haven't been overrun by the machines yet. If you happened to catch the news of the team that went to Greenland—that's right Greenland, they're getting awfully close to us now—then you know that the machines can be beaten by our military. I wonder though: Can we beat them in a full out attack? We've lost contact with China and Russia and all of Europe. Parts of Africa and India are out of contact and I'm hearing rumors from my friends in the South Pacific that Japan is under attack. What do we do, friends? I'm taking your calls and e-mails here tonight on the Truth Nationwide. Bart from Chicago, you're on the air.*

Caller: *Hello, Ret. I served in the 801st for six years*

and I have to tell you that this is something we've never trained for. As far as I can tell we've lost all satellite communications and GPS. We've lost our capabilities to use radar and radio comms. And it looks like even flying is now out of the picture. When was the last time you saw a plane in the sky?

Ret Ball: *That is a good point, Bart. I haven't seen a plane for at least a week now. What do you make of it?*

Caller: *My guess is that the Chinese and the Russians put up a good fight and tipped the machines off to human military technologies and tactics. If those things can take out our sats then why not our planes? I bet they're doing to us just what we did to Saddam in the Gulf Wars and putting the planet under a no-fly zone.*

Ret Ball: *Oh my gosh! I never thought of that. I bet you are right, caller. Thanks for the call. Aha, Megiddo is on line three! Hello, Megiddo you are on the Truth Nationwide. Tell us what you know.*

Caller: *Hi, Ret. My wife and I have taken to underground literally and I suggest that we all do this. I've been thinking about the Von Neumann probes' mode of attack.*

Ret Ball: *Yes, do tell.*

Caller: *Well, they're attacking the cities and the industrialized complexes. But they aren't doing this because they're militarily significant.*

Ret Ball: *Oh? Then why?*

Caller: *Materials. It's plain and simple. The alien machines must need raw materials to replicate themselves. And what better place to find a lot of already refined materials than in the big modern cities? Think about how much metal is in one office building alone. The thoughts of that are staggering because it must have taken them several years to transform the Martian surface. And then it took them more than a year to transform the Moon. But not Earth. We have so many materials available and ready for them that they probably can't eat it fast enough. That is probably the only thing slowing them down!*

Ret Ball: *My God! You speak truth, my friend!*

Caller: *Indeed! I suggest everybody get out of the cities and make as far into the wilderness as you can. Prepare by finding natural sources of water and foods and bring and store as much nonperishable foodstuffs as you can. I can only imagine what the poor people in the occupied regions are going through.*

Ret Ball: *Hey, you bring up another good point. Why have we heard nothing from survivors or refugees from the occupied zones? Are there no refugees or survivors? Thanks again for your call, Megiddo, as always you gave us a lot of food for thought. Next caller is Tina from Alabama. Hello Tina, you are on the Truth Nationwide.*

�֍   �֍   ✖

Alice Pike was good at what she did. In fact, there were those in certain circles that said when it came to developing microprocessor technologies and superminiature space-hardened electronics that there was no equal. Dr. Pike had taken the "brain tube" from the wrecked bot the Huntsville Redoubt was keeping and had it scanned with every type of analysis tool known to man. She had it put through X rays, electron microscopy, MRIs, electric field mapping, magnetic field mapping, acoustic mapping, heat conductivity, reflectivity, conductivity, superconductivity, diamagnetism, and a host of other tests.

The only thing she could figure was that there were patterns within the tube but they changed. After each successive X ray, the internal patterns looked different. So at least she knew that the brain was active in some way. The question was if it was changing on its own or if the X rays were changing it? Alice could think of no way to tell. She was stumped.

"This is impossible," she muttered to herself as she looked at the various diagrams and sensor images of the interior of the brain tube.

"What's impossible, Alice?" Roger Reynolds and Traci Adams had slipped in behind her to observe but not to disturb.

"Jesus, Roger! Don't sneak up on me like that. You nearly scared me to death." Alice looked away from the monitors for a second and rubbed her eyes.

"I thought you might need this." Traci handed Alice a cup of coffee.

"Thanks," Alice said as she grabbed the cup with both hands and held it beneath her face to savor the aroma and to feel the steamy warmth against her skin. The stimulus relaxed her and settled her nerves a bit. She took a big swig from the cup. "I really did need this."

"So, Alice, *what* is impossible?" Roger asked.

"This crazy thing!" she pointed at the brain tube. "I've scanned it in everyway I can think of and I can't make heads or tails of it. The electron microscopy shows these various regions of different densities and my guess is that these regions with the curvy bands here are some sort of interface or junction between different materials like the junctions in semiconductors. But these smaller spots that are peppered throughout the thing . . . I just have no idea. Oh, and every time they were X rayed some of them changed."

"Changed? How?" Traci sat down by Alice to get a better angle on the monitors.

"Well, that varies. Sometimes in size and sometimes in position." She shrugged. "I dunno."

"Roger, look here!" Traci pointed at the monitor. "You see that spot there and then over here there are these two spots in the subsequent photo."

"Yes, I see. So?" Roger could tell that Traci thought she was on to something but wasn't quite sure what.

"I noticed that earlier, Traci. But I can't make heads or tails of it." Alice pointed out two other similar sets of images.

"Don't you see . . . of course y'all don't, you're not that type of physicist. Those are like targets in a decay shower in an accelerator experiment or like we see in the atmosphere when cosmic rays hit it. It's a decay chain. That is something nuclear going on there, " Traci pointed out excitedly and smiled. "Uh . . . oh my."

"What, Traci?" Both Roger and Alice asked in unison.

"Was this thing checked with a Geiger counter?"

"Oh Jesus!" Alice gasped. "I didn't even think of that."

"Well, wait a minute. Don't get excited now. We checked this thing out thoroughly when it first came in." Roger calmed them. "There was no radiation."

"Yeah, I realize that Roger. But . . . some sort of decay has taken place in it since the X rays. It could be hot now." Traci shrugged her shoulders.

"Let's check it out." Roger picked up the lab phone and called the operator. "This is Dr. Reynolds, put me through to my secretary, please."

"One minute, Dr. Reynolds."

"Dr. Reynolds' office, this is Sarah, can I help you?"

"Sarah, this is Roger."

"Yes sir?"

"I need a Geiger counter in room 247B in the lab facility in two minutes. Would you see to that for me please?"

"Right awa,y Dr. Reynolds."

"Thanks."

"But I'm telling you that looks like a fission or a decay chain or an air shower of some sort. That is the result of something subatomic!" Traci argued.

"Well, then if it is, somehow the fragments are stable and not hot," Roger said. "Perhaps that is how this thing sends data or something."

"Oh hey, there's a thought! Statistical decays have been used for stable clocks for years. Why not use one for logic gates . . . hmmm?" Alice started scanning through the images more closely. "Not to be rude, but . . . I have an idea and I think better without interruption."

"Alice, is that your polite way of telling us to get the hell out of your hair?" Roger asked.

"Yes." Alice smiled sheepishly.

"Come on, Traci. We have other things to do. Alice, keep us posted."

Alice didn't respond. She was already too involved with her train of thought. *Decay chains for logic gates . . .*

The old copper mine had begun to take shape and was becoming more "lived in" every day. Helena had added some more homey touches to the main chamber once the electricity and plumbing were completed. She had brought down some of the decorative pieces from the cabin, including some picture frames, a painting or two, an afghan that her mother had knitted for her, a few throw pillows, and a couple of lamps.

The electrical wiring and plumbing that had been run along the floor and around the walls were now mostly covered up by two by fours and paneling on the walls and two by sixes and a combination of decking, plywood, and OSB particle board on the floor. It had taken more than thirty trips down the mountain to town to every hardware store and lumber yard to find enough materials to finish the interior of the shelter. Since the effective martial law on resources due to the alien threat, only minimal materials were available. He did manage several buckets of 10D nails, an assortment of woodscrews, sheetmetal screws, some nuts and bolts, a few cans of spray paint, and several gallons of leftover paints—Helena made him buy the paint. There would probably have been no way to gather enough materials to complete the interior of the mine shafts had he not come across an abandoned horse barn a few miles outside of town.

Richard had watched the barn for a couple of days as

he made trips to town and saw no activity there. Once he stopped he realized that the wood was probably more than fifty years old and nearly petrified to the point that it would never rot. There was some termite damage so he picked up some chemicals at the hardware store that took care of that. He had spent several weeks since he had begun the shelter in the mine tearing down the barn and hauling the materials up the mountain and down the mine shaft. Some of the materials he had used to repair some minor storm damage to the cabin that had been their home while the shelter was under construction. Helena still spent the majority of her time there, but Richard had convinced her that the time would come when she would be happy to be down in the old abandoned copper mine.

So, Helena had pitched in and helped make the underground environment more habitable. She had done almost all of the painting and decorating. In fact, Richard had seen no need for flooring or wall surfaces other than the rock and dirt the mine provided. Helena had "convinced" him to add the flooring. Richard had grown particularly fond of Helena's methods for convincing him to do things; there was always nudity involved—lots of it.

As it turned out, Richard was quite pleased with the flooring. He laid it down in a way that allowed him to run plumbing, electrical outlets, and Ethernet underneath safely and out of the way of foot traffic. This also gave him the ability to do repairs and upgrades underneath the false flooring as needed.

Richard was surfing through the software manual for the radio frequency spectrum analyzer control system. The damned thing was the only piece of equipment that he seemed to be having trouble bringing online. The ultraviolet/visible/infrared system he had bought gave him no trouble setting up. The mass spectrometer had given him no problems. The electron microscope had given him no problems except that he nearly pulled a muscle in his lower back trying to move it. He had had to upgrade to a larger pull cart and finally broke down and got the electric four-wheeled vehicle. Once he had that, his construction and moving went much faster. Helena had been telling him that for months, but he wouldn't listen. It was actually she who had *convinced* him to buy the thing—she had grown tired of the long walk.

Richard continued plowing through the software control manual for the RF spectrum analyzer and tapping in instructions. There was little success. He looked at the output on the computer screen and there was nothing but a line of white noise across the entire RF spectrum. He knew that was bogus because he had several multigigahertz microprocessors operating in the laboratory room of the mine at that moment . . . but nothing.

"All right, Dr. Horton, what are we forgetting?" he said to himself. He set the manual down and restarted the device—still no luck. Then he noticed the little omnidirectional antenna still in the clear plastic bag sitting on top of the monitor for the analyzer.

"No way, I'm that stupid . . ." He crawled under the folding table and noticed two coaxial cables lying on the floor. One was about six feet long and coiled up and not connected at either end. The other was the end of the cable that came from the other antenna hidden in the rocks outside on top of the mountain. Neither were connected so there was no antenna connected to the system. He slapped his forehead. "I guess I am."

Richard plugged the short cable into the back of the analyzer and the other to a two-port switch. He ran the test antenna into one port and the above-ground antenna into the other.

"That should do it." He pressed the reset button on the menu screen and *presto*! The computer processors in the room appeared on the screen as spikes around 2.4, 4.3, and 5.1 gigahertz. "Good, now let's take a look up top, shall we?" He flipped the two-port switch to the B port that was connected to the antenna above ground. The screen filled with radio noise and several peaks across the spectrum.

As he watched the radio noise spectral content, nine peaks that were just above the noise floor began to rise in amplitude. The peaks rose to only about ten percent above the noise floor and they also shifted in frequency from left to right in what appeared to be random order, all of them dancing around about 1.4 gigahertz or so.

"Hunh? What the hell is that?" he muttered and adjusted the gain on the receiver. The peaks rose from the noise floor slightly. "Spread spectrum? Hmm . . . centered around 1.4 gigahertz . . . I wonder if that means anything . . . hmmm." Richard rubbed his unruly and slightly graying beard thoughtfully. Then he nearly jumped out of his skin when his instant messenger alarm dinged at him.

RussianChick6300: *Come to cabin now!*
Megiddo: *Why?*
RussianChick6300: *Alien robots here!*
Megiddo: *B right there!*
RussianChick6300: *Hury they r everyw*

⌘   ⌘   ⌘

They must have cut the Internet connection to the cabin. Richard jumped into action and tripped over himself trying to get out of the computer desk chair he was sitting in. He nearly knocked himself out on the floor, but fortunately he was only dazed by the *thwack* his forehead made when it hit the decking. Rubbing between his eyes at the red mark forming there, he ran to the shaft main room and out the door to the four-wheeler. He started it up and motored up the shaft.

The briefings that he had read on the Internet and the few eyewitness accounts that had made it out of Europe came to mind, so he stopped the vehicle a good hundred meters or more inside the shaft and ran the rest of the way. Fortunately, he was in good shape from all those trips up and down the mine. He reached the mine's entrance and eased out into the pathway that led uphill to the cabin. There was no sign of alien robots that he could see, so he darted across the small clearing at the entrance where the logging road ran into the mine. He stayed near the edge of the road hoping that the trees would help cover him—but he didn't count on it.

One thing he couldn't understand was, why now? Richard had been preparing for the bots and all the intel and briefings that had been released to the public had suggested that they were not any farther than Greenland and that they would not be to the States for some time. Worse than that was the fact that the bots typically attacked the big cities first. So why in the hell were they here in the northwestern mountains of South Carolina in the middle of nowhere? This was too soon. He hadn't had time to bot-proof the cabin.

About a hundred feet down the logging road he turned

uphill on a footpath that they had worn as a shortcut up to the cabin. The path led him through the rocks and the oak trees that were typical of northwestern South Carolina woods along the Appalachian trail and wound its way to the rear of the small dovetail construction log cabin. As Richard turned the corner to the side of the cabin where the driveway ended there sat Helena. In front of her were pieces of four tires that looked like the steel belts had been ripped right out of the rubber—and the wheels were nowhere to be seen—and what appeared to be pieces of automobile carpet and upholstery, pieces of plastic, vinyl and rubber. The mess looked like a monster had eaten their pickup truck and vomited out anything that wasn't metal. There was nothing left of the Ford F-250. Ford tough was apparently not tough enough to withstand alien robots.

"Are you . . . harmed?" Richard touched Helena on the shoulder.

"Harmed, uh, *nyet*. Pissed to hell, *da!*" She was sitting down on the edge of the driveway fiddling with her jeans. The zipper and snaps had been torn away and the pants were basically ripped open at the crotch.

"Where are they?"

"Gone. Gone as quick as dey came. Goddamn tings took every pot and pan in de goddamn cabin. Even de sonovabitch bedsprings are gone. Look, my best goddamned jeans are ruined. Dey ate de televeesion, de forks and spoons, de couch springs, and even de goddamn truck. Dey ripped it to fuckin' bits." Helena sat shaking her head. "Tought you said no goddamn worries for long time?"

"Yeah, I don't understand that part. It doesn't make sense to me. What did they look like?" Richard could tell

Helena was shaken up. Not from her colorful use of the English language—that was her nature and Richard had long since gotten used to that—but the drained look on her face. She was pale and looked like she had spent every bit of energy in her body the way a marathoner looks at the end of the race. Or the way a soldier looks after a battle—afraid, exhausted, and just glad to still be alive.

Richard sat down beside her looking at the pieces of the truck—so much useless plastic, vinyl, and rubber. Even the rubber insulating coatings of the sparkplug and other wires were left behind, but the metal wires themselves had been pulled right out.

"Dey look like dat goddamned ting dere if you can put it back togedder. I tought you'd vant one so I beats the last one to fucking pieces with a stick of stove wood. Oh, dey took de goddamned stove too." Helena pointed at what appeared to be a metal boomerang about a meter across. Then she pointed at the hole in the roof and wall where the wood-burning stove had been yanked out. "Dat's gonna leak like hell."

"But you're not hurt? You certain?" Richard put his hand on her shoulder and glanced back and forth between her, the truck remains, the hole in the cabin, and the smashed bot. There was a trickle of blood on her right earlobe where an earring had once been. The lobe wasn't torn through but the hole had been treated roughly.

"I'm okay." She rubbed at her ears and looked at the blood on her thumb and forefinger. "Shit. Go look at de damned ting." Helena pulled her hair back behind her head and tied it into a ponytail. Then she patted the stick of stove wood that she had used as a battle club, "I'm gonna keep you, *da*."

Richard had to look at the bot—he *had* to. It was smashed to hell and gone—Helena had made certain of that. After a bit of inspection, Richard was fairly certain that the alien thing had once been a metal boomerang about a meter or so from tip to tip. It had been about ten to twenty centimeters thick and all of the surfaces were smooth and rounded and seamless. But now it was bent up and dented and had a couple of pieces busted off of it. On its underside was a smaller similar boomerang about a third the size. The smaller boomerang appeared to be molded seamlessly directly to the larger one. There was a large crack through both of them and there were several peripheral pieces scattered about it. Nothing about it, other than the fact that it was an alien Von Neumann probe, seemed to be unearthly—at least not from a quick visual inspection. But Richard had every intent of taking a closer look, a much closer look.

"This looks like common metals." Richard kicked at it.

"*Da*. Like a beer can. Oh, dey took dat too. And de refrigerator." Helena stood wielding her stove wood battle club, and carefully stepped beside Richard and the bot.

"You said they were eating anything metal, right?"

"*Da*. Dey even pulled de laptop right out of my hands. Not much metal dere?" she asked.

"Oh, plenty. The battery is most likely tasty to them if they eat metal." Richard kicked a broken piece of the alien probe over closer to the rest of it.

"I see. Den dey takes de faucets and the goddamned television, and de power wires from de walls all gone too."

"Then why didn't they eat *it* too?" Richard pointed at the bashed probe.

"Oh, dey had already gone. Dis one seemed fat or slow or something."

"Hmm . . . or pregnant," he said. Richard knelt down and rolled the probe back over and looked at the twinning pieces. "If that's what you want to call it."

"Well, I don't know what you would call it, but that performs like the womb, birthing canal, and whatever else these things need to replicate all in one." Alice pointed out to Roger, Alan, and Tom who had all crowded around her computer in her lab. This lab actually looked like a laboratory fit for a science fiction movie. Major Gries would have been more satisfied with the various computer monitors, instrument panels with flashing multicolored lights, and digital readouts. Of course, there were plenty of wires running around as well. In fact, the same metal octopus convention that had taken place in Roger's lab must have annexed part of Alice's laboratory as well.

"Do they actually have sexes?" Alan asked.

"No, no. If we continue to use biological analogies I would say it's more like cell division than anything. Somehow this thing here . . ." Alice highlighted a region of the electron microscope image on her computer screen. "Well, this is the region where I think the biological analog of the nucleus is and where it starts to fission."

"Fission—you mean it's radioactive?" Alan asked.

"Alan my boy, I think she means biological fission." Tom grinned at his colleague.

"Right, I would have never figured this out without examining the twinning bot that we have in the holding area downstairs. We were lucky Shane's group got that one." Alice continued to flip through images on her computer screen.

"When the bot was first picked apart that small portion near its center was detected but its purpose was unclear to us," Roger said.

"Yeah, we saw that. It's just a solid chunk of material as far as we could tell, " Alan added, waving his arms around.

"Well, it's a solid chunk of material, but with some apparently random microscopic hollow 'tubes' running through it. I think this is the central location for their reproduction system."

"We had no clue what it was for. You mean you think you know what it is now . . . that's a big improvement." Roger was excited to have made some progress.

"A big improvement indeed!" Tom agreed. "Do you know what the material is?"

"Well, I'm not completely certain, but at the atomic level it's common Earthly materials. The material was identified by the folks at NC State." Alice explained. She pointed at a window on the computer screen, a graph from a vaporization mass spectral analysis. "They took a sample I sent them and put it through spectral analysis. It turned out to be common stuff: carbon, iron, aluminum, titanium, nickel, silicon, trace amounts of cesium, strontium, sodium, lead, and uranium, but mostly aluminum. But, from X rays and electron microscopy of the solid piece, it appears to be some very complex heterogonous material with a structure similar to how a crystal grows but much more compacted and complex. And there are regions within the crystalline structure that are filled with pure elements—heavy elements."

"By heavy, you mean like uranium, cesium, etc.? Unstable elements?" Tom asked as he peered at the computer monitor.

"Right, most of them appear to be radioactive types, but none of them are decaying as far as I can tell. This is wild and amazingly detailed stuff." Alice scratched her head.

"So what do you think is going on, Alice?" Roger asked

"Well, I think that this is the machine's processor. What we're calling the *brain tube* is, I think, mislabeled. This is the core of the machine. The brain tube thing, I think is more like a command and data handling tube or a subprocessor. Somehow I think the brain tube is where external commands are received and stored. But this region here in the center of the bot, this is the real brain. This is what the bot uses to make decisions absent external commands and it's here where they split." Alice leaned back in her chair. "But . . ."

"But what?" Roger didn't like the uncertain tone of her voice.

"It's too much for me. I have no idea how the commands are implemented. This is more like DNA than logic gates. Only person I know that ever worked on anything even similar was Dr. Horton at Princeton back before they ran him off." Alice shook her head. "I'm pushing the limits of what I can do. We could use more help."

"Well, then why don't we find this Dr. Horton and bring him in?" Alan asked.

"Why not?" Tom agreed.

"Well, there is your problem," Alice said with a grimace. "After Richard left Princeton, oh, that was seven or eight years ago, he dropped off the face of the Earth. The only place anybody ever hears from him is on his favorite late night talk radio show."

"Yeah, okay, what radio show? Maybe we can have them put out a call for him if they're still broadcasting on the

Internet." Roger didn't believe that finding somebody would be difficult with the resources available to them. If they had to, the entire FBI could be brought to the task.

"Well, he calls in to that Ret Ball show, the Truth Nationwide, all the time as Megiddo," Alice said, smiling slightly. "He never realized that his students knew that was him, but it was always obvious to us."

"Oh my God. You mean that whacko is a real scientist?" Alan asked.

"You've heard of him."

"Mr. President, the Internet traffic across the country being monitored by the NSA project is turning up some interesting information." General Mitchell sat down at the conference table in the War Room. He put a jumpdrive into the laptop connected to the flat screen monitors and brought up a map of the country.

"The Internet is just fascinating isn't it?" the President said.

"What do you mean, sir?" Mitchell asked.

"Well, more than two-thirds of the world has been eaten by alien machines, most all phones are out, all telecommunications is out, but the damned Internet is still clicking away. There's probably still plenty of porn sites available." The President shrugged. "That damned Al Gore was brilliant. All those algorithms."

"Uh, right," Mitchell was, almost, sure that was the President's attempt at a joke. "This is actually the type of disaster that Dr. Licklider had in mind when he started the ARPANET concept back in 1962."

"He expected alien invasion?" The President raised an eyebrow.

"Uh, no sir, or at least not to my knowledge he didn't. I meant a massive global scale war that would knock out comms around the world. The ARPANET was to enable communications between various shelters and redoubt locations in the event that the Cold War ever got hot."

The President considered the general for a moment and the Chairman realized that his leg had been pulled. At least, he thought it had. Sometimes the President's sense of humor, and it could be quite black, was so dry that even his closest friends weren't sure if he was joking.

"What kind of interesting data has Dr. Licklider provided us, Kevin?" the President asked. He spent most of his time in the War Room nowadays. Planning, hoping, and praying that somebody would figure out a way to stop these damned menacing alien robots. So far, the Americas and Australia were about all that was left of the world, but nobody expected that to last much longer.

"Well, as you see the red dots scattered across the country sir, these are bot sightings or incidents."

"What do you mean?"

"In more than a thousand different locations, there have been boomerangs either sighted flying overhead, wandering through the terrain, or actually attacking and acquiring metal. One incident that was reported on the Internet to a radio show claims that his pickup truck was devoured by a swarm of bots leaving nothing behind but the plastic, vinyl, and rubber parts. There are several other similar cases."

"How long has this been going on?"

"From the report we just received from the NSA it appears that the first incident was reported about three days ago, and the sightings have picked up nonlinearly."

Mitchell flipped the screen to a graph of the bot sighting frequency versus date.

"What does this mean, Kevin?" The President didn't like the sound of this. A chill ran up and down his spine and his skin began to crawl.

"They're doing just like we would do before an attack sir. I think this is reconnaissance."

"No shit it's fricking recon," Gries responded to Roger after he read the report to him. "I don't need a brain the size of Chicago to figure that one out. We recon them, they recon us. The side with the big battalions still wins."

"Ronny agrees also. We're getting close to an all-out attack from the bots . . . and—"

"We're not any closer to figuring out how to beat 'em!" Shane finished Roger's sentence for him.

"Goddamnit! Goddamnit! Goddamnit!" Roger pounded his fist on his desk and then kicked his trash can across the office.

Chapter 21

"How in the hell did you get these things here?" Colonel Matthew "Bull" Ridley ran his fingers across the empennage of the sleek composite aircraft in front of him and whistled. "Nice."

"Yeah, I thought the damned bots were taking out all air traffic globally now." Sergeant Cady said looking at Alan and Dr. John Fisher, who were standing beside the squadron of sleek swept-wing and forward canard aircraft. Both Alan and John were looking like an opossum with a certified north Alabama shit-eating grin.

"The airframes and control systems were built by Scaled Composites out in the Mojave. The engines were delivered there and the aircraft were assembled and then flown here," John said.

"Yeah, but why didn't the bots eat them?" Gries asked.

"Magic?" Belgian RAF Flight-Lieutenant and Bull's right hand Rene Lejeune asked and shrugged his shoulders. "Luck?"

"Actually, y'all can blame the sergeant major there." Alan grinned and nodded to Top.

"No sir. I had nothing to do with such black magic and evil wizardry," Cady asserted.

"Well, Top, you remember talking about that ceramic car engine you saw on television back when I showed you the ceramic jet-propelled bullets for the M-240B?" Alan asked Top.

"Vaguely, Alan. I think that part of my memory got frost-bitten in Greenland."

"Well, I didn't go to Greenland so I remembered it just fine. Dr. Pike, Dr. Fisher, and I came up with a ceramic aircraft engine design. They're actually jet engines. The control surfaces are controlled by Kevlar wires and graphite composite pulleys and gearboxes. We also had a few larger cargo and troop transports delivered. The only metal in the whole thing is in the tiny computer chip that controls the ignition system and the ignition system itself. Alice used the same kind of design that she used for the little picosat. There ain't no more metal in this thing than in a dollar's worth of change." Alan waved his arms a bit and smiled.

"And, they flew tree-top high from California to here without getting compromised by the bots," Fisher added.

"No shit!" Gries said. "Good work, Sergeant Major Cady!"

"Sir!"

Alan and John seemed chagrinned. Of course it was Cady who sparked the idea in Alan, and Roger had told Alan to figure out how to build composite aircraft—completely composite. But had Cady not mentioned the ceramic engine he had seen on television years back they just might not have figured it out. Gries had to give Cady credit anyway just to goad the eggheads.

"So when do we get to try them out?" Rene asked.

"Thought you were never going to ask," John said. "The crew that flew them in are inside ready to debrief you and then take a well-deserved nap, I guess. Go get debriefed and then shake them down. These fighters belong to your squadron, Colonel. I suggest you start training in them. Scaled's test pilots also sent some information and video training guides. I suggest you take a look at those also."

"Hot damn! Rene, gather the clans," Bull ordered his sidekick.

"Yes, Colonel." Rene saluted and the two of them rushed toward the hangar where the debriefers awaited them.

"Wheeeww," Gries whistled. "You really outdid your-selves didn't you?" The major turned to Alan and Dr. Fisher.

"Oh, we're not done with you yet," Alan said. "Get back in your Humvee and follow us."

They drove back to a larger hangar building on the south side east of the airport. After they parked the vehicles, Alan and John led them inside to a row of motorcycles, buggies, and all-terrain-vehicles of various sizes and shapes.

"They're composite. Down to the lug nuts." Alan waved his arms at the vehicles.

"And they're yours," John added.

"That's right. Equip them however you see fit. This is *the* motorpool for these vehicles. If you want to do some-thing to them, the mechanics here are the ones to help you out. I will say this: be careful about drilling holes and how you mount things without asking first. Composite structures are funny and one hole in the wrong place and the entire vehicle might collapse. We did put hardpoints throughout them though, because we figured you'd want to mount stuff to them."

"Uh, Alan," Cady interrupted.

"Yeah, Thomas."

"These ceramic motors. What do they run on?"

"Ditto," Gries said.

"Oh, they run on regular gasoline, or kerosene, or alcohol, or just about anything that will combust good. They don't need oil either since the ceramics are already godawful slick."

"Sounds too good to be true." Gries seemed concerned.

"Oh, not at all," Dr. Fisher interjected. "There have been functioning ceramic engines for at least a decade and most of them can run on almost any combustible. You see, ceramics don't need the cooling that metal engines do so they can run a lot hotter."

"Uh huh." Gries and Cady nodded.

Surprise is in the mind of the combat commander, Gries thought to himself. He had to remind himself that it didn't matter why these tools worked. What mattered was how he was going to use them to win a war against alien machines that ate metal. They just might offer an advantage. What that advantage was he had no idea. But he would figure it out.

"As the colonel said, Sergeant Major, 'Gather the clans'!"

"Yes sir!"

❊   ❊   ❊

"Well, I think the DNA analogy is correct, Traci." Alice stood at the end of the conference room in front of the big screen nodding at Traci Adams. The PowerPoint slide showed images from the bot nucleus analysis.

Around the conference table were Dr. Ronny Guerrero, Dr. Roger Reynolds, Traci Adams, Alan Davis, Dr. Tom Powell, Dr. John Fisher, and a speakerphone. On the other end of the speakerphone were colleagues at redoubts across the country. They were also receiving pseudo real-time Internet video of the conference as well. There were several other scientists and engineers and technicians across the country at military locations and shelters listening in on the conversation via the Internet.

"Alice," Ronny said slowly, with his Cuban/American accent barely creeping through, "how does that help us?"

"Well, once I realized that the replication process of the probes is more like biological fission than anything else, the question of how they know how to replicate arose. Biological things have DNA for blueprints and this analogy led us down the path that the bots must have blueprints as well. Now what if, what if, mind you, we somehow figured out the bot DNA and mutated it?"

"Uh, Dr. Pike, this is Dr. Forrester in the AFRL redoubt in Albuquerque . . ." interrupted the speakerphone.

"Go ahead, Dr. Forrester." Alice said a little too loudly.

"I've reviewed the data and can't figure heads or tails about how the so-called DNA might work. Do you have any ideas there?"

"Unfortunately, no, Dr. Forrester. But, for now, let us

say that we figure it out. Then say we mutate the bots to eat themselves only and then release them back into the wild."

"Brilliant!" Roger slammed his hands down on the table. "That's it, Alice, THAT IS IT! Fight fire with fire, absolutely. We should focus all our efforts on doing just that! How do we figure out the bot DNA code?"

"Search me. Again, I say that Dr. Richard Horton was doing some things along the lines of machine DNA, and there is a chance he might have figured it out, but as for me I have no idea. I'm not giving up and I have some ideas, but I recall Dr. Horton really having a knack for this line of thinking." There was silence for a moment.

"This is the Wheeler Labs redoubt at Princeton. We knew Horton as you did, Alice. We wouldn't put much stock in what that crackpot has to say."

"This is DEPUTY SECRETARY REYNOLDS. Does anybody else at Princeton have an idea of how the bot DNA works?"

"Uh, sure we do, I mean . . ."

"Let's hear it now, then," Roger practically yelled into the speakerphone. Ronny grinned at him. Alan sniggered out loud. Traci patted his leg underneath the table.

"Uh, we'd have to think about it a bit more and get back to—"

"People, I'm not going to say this again. Most of the world has been eaten by alien machines. Hell, most of the solar system has been eaten by alien machines. And I will not for one second allow academic bigotry and egotism stand in the way of any possible idea or asset no matter how odd or wild it might seem. Even if it's a long shot billion to one chance of it working. What else do we have? Not a whole helluva lot that's what. At this point I'd piss on a sparkplug if I thought it'd help. *Understand me?*" Roger clenched his jaw, wishing he had that arrogant Ivy League prick on the other end of the speakerphone close enough to choke. His face was red and his head pounded and there was no telling what his blood pressure was.

There was no response from the other end of the line.

Ret Ball: *My friends you will not believe this but I have the Deputy Secretary of Defense for Advanced Defense Concepts and Testing, Dr. Roger P. Reynolds online with us this evening. Great to have you here on the Truth Nationwide, Mr. Deputy Secretary.*

Caller: *Thanks, Ret.*

Ret Ball: *Why are you contacting us tonight, sir?*

Caller: *Well, you see Ret we have posted all the information we have on the alien menace on our website at www.neighborhoodwatch.gov. Again, that is www.neighborhoodwatch.gov. We would like all the smart folks across the globe that can still access it to look it over. If you have any insights please contact us immediately through the contact lists on the site.*

Ret Ball: *That doesn't sound good, Mr. Deputy Secretary. If the United States Department of Defense is asking for help what does that mean?*

Caller: *Just the way it sounds, Ret. More than half, nearly two-thirds of the world, our planet, has been overtaken by these alien machines and we have lost contact with those occupied regions. We have rallied our troops, evacuated our cities, and gathered as many brilliant minds as we can find to help solve the problem and stop these alien machines. But we aren't certain of our chances and will listen to any, and I mean any, advice.*

Ret Ball: *I see. Anything else?*

Caller: *Yes Ret, there is one more thing. We desperately need to speak with one of your regular callers. He uses the name Megiddo on your show. We have reason to believe that Mr. Megiddo is actually a quite brilliant scientist and would very much like to speak with him.*

Ret Ball: *You heard it fans. Megiddo, if you are out there, your country, no, humanity needs you . . .*

Chapter 22

Richard and Helena had spent the better part of the last two weeks moving everything they wanted to keep—and everything the Von Neumann probes hadn't taken—into the mine. Richard patched the hole in the cabin where the stove had been but did not see the need to waste further time on fixing the interior. The cabin had been a convenience and a temporary location from the beginning, but Richard just could not see leaving a gaping hole in the side and roof for the weather to intrude through. It was still a decent shelter and had taken him months to find, fix up, and move into.

After her conflict with the alien machines, Helena had come around on the subject of leaving the cabin for more underground digs. The mine suited her just fine, although she did insist on carrying a large piece of stove wood around with her everywhere she went. She had even carved and sanded down one end of it for a handle and wrapped it with cloth and tape.

Richard at first had thought Helena would be a humorous sight wielding her oversized handmade billy club. But there was something about her slender five-nine Russian frame and accent, her long black hair, her insistence on wearing low cut worn-out jeans and skin-tight tank-tops, no bra, canvas sneakers, and toting around a mammoth war club that gave her a "warrior princess" quality that really got Richard going.

Other than science and solving problems, getting Richard excited was usually a hard thing to do. He even debated with himself at times whether he actually loved her—though he knew it was quite likely that she didn't really love him. Mutual convenience best described their marriage. He had needed companionship and she needed to get out of Russia. But he found he liked it a lot when she wandered around with her club.

The mine was fully operational at least to within the limitations of the power available by the waterwheel. The little hydroelectric plant that Richard had put together would power the water heater, refrigerator, freezer, a few lights, a television, a computer, and maybe one piece of scientific equipment at a time. Using the backup battery systems at the same time enabled him to power a few more of his scientific instruments. The batteries had to recharge all night. He had hoped for a little more horsepower out of the underground stream, but the flow rate was just too low to create enough torque for instantaneous power needs.

"I wish I could have found enough fissile material to go nuclear," he said to himself. As it was he didn't have the power to drive the electron microscope. "Would be nice to do some X rays and some microscopy of your friend." He nodded at the bot laid out across his workbench at the edge of the entrance into the lab shaft from the main chamber.

"You don't tink dat you could've stolen plutonium and gotten away with it?" Helena peered over the book she was reading and glanced at Richard. He had been quietly working for some time now, but when he spoke out loud to himself Helena had a hard time ignoring him. He was her *entertainment*.

"Huh? Plutonium? Oh, no. If I did, we would have it," he said nonchalantly and smiled through his thick, unruly graying beard at her. "Maybe I'll figure something else out."

"Well, de goddamned robots fly. Dey must have batteries or someting in dem." She popped a handful of shelled pecans in her mouth from the Ziploc bag on the folding end table near the couch. "Ought to use de goddamned ting for sometin," she said through a mouthful, brushed her bangs from her forehead, yawned, slipped her shoes off letting one dangle from her left big toe, and went back to reading.

"Yes, yes, power. They must have power, but where and how . . ." Richard had been examining the bot that Helena had killed for him but was not progressing as fast as he had hoped. He needed X rays and electron microscopy and he didn't have the power for those machines. So, he didn't have that detailed of data. That is, until he heard the latest posts on the Ret Ball show.

Fortunately, most of the data he wanted had been measured and compiled by a government program and was posted on a website for everyone to see. And oddly enough, *they* particularly wanted him, Dr. Richard Horton, a.k.a. Megiddo, to look at it and get back to *them*. Irony.

But Richard didn't trust the government. No sir, not as far as he could throw them. He knew that *they* had been covering up the knowledge of the alien probes for a long time. That was no different than the other conspiracies *they* had performed. There was the Kennedy assassination, the real reason behind Viet Nam and the Gulf Wars, Roswell, the giant floating black triangles, the secrets of the pyramids around the world, remote viewing, Watergate, alien stealth technologies discovered at Area 51, the real reason for double blind drug testing, and countless others.

Their mishandling of these technologies and this knowledge now had humanity in a bind. It was *their* fault. And now *they* wanted Megiddo to bail *them* out. Why didn't *they* want his help when he tried to operate within the confines of the system? Why had academia run him out of the community? It was their fault—a conspiracy to keep the truth from humanity! But Megiddo was a bigger man than that and he would save Helena and the rest of the world. Well, Helena probably didn't need saving, but the rest of the world most certainly did.

So he had downloaded the information carefully, analyzing it for government imbedded spybots and other tracking software. Fortunately, he didn't even have to use the government site. As soon as it was posted, it had been mirrored across multiple servers, including two in which he had inserted trojans that gave him full security control.

Once he had scrutinized it and was convinced that the data was real and bug free, he started studying it. He studied it intensely for several days, stopping only occasionally for a snack or a nap. Helena mostly ignored him and went about her business, but every now and then she would check on him or offer him a sandwich or tell him that he should come to bed.

Sleep was the last thing on Richard's mind. Occasionally Helena would bait him to come to bed with the allure of sex, but even that—as exciting and enjoyable as it was—was merely a distraction from studying the bots. In fact, his mind was so hot with new ideas and sizzling from the new information he had gotten that the pleasure he got from studying the details of the bot was perhaps even more enticing than Helena. Perhaps. *If only I had more power to drive my equipment.*

The government report was actually really good science and reverse engineering, but there was nothing there that Richard saw as the shining tidbit of information that would save humanity. It was only the groundwork. But somebody had to do the groundwork and having it already done and wrapped up in a nice four-hundred-and-seventy-three page pdf file package made getting to the real part of the work happen a lot faster.

There was a significant portion of the government research that seemed . . . familiar . . . to him. For some reason it triggered a sense of déjà vu. He couldn't really put his finger on it and he wasn't a hundred percent sure why at first until he came across the proposed idea that the bots used a form of machine DNA encoded at the subatomic level. He remembered one of his students from years ago at Princeton really intrigued by his work on that subject and this report had that kind of flare.

Richard followed that line of reasoning for a few days and finally he began to understand a general idea of how the alien machines system hierarchy and architecture flowed. There was a central nucleus that was the real controlling mechanism of the individual bot. Like a single celled organism this nucleus was where the replication blueprints resided. It was also there that the "messenger RNA"—an analogy of course—delivered instructions throughout the rest of the bot to the subsystems.

The actual messenger RNA were something rather amazing. Richard had a wild-ass-guess that the instructions were actually delivered via some sort of controlled nuclear decay process. How the bots kept the "pebbles" of unstable elements from decaying until they needed them to was a technology beyond anything humanity had discovered, but he was certain that was how the instruction packets were sent throughout the bot. His former student—what *was* her name?—was onto something there, but that was a harder problem. Then there was this tube the government had first wrongly labeled the "brain tube," which wasn't a brain tube at all. The government's second guess was a communications device.

Richard examined the "brain tube" of the alien bot that Helena had acquired for him. The twinning bot did not have a brain tube yet, but it did have a nucleus. Assuming that the biological analogy held, then a higher function organ would develop first in a fetus. This led him to the conclusion that the brain tube was not a first order function and that its "mother" was performing that function—whatever that was—for it.

He soon came to the realization that the government's

second guess was closer—communications. When does a fetus's vocal cords develop? The electron microscopy and X ray data in the government report led him to the conclusion that there were pseudorandom semiconductor and unlike metal junctions. These junctions only appeared to be random. After several fractal pattern overlays Richard discovered that there was a methodology to the junctions. They were logic gates. In fact, the logic gates of the tube shaped device appeared much like the circuitry—but on a much smaller and more complex scale—of a transceiver system.

The tube was a solid-state software ultra-wideband transceiver—it had to be. *That is where that spread spectrum signal must have come from.* Without having a powered and operational bot to study there was no way to really be certain. But, it looked like the type of device that might have created those odd signals that he had detected with his spectrum analyzer the day the bots attacked the cabin.

Those signals were spread spectrum and centered about 1.420 gigahertz—the so-called famous 21 centimeter line from radio astronomy and SETI circles. *Did that mean anything?* Richard was formulating that in the back of his mind.

The government had been monitoring the bots' signals for some time and a more detailed analysis of them was in their report. The fact that the center portion of their communications systems was around the band that hydrogen emitted and that astronomers thought would be the band that one day aliens would broadcast a message to us in could be just a coincidence. Horton thought it could be significant but none of the scientists and engineers from the government program had much to offer on that regard. He would think on that later. Right now he had more imminent and pressing matters; the bots were coming and he needed to find a way to stop them.

From the size of the microscopic conductor tube running from the power block of the bot's interior to the transceiver tube it didn't look like the bot was designed to transmit anything at large distances or at high bandwidths. At the same time there did not appear to be large receiver amplifiers within the thing's systems either. That told Richard that the bots were not receiving direct detailed data downloads from these mechanized central city locations that were discussed in the government reports. Not unless the other pieces of the bot like the motivator ball, the power section and so on had some sort of magical communication system. But Richard did not believe that to be the case. His theory was that the bots communicated large data dumps through physical contact and/or short-range dissemination of instructions. There was also the possibility of the DNA including built-in hardwired instructions.

It was possible that operating instruction upgrades were installed each time these things flew to some central city location or since they were analogous to biological cells, perhaps when they reached a particular cellular density they would evolve. He was speculating there.

One thing he was not speculating on was the main reason for the transceiver tube. He knew what it was, or at least he thought he did. But he needed some live ones to find out for certain. So he decided to "acquire" some more of them. The government reports told him all he needed to know to lure them. The bots liked radio. Something about radio attracted them; he had been right all along about that. The government analysis of the alien spread spectrum signal emissions also showed that the frequency shifting pulses were not truly randomly shifting in frequency. There was a method to the transmissions. In fact, they followed a 256 bit encryption sequence. That told Richard plenty. Unfortunately, what it told him was that without the key it wouldn't be likely they would decrypt the sequence by a simple hacker password dictionary attack. That is, continually insert all the passwords possible from a to z—not likely.

So, the government report suggested that they would attack the encryption algorithms themselves. Richard thought they might have luck there. After all they had the might of the CIA and the NSA with them, but a 256 bit encryption method was damned near impossible to break without the key. One note on one of the mirror sites said that hackers across the U.S. had combined forces to crack the code using a distributed system. They might even beat the government.

Richard had a different idea. He needed to watch the bots when they started "handshaking" and talking to each other. The handshaking was a simple process of passing binary code back and forth between the computer and the bot. Understanding an alien language was not necessary at this level of coding, only simple instructions would be needed. These instructions were to turn on or off certain functions and algorithms. It was simple ones and zeroes—math universal to all computers—that any code writer could understand. There was something about this handshaking that told the bots not to eat each other and therefore they must be passing the encryption key code. If he could watch them closely while they interacted with each other, he might be able to copy the encryption sequence without having to understand it. It was a long shot, perhaps. But he had used similar approaches to crack credit card company computers.

Chapter 23

"We have lost all contact with Manhattan Island, Mr. President," Dr. Vicki Johnson said calmly. The National Security Advisor had been with the current administration since before the President was governor of Oklahoma and they were good friends. Vicki feared that even speaking candidly as his friend now would not be enough to convince him what they should do. "General Mitchell and I think it's time to—"

"No! We're not going to nuke New York City!" The President pounded the conference table in the War Room. He looked at his friend in the eyes and shook his head. "I don't care if that entire map of the world turns red. We're not nuking our own cities." He pointed to the continuously updated world map that showed the occupied areas in red. All of New York City including the outer boroughs were under bot control.

"Sir," General Mitchell sighed. "It might slow them

down. We laced the major cities with enough HE, fuel air bombs, and nukes to vaporize them. We might wipe out millions of the bots. But we would have to do it now before we lost communications with the bombs or before the bots eat them or render them useless."

"What about our new fighters and bombers?" the President asked.

General Mitchell shrugged. "Sir, it's likely that there are nowhere near enough to support an all-out attack against the bots. There are just not enough of them. We will use them to support evacs and defense of the redoubts."

"Did it slow them down in China and in Russia and across the Asian continent? No, it didn't. If we ever take back our country, I don't want it to be so radioactive that we can't move back in."

"Then, uh, sir, what are your orders?" the general asked.

"We wait." President Colby hung his head and then leaned back in his chair. "That is all we do. We wait and hope the redoubt scientists figure out what to do."

Ronny Guerrero and Roger Reynolds were poring over the current intel data on the New York invasion hoping for some insight into stopping the alien machines. They were having very little luck. The two men had once only known each other through brief customer-to-contractor acquaintance and interaction. But over the last three years they had become coworkers, then friends, and now refugee scientists in a redoubt city hoping to find a way to stop the Von Neumann probes.

"I don't see any patterns, Rog. But what I do see is more of the same," Ronny said in his soft Cuban accent.

"What do you mean, Ronny?" Roger looked up from his laptop for a second.

"They land in a tubule and spread. Nothing different. We can expect a tubule to jump from New York City to some other major city soon." Ronny scribbled some notes on a pad in front of him and tapped wildly at a calculator. "See, following exponential growth, I'd say in a few more days we'll lose another city."

"Yeah, I was guessing that but hadn't run the simulation yet. I'll get Traci to work out the sims for the President in a bit."

"Good idea. But, what to do now? We need a strategy at least."

"Well, I guess we sort of have a strategy. I mean hide and survive as long as we can until we can figure out a way to stop them is a strategy. It's a tactical approach that we're completely lacking."

"Ah, yes. Should we try to defend the cities, blow them up, or let them fall?" Ronny nodded in agreement.

"Yeah. Well, of course the President's tactic is to let them fall. Perhaps he's right."

"I hate it, but you're goddamned right we should let the cities be." Sergeant Cady wiped the sweat off his forehead and continued loading the ceramic ammo into the composite troop buggy. "What the hell does it matter if they're evacuated?"

"I agree, Top." Shane Gries nodded. "We aren't gonna beat them by shooting them one on one. There ain't enough bullets. I think the President is doing the right thing here."

"Yeah, but I still hate it."

"Me, too."

⊠   ⊠   ⊠

The pickup truck loaded with what appeared to be everything the family owned had barely made it up the old logging road. The recon bots had stolen the gate weeks before so there was nothing stopping them from driving up the hill to the cabin or to the mine entrance.

It beat all Richard had ever seen. Were these people living in a vacuum? The Internet was all abuzz about how the bots eat metal and how you should stay away from metal and so on. But here was a young man in his late twenties, his wife of about the same age, a toddler maybe three years old, and an infant parading around in an old beat-up extended cab Toyota Tundra that was loaded down with everything from camping gear, mountain bikes, and firearms to strollers, baby gear and kitchen utensils, and cases and cases of canned goods, bottled water, baby food. Even a microwave and television set. There was probably a kitchen sink in it somewhere.

Their approach had tripped some of the fiber-optic sensor cable Richard had stretched out down the road for early warning of visitors, so he and Helena had walked up the mine shaft main tunnel to meet them. Richard hoped he could convince them to leave. He didn't need any liabilities or distractions from his work. His hope was that they were just lost and needed directions. The fact that these two adults were driving around with these kids and knowing those bots were out there made his skin crawl with fear and anger. He scratched at the nape of his neck and then just shook his head. Helena made no particular telltale signs of being upset that anybody except the man who had been living with her for the past couple of years would notice. She was pissed.

The young man parked the truck about twenty meters from the mine entrance and seemed a little nervous when he saw the odd couple coming out of the mine shaft entrance. To the young man, the old man approaching them appeared to be in his late forties to early fifties, was average size and had a wiry build with graying hair and graying beard. He guessed the woman was in her early to mid-twenties, could tell she had a light complexion since she was wearing cut-off jeans and a tank top; her milky white arms and legs revealed she spent little time in the sun, and her long dark hair suggested a slight "gothic" appearance. What frightened him most was the fact that the young woman was carrying a large homemade club in her left hand and from the looks of the dings in it she had used it on something before.

"Don't worry honey, I'll take care of this," he told his wife.

"Well, whatever. I've got to mix the baby a bottle. It's been nearly three hours since she's eaten anything." She shushed the baby and bounced her in her arms. The toddler was strapped in a car seat in the back of the pickup's extended cab. He was screaming bloody murder.

"Hello." The young man approached Richard and Helena and smiled timidly.

" 'Ello," Helena smiled and nodded at the children. "Look Richard, dey have a beebee with dem," she said rolling the "r" in Richard.

"Uh huh. Hello, what can I do for you? You are on private property, you know," Richard didn't like where this was going. *Why weren't these idiots at a shelter?*

"I'm Jeff and that's my wife Sara Jo. The one in the back screamin' there is little Jeff, Jr. and the one screamin' in the front is Precious Anne. We've been traveling for a long time. All the way down from Myrtle Beach and we haven't seen anybody. I took a wrong turn a few miles back, I guess. Where are we?" He offered Richard his hand.

"You are outside Spartanburg about twenty miles or so." Richard shook his hand guardedly. "You must be really lost to have wound up here. Where you headed?"

"Uh, we were headed to the national park down west of Greenville. Heard there was a campsite for refugees down there. I took that cutoff road at the bottom of the mountain thinking it would make the trip shorter. Guess not," Jeff said.

"Vwhy you vait til now to go to a shelter? Goddamned bots in New York and dem lovely babies don need in dat truck." Helena seemed concerned about the truck and from her experience she had every reason to be. "Don you know de tings eat trucks!"

"What, eat trucks . . ." Jeff looked confused. "Hey, you ain't from around here are you?"

"*Da.* I fuckin' live here."

"Sorry, uh, I'm just uh . . . tired . . . lost and . . ." He yawned and covered his mouth. Then he stretched. "Oh man, and the guy on the C.B. a while ago said . . ."

"C.B.!" Richard noticed the antenna on the truck. "You been talking on that thing!?"

"Uh, mostly I just listen to it, but I just told this fella that I was lost and nearly out of gas and—"

"Goddamn dummies don listen to de news." Helena looked at Richard who was already in a sprint to the truck. She followed him, "Right! De babies."

"Hey! Wait a minute!" Jeff said, startled and angry.

"Miss, you have to get these kids out of this vehicle right now. If you just used that radio they'll be coming." He held the rear door open and started unstrapping the screaming and kicking toddler. Jeff ran behind Richard and started to grab him around the neck in a barroom chokehold but Helena poked him pretty hard in the stomach with her club. Jeff let go of Richard's neck and gasped for air as he fell backwards on his ass.

"Hey!" Sara Jo screamed.

"Lady, you must get out of de damn truck now or dose goddamn tings'll eat it with you and your babies in it."

With a hundred *thuds* and the sound of screeching metal on metal, alien robotic machines attached themselves to the truck like a swarm of angry bees. Helena pulled Sara Jo and Precious through the passenger side doorway of the vehicle just as the seat cushion springs flew through the windshield into the underbelly of a cloud of bots. Metal fragments, plastic, rubber, vinyl, glass, automotive fluids of all sorts, and dirt and leaves were flung around them in a whirlwind of debris and noise. Once, the truck's horn even honked. The metal from the canned goods popped open and the various foodstuffs contained within them were flung aside as discarded useless waste to the bots. The gooey mess flew around them, splattering everything in the whirlwind's path.

Richard held the toddler under his bodyweight although the little tyke was kicking, screaming, and biting at him. But he was afraid if the kid got up a piece of flying debris would decapitate the little guy. Helena and Sara Jo used their bodies to shield Precious, who was also screaming the most gut-wrenching screeches. Between the children's screams and the hellacious noise the bots made destroying the truck, it was difficult to concentrate on anything but holding still. And the horrific sound was something along the lines of crossing an overcrowded preschool at recess with a monster truck rally.

As quickly as the bots had appeared they were flying away. Two of the bots were lagging behind and hovering about two feet above the ground flying sluggishly and waiting for something. They had both gathered enough raw materials from the truck and now were both twinning.

"Helena! Look!" Richard pointed to the twinning probe nearest to her.

Helena rose to her feet quickly, grabbing her club in a homerun hitter's stance, and knocked the boomerang-shaped probe skittering in a shower of sparks across the ground like a stone skipping on a pond. The boomerang-shaped machine twisted and twirled across the road as it bounced and landed in a briar patch on the far side. She spun and jumped the six feet or so over a pile of truck rubble to the second twinning probe and commenced smashing it.

"Goddamn alien tings coulda killed dese babies!" She bashed it again. That particular bot was for certain dead. "Goddamn it you all to hell!"

The first bot she had batted out of the park was skittering around and around, tangled up in the thick briars on the side of the old logging road and could not seem to break free. She started toward it to pound it some more.

"No! Helena, wait. I want it alive!" Richard grabbed a torn canvas duffle bag and some other material made of nylon that was left over from the remains of Jeff's tent. Richard rushed across the road, tossing the material in front of him, and tackled the bot, wrapping it in the bag. That didn't work worth a damn. The bot threw him and the bag head over heels deeper into the briar patch, scratching him from head to toe. "Shit!"

"Hold on, I'll get it!" Helena grabbed another large piece of the tent material that had been slung out of the bot's metal-eating whirlwind and she popped it like a bed sheet over the briars and the bot. "Grab de goddamn end!"

Richard forced his way up through the briars ignoring the pain of being cut and pricked by the briars just in time to snag the middle of the light green nylon material with his left hand. He pulled it to him and got purchase with both hands and then rolled over onto it and the wildly spinning bot. Helena fell face first into the back of his head, busting her lip and cussing with every breath. She shook her head twice and raised up pushup style so she could put her knees in the middle of the tent material and on top of the boomerang. She punched at it several times through the material, never once missing a chance to use an obscenity.

"Goddamn fuckin' sonovabitch ting!" She kicked at it. "It von't fuckin stop, Richard!"

"Good! Let's wrap it up more if we can and tie it off to something inside." He bear-hugged the boomerang and the wad of tent and duffel bag and rolled with it out of the briars. Helena grabbed at the other side when Richard came to a stop. Richard and Helena fought with the bot and it looked to Sara Jo and Jeff like two idiots wrestling a cougar in burlap sack. A cougar might have been easier.

The two held tight to both sides of the wad of bot and nylon and carefully moved toward the entrance to the mine. The propulsion system of the bot even in its damaged state was strong enough to lift both of them off the ground a few feet at a time, but it was no longer strong enough to get away from them. But it tossed them to and fro quite readily and was beating the two of them together, pushing them to their physical limits. Helena cursed some more.

They made it into the mine about thirty feet and tied the bot to the nearest support beam they came to that Richard thought could hold it. He pulled the tent material around the backside of the twelve-by-twelve beam between it and the rock wall of the mine shaft. He looped it through several times and tied it in a large knot. The wad of nylon and canvas material rose upward toward the ceiling of the shaft and pulled the material tight, looking like an odd shaped helium balloon tied off to the post—a helium balloon with a cougar trapped inside it. But it was holding.

Jeff and his family sat huddled together sobbing and hugging one another and trying to shush the infant. They were covered from head to toe in canned goods and radiator water. Fortunately, Jeff had about run out of gasoline or they'd have been covered in that, too. There was little left of his truck but there was a pile of supplies that were dried or powdered goods in plastic or cardboard containers strewn about. And things like pinto beans, creamed corn, baby food from jars, baby formula powder, and various other food stuffs all mixed up.

"Helena, stay with them. I'll be right back. Find out if they're hurt."

"Poor poor babies! De goddamn mean robots scare

you? Don vorry, dey gone now." She knelt beside Sara Jo and put her hand on the baby girl's head. The baby was still crying. "I tink she needs feeding?" Helena looked at Sara Jo.

"I need a bottle and the formula is all smashed!" Sara Jo cried. Tears rolled down her cheeks as she panicked.

"Don you worry, baby. Can you breastfeed her?"

"I can't produce enough milk," Sara Jo cried.

Helena looked at Jeff as she stood. He was still holding the toddler to him. Both of them were covered in a gooey mess but they seemed unharmed. "You okay?"

"Yes."

"De baby?"

"Yes."

Helena picked up an empty torn baby formula container. The cylindrical shaped container was cardboard but it had a metal top and bottom, both of which were gone. The coffee-can-sized container lay in a pile of white powder. She scooped it up with the cardboard container, holding it sideways so as not to spill. Sara Jo realized what she was doing and started scanning the pile of debris.

"There—the diaper bag. There's a bottle in it." Sara Jo pointed.

Helena rummaged through the little blue and white cloth bag until she found a clear plastic bottle with a nipple on the end. She unscrewed the nipple from the top of the bottle and then looked at the side of the formula container.

"It takes one scoop for two ounces of water."

"How much is a scoop? Dere is no scoop." Helena looked around the pile of foodstuffs for a scooper but did not see anything useful.

"Uh, about a heaping tablespoon. Shhh, Precious . . . it's all right, honey."

Helena found a bottle of water amongst the debris and mixed the formula per Sara Jo's instructions. She guessed at the amount of powder in a scoop by pouring the powder into her cupped hand. She handed the bottle to Sara Jo and watched as the little infant took to the bottle and almost immediately stopped crying.

"Thank you," Sara Jo sobbed.

"Told you. Fuckin' crazy you have dese babies out with dose goddamned aliens about."

Richard walked out of the mine shaft entranceway with an armload of things. He set a five gallon bucket in front of Jeff and handed him a ladle and a dustpan.

"These will have to do. Collect up all the foodstuffs you can. Beans, peas, creamed corn, all of it and dump it in this bucket. If it looks like it got any fluids from the truck on it don't take it."

"We can't eat this! It's, uh, it's ruined." Jeff looked confused.

"It hasn't been ruined. Oh, it has been exposed to the air. We'll have to cook it and can it or vacuum seal it, but we can save a lot of it. Believe me, from what I've been reading about the rest of the world there will come a day when this mess will look like a feast."

"Yuck, that is just gross." Jeff turned up his nose. It was all Helena could take.

"Listen here ya goddamn idiot." Helena stood in front of Jeff looking down at him. She could not help but think how badly her family in St. Petersburg must have suffered once the aliens took over. Thanks to Richard, she might be the only member of her family still alive.

She cocked her head and leaned on her war club. "We're tirty or fordy miles up de goddamned mountain and don have no way to get back. Where we gonna go anyway, huh? You should have taken dese babies to a shelter months ago you fuckin' dumbass hick. Goddamn if you don listen to Dr. Richard now. He de only ting gonna save your babies, your wife, and your goddamn dumb ass. So shut your fuckin' mouth and go an do what de fuck he says."

"Just do it, Jeff." Sara Jo frowned at her husband but kept her voice low so she wouldn't upset Precious.

Richard took a smaller three-gallon pail from inside the larger bucket and handed it to Helena. "See how much of the baby formula you can salvage. If you get a little dirt in it, so what, don't worry about it. We'll sift it later." Richard looked at the small amount of the white powder scattered throughout the pile. There couldn't be more than three gallons of it. He was not quite sure how much of it got mixed with water but he knew damned well it was a long way from being enough to feed that little baby for more than maybe a month. These two fools had no idea how bad a situation they had put themselves and their helpless children in.

He reached in the smaller pail and pulled out a roll of heavy-duty garbage bags. "Mommy, when you are done feeding the baby start gathering up everything you can find that is still useful or might be salvaged."

"We . . . we can't stay here!" Jeff said looking around for more of the alien machines.

"You can stay in the old cabin up the road if you want," Richard grunted. He didn't much care for these two stupid adults or at least the male.

"Richard!" Helena stamped her right foot into the ground. "Dey will do no such a fucking ting and you goddamn know it."

"But Helena dear—"

"Don you goddamned 'Helena dear' me. No way dese babies gonna stay up dere in dat drafty old cabin with no lectricity and water."

"But—"

"You're being an asshole. Dey stay down de hole with us and dat is goddamn dat!"

"So you are absolutely certain this is the frequency distribution of the alien transmissions?" Roger Reynolds turned and glanced at Ronny Guerrero excitedly and then back to the NSA MASINT specialist giving the briefing.

"Absolutely, Mr. Deputy Secretary. We have verified it against the bots currently occupying recon herds in this area. This is the sequence of frequencies they're using."

"Then are you saying we can understand their communications?" Ronny asked.

"No. They're high-bit encrypted, over 256, and we haven't cracked that. For that matter, they seem to cycle their encryption with higher encryption bursts. But it's at least a start. We now know exactly what the frequency spectrum of their transmissions is. Without that, decryption would never be possible." The technician pointed out the several spikes of the transmission frequencies and continued to explain how they hopped based on a fractal basis across the spectrum. But, and it was the big but, they still needed the decryption key.

"All right. Post all this on the website immediately," Roger ordered.

❈   ❈   ❈

"Mr. President," General Mitchell said, looking around the War Room Advisory Committee, "latest intel shows that the bots have jumped tubes from NYC to Boston, Philadelphia, and Baltimore as well as all the smaller cities in between. We're still in communication with the MIT redoubt at Hanscomb Air Force Base, but we're hearing that the battle is not going well. They anticipate being overrun within the hour."

"The cities have been evacuated and the loss of civilian lives should be basically nil, sir." Vicki reminded him. "There were holdouts, but less than ten percent of the population. And, of course, the forces in the redoubt."

"We can't maintain people in those refugee camps forever, Vicki. There simply isn't enough food and supplies. What's the time frame we're looking at?"

"Sixty days," the director of FEMA replied. "And those tent cities aren't entirely metal free. If the bots hit them, there is going to be reduced impact but not zero impact. Among other things, any large population requires security forces. The security is provided by National Guard at the moment, but if you rip away their weapons they're just a bunch of kids with uniforms."

"We anticipated that issue," General Mitchell replied, smiling faintly. "We're implementing training in nonprojectile and zero-metal projectile weapons."

"Care to translate that for me?" the President asked, frowning.

"The units are being rearmed with staffs, quarterstaffs, and bows," General Mitchell said, shrugging. "We're also falling back on historical communications models." He looked over at the aide de camp at his shoulder and then back.

"The *original* purpose of an aide de camp was to carry messages, and messengers were a primary communications method as late as the First World War. We've established cavalry messenger posts across a large area and we're slowly expanding that area. Even if the Internet goes down *entirely* we should be able to maintain communications across the U.S. *Slow* communications, but communications. The Army has extensive experience in continuing under rather odd conditions, Mr. President. I mean, we've got *manuals* that cover most of the conditions we're going to be running into. As long as the food holds out, we're going to *stay* an Army."

"Good to hear that at least one thing is working," the President said, nodding. "Any projections as to what cities might be next?"

"Not at this time," General Mitchell said. "So far they're hitting the East Coast and seem to be working south and east. We've established lidar sites across the country hooked into the internet and SIPARNET."

"Lidar is . . ." the President said, holding up a hand to forestall response. "That's using lasers as radar, right?"

"Yes, Mr. President," Mitchell said, trying not to grin. "Close enough. The problem is that it's limited as hell. But, on the other hand, the bots don't seem to detect low-power laser. The lidar is where we're getting some of the data on spread. We got the idea from the satellites that NRO managed to field." He paused as an aide entered the room and handed him a message. He looked at it for a moment and then frowned.

"Speaking of lidar, we just picked up a . . . call it one of

the 'main' tubes lifting off from near where Trenton used
to be. The other attacks came in on relatively low vectors, that is they didn't get very high since the other cities
were relatively close. This one is heading for altitude."

"Where's it headed?" the President asked, frowning.

"Unknown at this time," the general said. "West. But
that's the rest of the country. Chicago? St. Louis? Here?
The West Coast? Unknown at this time."

Another aide came in and gestured at the plasma screen
on the wall.

"We've finally gotten the lidar software working, sir,"
the female aide said in a soft voice. "Channel ninety-two
should give you a view. It's controlled from the battle center; if you— "

The view on the screen was of a map of the North
American continent. The tube, big as it was, wouldn't have
been visible, but there was a large karat over it as well as
smaller ones over the lesser tubes spreading along the
eastern seaboard.

"There goes Baltimore," the President said. "I don't
know if I'm grateful or hate the fact that we've got real-
time information. Not much we can do about it, is there?"

"Something coming in on Fox," Vicki said nodding to
an aide. The screen was changed to a view of a reporter
trying to describe what was going on behind him. The
sound was off, but they didn't really need it.

Two ships, liners by the looks of them, were visible at
sea. A swarm of bots was in pursuit, but even as they
headed for the undefended ships another, larger, ship
came into view. It was a carrier, from the perspective on
the shot it wasn't clear which, that was interposing its bulk
between the fleeing cruise ships and the bot swarm.

Flickers of tracers from the carrier's Phalanx guns reached out towards the bot swarm but the depleted uranium rounds were swallowed to no effect. Then the swarm reached the carrier and began to cover it. And the ship began to disintegrate.

The last shot was of the carrier's island slumping off and splashing into the sea. By that time the ship had been eaten down below the flight deck, and fires from ruptured fuel bunkers had turned it into an inferno from which small, burning, figures could be seen falling. But the liners were well out to sea, probably beyond the range of the bots' interest.

"That was the *Carl Vinson*," General Mitchell said to the hushed room. "Five thousand men and women. Those liners are filled with the last refugees from Washington and Baltimore. They're headed for Bermuda. For all the good it will do them."

"Turn it off," the President said quietly. "We're just eating ourselves up watching it. But as soon as they know where that main tube is going, get me the information. And tell Dr. Reynolds that we need more than just cool toys. We need to *stop* them."

The frequency spectrum analysis the government had made was just what Richard needed to find the key to the encryption. He generated an algorithm that would set his spectrum analyzer to follow the hopping frequency of the bots' transmissions at maximum frequency resolution. After days of listening to the bots at those hopping frequencies he finally picked up two signals that must have been close enough for his system to pull out of the noise floor.

As plain as day he watched the frequency modulation of each of the individual frequency spikes jitter up and down the band around the main center spike. It was that jittering signal, that frequency modulated signal embedded in the hopping frequencies that was the handshaking key.

Richard watched as the frequency modulated signal looped and repeated a few times and then a stream of different modulations were sent. He figured that this was the exchange of encryption data between the communicating bots. He ran this data through his credit card hacking code and there was the crypt key. Richard programmed in the algorithm to implement the key and decrypt the signals real time. He then watched a string of ones and zeroes fill the computer screen.

He had broken the bots' communication scheme. Now he just needed to figure out what the hell all that binary code meant. What were the alien things saying to each other? He decided to upload his data to the government with hopes that they could do something with it. Besides, he wanted to play around with the flying bot that he and Helena had caught. There was bound to be a use for it. The damaged bot was still propelling itself in the forward direction and had yet to completely fail or stop its propulsion. Richard had made some preliminary scans of the bot and could tell its communications tube was working, so he kept the thing wrapped in aluminum foil and at the lowest point of the mineshaft at the bottom of the underground river when he wasn't analyzing it.

Major Shane Gries and Sergeant Major Thomas Cady stood guard around the wheeled cart. The wounded but still functional bot they had captured in Greenland was being moved down one floor of the Huntsville redoubt from where it had been stored. The thing's propulsion unit was shot but it was still broadcasting, so they had to store it at least three stories down below the surface. Measurements of the bot emissions showed that three stories of concrete was plenty to shield the thing from its friends.

Other than bot topography, initial analyses had only led to minimal breakthroughs in the alien mechanisms. But since Dr. Richard Horton had been in continuous contact with Dr. Alice Pike the momentum had changed for the better.

Alice had been right all along. The program had needed Dr. Horton's unique perspective on things. He had taken the frequency sequence discovered by Roger's ELINT team and then used it to crack the encryption key for the alien bot's handshaking protocols. He had e-mailed that data to her with a prospect strawman design for a bot communication device. But he had yet to figure out what to communicate to the bots that would be useful. Alice was working on that herself, but wasn't quite there yet. She was thinking and hopefully an idea would come.

Alice pushed the cart forward while Gries and Cady walked carefully along each side of the cart with both eyes on the alien boomerang-shaped menace and both eyes scanning the hallway for unforeseen events.

"Surprise is in the mind of the combat commander," Gries muttered to himself, thumbing the safety of his HE paintball machine gun.

"Sir," Cady nodded keeping one hand on his HE gun and one on his handmade war club.

"I don't know why you two are so edgy. We're three stories underground. What could happen?" Alice shrugged, stopped the cart in front of the elevator door and pressed the down button.

"Anything," Cady grunted.

"What?" Alice asked.

"The sergeant major means that anything could happen at any time. If you fixate on specific likelihoods, you're going to be surprised by the *un*likelihood that actually happens. So be ready for *anything*. If you expect *anything*, Dr. Pike, then you are prepared for it. And if nothing happens, well, I'm prepared for that too. In fact would prefer it that way," Shane said.

"Elevator is clear, sir. But nothing is boring, sir," Top said.

Gries nodded at Alice to push the cart in and then he followed in behind her. Cady was standing with his back to the far wall of the elevator scanning for trouble.

The doors to the elevator closed and elevator music began playing. The song was familiar to Alice and she started humming along with the tune. She seemed to recall it being an old sixties or seventies song about a transvestite. Gries seemed to relax and lean his left shoulder against the elevator wall, but he still kept a watchful eye. The sergeant major was lightly nodding his head up and down with the tune but other than the slight nodding he was solid as a rock. Alice relaxed a little more as the elevator came to a stop.

The doors opened and immediately the major was standing alert and Top worked his way in front of the cart, the elevator music no longer even a memory to him. Then the idea hit Alice like a dam bursting and flooding a valley below it. Her eyes widened and she was caught up in the idea that flooded her mind.

"Elevator music!"

⌘   ⌘   ⌘

"So what is it?" Alan Davis held the tiny circular shaped circuit board in his hand. The tiny printed circuit board was about the size of five pennies stacked on top of each other with several small chips and components soldered to it. There was a membrane switch on one side and what appeared to be a small watch battery on the other.

Alice smiled. "I call it an IBot."

"An IBot?" Roger took the device from Alan and looked closer at it.

"You mean like an IPod?" Traci asked, nudging up closer to Roger to get a better look at the thing and to be closer to Roger.

"Bingo, Hooters Girl." Alice continued to be impressed by the former Hooters waitress. "Using the codekey and the bot handshaking protocol that Dr. Horton discovered and the frequency modulation your guys found, Roger, I constructed a little music box for the bots. Any bot that gets within ten or twenty meters of this thing, the range is depending on terrain of course, will try to handshake with it. The IBot will respond with the proper codekey for the handshaking protocol and send the 'prepare to receive' code that I isolated from the decrypted data Dr. Horton sent us.

"Ah, and then you play it a song?" Roger scratched his head.

"Yes. And since the little memory chip on board the IBot is only large enough to store about one song, I programmed it to continually loop."

"Ha! So the damned things get a song stuck in their head?" Alan laughed. "That is freakin' brilliant."

"But what does that do for us?" Roger asked, pretty sure he understood but he wanted to be positive.

"Well, the data we have on the bots tells us that while they're handshaking and downloading they stop other activities." Alice explained. "It's like getting in the elevator and hearing the elevator music. You are a captive audience so you stop what you are doing and listen to it."

"Have you tried it on our bot yet?" Roger asked.

"Oh yes. Watch this." Alice tapped a few keys on her laptop and pressed a button on the overhead projector. The projector displayed what her laptop monitor displayed on a blank wall of the lab. "See, this is the output from the spectrum analyzer box connected to my USB port. Here around 1.4 gigahertz you see the com signal from the bot hopping around. Now watch this." Alice took the IBot from Roger and pressed the membrane on-switch of the IBot and a second signal appeared on the screen. Then the bot's signal began to shift and change and the handshaking protocol appeared.

Alice tapped another window open that displayed the decrypted datalink between the bot and the IBot. Strings of ones and zeroes scrolled down the window.

"It's working!" Alan said. "Look, this string here. That is the song right? And the bot is just humming along with it. Check out the mimicking signal."

"Yeah, I haven't figured that part out yet, but who cares. Maybe it really is getting stuck in the thing's head. Who knows?" Alice shrugged and smiled. "The main thing is—"

"It works!" Roger rubbed his hands together.

"What song are you playing them, Alice?" Traci asked.

" 'Lola.' " You know, 'We drank champagne and danced all night . . . ' That one."

Alan laughed. "Goddamned hippie stuff. Why couldn't y'all used some Skynyrd or some Guns'n'Roses or something?"

"Well, you could program it however you want—" Alice started.

"No! Leave it just the way it is and get the blueprints to every redoubt left. Alan, figure out a way to harden it. I want as many of these things as the human race can manufacture. Put everybody making them." Roger went into deputy secretary of defense mode. "I have to call the President. Traci, go find Ronny and Danny and have them meet me in the red-phone conference room."

"Sure." She nodded and left.

"Alan, get Top and Gries down here and get them thinking of a plan."

"Let's get on this!"

"So why not broadcast it worldwide and shut them all down at once?" the President asked.

"The problem, Mr. President, is that this type of communication signal is not like standard radio. It's more like a broadband wireless connection. You see, you can pump out a lot of data over the link, but due to the physics of how they work even higher power transceivers are limited to a few hundred meters or so." Of course it was more complicated even than the most sophisticated human broadband technologies, but the principle and the physics were the same. This wasn't the final answer to ridding humanity of the alien Von Neumann probes but it was a start and Roger wanted to get this information out to the President as soon as he could. Which was why they were using an Internet video call.

"So, could we set up safe zones the way the airports and cybercafés used to have wifi zones?" the NSA asked.

"Absolutely. And I'm even thinking we could mount them on vehicles and they might work," Ronny Guerrero added. "We're effectively spoofing the bots' IFF capabilities."

"That's right, Ronny. I've got my team modifying some broadband wireless routers to transmit the signal. It should work. We have to hope the bots don't get wise to our plan."

Roger had finally done something that might help. Oh, he knew he didn't do it himself. But his project had. He had put the right team together, found the right experts when they needed them, and acquired the right resources. It had worked at least enough to offer some hope. The first hope he had felt in the months since he saw the intel on what was left of Europe and how people were living— no, surviving—there.

"We should use this IBot thing and start a plan of action and go after these things," General Mitchell suggested.

"Well, we can't mass produce them fast enough for an all-out invasion. But we believe we can produce enough to set up a perimeter over four or five redoubt areas within the next month," Roger said.

"A month! Those things will have eaten more than a hundred cities by then!" the secretary of defense shouted. "We found out where the major tube was headed; it dropped square on Oakland. Now they're spreading on the *west* coast as well!"

"Actually, a hundred and twenty-five cities at the current rate of growth," Roger replied. "But I'm sorry, sir, that is best we can do for now. We can choose the redoubts and start evacuating everybody to them now."

"Then how long will it take to manufacture enough of these, uh, IBots did you call them? How long will it take to make enough of them to go after the invaders?"

"Current rate of growth versus our manufacturing capabilities suggest perhaps a few years, sir," Roger admitted with a sigh. "We're behind the eight ball. But it will help with local defense. Just getting the darn things to *slow down* is a miracle."

"Don't forget, Mr. President, that this is a defense mechanism and we just now learned how the bots communicate," Ronnie added. "We might develop new technologies and strategies sooner. But right now, this is the best chance we've got to slow them down."

"I guess this is something. So, Kevin, you and Jim and Vicki get the rest of the Joint Chiefs together and determine which are the most strategic redoubts and let's get this move started now." For so long he had been sitting idle with little hope and no plan of action. At least now they had something. It wasn't much, but not-zero was entirely different from zero.

"Richard." Jeff handed him the last of the strapping material. "I can't tell you how grateful Sara Jo and I are to you and Helena. We . . . uh . . . we would . . ."

"You'd be dead, Jeff," Richard said emotionlessly. "You'd be dead, your wife would be dead and your kids would be dead. Hand me the RoboGrips . . . uh, no the big ones." Jeff handed him the grips, trying not to shake his head over Richard's entire lack of tact. Richard tightened down the last of the lag bolts through the bot's midsection to the waterwheel and then he tightened the strapping material down. "There. That should just about do it." He crawled back down the ladder to the platform below the waterwheel. The cool mist of the waterfall soaked his skin refreshingly.

"Well, we're running out of baby formula for Precious. I know there is some canned milk here but I don't know if that's good enough for a baby." Jeff backed down the steps off the platform looking at Richard, who was paying him little attention.

"Okay let's see if this works," Richard said, ignoring the problem of Jeff's baby. He tapped a few keys on his laptop and stopped the IBot transmission to the bot. The damaged bot stopped handshaking with the IBot and resumed its functions. Its damaged propulsion drive kicked on.

The waterwheel that Richard and Jeff had strapped the bot to began to whirl forward as the bot propelled itself. Richard watched the torque encoders and rotation speed on his laptop to make sure the bot's propulsion was not too much for the waterwheel. The wheel kicked up to several hundred revolutions per minute and then its speed topped out against the gear and bearing friction. The generator was now producing power at about an order of magnitude higher level than it did with just the underground river turning the wheel. Richard was pleased.

"That was clever, Richard," Jeff said watching the man in awe.

"Yes, I know. I am very clever. I am not friendly, I am not a people-person. But I *am* very clever."

"So what do you think about Precious?" Jeff asked.

"Precious? Oh, the infant. Yes, yes. I calculated weeks ago that you would be out of formula about a week ago.

I'm surprised it lasted this long," Richard said nonchalantly.

"Uh, we've been mixing it weaker than normal." Jeff said embarrassed and nervous.

"Jesus Christ, you idiot," Richard snapped. "This is the most important part of an infant's development and you could be doing major harm by not feeding it properly! It would have made more sense to use it all up at full strength! You're making the sort of mistake I'd expect out of some third world moron!"

Richard looked at his laptop one last time and checked the parameters of the generator and the waterwheel. He looked up at the wheel that was now just a blur. The water from the fall was spraying forward off the top of it each time the bot or the counterweight on the other side of the wheel splashed through it.

"Good."

"What?" Jeff could never tell if Richard was talking to himself or addressing him.

"Come on." He led Jeff back up the mine shaft to the edge of the corridor where most of the long duration dry goods and foodstuffs were stored. "Here, take these. And grow up."

He handed Jeff a large storage box with a printout taped to the top of it. The printout was a list of the nutritional information from the back of one of the destroyed baby formula canisters with an arrow from each to an ingredient in the box. At the bottom of the page was the recipe and cooking instructions for the homemade baby formula.

Jeff looked in the box, shaking his head at the ingredients. There was a twenty pound bag of long grain dried rice, a quart bottle of sunflower cooking oil, about a hundred

single-serving containers of pancake syrup from several
different restaurants and hotels, two large Ziploc bags full
of sun-dried persimmons, two Ziploc bags of shelled pecans, a restaurant salt shaker full of salt, and a ceramic bowl
and stick thing that Jeff assumed must be the mortar and
pestle described in the cooking instructions.

"This will work?" Jeff looked from the box back to
Richard several times.

"Of course it will. It's just simple cooking and no chemistry. Even you should be able to understand it. I started
to add a yeast culture but you'd screw it up and poison
that poor baby." Richard looked annoyed. "She'll do fine
with what you have there."

"Amazing," Jeff whispered to himself and hefted the
box with both arms. "Thank you."

"You should ask for things when you need them or learn
to do things for yourself. Now leave me alone, I have work
to do."

"Richard, you gonna be up all de goddamn night
again?" Helena startled him as she put her hand on his
shoulder and looked over it at the computer screen. Since
he had gotten the generator going at bot power, the X-ray
and electron microscope machines were up and running
and Richard hadn't slept much in at least a week. Helena
was glad though about the better power situation because
it also meant they could turn the electric heaters up. The
mine stayed a constant sixty-five degrees, which she
thought was way too cold for the babies. But having grown
up in St. Petersburg it was short-sleeve weather for her,
so she was typically wearing nothing but shorts and a tank
top around the mine.

"Probably. I think I'm on to something here," he said, continuing to stare at the X-ray image on the monitor. He had been saying that for the last five days.

"What is dat?"

"I think it's the replication code of the alien bot." He stroked his beard and yawned.

"Here, drink dis." Helena handed him a cup of hot coffee.

"Thanks, dear." Richard paused and sipped the coffee.

"You did a good ting with de baby's milk, you know," she said, sitting down beside him. "Little Precious, she took right to it."

"Uh," Richard just grunted.

"You tink you gonna save de world with dis? What are you gonna do with dis replication code thing?" She watched him for a moment silently.

"I dunno," he said. "But it looks like these things can build almost anything. They can manipulate this invisible force field of theirs down to a molecular level and build, well, anything from the molecule up."

"What, you mean if dey had a bunch of wood dey could build a goddamn house or something?" Helena asked. "Dat'd be nice."

"Well, yes I guess so. They would need the blueprints though. The only blueprint the one we caught has is for building a copy of itself." Richard took another sip of the coffee.

"Well, why don you make de goddamn ting make copies of itself and tell it to go eat all its fuckin' buddies?" Helena said, angry at the bots.

"Well, the government thought of that, but they don't know how to reprogram the . . . Hey that's it!" Richard finished his coffee. "I think we could do that! Helena you *are* a genius."

"*Da*. And pretty goddamn goodlookin' too." She kissed him on the cheek, wrinkling her nose as his beard tickled it, and stood up. "You come to de goddamn bed every now and a fuckin' den an' I'll show you. But take a shower first. You stink."

Richard took the subtle hint, took a shower and then joined her in bed. But he didn't sleep. Helena made love to him passionately and like a woman who doesn't see the man she loves as often as she would like. They lay silently in their bed for a few moments after and Helena drifted happily off to sleep. Once Richard was certain she was sleeping soundly, he eased himself out of bed, pulled up his shorts, and slipped out of their bedchamber, through the main shaft living room, and back to his laboratory. He tapped the computer on and booted up the work he had been looking at before.

"Now let me see. How would you wipe the mind of the bot and change its programming . . . hmmm? You will be mine, little robots, for I am very *clever* and you are not."

"We just got word from Atlanta," General Riggs said as Roger walked into the command center. "Last word, that is. Tech's redoubt put in a last call and then went off the air. The laser station on Stone Mountain was still in operation, but they expected to get overwhelmed shortly. And lidar reports that the swarm is already twinning. One group seems to be headed our way."

Roger nodded and thought about the defenses. Huntsville was the first redoubt to be hit that had *everything* that had been envisioned. They didn't have as much of everything as he would have liked, and not all of it was produced within the redoubt, but they were the first redoubt to have a chance of holding out.

"Your transport is spooling up at the field," Riggs continued. "You'd better hurry."

"What?" Roger replied, confused by the sudden, to him, nonsequitur. "Like hell. Huntsville's my *home*. And my team came up with most of the defenses. I'll get Alice and the rest out of here—their designated retreat is Denver—but I'm staying."

"Like hell, as you said," Riggs replied. "You're the guy who *runs* everything. You should have been in Cheyenne days ago."

"Too bad," Roger replied. "You can't order me to leave and by the time you could get ahold of the SecDef it'd be too late. Get the rest out; I'm a stayin'. Besides, I want to see how it all works."

"Oh, hell," the general said, shrugging. "Have it your way; I've got a war to run."

"What the hell are you doing here?" Roger asked as he entered his own "command center."

Traci spun around in her chair and grinned, shrugging one shoulder as if to say "What are you gonna do?"

"I made sure everybody was on the transport and then . . . opted out," she said. "So did Alan and Tom. They said they'd be down in a minute."

The underground bunker had been highly modified since the first time they sheltered in it. The outer doors were now nonmetallic. Some were carbon composite but most were thick wood assembled with glue and dowels.

Even the hinges and locks were composites. The bunker had loads of communications links but even those were nonmetallic fiber-optic cables. The rooms had been upgraded as well and the "command center" for the Neighborhood Watch group was more than comfortable. There were two fold-out couches, recliners and three computer station chairs to control the bank of nine plasma screens on one wall. Currently they were showing views from remote pickups on Monte Sano Mountain, downtown Huntsville, the airfield and Weeden Mountain, which directly overlooked the arsenal, as well as lidar data from the surrounding area.

"They're almost to Fort Payne," Traci continued, naming a town halfway between Atlanta and Huntsville in a direct line. "Another group just dropped on Chattanooga."

"Bull should be rolling," Roger said, taking a seat at one of the station chairs and toggling for a different view of the airfield. Sure enough, a flight of the new Goshawk composite fighters was rolling out of their bunker. "Go for it, Bull."

"I'm sure they'll have fun," Traci said, toggling a different view from Monte Sano Mountain. The high ridge was directly to the east of Huntsville and had a long view of the area between Huntsville and Atlanta. Faint on the horizon was what looked like a large cloud of birds. "And so it starts."

Colonel Ridley loitered at altitude until the last of the Goshawks got into formation and then used hand signals to indicate their direction of flight. The one thing that nobody had managed to do was put a "zero metal" radio into the damned birds. All they could use was hand signals. And forget an automated navigation system. In a way, the Goshawks harkened back to the "good old days" of flying. Gone were complex "fly by wire" controls and automated aiming systems, replaced by manual controls and brute strength. In many ways, except for the fact that they rode a ceramic composite jet engine that was barely tested, the planes were more like flying a Mustang from WWII than a Falcon.

They definitely had the "Burt Rutan Look," though, with forward canards and fore-swept wings. In tests he'd managed to get them right past supersonic but not by much. That was okay, though, the enemy was subsonic as well. And the birds *could* loft a fine load of modified Sparrows.

Fortunately, the incoming enemy had waited until late in the day to approach. If they'd hit in the morning, the battle would have been hell since the sun would have been directly in the face of the human pilots.

The plane didn't even have a compass. So far, nobody had come up with a compass that *didn't* have a scrap of metal in it. Instead he had some very detailed aerial, satellite actually, photographs of the area and the sun behind them to find their way home. One sortie to launch the missiles into the bulk of the oncoming enemy and then go home. It was really up to the lasers and mines to *stop* the probes.

He banked again as they reached Monte Sano Mountain. If they engaged much farther out than the defenses on the mountain, the probes would just pick up their "dead" and continue on. The trick was to hit them so hard they didn't have time. That was one of the key pieces of data that Shane had picked up in Greenland. The probes stopped to recover their wounded and rebuild from them. If you hit them hard enough while that was going on you could stop the whole process.

When he finally glimpsed the probe swarm, he doubted, though, whether that was going to be possible. It looked like a hurricane on the horizon.

He gave the signal for the group to bank around again, killing time until the probes got into the killzone. They came around to the north, the flight of fighters banking over Huntsville in perfect formation at no more than three thousand feet AGL, then turned back to the east. He powered down, dropping to just above stall speed, giving the probes time to get into the killbox. The lasers and missiles couldn't fire until his flight engaged. They were, in a way, the signal for the engagement to start. And he had to wait.

He hated waiting.

A flicker out the corner of his eye made him turn. Rene was signaling that they were close enough but he shook his head. Closer. They had to hit them with a solid punch or not at all.

"Come *on*," Alan bitched. "What the hell are they waiting for?"

"They have to get them to the programmed distance," Roger said, shrugging. He was nervous as well. Even with the magnification dialed all the way back, the cloud of machines filled the sky. "The Sparrows aren't going to do much against that formation. What they *will* do is slow some of the probes down. The trick is to get them to trickle in. If that whole mass fell on us, nothing we could do would stop it. But if we can get them to come in in smaller groups, and if we can destroy enough of the smaller groups faster than they can reconstruct, we'll win. They need to be this side of Gurley for them to have a chance of doing that. We're figuring we're going to lose the Monte Sano Mountain defenses. But if they can *slow them down,* we might have a chance."

"There," Tom said, setting down his beer. "There it goes."

The missiles weren't even fired by electricity. Instead, an airtube led to an igniter switch. As he closed, Bull fired off all six Sparrows, then closed with guns. The flight of fighters had moved to a staggered formation and they banked upwards as they closed, cutting a swath across the front of the massive formation of probes. It still was a pinprick, but every pinprick helped.

The cloud of probes wasn't as solid as it appeared from the distance. There were some probes that had spread out to the front. It was those that the fighters engaged, their ceramic ramjet rounds slamming into the lead probes and tearing them to shreds. It was also a necessity as the swarm got closer and closer. The probes were close enough together that the fighters were, as much as anything, "plowing the road" in an effort to cut through the edges of the cloud.

Bull had more than once started up a flock of birds. Generally, birds couldn't hurt a fighter. But *these* birds were made of metal. He triggered his guns desperately as one of the probes lurched into his path, already ravaged by somebody else's fire. The probe disintegrated in midair but pieces of it still slammed into his wingroot hard enough that he was surprised the jet held together.

Finally they were through the outliers and headed home. Now to see if the wing stayed on. As planned, they poured on the gas and headed for altitude at the same time. They had to get out of the way of the next line of defense.

Roger zoomed in Plasma Six on the front of the probe cloud and grunted in satisfaction.

"They're picking up their wounded," Shane said, nodding. "Just like I said."

Some of the probes who had picked up enough metal from their deceased brethren had stopped to twin. They were quickly lost from view but it was apparent what was happening.

"Now to see if a solid punch works better," Roger said, zooming the magnification back. The video camera was located on the observatory on Monte Sano Mountain and as he zoomed back he got one flash of the fighters screaming by not far overhead. Then it was as if the mountain erupted in fire.

On the 15th of April, 1950, Redstone Arsenal had become the Army's premier rocket production and design facility. Since that time, every major category of rocket produced in the U.S. had some link to Redstone Arsenal and Huntsville. Huntsville, in fact, was a town of little *but* "rocket scientists." Just as L.A. focused on the movie industry and had the byproduct of being filled with out-of-work actors, Huntsville was overrun with people *obsessed* by things that flew on a pillar of flame. And just as there were dozens, hundreds, of little production companies churning out small movies in L.A., there were dozens of companies that, with a little funding, could make things that went WHOOSH around Huntsville.

Starting with Rocket Ram-Jets, Roger had organized those companies into a minor rocket-building empire. And they had responded. Despite numerous shortages, there was still plenty of potassium nitrate, charcoal, carbon composite materials and resins, and hydroxyl-terminated polybutadiene (HTBP) to be had. When specific shortages turned up, here a thermocouple, there a specialized form of paper, the companies had adjusted, adapted and overcome. After all, they *were* rocket scientists.

And over the course of a few months they had churned out an enormous number of very simple rockets. Those rockets had only one purpose in life: deliver a small payload to a location not very far away and then die.

Therefore when the signal was given, over one thousand K type Estes rockets launched nearly simultaneously. Atop each of them was a small payload consisting of fourteen "metal mines" and a timer. Some of them met "leakers" ahead of the swarm on their way to their rendezvous with destiny. That was okay since every dead bot was a good bot. But most of them penetrated into the edge of the swarm and then "dropped" their payload. However, they weren't done. The bots seemed to have some sense of their oncoming wrath because a few swerved to avoid the tearing missiles. But the swarm was deep and crowded. It was impossible to move too much within the swarm and just as impossible to *miss* hitting *something*. Every single missile, either before dropping their payload or after, managed to hit, and destroy, at least one bot. In many cases they hit more than one before being mangled out of functional existence. When a rocket flying at five hundred kilometers per hour hit a bot, rarely did either escape unscathed.

Of the thousand missiles fired from the Monte Sano Mountain defenses, seven hundred and ninety-two managed to drop their payload. Each of them carried fourteen "metal mines." Since the rockets themselves had little or no metal content, the bots instantly gravitated to the mines, pulled the little metal bits out of this flying bonanza and then . . . died.

The effect, being watched from deep underground, was very much like watching fireworks, except by day. There was a small charge in the center of the payload that spread the mines out. This was noticeable by a brief puff of smoke. Then, as the bots pulled the metal tabs out of the mines and detonated them, there was a series of explosions, flowering outward from the smaller puff.

"Damn," Alan muttered, munching on a handful of potato chips. "That's cool. I wish it was nighttime."

"Sun's going down," Roger pointed out. "Just in time for the laser light-show."

With the fighters gone and the rockets having done their job, the lasers could open up.

There were two laser projectors on Monte Sano Mountain, one right by the observatory and another by the Forestry Department lookout tower. Both were powered by nine very large General Electric diesel generators. The combined output of the generators was over seventy megawatts and the vast majority of it was pumped through a massive array of liquid cooled laser diodes.

The laser systems themselves were mostly large laser diode arrays made of semiconductor material mixtures of indium gallium arsenide and phosphate. The individual diode laser measured only a millimeter thick, a few tens of millimeters long, and a few microns wide. Millions of the tiny devices were stacked side by side to create a massive laser array with an optical output in the megawatts of photon energy. The photons were of a wavelength of about 1.3 microns and were therefore infrared and invisible to the naked eye.

Laser power is limited by atmosphere. While there were various ways of reducing the effect, the Redstone group hadn't had the time to try for finesse. Thus it was a matter of letting the probes get *close* before the projectors opened fire. The lasers went off when the probes were less than five miles away.

The lasers began to "paint" the sky, tracking back and forth across the entire zone that the probes occupied, moving much faster than the eye could follow. This created "lines" of fire that dithered across the front of the cloud, zooming up and down and up and down across the entire front. The pointing and tracking system for the array steering maintained a centroid lock on the cloud and randomly dithered within the bounds of the cloud. Pinpoint shots could be made to within accuracies of a few centimeters at that range but the beam was a half meter wide by then due to diffraction and there were plenty of targets to shoot at anyway. So accuracy was not a problem.

The powerful lasers tracked back and forth, pumping megawatts of coherent light into the mass of probes.

And the entire front of the cloud of probes began to . . . fog.

"What the hell is that?" Shane asked. "It looks like a smoke screen. Are they doing that to cut down on the lasers?"

"No, but it's having that effect," Roger replied. "That, my friend, is gaseous metal. The lasers are burning the probes apart, but they're releasing clouds of metal gas in the process. That's going to be a very unhealthy place to be after this is all done."

He zoomed in on the cloud and managed to catch a view of a bot just as the laser, which was quite invisible to the eye, cut across it. The laser caught the bot on the edge of one "wing" and sliced upwards. The beam wasn't powerful enough to cut all the way through but the effect was to cause the bot to begin spiraling downward. Another bot caught it after it had fallen no more than a hundred feet, and along with some others began tearing it apart. But even as Roger watched, the remorseless laser plowed through *that* group, cutting the four clustered bots apart and causing the whole group to begin spiraling towards the ground.

"It's slowin' 'em down, though," Alan said, looking at Plasma Two, which was carrying lidar data. "Damn if it isn't slowing them down."

"But they're spreading out, too," Roger pointed out, zooming back the lidar data. The cloud was spreading upward and to the north and south. He wasn't sure if it was thought out or simply a result of crowding. It was apparent, though, on the remote vids that the laser operators had noticed the spread and had spread their own beams as well. However . . .

"They're getting through, now," Shane said, shaking his head. "The lasers can't cover that much sky and still keep them back."

Remorselessly, the mindless bots were advancing through the laser fire. They could barely make headway, but they were forcing their way forward and fanning out the sides and over the defenses. The latter two were the most important and dangerous, through. The bots to the side and top were able to use those between them and the laser projectors as screens and were continuing on towards Huntsville.

The video from Monte Sano Mountain had gotten . . . dark. The projectors now had probes on every side and had spread their fire to deal with it. That meant less fire per square meter but despite that there was only so close the probes could get. As they closed, the space between the laser "lines" became smaller and smaller. More of the power was being pushed into a smaller and smaller space, creating a dome of probes trying, now coherently, to get at the projectors and the projectors tearing them apart.

Roger frowned as something dropped past the pickup, then he began noticing more and more objects. But it was *dark* in the dome, the only light now coming from the occasional flash of lightning as a probe died. In the stroboscopic effect of thousands of the probes flashing their death light, he tried to figure out what was happening. Then, suddenly, the video pickup rocked and then tilted downward, its mounting apparently destroyed. In the dim strobing from dying probes, and now a strange red light from burning metal, he could see pieces of probes littering the ground in every direction. The ground was *covered* in smashed probes, many of them strobing and adding to the overall lighting effect. Indeed, the quality of the light was improving as more and more of the probes added their death flickers, creating an ambient light that was weird beyond all imagining. Then the camera went dark.

He switched to the last pickup on the mountain that collocated with the laser projector. There was a steam rising in the area, probably from the cooling system that had to be working overtime. And in every direction there was a weird glow from atmospheric breakdown and ionization. The laser itself was infrared, in a band of light that the human eye couldn't see. Despite that, he could clearly see it tracking across the sky. *Close.* It was hard to get perspective, the fog of gas around the projector limited the ability to see actual probes, but it looked as if the laser was hitting something no more than fifty meters away. And besides the weird green-white light from the dying probes, the sky over the projector was the strangest purple-orange Roger had ever seen in his life.

"What the hell is that?" Roger asked, dazzled, confused and awed. *They* had created this . . . this . . . wonderful, glorious *nightmare*.

"Excited gas," Tom said after a moment. "It's a good thing there aren't *people* up there or they'd be choking to death. The laser shoots a probe. Probe breaks up. Falls towards projector. Laser cuts it again. And again. Before long you've mostly got gaseous metal. That blocks the laser. We should have thought of that. Not sure what we could have done."

"Wind generators," Shane said instantly. "Big damned fans. Blow it away. Maybe something like ceramic jet engines."

"See, this is why I wanted to stay," Roger said. "To watch. Not just for kicks, mind you. But . . . Damn, this is . . ."

"Apocalyptic?" Tom finished for him. "Certainly awesome. But . . . ah . . ."

Suddenly, the laser stopped tracking. And in seconds, the video went dead.

"And that's that," Tom said, sounding almost satisfied to have the laser finally die. "At some point, the oxygen level was going to drop too low for the generators—"

"Told you we should have used nukes," Alan pointed out. "No problem there."

"And so it goes," Shane added. "Monte Sano Mountain falls at last."

"Yeah, but those aren't the only projectors we have," Roger said, smiling faintly. "Here comes . . . Weeden."

Monte Sano Mountain had two projectors. Atop Weeden Mountain, which sat in the middle of the Arsenal, there were *nine*.

There were actually three peaks to the ridge that ran down the center of the arsenal: Weeden Mountain, Madkin Mountain and Ward Mountain. None of them technically met the definition of a mountain, since none of them rose to more than six hundred feet over the surrounding terrain and barely 1200 feet above sea level. On the north was Ward, the lowest at barely 900 feet, then Weeden then Madkin, both at 1200 feet. Ward had one battery of one thousand "mine" rockets and a laser projector. Ditto Madkin. The rockets on Ward Mountain faced north, the rockets on Madkin faced south. On Weeden, centermost, there were two batteries, east and west, and seven projectors. These three peaks, overlooking NASA Marshall Space Flight Center, the Arsenal and Huntsville itself, held the hopes and dreams of the survival of the human race.

Most of the critical equipment for Asymmetric Soldier

had been moved into newly dug tunnels in Weeden Mountain. But the major facilities, the buildings and shops scattered across the Arsenal, were nearly impossible to replace. Holding the probes at the line of the Arsenal border was, therefore, a high priority.

The main defense command center was located in Weeden as well, in a heavily reinforced bunker buried in the heart of the mountain. Since the day when General Riggs had pointed out that "we're not part of FORCECOM," things had changed. Besides commanding the Arsenal he now had under his direct control a brigade of light infantry from the 82nd Airborne Division. And, of course, Shane Gries's "special security detail." The brigade was scattered around the mountain, holding critical positions in the hopes that they could stop the probes if they broke through the main defense line. But the main doors to the command center were held by the short platoon under Major Gries.

Which was why Jones and Mahoney were watching the fun from a bunker just to the north of the main entrance.

"Security Team," Gries said over the speaker behind them. "Listen up. Probes have hit the Monte Sano Mountain defenses. Expect to have them in sight over the mountain in about five minutes. Out."

"It's gonna be dark soon," Jones growsed. "How the hell are we suppose to shoot these things in the dark?"

"All life is the darkness of the cave through which we, as searchers, must stumble using only the reflected reality of truth as, as such, a figure shown upon the wall," Mahoney intoned.

"You've been reading again, haven't you?" Jones said, sighing. "What is it this time?"

"Plato," Mahoney admitted. "But he's got a point. What is Truth? Is it, in fact, truth that we will see the enemy in a bare five minutes? Are they even reality?"

"The *reality* is that you're going to have a carbon ceramic knife cut your throat if you don't quit reading philosophy," Jones snapped. "The *reality* is that if these things take out the mountain we're gonna be *walking* to the next redoubt. So pay attention to your sector."

"Don't I always?" Mahoney said. "And, in fact, it turns out that the captain's estimate *was* illusion."

"Huh?" Jones said, leaning towards the firing slit to get a glimpse in the direction Mahoney faced. Mahoney's position faced northeast whereas his faced due east. And there, to the northeast, was a glittering *wall* of metal shining above the distant mountain in the light of the dying sun, a red cloud of an approaching storm as pregnant with menace as any hurricane wall. "*Damn.*"

"Couldn't have put it better myself," Mahoney said, cocking his M-240R. The R version of the machine gun was a special modification of the local machine shops. A water-filled shroud surrounded the barrel for the purpose of cooling. The fire rate of most modern machine guns was limited by the fact that when fired at high rates the barrel and breech would overheat. This caused various unpleasant effects from jamming to "cookoff" of the ammunition as it touched the super-hot breech to barrel warping, which could cause an explosion. Modern machine guns were, by and large, designed to be mobile and thus were "air-cooled." But since the defense of the mountain had become a matter of bunkers and holding position, the machine guns had been retrofitted with the water-cooling shrouds. They could, effectively, be fired indefinitely without the need to use carefully controlled bursts and constant barrel replacements.

Thus the machine gun itself was set up on a box of ammunition the size of a large motorcycle. Jones figured if he ended up firing the whole box he should be able to take the rest of the day off. He watched the swarming horde for a moment as it crossed the mountain and dropped onto the city below. At the very top there was a plume of strange smoke, as if the mountain had suddenly erupted. That, too, was caught in the red light of the sun, making it appear to be lava spewing into the air.

"I think it's time that the Greyhound started playing our song," Mahoney muttered.

"Nah, it's not that bad," Jones replied. "Yet."

"If that's not a tempest at the gates I don't know what is."

"I got it," Jones added after a moment. "I got it."

"Got what, the clap?" Mahoney asked. He might be introspective when the enemy was out of sight, but when the probes were in view he was all business.

"What you were saying before," Jones replied, excitedly. "We're like, in a cave, right? Sort of. A bunker anyway. And the light's shining on the probes, reflecting off of them. That was what you were talking about, right?"

Mahoney sighed. "I am surrounded by Philistines."

"Now *that* I just don't get," Jones said, frowning. "I mean, we're not even surrounded, yet, and those are like . . . alien probes. Is whatever you just said something like that?"

"Interesting," Shane mused, tapping his mouse to bring up a readout.

"What?" Cady asked, leaning over from his own position.

Shane was much more used to leading from the front than from deep in the heart of a mountain. But any modern infantry officer was more than well versed on using computer networks for what the military termed "C3I," communications, control, command and intelligence.

Technically Shane should have been using the C3I system in the command post to maintain control over the troops in his area. That area was defined as the distance of the weapons that he had at his command. Since all long-range weapons were at General Riggs's command, that area wasn't much. But he had Sergeant Major Cady to handle that and when all was said and done he had less than a platoon to manage. It didn't take up a lot of his time. So he'd "expanded" the area, both informationally and terrain-wise, that he was viewing. In other words, he wasn't just looking at the remaining sensors, visual and lidar, that were telling the general what the probes were doing, he was monitoring the whole spectrum.

"General," the electronic warfare officer said, "probe transmissions have just picked up by fifteen percent. Pretty much across the board."

"That," Shane said, quietly, in response to Cady. "They're generating like mad."

"What does that *mean*?" the general asked, spinning in his chair to look over at the EWO.

The command center had been designed by a local firm. It turned out to be the firm that had *also* designed every NASA control center since the Mercury capsules. So there was a very similar feel. The general's position was two thirds of the way towards the back at a terminal with various other controlling officers and enlisted men scattered around. Shane, as one of the lowest priority positions, was towards the back and rear. On the other hand, it gave him a great view of the forward information screens and everyone else's positions.

"Don't know, sir," the EWO admitted. "We don't have a hard fix on how they talk, so we can't exactly translate it."

"Updating," Shane said to Cady. He'd meant for it to be a quiet and personal conversation with his NCO. But it hit one of those dead silences that sometimes fall over a group and it rebounded around the room.

"Say again?" the general said, looking around. "Who said that?"

"Me, sir," Shane replied, cursing himself. He wasn't *supposed* to be looking at signal data at all. The glare that he got from Colonel Summers, the commander of the 82nd brigade, said it all. But he'd already stepped on his hooter; might as well jam it into the ground. "The signals picked up by about five percent when they got close to the lasers. They stayed that way until just a moment ago, then they *really* picked up. They got some information processed, probably what to do about lasers if they hit them again, and passed it around. Signal level is now back to nearly normal."

"Good possibility," the general said, spinning around to look over at the major. "Extrapolate."

Damn, damn, damn. Surprise is in the mind of the commander, even the surprise of trying to answer a question. What was the update?

"Somewhere they have a higher level battle processor, sir," Shane replied, after keying the controls so that he was talking directly to the general. He noticed right away that the general had keyed it for general distribution so he might as well have just yelled. "It might be distributed in the probes or it might be one of those big cities over in Europe. That processor told them that they had to do something about the lasers. So far we've only seen them tear stuff apart. There's no reason that they wouldn't have a higher level ability than we've seen. In Greenland we saw them begin destroying carbon to escape traps. Perhaps they'll use a longer range weapon we haven't seen before." He paused for a moment as his mind raced.

"They'll want to keep most of their systems as extractors. To change will take time. I would look for a group that falls away from the main body to modify itself and then goes for the first laser that fires."

"Good possibility," Riggs said, spinning back around. "Hammond," he continued, looking over at the Information and Intelligence section, "keep an eye on that."

"Roger," the J-2 replied. "We won't be able to code for it. We'll have to use eyeballs."

"Do it," the general replied.

"Probes have entered Huntsville city limits," the J-3 reporter said. "Approaching Phase Line Deadite."

Shane smiled at that. When he'd seen the op-plan for the engagement, he laughed his butt off and wondered which staff weenie was an Army of Darkness fan and *how* they had gotten the codes past the general. A little digging turned up that it was General *Riggs* who was an Army of Darkness fan.

"Initiate Op-plan Ash when ten percent of the probes have crossed Phase Line Deadite," Riggs said. "And may God be with the just."

⌖   ⌖   ⌖

"Hmmm . . ." Richard mused, watching the alien probe slow down and then speed up as he tapped the keys of the laptop. "That seems . . . to have done it."

"Dat's nice," Helena said. "But don't you want it runnin' full speed?"

"Absolutely," Richard replied. "But if I can control *one* bot I can control many. Or, rather, the military can. Much as I hate giving my secrets to the military-industrial complex, this is one area where they are a utility. And this Dr. Reynolds who is a deputy secretary of defense seems to be an honorable man."

"Dat's da guy in Huntsville, right?" Helena said, raising an eyebrow.

"The same," Richard replied, shutting down the laptop. "I finally determined that he was working with Dr. Alice Pike, which explains many things. She was a bright girl, Alice."

"Well, if you wanna tell Huntsville somet'ing, you better hurry," Helena said. "Dey're under attack."

"Good Lord," Richard said, picking up the laptop and hurrying towards the laboratory. "You could have told me!"

"I jus' did," Helena pointed out.

"Ten percent and climbing past Phase Line Deadite," the J-3 tac NCO said.

"Fire rockets," General Riggs responded.

"Firing."

Jones slapped his hand over his ears as one thousand J-type rockets launched with near simultaneity.

"Jeeze that was loud!" he yelled over the ringing in his ears. "They could have warned us!"

"Go baby go," Mahoney said, ignoring his bunker mate.

"I wonder how they'll . . ." Jones said and then paused. "Aw . . . shit."

"Oh, yeah, and updating their defenses against the rockets," Shane added to himself, grimacing.

The mass of probes was rapidly spreading across Huntsville and on the vids it was easy to see the buildings crumbling as they passed. The wide-angle vid had a great shot of the rockets flying towards their mass, currently passing over and spreading out along South Memorial Parkway, or "Phase Line Deadite." It also had a great view of the odd . . . tubes that extended from the mass, spreading out around the incoming rockets. The tubes were about ten meters across, probes making up the wall of the tubes, and extended along the ballistic flight path of the rockets so that the rockets had to fly down the center. As he watched, the rockets also began to shred and then disappear, without so much as the slightest explosion.

"Major Gries," the general said quietly over his headset. "Comments?"

"We can now anticipate *some* reaction against the lasers, sir," Shane replied tightly. "They didn't hit the mines on this attack, so those might have an immediate effect. And they haven't run into IBot yet."

"Concur," General Riggs said. "On the eventuality that they will attempt to close with the lasers, I want you to pull your platoon and redeploy them around the East Weeden laser site. Make sure they carry breath-masks."

"Yes, sir," Shane said, starting to stand up.

"Turn over control to your sergeant major," Riggs interjected quickly. "I want you here."

"Yes, sir," Shane said with a grimace.

"On it," Cady added, keying his mike. "Platoon, unass your positions. Move to the armory. Draw nonmetallic weaponry and masks. You got two minutes. Haul!" He reached under the console and pulled out his war-stick. "Time to go swat some bugs."

Fortunately there were elevators to the summit position where the lasers were mounted. Just as fortunately, the probes were taking their time stripping Huntsville of all its useable metal. But the troops were still panting by the time they got to the summit.

"Top, now that we're here, what are we doing here?" Mahoney asked as the platoon spread out from the flush-mounted stairwell by the laser bunker. The same guys who had designed the whole mountain complex had designed the laser position and, in keeping with the NASA theme, Mahoney recognized the design from a trip to Kennedy Space Center. It was the same sort of massive structure as the ones used for observers of the Apollo launches. The two-story structure consisted mostly of *very* large concrete-filled sandbags. More and stronger seemed to be the idea. The tiny projector was mostly hidden on the very top, a glittering ball of crystal catching the last rays of the sun.

"The Old Man and the general think the probes are gonna go for the laser as soon as it opens up," Cady answered. "Our job is to make sure they don't get here."

"Top," Jones argued, "if they can take out the laser, we're not going to be able to do much."

"That's to be seen," Cady answered equanimably. "There's a dead zone here under where the lasers can fire. That's our priority. You let the big boys handle the rest. For now, spread out around the laser. Everybody gets a zone. If a probe comes into your zone, kill it. It's that simple."

"Simple," Jones muttered as Cady and Staff Sergeant Gregory spread the short platoon around the perimeter.

"Very," Mahoney said from his position. He and Jones had managed to snag the best view, which also meant they were probably going to be the first hit. "Very simple. But important point, keep your head down." Mahoney was leaning up against the concrete bunker, apparently enjoying the view of Huntsville being chewed to bits. The laser bunker was mounted on the very summit of Mount Weeden. Off to their left was a lower bit with, of all things, a small swamp. It was an odd feature to see on the top of a mountain.

"Why?" Jones asked.

"Because, if your head gets too high . . ." the other specialist said and then thumbed over his shoulder. "Those lasers don't have target discriminators. They'll shoot you just as soon as one of the probes. And it'll go through you easier."

"Ouch," Jones said, glancing nervously over his shoulder. "I don't like being out here; we're exposed as hell."

"Tell me about it," Mahoney replied as Sergeant Gregory came back around.

"Listen up," Gregory said, waving them over to huddle around him. "Couple of safety points. Top was watching the video from Monte Sano Mountain. First point, watch where you move. The laser's not going to miss you if you get in its path—"

"I already pointed that out to Jones," Mahoney said.

"Right, good . . ." the staff sergeant replied. "Stay close into the bunker. The laser is set to skim the edge of this ridge. If you're close into the bunker, you're out of its line of fire. Second point, when the laser hits these things it chops them up. When they get close, we're going to have pieces of probe slamming into the ground all around here. And into us. Keep your damned helmets and armor on. It might keep the damage down. When they get real close, the air starts getting filled with burned up metal. It'll rip up your lungs. When they close with us, go to MOPP one, mask only. The mask will keep you alive. Clear?"

"Clear," Jones said. "How'd we draw this shit detail, Sergeant?"

"Somebody's got to do it," Gregory replied with a grin. "You don't expect them wind-dummies to get their berets all dirty, now do you?"

"Got it," Shane said, keying the com for the intel section. "Sir, would you take a look at the group of probes located at 5413 by 3845? That's right by the Oak Park athletic field. Looks like about . . . hell, maybe a thousand of them. I don't have backtrack, but it looks as if they stopped there and are just . . . sitting."

"Good eye, Major," the J-2 colonel said. "Let me get a couple of people to eyeball them."

"Over fifty percent across Phase Line Groovy," J-3 reported.

"Prepare to lase—" General Riggs said and then stopped, holding his hand to his earbud. "Roger." He looked up and then clicked a control, zooming the main viewscreen into the group that Shane had spotted. With the zoom cranked up, it was apparent that the probes had changed shape slightly. There was now a circular opening that looked very much like a cannon mouth on the front of the probes.

"Laser targeting, Weeden East only, designate that group of modified probes as high priority."

"Roger," Lasing called. "Slewing. We have the group targeted."

"Initiate lase," General Riggs said.

There were a few probes between the laser and the presumed "anti-laser" group. They didn't really pose much of a problem except for creating small clouds of gaseous metal. But as soon as the lasers hit the first probe, the modified group began to move, dropping down to the deck and accelerating towards Weeden Mountain.

They also began jinking in and out of the shadow of the remaining buildings, flying down roads not much off the ground. There were enough buildings, and enough rubble from buildings, that the group was able to an extent to avoid the lasers. For that matter, it was hard to tell, but it appeared that some of the laser-killers might have taken brief hits and kept going. And they weren't the only group headed for the mountain. It seemed as if the lasers were the signal for most of the probes to drop what they were doing and head for the Arsenal.

"That got their attention," General Riggs said. "Where'd the killer group go?"

"Disappeared into the mass," J-3 responded.

"We're trying to pick them up again," Lasing called.

"Negative," General Riggs replied. "Open up full lasing across the area. Engage at will."

"Roger."

"There they are," Shane called as the killer probes exited a corporate park and started crossing the "no-man's land" that had been established around the perimeter of the Arsenal. Among other things, the "no-man's land" was the first line of anti-probe mines. But those mines depended on the probes pulling the metal out of them to function. And the "killer bots" weren't interested in metal, just lasers.

The inner edge of the no-man's land was also where the lasing stopped. Once the probes crossed it, and more than half made it across since the lasers were targeting the whole sky, they were under the fire basket of the lasers. The only thing between them and the lasers were the few troops on the mountain and the platoon around the laser site.

"Vampire, vampire," Shane called on the platoon net. "Approximately four *hundred* bots with unknown weapon approaching from the northeast, coming in low. Top, shift to heavy on the northeast."

"Sir," the EWO officer said over the channel to the general, "we can initiate IBot at any time."

"Hold it," Riggs said, nodding. "If we can stop them from getting the lasers and let more of them come into the basket I'd prefer it. I don't want them outside the basket and passing on that we're spoofing them."

"Roger."

"Start broadcasting."

Weeden Mountain had long been known to the general Arsenal public as "Antenna Hill." It had a vast array of antennas on it used for everything from cell phones to satellite uplinks. And the probes *liked* radio.

On command, every single antenna started broadcasting. And those few probes that were still eating Huntsville dropped what they were doing and headed for the redoubt.

Private First Class Jason Soldiers had lived with his name his whole life. But *despite* his name, he had enlisted in the 82nd Airborne at the ripe age of eighteen. One of the few books he had ever read, and enjoyed, was called *Starship Troopers*. In it he ran across a point that really resonated with him. The main character had just joined the military in that book and, much to his chagrin, had ended up as a simple infantryman. He had told this to the one NCO he had met, the recruiting NCO, and gotten a very odd, to him, reaction. The recruiting NCO, a former infantryman missing a couple of limbs, had told him that "the infantry's the only really important arm. Everybody else supports *us*. Because we're where the rubber meets the road."

That was what he'd told the recruiter when he signed up. He wanted to be where the rubber meets the road.

At the moment, though, he really wished he'd gone in for radar technician or computer repair. He'd gotten the word that there was a group of bots headed for the lasers. And they had orders to take them out.

The only problem being that it seemed like every single one was headed for his bunker. There seemed to be a million of them and they were coming in very low, very fast, and very *very* hard.

There seemed to be only one thing to do, so he toggled off the safety on the M-240R, picked a point in space over the bots and pulled the trigger.

⌘   ⌘   ⌘

The remaining problem of the M-240R, after it was cooled, was ammunition. The best choice would have been the ramjet rounds demonstrated by Dr. Reynolds and Alan Davis. However, producing enough of them in any reasonable time had proved to be impossible. Instead, a modified sabot round was the best that could be created. Since the probes ate metal as it flew towards them, the new round consisted of a plastic outer "shoe," or sabot, with an inner ceramic round. As the round left the machine gun, the plastic sabot fell away, leaving the ceramic round to do the damage, however the relatively low-density ceramic round tended to tumble beyond about four hundred yards and lost velocity rapidly.

The probes, on the other hand, had a momentum of their own. And the ceramic rounds, while lightweight, could still shatter the metal facing of the probes in tests.

Against the killer probes, however, things did not go as well as planned. Soldiers watched in disbelief as the rounds sparked and crashed into the probes, but seemed to have little or no effect. A few of the probes lost control and slammed into the mountainside in a shower of sparks. But the majority, even when they were struck by the ceramic rounds, continued on as if nothing had happened.

Soldiers stopped firing and spun around, pressing a button he had been told *not* to use under any circumstances. It was the button that put him through directly to the brigade commander in the bunker.

"This is Soldiers, Bunker One-Niner-Five. Sir, the killer probes are *armored*, repeat *armored*. Ceramic rounds have no effect, repeat no effect."

⌦　　　⌦　　　⌦

"Move it!" Cady yelled, redeploying the platoon so that most of them were on the northeast side. "Shag *ass*!"

"Sergeant Major!"

Cady looked up in surprise as the voice of the major boomed out of the sky and then realized there must be a PA system on the laser bunker.

"Platoon! The killer bots are armored, repeat armored. Try to hit them on the underside and see if that works."

"Oh, this just gets better and better," Jones said, taking a knee and hefting his rifle. The platoon had been armed with the latest version of the sergeant major's "super-gun." Thanks to Alan, Lurch and a local paintball company, the gun was capable of firing more powerful rounds, faster.

"Time to cue the music, sir," Cady muttered. As he did the speakers began to crackle with the sound of thunder and lightning.

"What are you doing, Major?" the general asked quietly.

"I hope you don't mind, sir," Shane said, gulping. "It's something we would do in Iraq when we knew we were in the deep. Motivational material, sir. Just a song one of the troops liked and we picked it up as a unit thing."

" 'Citadel' by Crüxshadows," the general said, smiling faintly. "You do think we're in the deep."

"I see a citadel alone," Shane replied. *"Clinging brave, defying fate.* Not sure there's a better description. Sir, permission to speak to Lasing?"

"Do it. Out here."

⌗　　⌗　　⌗

"Lasing, this is Major Gries," Shane said. "Can you make a bubble to the northeast of the bunker? We've got dead ground under your laser. I need to move my troops to cover it."

"I can give you a bubble," the lasing officer replied. "Five meters wide and, say, three and a half high call it? That do?"

"Fine, and I'd suggest tightening your fire into that area."

"Teach your granma to suck eggs, Major," the lasing officer said, with grim humor in his voice. "Already done. Those things are our main threat at the moment."

"Any way to point out where it is?" Shane asked.

"They'll know."

"Crap, look at that," Jones said as a small bush directly in front of them exploded.

"Laser," Mahoney replied over the music. "That's why you don't want to go forward. You'll be the burning bush. There," he added, waving at what appeared to be thin air. But there was a faint glow as the laser ionized the atmosphere. "That's what you've got to avoid."

"*Top, move forward*," the speaker boomed, cutting off the music. "*There's a hole in the lasing, due northeast of the bunker, five meters wide, two plus high. You should be able to spot it. Move forward to cover the dead ground! You need to stop them before they get to the top of the mountain!*"

It was the first time that Jones had actually seen the sergeant major shocked. Everyone looked over at the

NCO and could see him with his jaw wagging up and down, trying to find something to say. Jones wasn't sure whether to be terrified or laugh out loud. He decided a hysterical chuckle was called for. Okay, cackle.

The, more than one, hysterical cackle seemed to center the big NCO.

"What the fuck are you doing still sitting here with your thumbs up your ass?" Cady roared. "You heard the man! Gregory, take right, I'll take left. Tighten up and stay low. *Forward!*"

Cady swung left and duckwalked forward, keeping one eye on the occasional strikes on the ridgeline and the other over his shoulder, trying to use the two points to get some idea of the line the deadly, and invisible, beams were following. After a brief pause Staff Sergeant Gregory headed right, doing the same.

"Jones, Mahoney, Nelms," Gregory said, expanding on the sergeant major's orders. "You three front rank, between the S'maj and me. Crawl it. When you get to the edge, poke your head over. Shag ass."

Mahoney and Nelms both looked at Jones, who shrugged and grimaced.

"Bugger this for a game of soldiers," he hissed but then threw himself prone and started fast-crawling forward on elbows and knees with the other two following and then catching up to flank him.

The rest of the platoon followed, more or less in groups of three.

"Second and third ranks," Cady said, still sidling towards the edge and trying to stay out of the beams, "get ready to fire upwards. When those things come over the edge, just fucking *hose* it until you're out of ammo!"

"Fuck, fuck, fuck," Jones said as he reached the edge of the summit. It had been a fairly abrupt drop to a short bluff. Now it was as perfectly cut as if it had been carved away . . . well, it *had* been carved away by a laser. The fact that the laser wasn't, *at the moment*, shaving it seemed a minor point. "This is fucking nuts!"

"We gonna do this?" Nelms asked nervously. The normally sanguine sniper seemed unusually perturbed.

"No," Jones said, then shrugged. "One . . . two . . ."

"What the fuck?"

Staff Sergeant Richard Simone was a data security specialist code five, about the highest level available. He'd previously been assigned to the Pentagon after several minor but politically embarassing hacking attacks on secure systems. Dick Simone had been coding at the age of eight and "script kiddying" by the time he was ten. But after a while he realized that it was *much* more fun trying to *stop* hacking than actually doing it. He still maintained his connections with the cracker community, if for no other reason than to keep up on the latest slang. A few of the cooler elements even knew that he'd gone "legit;" there was a certain cachet among the really good crackers out there when they found an "enemy" that was their class.

Dick could have made much more money in the civilian world, especially since the military mostly left data security to relatively low-paid noncoms. But he had the "*mentat civitas*," that sense of honor and duty that was the core of being a soldier. Eventually he'd stop reenlisting and go get a job where he could make some real money.

Well, he *had* had that as an option until the bots got

here. Now, being in Weeden Mountain was about as safe, and well paid, as it got.

But despite the total chaos in the world the Internet was still, more or less, functioning and there was *still* the occasional jackass that tried to crack the system. And he'd just spotted one.

The guy was using a fairly simple buffer overflow attack but with a nice little fillip of an encryption packet designed to overcome Blowfish. The point seemed to be to create a zero day exploit, which he didn't have a chance of managing. So far, nobody had cracked Blowfish. A "zero day exploit" was trying to crack it on the fly. Wasn't going to happen. The cracker had hit the first firewall and thought he'd made it past. But Dick had set that one up as a trap; when a cracker using any of a thousand or so methods cracked the firewall it set off an alarm. Then Dick could watch them try to crack the second wall. And the second wall, if it detected the cracking, actually sent the cracker into a bypass loop that *looked* like a computer system but was really a very elaborate ruse, a honey trap. And all the while, Dick could be backtracking the crack and cracking the *other* guy's computer.

Dick called up a spider to follow the cracking back and got his first shock of the incident when a message popped up.

"Ah, thank you for detecting me. I need, very very urgently, to contact Dr. Reynolds. Tell him this is Megiddo and I've got the codes he needs. This is urgent since I understand that you are under attack."

❈ ❈ ❈

RocketRog: *Megiddo?*

Megiddo: *The same. I have completed a program that I believe will permit you to control the bots. It uses the same frequency spectrum as the IBot program that Dr. Pike developed. However, this one gives you the ability to stop them, have them land and reset their passwords so that you can lock out higher controls. I'm working on further refinements, however this should do for the time.*

Rocket Rog: *Boss. When can I get it?*

Megiddo: *The kind sergeant that contacted you gave me a secure point to which I might upload the program. It is currently uploading from a mirror site I placed a trojan on some time ago. And tell the nice sergeant that the tracer bot he just sent goes to one of the few remaining servers in Australia. Good luck.*

<Meggido has signed off>

". . . three! AAAHHH!"

There wasn't much to do but scream and pull the trigger. As soon as Jones put his head over the edge of the bluff all he saw was a wall of metal. The bots were actually flying through the tops of the trees, which had been sheared off by the laser, just under the beam. And the lead wave was no more than a pickup-truck's length from the edge of the bluff, headed, as far as he could tell, right for his face.

The exploding rounds were not designed to penetrate armor, and Jones could see even in the split second that he had, that these bots were *much* heavier than the ones that they'd brought back from Greenland. They were thicker top to bottom and the metal had an odd sheen to it. For some reason a battlefield in Iraq came to mind but he couldn't figure out *why*. The thing that went through his head in a flicker was a *smell* of all things. A hot, metallic stink that he couldn't quite place in the chaos that was this moment's existence.

Despite the fact that they were not armor penetrators, the explosive rounds had an effect. Enough small explosives in a small area can sometimes make up for larger explosives, even if in very odd ways. The main thing that they did was throw the bots *off course*. The probes were packed in wingtip-to-wingtip and running in a narrow gap between the ground and the lasers overhead.

As the rounds, hosing out of the modified paintball guns at over six hundred rounds per minute, began to slam into the packed-together probes it created chaos. For the *probes*. Probes hit on a wingtip tumbled sideways, slamming into the probe next to them or jinked up or down or knocked even into a spin. Up meant a brief shower of crackling electric metal as the probe, armored as it was, hit a multimegawatt laser at *very* short range. Down meant slamming into a tree, the ground or the onrushing bluff. Probes crashed into each other in a shower of metal, turning into nearly ton-weight balls of shattered metal and electrical discharge.

But momentum wins every time, and the probes had been headed for the cliff. Which meant that *all* that shattered metal was headed for the five people lining the cliff-top.

Jones couldn't look sideways as he saw a chunk of probe the size of a large bicycle pass through the space to his right but he didn't really have to; there was a sudden spray of arterial blood that wasn't really survivable. Whatever had happened to Nelms, the sniper wasn't going to be going home to Des Moines, Iowa.

Top was next to him, hosing just as he was and screaming just as loud. There was just something about the situation, a seemingly unstoppable wall of metal winging towards them at four hundred miles per hour with only a wall of *very* small exploding rounds keeping the metal from hitting them, that called for one primal scream after another. Top's was just a lot deeper than everyone else's.

One of the vids on the laser bunker had a good shot of the firefight going on at the edge of the cliff and Shane nodded to himself as he watched. There was only one thing wrong with the picture from his perspective. Too many of the probes were getting too high before being hit by the laser. Two had made it over the edge of the bluff but the backup team had managed to hit them before they did whatever they intended to do to the laser bunker. So he keyed his mike.

"Platoon, get *lower*. The laser is coming *down*."

Jones didn't really hear the CO. He could only focus on the onrushing wall of metal. But he *did* notice when the probes started exploding *much* closer overhead.

This led to *louder* screaming. But he kept his finger firmly planted on the trigger.

Two thousand rounds. Six hundred rounds per minute. Three and a half minutes. How long as this been going on? It seems like about a year . . . I think I'm already in hell.

⌘   ⌘   ⌘

"Colonel," Shane said over the link to the 82nd Brigade commander. "I very much need someone to get some ammo up to my platoon, sir."

"Already on it, Major."

Suddenly the gun stopped spitting little plastic death and Jones pulled the trigger in shock. His extensive experience told him there should be more rounds in the massive box he was carrying.

He quickly looked right and realized that Letorres had replaced Nelms. On the other side of Letorres a trooper he didn't recognize was holding one of the big ammo boxes and preparing to replace the one on Mahoney's back. A quick check back and he realized that another troop, from the 82nd by his shoulder patch, and Private Gibson were both working to replace his. The 82nd trooper grinned at him and tapped him on the shoulder.

"You're up," the trooper said, standing up.

Jones jerked his head around in time to keep the splash of superheated fluids out of his face, but he heard the thump and felt something warm and very wet land on his legs as part of the trooper's helmet, and some skull, landed next to him.

The scream he let out segued nicely into opening fire.

"Damn," Shane muttered.

The probes attacking the laser site seemed to realize they were losing. Or, at least, were very close to stalemated. So they'd changed tactics. He'd always suspected that at the top of the slope they would sacrifice the lead

ranks to cover for the followers. As he watched, they
started doing just that, but created two cover groups, one
against the fire at the top of the hill and one against the
lasers. About fifty meters downslope, the probes began
rotating their bodies so that their upper portion was
pointed towards the fire. They also began to slow, perhaps as a function of air resistance but more likely as
deliberation. The combination of the laser and the
troopers on the ridgeline hammered this wall of metal,
but the upper portion, at least, of the probes was armored.
And in this more deliberate formation they were no longer
slamming into each other catastrophically. Probes were
dying, but not faster than the overall group was making it
up the mountain.

"Major," one of the intelligence NCO's said over the
link. "You might want to know that we now have four
groups spotted that have stopped assimilation of Huntsville and appear to be reconfiguring."

And they had plenty of probes to throw away.

"Fuck, fuck, fuck, fuck, FUUUCK!" Jones shouted
as the wall of flipped up probes rode over his position. At
that point they were taking the direct fire of the laser,
which had been narrowed down to *only* fire on the vector
the probes were attacking from.

The laser was destroying rank after rank of the probes,
but the result was air full of melted metal showering down
on the few survivors of the platoon.

The sound was indescribable, a screaming maelstrom
of shrieking metal unlike anything Jones had ever heard.
He was being continuously pounded with chunks of metal
falling on his arms, his head, his legs. He tucked into a

ball, trying to take as much of the impacts on his armor and helmet as possible, his hands tucked into his stomach and legs drawn up under him. But some of the "chunks" were spitting enough electricity to supply a large home and much of it was arching into the bodies of the survivors. He was continuously jolted with lighting bolts. If he survived this he swore he would *never* come near anything electrical again. Other chunks were nearly full sized probes and when one of *those* slammed into him he felt at least one bone in his arm crack, which elicited another scream.

Life had become trying to survive the clash of two behemoths of destruction. There was nothing to do but try to live through it.

Corporal Zirnheld can kiss my ass. I just want a nice quiet house someplace with a garden and pool . . .

The scenario on Monte Sano Mountain was being repeated. But this time his troops were caught in the maelstrom and Shane could see them being covered in chunks of metal. They hadn't had time to get their masks on so even if they survived, they were liable to die from the gaseous metal they were breathing.

The worst part was, the probes were now *over* the rim and they were starting to flip upwards. Most of them were being killed but he watched as one group finally managed to flip so that those cannon-like projectors faced the bunker.

And then the screen went blank.

With a final series of rending crashes, all the sound stopped.

Jones just lay still for a moment wishing that whoever

was screaming in pain right by his ear would just *stop* for the love of God. Then he realized that it was him. The sound was being reflected back by the piles of melted bots covering him.

The air tasted and smelled foul with metal so he reached for his gas mask and let out another, quieter, scream when he realized that his *left* arm was the one that was broken. He reached across his body and got the bag open, then pulled the mask out and fitted it. He had to take off his helmet. This required moving a few bits of probe wreckage.

He finally managed to get the mask fitted and sealed one-handed, then pushed up with his right hand, shoving upwards and shedding off the cloaking layer of metal.

The first thing he noticed was metal. Lots of it. Scattered. Metal. Lots. Ouch. Some of it was still sputtering with electricity.

Looking around he realized why the bots had left. The bunker had been *chewed*. Either they were using some sort of explosive round or a gee-whiz science-fiction ray that they hadn't shown off before. It was *definitely* something explosive; the chunks taken out of it weren't uniform like they'd been cut out by the probe recycler beam or whatever. They were big, nasty explosive holes.

The line of bodies at the base of the bunker he almost didn't notice. Apparently the 82nd guys had taken shelter by the bunker. Fat lot of good it did them; it looked like the bunker buster beams or whatever had hit some of them. And the rest had probably been killed by spalling.

"Top?" he croaked, "'Torres?" then was shaken by a round of hacking coughing. He managed to get his mask off and spit out the nasty metallic-tasting phlegm, sealed the mask, got a breath of air, unsealed, got a drink, sealed and got another breath. Then another set of coughing, repeat.

"Top? Torres? Mahoney?"

"Fug ib," he heard from under the rubble and then Mahoney slowly pushed his way to the surface. He had a mask on as well. "Fug *ibs*!"

"Yeah," Jones replied, looking at where Letorres and Top had been. He wasn't sure about anyone else. There was a *big* pile where Top had been and one of the bots . . .

"Oh . . . fuck," he muttered, stumbling towards the spot.

"General, Laser One is down," the J-3 said. "Forty percent of the defense points on the mountain are out of communication. Penetrations on tunnels four and nine. Penetration halted, temporarily. Forty percent penetration across Phase Line Ugly. And there's a new wave of bots headed for the mountain. Some of them are configured for antilaser attack and they appear to be vectoring for the discovered tunnels."

"Play the music," the general said, leaning back in his chair and steepling his fingers. Like a gambler who has turned his last card, tossed his last chip and thrown his wallet on the pile, all he could do now was see what Lady Luck would turn up in the other player's hand. He'd keep his poker face on to the end.

Jones looked down into the valley and tried not to throw in the towel. The entire mass of probes had risen up from Huntsville, like a Krystal burger after a late night of drinking, and was headed for the mountain. Clearly, however, the bots "thought" on an operational level; they'd decided that the mountain was the center of the defenses and needed to be eliminated.

He was less worried about them at the moment, though, than the pile of metal around the sergeant major. One of the chunks was most of a bot, and the "wing" had fallen downward, directly onto where he remembered the sergeant major being.

He began digging at the pile frantically, trying to get under the heap as the cloud of probes rose up the mountain like an evil fog.

Shane swore, softly, as most of the bots in view stopped moving. Those that had been screaming through the air towards the mountain drifted to a stop with a certain amount of jostling and then just . . . hung as if waiting for something.

"IBot is working," the J-3 called. "Probe advance halted."

"Open up with lasers three and four," General Riggs said. "Have them engage all bots in the valley."

"Yes! Yes!" "Hot Fuckin' Damn!"

The control center erupted in cheering soldiers as the lasers began tracking across the still probes, blasting them out of the air. Shane, however, still was glued to his seat, unable or unwilling to believe that this was as complete a victory as it appeared. So he was one of the few to hear the J-2 section.

"Increase in traffic," J-2 reported. "Signal strength increasing. Something's going—"

Suddenly, the halted bots started moving again. And *every* bot in the valley was now headed for Weeden Mountain.

"Lidar reports probes lifting off from Chattanooga, Tuscaloosa, Atlanta area—Christ, every damned probe in the Southeast is headed for us!"

Sergeant Simone was pleased that this Megiddo guy, who looked to be a better cracker than it had first appeared, had something useful for Dr. Reynolds. Dick wasn't sure what it was or how the battle was going; he worked another front. The "Real World" had its warriors and the electronic world had its own. Dick Simone knew where he sat on that divide.

There was a ping from his system as somebody *else* tried to penetrate the system. As he was bringing up the program to track them, another ping went off, then a series that sounded very much like an alarm.

As far as he could tell, at first, it was a simple Denial of Service attack. A DOS occurred when someone, usually using various controlled remote systems, hammered an ISP's servers with pings, effectively shutting down service from the server. But this one was different. *Every single packet* contained some sort of cracking program, most of them things Dick, who thought he had seen them all, had never vaguely encountered. Most had dumped to the honey trap, but they were running rampant through there, while others had managed to hammer past two firewalls and were getting to his final line of defense. Somebody *had* managed a zero day exploit on Blowfish. And *more* were coming in!

He barely had time to look as the tracker program popped up with the source of at least one of the attacks, but he was glad that he'd spared it a glance. As soon as he did, he swore, stopped what he was doing and slammed his chair backwards towards the server wall.

"What's going on?" Lieutenant Gathers asked. The data security officer was a nice guy and pretty good at running the show, but Dick wasn't going to take the time to answer. Instead, he flipped open the server door, slid to the floor and hurriedly yanked the main cable connecting the system to the Internet then did the same for SIPARNET.

"Sergeant Simone, would you please explain—" the lieutenant started to say then froze as the computer in front of him started to go haywire.

"We're under attack," Simone replied, slamming back into place and starting diagnostics on the computer network. It was clear that there were worms in the system; the only question was whether he could get ahead of them and start isolating them.

"I know we're under attack," the officer replied, looking at his system. "There are about a billion probes—"

"No, I mean *we* are under *attack*, sir!" Dick yelled. "And it's coming from *France*!"

"Can we use this?" Roger asked, looking at the code of the program. It was . . . complicated.

"Megiddo's not going to send us something that would be harmful," Traci said definitely. "Everything he's sent so far has been useful."

"We ain't got much choice, Roger," Alan pointed out. "We're kinda outnumbered, Kemosabe."

"Agreed, okay we'll—"

"Whoa!" Traci said. "We're under electronic attack. I mean, there's something in the *base* system that just hit our internal wall and bounced."

"Huh?" Roger said. The Asymetric Soldier group used

a network separate from the main base network. They used the same physical systems for accessing SIPARNET and the Internet, but their internal working server was of a higher classification than the standard base system, so it was internally sealed off from most of the base systems.

"We're getting more hits," Traci said. "Something's in the internal base system and trying to get through to ours. Damn," she added, clicking a pop-up. "Add that it nearly made it. I just cut us off from the main base system."

"We can't upload this to the base computers, now," Tom pointed out. "Even if it worked."

"The hell we can't," Roger said. "The computer controlling the IBot program is up in the antenna farm. All we have to do is run this program up and load it to it."

"Roger, that's the top of the damned *mountain*," Traci pointed out, hitting another key. "I didn't even know we *had* that connection. What the hell *is* this thing?"

"Pull the physical connections," Roger said, sliding a USB memory card into the side of the laptop he'd moved the Megiddo program to. "I'll give you two guesses where that attack is coming from, and only one counts."

Shane blinked as the lights in the room went off then back on, then off, leaving the room lit only by red safety lights. His monitor flickered as well, changing views without command several times then went off. He looked over to the general just as a heavyset Air Force officer burst through the doors to the command center and stumbled down to the J-2 desk.

Most of the officers and NCOs in the room were muttering or questioning what had happened but Shane leaned back in his chair to watch the general. The major knew that there wasn't anything in his area of control, or expertise, to be done about whatever was happening. All he could do was wait a few moments to see if things calmed down. And he wanted to watch what Riggs was going to do.

The J-2 listened to the heavyset lieutenant and then swore and got up and headed for the general. Other senior officers were closing in around the commander but the J-2, despite being a shrimp and outranked by most of them, shoved his way through and leaned over to whisper in Riggs's ear. Given that a colonel was whispering in the other ear at the same time, Riggs seemed to be taking both conversations in.

Riggs nodded for a moment, then waved the J-2 and the colonel away and stood up.

"Listen up," the general said. "We just got hammered, electronically, by the enemy. They got past most of our electronic defenses. They've got trojans and worms in the system which is why everything is shut down: what wasn't corrupted by the attack has been taken off-line to prevent them getting into it. Data Security has most of it isolated and stopped the attack from the outside. Which is good: given that these things are ahead of us technologically and they are, after all, flying computers, the fact that we could stop them at all is surprising.

"Lasing. Your remotes have been physically pulled to prevent the machines from taking over the lasers. Data Security did that first thing. Get up there, physically, and take control of the lasers. I'll set up runners to manage control. Colonel Guthrie! Your troops and those lasers are all that stands between this mountain and those probes, if they get going again. Get out there with your

unit. Tell them: Hold The Line. J-3. I want paper maps
and markers up on the walls in two minutes. We're going
to have to do this the old-fashioned way. Everyone else,
we are shut down electronically. Get manual commo in
place. Runners. Field phones. I don't care if you're using
two tin cans and a string. Try to coordinate through the
commo officer but *get us commo* until DS can get the
systems back up. Go."

Dick was pretty sure he had gotten ahead of the tide.
At the first sign that a worm or trojan had gotten into
the base system, he had set up a program he'd named
"Babel Blaster" that shut down every link in the network.
Dealing with the various worms and trojans like the MS
Blaster had taught him that. As soon as the first trigger
on the internal system went off, Blaster went on and began
operating automatically. While Babel Blaster was running,
he went into the server room and *physically* pulled every
single cable connecting the entire base. Getting everything back in place would be a bastard. But he had written
bots to manage that, as well.

Fortunately, the worms hadn't managed to penetrate
his master controls. Those were on a 256 bit encryption.
The weakness of encryption was usually at the password
level. If you used a high numeric encryption scheme and
then used a simple four alphanumeric password, say your
birth year and month, the attacker only had to break the
password. And there were only so many children's names
and so many birthdays to go around.

Dick's master control password was a 196 character
string of random high ascii. And he never wrote it down.
He may have just been a staff sergeant, but that didn't

interfere with having an eidetic memory.

When he was sure that his master server was safe, he stopped and sat, elbow on table, chin in hand, looking at his screen. He wasn't sure what he was dealing with but he had certain verities in life. He watched science fiction movies and TV, so he had those to go on. But he disagreed with some of it, based on his personal knowledge and training. One thing that he could simply not believe was that you could cram a full, functional, artificial intelligence into a tiny data packet. No matter how compressed the information, you still were dealing with a limited number of ones and zeros. And *all* the data packets that got through were small. Ergo, what he was dealing with were fucking viruses, worms and trojans. And he'd been writing those, and fighting those, for twenty years. He couldn't say that he knew *all* the tricks, but he did know how to *think* about the tricks, how they could and could not work. How they could and could not hide.

The problem being that most viruses, trojans and worms were detectable by "signatures," bits of code that were really variants of earlier versions. But he was pretty sure these weren't going to use legacy code. And he was the only person who was looking at them: Symantec's facilities were trashed. Ditto the National Information Security site. Even "heuristic" checking wasn't going to do it.

He'd have to start from scratch. Okay, he could do that. And he could do more.

"Simone, what the *hell* are you doing!" Lieutenant Gathers asked as he hurried into the server room. "Everybody else is running around trying to work the problem. What the hell are you doing just *sitting* there?"

"Working the problem, Lieutenant," the sergeant said, not bothering to look up. "And I gotta start somewhere. So gimme your laptop."

Richard frowned at the incoming packet. The packet alleged to be a jpg, but it was clearly corrupted. However, when the "corruption" was analyzed, it turned out to be a short communique from the nice sergeant in Huntsville. The nice, apparently *very* clever, sergeant.

Richard finished reading the data and then smiled. Any of his former students who had seen that smile would have dropped his class abruptly. And probably left town, taken an assumed name in a foreign country and tried *very* hard never to be noticed.

Richard had never considered being a soldier. But it appeared that he had just been recruited.

On the other hand, it was a war that he was both predisposed to and capable of fighting.

He flexed his fingers and for just a moment wondered how clever he really was.

He finally decided that he was clever enough. And if not, there was always the brute force approach. There were other clever people left in the world. Presumably a computer could not disconnect *itself*.

Dick looked up as a harried Dr. Reynolds ran into the room.

"IBot transmitter computer?" Roger asked.

"Clean as far as I know," Simone replied. "I pulled the connections before the server that it's hooked to got corrupted. Is it still transmitting?"

"I think so," Roger said.

"It's still clean," Dick replied. "If these bastards got in it it wouldn't be transmitting."

"Good," Roger said, running out of the room.

"Everyone rushing about," Dick said, shaking his head. "Don't they know there's a war on?" He hit "Enter" and leaned back. All four of the attacking programs that he'd found so far had certain bits of data loaded into them. Most of the data was what to do in the event that they were discovered. But they also were supposed to report back on what they found. As far as Simone could tell, he'd prevented that. However, the data told them *where* to report back.

Intelligence flows two ways. And there were still *lots* of people on Earth who could do something with things like the electronic location of one of the probes' master computers and information on what protocols it expected when information was being sent in. And the difference between information and sabotage in the computer world was . . . very, very small.

With one click of a keystoke, Dick had just sent the data to all of them.

"You wanna play games, motherfucker? I'm a master of playing games."

"General, the probes are coming live again," the lieutenant said, breathlessly. "Not all of them, but quite a few. We're engaging them as they approach, but we can't get all of them. Some of them are headed for the antenna farm. Others are hitting places further down the mountain."

"They're taking out the IBot transmitters," the J-2 said. "At a guess. We've got transmitters lower down the slopes as well as the main transmitter up on the hill. And bots scattered in the minefield."

"Some of them are blowing up down there, but not all," the lieutenant added.

"The big brains on their side are overcoming the IBot transmission, somehow," Riggs said, shaking his head. "We need somebody down here who understands the electronic assault field. Can we jam them?"

"I can try," the J-2 said. "But if they're working from short range we might not be able to step on their signal. And if they're using contact it won't work at all. I'll have to physically go up to the antenna park and set it to jam."

"Go," the general said. "Run."

Roger stopped at the top of the stairs and panted for just a second. Among other things, the elevators were out. And what with everything that had been going on the last few months, he hadn't gotten much time to work out.

The antenna farm had a small maintenance shed with its own computer for local testing and maintenance. It was padlocked, but Roger had brought a skeleton key in the form of a crowbar. In a few seconds he was sitting at the computer. He jacked in the USB drive and pulled out the program, then went looking for the Lola program.

The Lola system was hooked into the 1.4 Ghz transmitter program. Roger frowned for a moment, then simply pulled it out and dropped in the Megiddo program.

As he was initializing the transmission, the J-2 burst through the door.

"Who the hell pulled the lock off the door?" the angry lieutenant colonel asked.

"Me?" Roger replied, spinning around in the chair. "Deputy Secretary of Defense Reynolds?"

"Oh," the colonel replied, abashed. "Sorry, sir. But the general wants me to start jamming the bots. They're beating the IBot system."

"I just replaced it," Roger replied, looking out the window. "As a deputy secretary of defense, I know that I'm not supposed to be involved in something directly operational. But as Dr. Reynolds, would you mind if I overrode the general's order temporarily to see if this works?

"Uh . . ." the colonel said then paused. "Go for it."

"Going for it," Roger said, smiling.

Four bots were in view through the door, hanging over the mountain. Roger pulled up the Megiddo program and tapped a key. All four started drifting downward until they impacted the ground. He tapped another key and they started to rise up.

"And now . . ." he continued, looking over the transmitter system. "Ah, power increase. That should cover most of the valley."

"What the fuck?"

Soldiers had found that the machine gun worked just fine on the regular bots. He'd shot up most of the ones in range from his position but shooting the ones more than about five hundred meters away hadn't done a damned thing. However, he took his finger off the machine gun as the probes started acting funny. First they drifted down to the ground, then up, then down and finally landed and stayed there.

"Okay, would somebody *please* tell me what the fuck is going on around here?"

⊠   ⊠   ⊠

Shane sat back down at his computer just as the power came back on. General Riggs appeared to be listening to his earbud for a second and then nodded and hit a key.

"Attention," the general said through the room's PA system. "Data Security has our systems back online. We don't have access outside the base, yet, but they tell us that reports from lidar stations indicate that the probe waves headed for us have turned around. And the probes in our area now *appear* to be under our control due to Dr. Reynolds' team."

Instead of the earlier cheering he got a round of skeptical faces.

"Agreed," he said to the unspoken majority opinion. "Colonel Guthrie, have your boys get out of the bunkers. Destroy every probe along the mountainside. Lasing, you have every probe that's to the north and south, but use manual aiming and don't shoot the colonel's soldiers. Keep a few functional, but get them under wraps. Get with Major Gries to cover those protocols. I *think* we won. Let's make sure that we hold onto that win."

"Major Gries?" the general continued on the direct link.

"Sir?" Shane said. He'd almost taken off the headset and was already on his feet.

"I'm sorry to hear about your loss."

Shane started to answer and then simply nodded, taking off the headset and shutting down his station.

Epilogue

"What are you doing, now, Richard?" Helena asked, setting down a reheated TV dinner by his computer.

"Fighting a war, my dear," Horton replied, smiling. "Creating weapons of great subtlety and power. And updating some data I sent to Huntsville."

"Dat's good," Helena replied, looking in incomprehension at the strings of ones and zeros sliding across the screen. "But you gotta eat. An army travels on its stomach."

Ret Ball: *You are listening to the Truth Nationwide, the only surviving radio program across this great mostly alien-bot-free country. We have open callers tonight. God Bless us! We have Tina and Charlotte from the great battleground in Huntsville, Alabama! We are thankful that you girls are still with us! What do you want to tell us?*

Caller: *Oh my gosh, it's so great that we can still talk to you, Ret! The entire city was destroyed and covered with alien bots and stuff! But WE ARE STILL HERE!*

Caller: *That's right. The Internet is still working and everybody needs to know that there is a bot intelligence trying to attack all our servers!*

Ret Ball: *How do you know this, girls?*

Caller: *Our parents are part of the defense scientists and told us.*

Ret Ball: *Is there anything we can do to help?*

Caller: *Uh, sure, like, all you hackers out there could start hacking back at the thing or at least that's what my mom says.*

Ret Ball: *You heard it here folks. Any hackers out there start attacking the alien intelligence on what is left of the Internet.*

"Internet's under full-scale assault," Traci said, munching on a sandwich and watching her monitor. "On the other hand, I think every hacker on Earth is going after that source from France. And they seem to be fighting the attacks against servers here, too. There's probably a lot of them in the refugee camps; you oughta see about getting them some support. Too bad we can't just send The Atom and the rest of the Justice League of America, huh?"

"The Atom? Hmmm . . ." That gave Roger an idea. "Put it in my to-do file and make a reminder note about The Atom. That's a good idea," Roger said. "But right now we have some heroes to say goodbye to. Right after the funerals."

Most of the lost soldiers had family requests to be buried at the Huntsville memorial site. A few, including posthumously promoted Sergeant Allen Nelms, had family requests to be buried at other locations. A memorial service would be held for those at the Huntsville site later in the day.

Two probes, their surface now shifted from glittering steel to bands of red, white and blue, held the coffin a meter off the ground as honorary pallbearers walked on either side.

On command, they gently lowered it into the hole blasted into the top of the mountain by other probes. Sergeants Jones and Mahoney held onto the flag, both one-handed since Mahoney had a fractured wrist, as the casket was lowered into the ground. The remaining pallbearers fell into line, holding their weapons, standard M-4 rifles, at salute. There was supposed to be a separate honor guard, but nobody was willing to give up either slot.

"It is fitting that this soldier be laid to rest, here on the site of his last battle," General Riggs said to the gathered soldiers and civilians. "Many fell this day, but none led the way so well or with such conviction as this soldier. He stood at the gates, defending his home, his honor and his land as sternly as any Trojan and leading by example so that others stood there with him. By holding this line they gave everyone else the most precious thing possible in war: time. Today, the enemy that killed him works for us. Through the efforts of many people, some here today and others far away, we found the Achilles' heel and Paris's arrow flew true.

"Sergeant Gregory will be missed. But others take up the battle in his stead. They continue to shine in the light of his leadership and devotion, and they will continue to carry the battle to the enemy. No soldier could ask for more.

"Sergeant Major."

Cady's right arm, which had been almost severed by the falling probe, was neatly capped by a black cloth. Dr. Reynolds had assured him that the remaining resources of Asymetric Soldier could craft him a prosthetic that was damned near as good as new. Maybe a little better. But he didn't need it for this duty, only his voice.

"Detail, prepare to render salute! Present Arms! Fire! . . . Load Arms! . . . Fire! Load Arms! . . . Fire! Order Arms!"

Jones and Mahoney had to get help folding the flag. But after it had been presented to the general—Gregory's wife and kids were somewhere in a refugee camp in Kentucky—they got in line to drop dirt into the hole.

"So long, Sergeant," Jones said. "Keep the fire warm."

"Yeah," Mahoney added, trying to think of something appropriately clever and philosophical.

Overhead four of the new bot propulsion fighters flew by. The sleek craft were piloted by the only surviving "Rednecks." One, piloted by Colonel "Bull" Ridley, banked off into the missing man formation. All four of the swept wing forward canard fighters glittered red, white and blue in the bright afternoon sun. Behind them came rank upon rank upon rank of red white and blue flying machines, all under the control of humanity. They filled the skies momentarily and then banked down into the valley to land on the remains of Huntsville, there to await their next command.

Mahoney looked back down and gave up. In the end, all the philosophical words were hollow, so he said goodbye as a soldier.

"We are *so* going to kick those machine bastards' asses."

Citadel

Languid waves of desperation
fall before the rains
A vanguard to approaching war
is borne upon the sea
The icy breath of cyclones bent
on waging our destruction
Drills hard against the hearts of heroes
called here to defend

I see storms on the horizon
I see the tempest at the gates
I see storms on the horizon,
and a citadel alone
Clinging brave, defying fate

And I will stand here at the gates to face the
    onslaught fighting
Without surrender or defeat
With Troy besieged by tyrants' greed—
In Hector's memory, God willing
We shall save this victory
Without surrender or defeat

✠ ✠ ✠

Sudden silence—I realize
breaking teardrops in the rain
With every breathing moment
the pillars are sustained
And waking hands attached to nothing
tightly clutching close
Each sleeping vision speaks unheard
and heaven only knows

And I see storms on the horizon
I see the tempest at the gates
I see storms on the horizon,
and a citadel alone
Clinging brave, defying fate

And I will stand here at the gates to face the
onslaught fighting
Without surrender or defeat
With Troy besieged by tyrants' greed—
In Hector's memory, God willing
We shall save this victory
Without surrender or defeat

Paris' arrow landed true
Paris' arrow landed true
Paris' arrow landed true
Down upon your heel . . .

✠ ✠ ✠

This Troy . . .
she will not fall again
This Troy . . .
she will not fall!

And I see storms on the horizon
I see the tempest at the gates
I see storms on the horizon,
and a citadel alone
Clinging brave, defying fate

And I will stand here at the gates to face the
*   onslaught fighting*
Without surrender or defeat
With Troy besieged by tyrants' greed—
In Hector's memory, God willing
We shall save this victory
Without surrender or defeat!

*The following is an excerpt from
the sequel to* **Vorpal Blade**:

MANXOME FOE

By

JOHN RINGO
&

TRAVIS S. TAYLOR

Available from Baen Books
February 2008
hardcover

1

"I'd only do this for Mom, you know."

Sergeant Eric Bergstresser adjusted the high collar of the Marine dress blues and shrugged his shoulders, again, trying to get the uniform to feel right. But since he spent most of his time in digi-cam or jeans, it never quite did.

"You've skipped out of it the last two visits, bro," Joshua Bergstresser said, shrugging. Josh, just turned sixteen and decidedly civilian given the earring he was sporting, was wearing Dockers and a polo shirt, as dressed up as he was going to get for church. "Besides, you look good. You're going to attract the ladies like flypaper. Maybe I should get a set of those."

Eric winced and then shrugged.

"Don't do it unless you're sure," Eric said, frowning. "As long as you're not in my outfit, Mom probably won't get two telegrams."

"Not a good way to talk, bro," Josh said. "You'll be fine. Tell me you'll be fine."

"Ain't gonna lie, bro," Eric replied. "Not something I can talk about. But I will tell you that on my last mission, we went out with forty-one Marines and landed with five."

"Are you serious?" Josh asked angrily. "That never made the news!"

"Yes, it did," Eric said, one cheek twitching up in an ironic smile. "Thirty-six Marines killed in helicopter crash. News at Six."

"That was out west somewhere," Josh replied, furrowing his brow thoughtfully. "That was your unit? Eric, crashes, well . . ."

"There wasn't a crash." Eric chuckled grimly. "They all died in combat. But a helicopter crash was a convenient cover. Among other things, it explained why most of them had closed casket funerals. Hell, there weren't even bodies in most of the caskets, just sandbags. We didn't lose them all at once and quite a few weren't recoverable."

"And that was your unit?" Josh asked.

"Yep."

"And you're going back?"

"Yep."

"That's insane."

"Yep."

"Eric," Josh said desperately. "You cannot go do . . . whatever it is you do, again. Forget what I said about the uniform. De-volunteer or something. Hell, I'll hide you under my bed. With casualties like that . . ."

"Not much chance of believing I'll survive, right?" Eric asked, finally turning away from the mirror.

"YES!"

"Believe it or not, on the last cruise I started to get

into Goth and heavy metal," Eric said, talking around the point.

"And I was happy, happy, happy," Josh replied. "Since I no longer had to listen to Hank Williams, Jr. What's it got to do with the statistical certainty you're going to die?"

"I still listen to Hank," Eric said. "But one of the songs I got into was called 'Winterborn.' You've never heard of Crüxshadows, have you?"

"Bit indy for me, man," Josh said. "What's wrong with Metallica?"

"Besides that they haven't had an album out in ten years?" Eric replied. "But this song, it's about the Trojans. There's a line in the chorus: *In the fury of this darkest hour, I will be your light. You've asked me for my sacrifice, and I am Winterborn.* I'm good at what I do, Josh. Very good."

"I didn't figure you got the Navy Cross for being incompetent," Josh said quietly. "But there's these things called odds."

"And if I didn't do it, somebody else would have to," Eric continued as if he hadn't heard his brother. "From experience, probably somebody who wasn't as good, who has less of a chance of coming back. You want me to put them on the chopping block, bro?"

"Hell, yes!" Josh said, his jaw working. "They're not my brother!"

"They're somebody's brother," the sergeant said, picking up his cover. "They were brothers and sons. Some lady just like Mom carried them in her womb and nursed them and loved them. And most of them we couldn't even bring home. There wasn't anything to bring. I've got a better chance than any replacement." He tucked his cover under his arm and curtly nodded at his reflection. "So, this is my sacrifice. As my first sergeant once said, if I was worried about where I was going to die, I never should have joined the Marines in the first place."

Commander William Weaver, Ph.D., topped out on the climb and stood up on the pedals, clutching the saddle between his thighs as he coasted downwards to catch his breath. The roots on the trail were still slick from the morning dew that had yet to be burned off by the mid-morning Alabama sun. The canopy of oak trees and the dense green foliage around the trail would prevent that for several more hours. The rear wheel spinning and slipping on the roots had made the climbs more difficult than Bill was hoping and he was getting totally worked.

Leaning his center of gravity behind the saddle as the screaming downhill rushed up at him, he managed to keep the bike in control just long enough to hop over a small oak that had been dropped across the trail to prevent it from washing out. Bill looked at his heart rate monitor on the center of the handlebars—185. He was working way too hard for this part of the trail. The ride was fun and had let him take his mind off of, well, off of a lot of things, but his heart just wasn't really in it. The climb on the other side had severely kicked his ass. He should be able to get his heart rate back down to at least the 160s, but it was dropping slower than he'd expected and his heart pounded like a bass drum in his throat. He felt so out of shape. And the ride back up the mountain to the parking lot was going to be hell.

Eight years ago he would have kicked this ride's butt and been up for another lap or two, but eight years ago was . . . eight years ago.

Eight years ago was when he'd put his ass on the line to save the world. Eight years ago was before there was any concept of the Vorpal Blade. Eight years ago was . . . eight years ago when the world was a relatively simple place and a little slope like that last one wouldn't have bothered him one bit.

Eight years ago he'd been working for a defense contractor, fixing problems for the military and other government agencies with acronyms, mostly ending in A. DIA, CIA, NSA. Then an explosion blew out the University of Central Florida physics lab. Not to mention the rest of the university. Two hundred fifty-one times ten to the twelfth power joules would do that. Call it sixty kilotons and be done.

Subsequent to the blast that flattened UCF and a goodly space around it he'd been blasted into other dimensions, died he was pretty sure, resurrected he was absolutely sure and generally had a hell of a time running around saving the planet. The blast had opened up gates to other worlds, some of them inhabited by hostiles with seriously negative intent. Called the Dreen, they consumed organic matter to create more copies of themselves. They had conquered multiple worlds and Earth was next on the list. Weaver, with the help of a SEAL master chief and sundry others had managed to close the gates the Dreen used. But the anomaly where UCF physics department used to be kept pumping out more gates.

In time Weaver, among others, had figured out how to create gates on Earth, shutting down the gate forming bosons that were the culprits. Instantaneous teleportation from point to point was now a reality, with more and more gates being opened every day. The now defunct airlines had been less than thrilled. After almost ten years it was getting to the point that auto makers were less than thrilled.

The Dreen were not the only alien species encountered. One of their subject races, the catlike Mreee, had pretended to be friends just long enough to scout out the new human prey. The destruction of the Dreen gates had almost certainly wiped out the Mreee as well. Contact with them had certainly been cut off. But the survivor Mreee, part of the Dreen invasion force, had been less upset about that than many expected. They were a proud race that had seen themselves fall into slavery to masters who took not only their planet's resources but the very bodies of their citizens for conversion into Dreen. A clean death at the hands of an honorable foe was preferable.

One friendly race had been encountered, as well. The Adar were in advance of humans technologically but had nearly as much trouble with the Dreen. It was the Adar, though, who had passed on two items. One was a bomb big enough to shut down the Dreen gates. They hadn't used it themselves because the only way to crack the gates was for the bomb to go off very close to one. If it went off on the wrong side, the planet wasn't going to be habitable. The humans were desperate enough to use it and it worked, shutting down not only the gate that it was sent through but all other Dreen gates.

The second device, though, was in a way more useful. The Adar had found it on an ancient planet whose sun was just about dead. Nothing more than an enigmatic black box the size of a deck of cards, it had surprising properties. Any electrical charge caused it to release orders of magnitude more energy than inputted. Weaver eventually guessed that it was at least in part a warp drive. And he was right.

Using the box, which was not only a warp generator but a reactionless drive generator, the U.S. government had converted a submarine, the USS Nebraska, into a spaceship. It had taken seven years, and Weaver had jumped ship into the Navy early in the process. One of the problems he was having with this hill, admittedly, had been caused by too much time in a swivel chair redesigning a submarine to go where no man had gone before.

But Weaver, and a team of thousands, had eventually done it. And then Weaver, acting as astrogator, had gone out with the rechristened Vorpal Blade. Humans, seeing the first mirrorlike gates, had christened them Looking Glasses. The Adar found human thought process fascinating and had insisted that this ship be named in accordance with that thought. Since the ship was an Alliance spaceship, they'd had enough pull to push the name through.

Unfortunately, the Adar, while fine scientists and philosophers, had very little understanding of human humor or thought processes. So the acronym for Alliance Space Ship had slipped past their filters before it was too late.

On the ASS Vorpal Blade, Weaver, a crew of one hundred and fifty-four officers, NCOs and enlisted, forty-one Marines, and a handful of scientists had ventured forth on a local survey. They had limped back with five Marines, a couple of scientists and a hundred and twenty crew. But they'd found out what they were sent to find out: Space may be an unforgiving Bitch but She was nothing compared to landings. On the other hand, they'd also found allies and some interesting technology.

On a moon of a gas giant circling the otherwise unremarkable star 61 Cygni Alpha they'd encountered a race of rodentlike mammaloids. Named the Cheerick in the language of the country the Vorpal Blade contacted, they were similar in form to chinchillas or hamsters and at their highest level of technology were about at War of the Roses level. In other words, they'd just started to press the edges of real science, climbing out of the darkness of alchemy. However, they also had records dating back thousands of years that indicated that from time to time, for reasons unknown, another race would rise up and destroy them. Dubbed "The Demons" they had begun to show up shortly before the arrival of the Vorpal Blade. The Blade had, fortunately, been forty light-years away at the time of their first sighting so it was innocent.

Eventually, through about half of their casualties, the scientists of the Blade had determined that the "Demons" were some sort of biological defense mechanism that targeted electrical emissions. By that time, the majority of the science team and a goodly number of Marines had bought the farm. But before they died, the science team had gotten a lock on the source of the Demons.

It was left to Weaver, Chief Warrant Officer Miller, USN, a handful of local Royal Guardsmen and a small team of the remaining Marines to stop the scourge. Fortunately, they'd been accompanied by the ship's linguist, Miriam Moon. Normally as nervous as a rabbit, Miss Moon had been the person who figured out how the system worked and, using a local, shut it down.

While Weaver was away on his forlorn hope, though, the ship had been under attack. Most of the "Demons" were ground mounted but there was an aerospace component as well, giant red and blue "dragonflies" with a very fast reactionless drive system and lasers that shot out of compound eyes. The Blade had been chased into space by them and ripped very nearly to shreds. The local who had taken control of the system, Lady Che-Chee, had had to tow the ship back to the planet using the same flies that had ravaged it.

Enough repairs had been enacted to allow the ship to limp back to Earth, but making it spaceworthy again had been a half-year process. Weaver had acted as the ship's executive officer on the trip back but gratefully turned over the job on arrival to a more experienced officer. Since then, though, he'd been deeply involved in the repairs and upgrades. Like, pretty constant sixteen-hour days involved.

This was his first real break, since the major repairs were completed and all that was left was details. He'd grabbed at the new CO's suggestion, more like order, to take some leave. The ship wasn't due to leave for its next mission for two months. So he'd headed down to his real home in Huntsville to visit friends and reacquaint himself with the trails, baby-head sized rocks, roots, boulders, downed trees, screaming downhills, and extremely rough and technical climbs of Monte Sano Mountain.

He pulled his left foot out of the pedal and planted it as he braked just before the whoopdie-doos. Just as he started down, his cell phone rang. The ringtone—"Welcome to the Jungle" by Guns'n'Roses—was barely audible over his pounding heartbeat. Bill welcomed the break, he was that fragged. He bit the tube hanging from the helmet strap in front of his face and sucked down water from his CamelBak between gasps for air.

Despite the fact that he was on leave, he was required to be on call. Since he not only had a deeper grasp of the science behind the drive but a knowledge of every bolt and system in the ship that was unsurpassed by even its commander and XO, sometimes there were questions that only he could answer. And it appeared that there was another one.

"Weaver," he said, panting for breath. The earbud he was wearing automatically activated at his voice.

"Commander Weaver, Captain Jeller, SpacComOps. You're required to report at the earliest possible moment to your ship."

"Shit," Bill muttered. "Uniform?"

"Whatever you're wearing at the moment, Commander," the captain on the phone said. "There has been an incident . . ."

Eric tuned out the priest as the sermon started. It was a new one since he'd left for the Corps, a woman of all things. His family was Episcopal but while Eric had heard there were no atheists in foxholes, he didn't recall praying much on the last mission. Mostly he'd been too scared spitless to remember any.

He spent most of the sermon checking out the congregation. It was pretty much the same faces he'd seen most of his life. He was born in Fayetteville, NC, when his dad was still in the Army, a "leg" who did something in logistics Eric had never quite understood. But Eric didn't remember North Carolina as a kid. His dad had moved to Crab Orchard to work in the, then new, plastic plant as a dispatcher. Josh had been born in the Arh Beckley Hospital as had his sister Janna.

Most of the people in the church had been born in Arh Beckley, those that hadn't used a midwife. And he'd seen the same faces every Sunday for as long as he could remember. So was it his eyes that had changed or the people around him?

Coach Radner had been a nightmare during high school. The head coach for the phys ed department and the lead coach for the Crab Orchard High School football team, the former paratrooper was missing two middle fingers from some industrial accident back in time. One time Bob Arnold had mocked him as the coach was instructing him on the fine point of the three-point stance of a blocker. Bob, thinking he was being funny, had taken up a three point stance with those same fingers folded back as if they'd been cut off. Radner, half Arnold's weight, had knocked the tackle flat on his ass with that same damaged hand. You did not cross Coach Radner.

Looking at him now, Eric saw a man who was relatively out of shape and on the back side of fifty. He looked satisfied with his life but not the demon that Eric recalled.

Bob Arnold was in the audience, too, with his wife Jessie. Jessie was one of the co-heads of the cheerleading team; Bob was the school's top tackle. It had been a natural match. Now, they both looked worn and washed out, with two kids already; Bob's muscle was turning to fat quick and Jessie wasn't exactly svelte anymore. Eric heard Bob was in construction framing down in Beckley. Eric had a hard time adjusting the picture of the two in high school.

Behind them were the Piersons. Mr. Pierson and Mrs. Pierson looked pretty much the same as they always had, a good looking couple. Mr. Pierson was the local veterinarian, Mrs. Pierson had been a legal secretary to one of the town's lawyers for years. But Eric stopped and blinked for a moment at the people with them. The Piersons had four children. Paul had been a year ahead of Eric in school and Eric heard he'd gone to college so he wasn't around. The youngest girl had to be Linda, but she'd really grown. She must be ten or so by now and had shot up. Then there was Hector. He was recognizable by the shock of white hair but that was about it. Where'd the pimples come from?

But the one that really caught him was the teenage girl with them. The other Pierson child would be Brooke but . . . that couldn't be Brooke. He conjured up a vague memory of a gawky and awkward blonde girl who had just entered high school the year he was graduating. She'd had a serious overbite that mildly affected her speech and a mass of metal to go with it. Nice hair, a mass of naturally curly blonde locks, but . . .

Jesus! It had to be Brooke Pierson. But the maulking vision in a pink dress sitting with them couldn't . . . Same damned hair, though. Shit, it was Brooke . . . She'd sure shot more than up.

He turned away as the girl in question looked his way, as if divining that he'd been staring. It wasn't that, though. He'd caught other looks from the congregation as the service had gone on. The dress blues certainly stood out and Dad had told him that the decoration had been written up in the local paper. Given that they weren't, as far as anyone knew, at war, the award of the Navy Cross had been big news in a very small town.

Looking away from the girl who . . . hell, she'd be seventeen, which would get you twenty even in West Virginia . . . he saw Coach Radner looking his way. The old paratrooper gave him a respectful nod, one former warrior to the present generation, and turned back to ignoring the sermon.

It was times like this that got Eric thinking. Looking around the congregation he picked out the veterans. There were a bunch: small towns like Crab Orchard had always provided more than their fair share of soldiers and Marines. But they left quite a few behind, too. The annual Memorial Day celebrations pointed that out, the roads lined with crosses with names on them. More crosses than there were people who lived in the town it sometimes seemed. WWII, WWI, Korea, Vietnam, the aborted "War on Terror," the Dreen War . . .

Would one of those crosses one day say "Eric Bergstresser"? Or would he be one of the guys in the congregation, running to fat but there to see their grandkids? Would he sit around in the VFW hall and tell stories about crabpus and Demons? Or would he be an empty box in a grave, a guy people sort of recalled on Memorial Day, but really nothing but a fading memory?

He shook his head to clear the thought as the sermon finally droned to a close. The new priest, priestess, whatever, sure seemed devoted but my God she was boring. There had to be better uses of his time but Mom wanted to show off her Marine-hero son. Given that it might be the last chance she got, he owed her that. It was that that had decided him on coming. Not that he was going to put it to her that way.

Since he was in church he figured he ought to pray, some, for a chance to come back to it. But he was blanking on prayers. No, there was one.

For heathen heart that puts her trust
In reeking tube and iron shard—
All valiant dust that builds on dust,
And, guarding, calls not Thee to guard.
For frantic boast and foolish word,
Thy Mercy on Thy People, Lord!

"What was that, Eric?" his mom asked, as the congregation rose to do what Eric thought of as "the huggy" thing.

"Just a prayer, Mom," Eric said as the lady in front of him, whom he didn't recognize, turned around to get a hug and a welcome. "It's called 'Recessional.'"

—end excerpt—

from *MANXOME FOE*
available in hardcover,
February 2008, from Baen Books

The following is an excerpt from:

CALIPHATE

by

TOM KRATMAN

Available from Baen Books

PROLOGUE

Hidden in the grass, the hare froze as the shadow passed over it. Even with its little brain, still it knew that the shadow was not just some passing puff of cloud. It was too small, too quick, too purposeful. And, too, something in half-seen glimpse of the dark outline undulating over the uneven ground told of a raptor soaring above.

The hare was a naturally shy and timid creature, rarely venturing out into the meadows and pastures that covered the land. But this was spring. Instinct told the animal to find a mate. Instinct ruled. It could hardly help itself from gamboling about in search of a female.

It had found one, too, or thought it had. When he'd approached, though, the female had slapped him repeatedly to drive him away. Either she didn't want him for a mate or she wasn't quite ready yet. No matter to the hare, it would hang around until the female was in a more accommodating and receptive frame of mind. He could still smell her; she wasn't far. Time, it had seemed, was on his side.

But there was that shadow overhead.

The raptor's eyes were large and keen. With them she saw her lifetime mate, even at his scouting distance. Though she was the better hunter, still the pair took turns, scouting and driving, diving and killing. Now it was the mate's turn to scout.

From her high post she thought she'd seen prey, some smallish brown animal. A hare, she thought. *Good eating . . . and the young hunger.*

She'd turned in her flight then and lost sight of the thing. It couldn't have gone far though. There . . . *Yes, there,* it probably was, down there in the patch of grass. It was rare to find grass so thick now, what with the depredations of the goats. The raptor thought only of the advantages to hunting that lack of cover provided. It never considered what would happen when there was no grass anymore, nor anything else for the prey to eat. In this, at least, the raptor and its master—the man below on horseback with the outstretched arm and the thick, heavy glove—were in agreement: Let the future take care of itself; live for today.

The raptor—it was a golden eagle—gave a cry. *Eeek . . . eeek . . . eeek.* This told her mate all he needed to know.

The hare heard the cry and began to tremble with fright. Should it move from its hide and open itself up to attack from above? Should it stay there and risk being isolated, uncovered and eaten? And then there was the female to think about. Where was she? The male thought it could still smell her. Was she, too, hiding and trembling?

The male hare wasn't concerned with protecting the female. It would have gladly offered her up to the raptors' feast if only it had known how. Yes, the urge to mate was strong. But the urge to live was stronger still and another mate could probably be found. It would probably have offered up its own offspring rather than face the ripping talons and tearing beak.

The female gave another cry, subtly different from the first. She saw, with satisfaction, her mate swoop down with a terrorizing cry of his own. *Aha . . . there's the prey!* She swooped, exulting in her own ferocity.

How the contemptible thing tries to avoid me, to save its miserable life. No use, little one, for the God of Eagles has placed you here for me.

The eagle's feathers strained as they bent under the braking maneuver. Then came the satisfying strike of talons, the delightful spray of blood and the high pitched scream, so like a baby of one of the bipeds that dominated the ground here and guarded the goats that consumed the grass.

The female called to her mate. *Eeek . . . ee-ee-eeek. Come and feast, my love.*

Slowly the trembling subsided. The hare wasted no tears for the one that might have been its mate. Though the female was dead, the male would live, for the nonce. It would feed, even as the raptors fed on the corpse of the female.

How much better then, a man than a hare?

PART I

CHAPTER ONE

Where now is the ancient wealth and dignity of the Romans? The Romans of old were most powerful; now we are without strength. They were feared; now it is we who are fearful. The barbarians paid them tribute; now we are the tributaries of the barbarians. Our enemies make us pay for the very light of day and our right to life has to be bought. Oh, what miseries are ours! To what a state we have descended! We even have to thank the barbarians for the right to buy ourselves off them. What could be more humiliating and miserable?

—Salvian of Marseilles, 5th Century AD

Grolanhei, Province of Affrankon, 12 Safar, 1527 AH (23 March, 2103)

"Wonderful strike!" applauded the man on horseback, slapping the stock of the rifle in the saddle holster at the horse's right. Mohammad was his name, though, as Mohammad was the most common name in Europe, this was less than significant, individually. "Wonderful strike, Rashid," he repeated. A third man, Bashir, agreed.

Bashir's rifle was in his arms. It was hardly necessary. The *Nazrani* were like rabbits and no man needed a rifle to ward off rabbits. Even so, the presence of the weapon, and its display, was a badge of the superiority of the faithful and the inferiority—the *helpless* inferiority—of the infidel. Virtually all of the masters carried them almost all the time they were in public. There was quite a lively trade in personal arms, too. Nearly every town with any numbers of the faithful had a shop full of shotguns, rifles, and even automatic weapons for sale.

Rashid, their companion, just nodded. Like Mohammad and Bashir, Rashid also sat astride a horse, in his case a magnificent white animal. In truth, Rashid's attention was not on the birds, nor even on their prey. Rather, he watched the little hamlet of Grolanhei, part of his personal domain as one of the tax gatherers for the emirate of Kitznen.

Grolanhei did *not* have an arms dealer.

All my little helpless rabbits, Rashid thought. *All you disgusting filthy* Nazrani *are my prey.*

As light skinned and blue eyed as the wretched heretics that peopled the town, still Rashid more resembled his hawks than he did them. His eyes were bright, keen and avaricious; his nose a beak jutting from his face. Inside, too, he resembled a hawk, all fierce and selfish appetite, all blood-lust and drive to dominate.

Every year, at tax time, Rashid made sure to collect a few children in lieu of the taxes he deliberately set too high. He received a direct bounty from the *bundejaysh*, the army, for the boys he collected for the Corps of

Janissaries. The girls went on the market to whosoever might want a female child for service. Sometimes that service was domestic. Other girls, especially the prettiest ones, could be sold for other purposes.

But the bastard Nazrani *hide their women and girls now,* Rashid mentally cursed. *It's become altogether too difficult to tell which of their little bitches might fetch a decent price. Shameful for them to pervert the law like that. Bastards.*

"Stop being such a *girl*, Petra," the young boy said to his sister as the two watched the bird of prey swoop and strike.

Petra bint Minden, aged six, had shuddered at the swooping hawk's cry. She shuddered again, shielding her eyes with tiny hands, as the hare screamed out in pain and terror. Barely, she forced her fingers apart to see the eagle carry off its limp and bloody prey. Again she shuddered, pleased that *she* was not so small as to be the prey of a raptor.

Petra felt her brother tug at her arm. His voice commanded, "Come *on*. The masters are coming. And we're almost late for school."

Turning away from the pasture where the eagle had struck, Petra followed after her brother on little legs. It was hard to keep up, what with the enveloping cloth sack the girl wore that covered her from head to heel. The covering was whole, though her mother had spent long hours patching and mending it. For it wasn't the law that required Petra to be so enclosed; she was too young for it to matter.

Rather, she wore the burka at her mother's insistence. As the mother had said, "Some of the masters take a long view of things. You're a beautiful child, Petra, though you're too young to know what that means. Even so, no sense in letting them see you and put you on a list for when you've turned nine."

Behind her, Petra heard a horse neigh, the sound echoed by several more of them. Turning quickly, she spied a group of three riding across the bare and open field. Two held their arms out, she saw, as another twirled something overhead. Two great hunting birds came to rest on the outstretched arms, one of them bearing the corpse of the hare. Petra knew they must be from the masters; *Nazrani* weren't allowed to ride horseback.

"Come along, Petra," insisted her older brother, Hans. Hans was nine, big for his age and strong. He was her protector and the hero of Petra's existence. Like his sister, the boy was blond with bright blue eyes. Folk of the town were already whispering that he was sure to be gathered for the janissaries within a few years. Unlike their father, Hans was too young to have the bowed back of the *dhimmi*, those who submitted by treaty to the rule of the masters, their taxes, and their laws.

There were several *orta* of janissaries in the old al Harv barracks set roughly between the town of Grolanhei and the larger one of Kitznen. They sometimes came to the smaller town to drink forbidden beer or make use of the town's dozen or so whores. (For the janissaries were well disciplined and rarely indulged in rape.) Petra found their black uniforms with silver insignia strangely compelling.

"Come along," Hans commanded again, grabbing her by her arm and pulling her back to the town that edged the open field. "We don't want them to notice us."

Bad things, so it was whispered, sometimes happened

to blond and blue-eyed children who attracted the notice of the masters. Petra shuddered again and followed her brother, stopping only once more to turn and peer at the magnificent horsemen.

The way to school, up the cobblestoned Haupstrasse, led past a fountain and a crumbling monument, a painted wall, which listed the names of the town's war dead going back centuries. No names had been added to the monument in over one hundred and fifty years. Few of those old names were visible now. The picture, painted on a wall over the town fountain, was of an angel lifting a fallen soldier to Heaven. It was part of the back of the Catholic church. As such, under the rules of protection imposed by the masters, the treaty of *dhimmitude*, neither it, nor the church, could be repaired.

It didn't really matter anyway. Petra couldn't read yet, though Hans was trying to teach her, no matter that the law forbade it. Left to the masters she would never learn to read. She was, after all, a mere female. In their view, her ultimate value was in her body, in the pleasure it might someday bring to a man, in the household work she would do, and in the children she would bear. For all practical purposes, she—like virtually all the females of the Caliphate, to include the Moslem ones—was considered to be not much more than a donkey who could speak and bear children.

Instead, her school taught her only basic theology—to include, by law, a theology not her own—and home-making, as well as the rules under which she must live out her life. That last was a part of that theology not her own.

As she had nearly every day since she had learned to

walk, Petra looked without understanding at the wretched and abandoned memorial, then turned and continued on her way. She expressly did not look across the street from the monument to the crude wooden gallows where the remains of two teenaged boys swung in the breeze by ropes around their stretched necks. The boys were dressed in girls' clothing, minus the hijab.

Petra had known both boys. Their names were—had been— Martin Müller and Ernst Ackermann. She, like the other women and girls of the town, had cried when the masters took the boys and hanged them before the crowd last Sunday after church. The dry-eyed Catholic priest had stood by and blessed the masters' work. The boys would sway there, if history was a guide, until the following Sunday, just before church. (For while the masters had firm rules for the timing of the burial of their own dead, *Nazrani* bodies could be left unburied for educational reasons.)

Petra remembered the pleading as the executioner had forced the boys onto the stools under the gallows' crosspiece, the tears on the boys' faces as they were noosed and then the flailing legs, the eyes bugging and the tongues swelling out past blackening lips. That's why she couldn't look; she remembered it too well.

She didn't know why the boys had been executed. They'd always seemed very nice to her, especially nice in comparison to most of the other boys of the town, her Hans, only, excepted. After the hanging, all the girls had agreed that, among a pretty rowdy lot, those two had been much kinder and more decent to them than were any of the other boys of the town. Indeed, they'd been so sweet that they might almost have been girls themselves.

There was too much in the world that Petra really didn't understand. Shaking her head, she followed her brother to the small schoolhouse where she would spend half her day before hurrying home to help mother with the daily chores.

At the schoolhouse, Petra and Hans split up, he going in by the front door, she walking around back to the girls' entrance. Inside, she doffed her coat and her confining burka, hung them on her own peg, and walked into the classroom. A set of solid and pretty much soundproof walls separated the girls, all in one room, from the boy's seven classes. That was not so bad, really. Though the classroom was overcrowded, a little, education for girls wasn't mandatory and so there were only about a fifth as many girls in the school as boys.

Sister Margarete, the sole teacher for the girls of the town, was old enough to have learned to read as a girl herself. What would happen to the girls, once she died, the nun didn't know. The masters had granted the church a local exemption to the strictures against educating Christian females, but it was at best a partial and limited exemption. Margarete didn't know if it stretched enough to provide a replacement for herself once she'd gone to her final reward.

Tapping a wooden pointer on the podium, Sister Margarete directed the girls to sit, then began with a review of the previous day's lesson:

"We must pay the *jizya* . . . we must submit to the Sharia . . . Slavery is a part of *jihad* and *jihad* a part of Islam . . . we must cover ourselves in accordance with the Sharia . . . We must submit to our fathers and husbands or any other masters the Almighty may decree for us . . .

No one not of the True Faith may ride a horse or an automobile, except at the order of one of the faithful . . . " Petra knew what an automobile was but had only seen one occasionally in her life. She knew no one who had ever ridden one. . . . "No Christian may live in a house better, larger or higher than any lived in by a Moslem . . . In a court of Sharia a Christian's testimony"— Petra wasn't too sure what "testimony" meant—"counts for only half that of a Moslem, and a woman's for only half a man's. . . . No Christian or Jew"—Petra had no clue what a Jew was, either—"may possess a weapon . . . If the masters demand silver we must humbly offer gold . . . If a master wishes to fill our mouths with dirt we must open them to receive it . . . "

Along with the others, Petra recited. Like the other young girls, she didn't understand more than half of what she recited meant. Maybe it would come in time; she knew she was only six and that older people understood more than she did. Besides, her town was entirely Catholic, for the most part ruling itself. The Moslems all lived far away in the provincial capital of Kitznen or with the janissaries at the barracks of al Harv.

"Okay, children, school's over," announced Sister Margerete as she stood near the door. "You older girls, don't forget your burkas. Though you are not of the masters still you are subject to the same rules as the Moslem women."

This only made sense. How, after all, was one of the masters to have any peace at home if the shameless Christian hussies had more privileges than their own wives and daughters? Even many of the younger girls, such as Petra, wore burkas for the same reasons Petra's mother had for forcing it on her daughter.

School got out early. School, for girls, *always* got out early. After all, most of what they needed to know in this year of someone else's Lord, 1527, they would learn better at their mothers' knees than in a school. Pulling on her gray covering, Petra filed out with the other girls. Since Hans would be several hours more, Petra walked home alone. She took back streets, dirty and muddy, rather than the cobblestoned main street. That way she didn't have to walk by the swaying and soon to be rotting bodies of Martin and Ernst.

As she walked, Petra chanced to look to her right, out into the open fields. A small herd of goats was out there, property of one of the masters in Kitznen, no doubt. The goats were eating the shoots from a field of barley.

Imperial Military Academy, West Point, New York, 26 March, 2106

"Knock it off on the Area!" the corporal bellowed. Immediately, some fifty-odd stamping cadets took themselves out of step and ceased their illicit, cadenced marching on the asphalt. Hours were punishment, to be walked alone and not marched as a group.

Fun while it lasted, for some constrained values of "fun," thought the gray-clad, overcoated, white-crossbelted, biochemistry major and Cadet First Classman John Hamilton. (Hamilton, despite being a first classman, was also Cadet *Private*, but that was a different story, an altogether sadder story, involving an illicit tryst in a little-used alcove down in the Sinks.)

Hamilton was a native of Maine. He'd had an ancestor, as a matter of fact, in the famous 20th Maine, during the Civil War—a Canadian who'd come south from New Brunswick to enlist and decided to stay on after the war. (Though one couldn't tell from his color or his eyes, he'd also had an ancestor from Toronto who'd enlisted in Company G of the equally famous 54th Massachusetts. That might have accounted for the wave in his hair.) For more than four centuries, in every generation that was called, Hamilton's generations had answered. He'd answered, too.

Coming to a halt a few yards from the stone wall of Bradley Barracks, Hamilton transferred his rifle—now, in an exercise in deliberate anachronism, a reproduction Model 1861 Springfield— from one shoulder to the other, turned about, and began walking in the other direction.

Already, Hamilton could hear the plaintive cries of "Odinnn!" arising from the surrounding barracks to echo off the stone walls.

Much like the empire it supported and defended, the school had grown considerably from its rather humble beginnings. For example, while its first class, that of 1806, had graduated and commissioned fifteen cadets, the current class, that of 2106, was more than one hundred times greater. The Class of 2106 was expected to send forth some fifteen hundred and twenty-seven newly commissioned second lieutenants, or roughly one-fortieth of all new officers accessed by the Army in this year.

Or, thought the gray-clad Cadet John Hamilton, as he paced off his four hundred and seventy-seventh hour of punishment tours, *One-thousand, five hundred and twenty-six if I get too many more demerits. I must be a shoo-in for the Martinez Award by now. If, that is, I don't get found*—booted from the Academy—*on demerits.*

As West Point traditions went, the Martinez Award was, at about one hundred years since founding, relatively new. Like being the goat—the last ranking man or woman of the class—it was a distinction not avidly sought. Still, there had been a fair number of general officers who had, in their time, been recipients of the award, just as there had been through history a fair number of goats who rose to stars, George Edward Pickett (1849) and George Armstrong Custer (1861) being neither the least significant nor the most successful among them.

Hamilton, though, wasn't interested in stars. He wasn't really all that interested in the Army, certainly not as a career. If he ever had been, the Imperial Military Academy had knocked such ambition out of him. Instead, he saw it as a way to pay for school and to serve out his mandatory service obligation. Whether that service would see him on the coasts of the Empire's British allies, more or less comfortably, if chillily, watching the Moslem janissaries across the Channel, or hunting *Luminosos* or *Bolivanos* in the mountains or jungles of the South American Territories, or policing the Philippine Islands, or any of the dozens of other places across the globe where the Empire held or fought for sway, he couldn't predict.

Anything, Lord, anything but freezing my balls off hunting Canadians in northern Quebec or Ontario, please. I'm too tall and skinny for the cold. Even Chechnya on the exchange program would be better.

"Ooodddiiinnn!" sounded again from out the barracks windows.

Hamilton already had his branch assignment, infantry. Yet he lacked for a unit assignment yet, and that must depend on the latest casualty figures and some schooling.

As a matter of fact, he wouldn't find out his first assignment until he graduated Ranger School— assuming he did, of course; many did not—just before reporting in for the Basic Course at either Fort Benning (Light Infantry and Suited Heavy Infantry Officers Basic Course) or Fort Bliss (Mechanized Infantry Officer Basic Course) or Fort Stewart (Constabulary Infantry Officers Basic Course). And even then it might change if casualties in, say, Mindanao suddenly soared.

And the casualty lists are never short, Hamilton mused. *They never have been; not in my lifetime, anyway.* He stopped, again facing a stone wall, then transferred his rifle and executed an about face. *Then again, when you've got a population of your own in excess of five hundred million, and control more than another billion, what's a few thousand a month? Except that one of them, sometime in the next five years, might be me. Oh, well . . . buy your ticket and take your chances. And it isn't as if we've a lot of choice about fighting. Maybe once we had that kind of choice. Not anymore.*

Hamilton took a surreptitious glance overhead. Yes, clouds were gathering. The prayers were working. *Perhaps no parade tomorrow.*

"OOODDDIIINNN!"

One of the nice things about walking hours in the Area was that it gave one time to think, though the weather could sometimes be all that one was able to think about. Weather permitting though, and today was merely brisk rather than outright miserable, one could really do some interior soul searching and reflection. Hamilton wondered, sometimes, if he didn't court demerits just so he could have that time alone.

I wonder what it was really like here, before the Empire. The histories don't discuss it much, beyond showing the before and after pictures of Los Angeles, Boston, and Kansas City. I've read the Constitution, all through the Thirty-Sixth Amendment, but the words don't really give me a feel for what it was like back then. Different . . . it must have been different. Did Free Speech really mean people were free to criticize the wars of defense? To protest them in public? Did Freedom of Religion accept even the enemy here? Well, that was before the Three Cities. Was military service really voluntary? For everybody? How the Hell could they maintain the hundred divisions we need that way? Then again, did we need a hundred divisions the old way? But after we were hit here, did we have any choice, really?

Despite being at war, and having been at war—even if it wasn't always recognized as such—for over a century, the emphasis at the IMA was still more on "Academy" than on "Military." Even so, there was a fair amount of military training, some practical, some theoretical. Hamilton had signed up for several practical electives over the last two academic years. One of these was "The Fighting Suit," the basic equipage of the Suited Heavy Infantry. (And, yes, when Hamilton had been the roughly four-millionth to publicly note the convenient acronym that came along with Suited Heavy Infantry Troops, he'd been slugged with a whopping forty hours of walking the Area.)

In any case, the Exo wasn't really a suit, not in the sense that it covered its wearer completely. Rather, it was an exoskeleton to which some considerable degree of armor protection could be added, at a cost in speed, range and supplies carried.

"Remember, it's not a cure-all," the sergeant-instructor, Master Sergeant Webster, had told the cadets the first day of class. Grizzled and old, Webster was the color of strong coffee. He was, so far as Hamilton could tell, the platonic ideal of a noncommissioned officer as such existed in the mind of God: tough, dedicated, no nonsense, and with just enough sense of humor to be, or at least *seem*, human.

"The suit is a bludgeon, not a rapier. It can get you to the objective," Webster had added. "It can get you there reasonably fresh and well supplied, but without much armor. Or it can get you across the objective, with full armor and reduced supply. Or it can do both if, and only if, something else carries you to near the objective.

"It's also a guarantee that, if you wear it while setting up an ambush somewhere in the Caucasus, the enemy will smell it from a mile away and never come near you. So why bother? And if you think you can use it for a recon patrol, I'll also guarantee you that the enemy will *hear* it from half a mile away. So why bother?"

"Because with full armor and a winterizing pack it will keep me warm while hunting Canadian rebels in Northern Ontario?" Hamilton had suggested, one inquisitive finger in the air.

"Mister Hamilton," Sergeant Webster had answered, "there is no such thing as a 'Canadian.' There are Americans. Then there are imperial subjects. There are also rebels, allies, and enemies. *No* Canadians, however. Write yourself up for an eight and four: minor lack of judgment."

Story of my life, Hamilton thought. *Ask a question; get some time in the Area. Try to think and—*

The thought was interrupted by the Area sergeant.

"Attention on the Area. The hour is over. Fall out and fall in on your company areas."

Young Cadet John Hamilton, and many another, hastened to get on with something that passed for a more normal and fruitful life.

Why the fuck didn't I apply to Annapolis? I love boats. I grew up around boats. But nooo. Family tradition was Army and so I just had to follow along. Jackass.

"What will kill or take out an exoskeleton?" Webster asked rhetorically, after the class had taken seats. His finger pointed, "Mr. Hamilton?"

"Kill the man wearing it, Sergeant."

"How? Ms. Hodge."

That cadet, cute, strawberry blonde and—Hamilton reluctantly admitted—probably tougher than he was, answered. "Without armor, Master Sergeant, shooting the wearer in a vital organ is sufficient. Assuming armor is worn, however, the armor can be penetrated by a .41-caliber or better uranium or tungsten discarding sabot projectile. The joints are subject to derangement by large explosive devices or near-impacting heavy artillery or mortar fire. The power pack can similarly be fractured or penetrated. This will also contaminate the exoskeleton such that it cannot again be worn short of depot level decontamination. If the enemy is very clever, and the situation on the ground very bad, it can be worn out of power—"

"At which point," Webster interrupted, "you will have made a present of some very expensive gear to some very bad people. Very good, Cadet Hodge."

Hamilton leaned over and whispered in Hodge's ear, "Ass kisser."

"Better his than yours," Hodge whispered back. "*He* probably washes."

Webster, more amused than anything, let the byplay go without comment. He continued with the lesson, "The point is, however, that almost anything that will kill you in your bare skin *can* kill you while wearing the exoskeleton, even with maximum armor. It's just harder to do.

"However, unlike armored personnel carriers and infantry fighting vehicles, the Exo allows the member of a unit to take maximum advantage of small bits of cover and concealment. It does not, individually, present as tempting and lucrative a target as a tracked vehicle carrying nine to twelve men. This is true even though at half a million IND"—Imperial New Dollars—"each, nine Exos cost slightly more than one infantry fighting vehicle. Men are not potatoes, after all. Their lives matter."

Webster noticed Hodge fidgeting in her chair. "You had a question, Ms. Hodge?"

"Not a question, Master Sergeant, just an observation. Whatever the cost, whatever the risks and whatever the downsides, the Exo makes sense for me because I'm a woman. Nothing else allows me to be a full equal of men in combat."

"Not quite, Ms. Hodge," Webster corrected. "Because you're the bottleneck . . . not you, personally; I mean women are the bottleneck . . . in the production of the next generation, the Exo cannot *reduce* your overall value to that of a man."

"God knows, *I* value you, sweetie," Hamilton said, no longer in a whisper but at least *sotto voce*.

Webster's voice thundered, "Mr. Hamilton, write yourself up for another eight and four: public display of affection."

Grolanhei, Province of Affrankon, 2 Shawwal, 1530
AH (1 October, 2106)

"*Jizya!*" demanded Rashid, the tax gatherer, his fist
pounding the old oaken table in the Minden's kitchen.
But for his beak of a nose, the gatherer did not look notice-
ably different from the *Nazranis*. Rashid's ancestors had
converted early and then married into the dominant
group.

"But, sir," Petra's father began to explain, "the harvest
has been bad this year. The early frost . . . the rain . . . "

"Silence, pig of an infidel!" The *jizya* is a head tax. It is
flat. It is fixed." *Fixed by me.* "It makes no account of the
piddling troubles Allah sends you filth to encourage you
to give up your decayed and false faith."

Seeing that Minden was still minded to dispute the
collection, the tax gatherer's lip curled in a sneer. Cutting
off further discussion, he said, "You realize, do you not,
that the *jizya* is what permits you the status of *dhimmis*?
That without it, without the pact, the *dhimma*, we are in
a state of war, of holy war, of *jihad* with you and yours?
That your lives are forfeit? Your property forfeit?"

"But . . . please, sir . . . "

Being inside the walls of her own home, Petra was
uncovered. Neither she, nor her mother, had anticipated
the arrival of the taxman today. Indeed, they'd all been so
distraught and overworked with the gathering of the very
skimpy harvest, they'd not thought of much of anything
but how they were going to eke out an existence over the
winter. They had to hope others had had better luck this
year. If it was a question of letting the *Nazrani* farmers

eat, or taking the food to feed their own, the masters had no compunction about letting filthy *Nazrani* starve.

Though only nine, and though she feared hunger as much as the next, Petra was ashamed to see her father beg. She was ashamed of his *dhimmi* status, now that she'd grown and learned enough to understand what that meant. She was ashamed of her people who submitted to this humiliation. And, when the tax gatherer looked over at her—more accurately, so she saw, looked her over—she was ashamed of herself. She remembered something Sister Margerete had told her class:

"Mohammad consummated his marriage with his favorite wife, Aisha, when she was nine years old."

Petra hadn't quite understood what "consummated" meant.

"Mark down the boy for gathering to the janissaries," Rashid told the chief of his four guards. "Take the girl now.

"And next year, you filthy swine, when I come for our taxes and demand silver, you had best give me gold or you'll see yourselves joining your daughter on the auction block."

One of Rashid's guards went to Petra. He took handcuffs and a chain from a pouch that hung at his side. The cuffs he ratcheted shut around her wrists, tightly enough to make her wince. The chain he attached to the cuffs.

Hans lunged. "Get your hands off my sister!"

The guard with Petra ignored the boy; that's what the other guard was for. That other guard caught Hans halfway through his lunge, wrapping one arm around the boy's waist. He then put Hans' feet back on the floor, stood and slapped him across the face several times, hard enough to stun and draw blood. The guard then knocked the boy down as his mother wailed and his stoop-shouldered father hung his head in helpless shame.

Petra, who had begun to cry when the cuffs were put on her, screamed when she saw her brother hurt. A slap from Rashid—hard enough to hurt without damaging the merchandise—quieted her.

She was sobbing as they led her away for her first ride in an automobile.

A crowd gathered outside the Minden's hovel, curious but too frightened to help. After all, what help could they give in a country no longer their own?

—end excerpt—

from *CALIPHATE*
available in hardcover,
April 2008, from Baen Books

If you liked Heinlein's *Starship Troopers*, read John Ringo now!
"Marvelous!"—David Weber

A HYMN BEFORE BATTLE

Our choice was simple: We could send human forces to strange planets to fight and die (as only humans can) against a ravening horde that was literally feeding on its interstellar conquests—or remain as we were, virtually weaponless and next in line for brunch. We chose to fight.

PB • 0-671-31841-1 • $7.99

GUST FRONT

The aliens have arrived with gifts, warnings, and an offer we couldn't refuse. And now the enemy is taking the battle to Earth.... "If you want military SF with a difference, read John Ringo." —Eric Flint

PB • 0-7434-3525-7 • $7.99

WHEN THE DEVIL DANCES

"John Ringo's novel has bad guys from the wrong side of hell, 'good guys' you wouldn't buy a used car from, heroism, cowardice, military stupidity and genius, millennia-old plots, Leopard tank versus plasma cannon, and a kick-butt suit of powered armor." —David Weber

PB • 0-7434-3602-4 • $7.99

HELL'S FAIRE

"One of the best new practitioners of military SF." —*Publishers Weekly*

HC • 0-7434-3604-0 • $25.00
PB • 0-7434-8842-3 • $7.99

And don't miss these bestsellers in the same series:
CALLY'S WAR
by John Ringo & Julie Cochrane
HC • 0-7434-8845-8 • $25.00
PB • 1-4165-2052-X • $7.99

THE HERO
by John Ringo & Michael Z. Williamson
HC • 0-7434-8827-X • $24.00
PB • 1-4165-0914-3 • $7.99

WATCH ON THE RHINE
by John Ringo & Tom Kratman
HC • 0-7434-9918-2 • $25.00

Available in bookstores everywhere.
Or order online at our secure, easy to use website:
www.baen.com